A NOBLE SACRIFICE

Morgan had to save his clan. Even if, in the end, it required a sacrifice.

"Jenefer!" he shouted, loping after her.

He caught her by the shoulder and whipped her around toward him. Her expression was full of fire and determination.

"What?" she snarled.

Her anger disappeared when she saw the genuine concern in his eyes.

"Do as I say," he pleaded, "I'm beggin' ye."

"Damn it, Morgan, I can do this," she told him. "I can fight."

"Aye, ye can," he admitted, "better than most o' my men. But I need to know ye're safe, because…"

He looked into her spark-filled green eyes, burning with a passion for justice. And honor. And life.

And he told her the truth.

"Because I love ye."

BRIDE OF FIRE

Copyright © 2019 by Glynnis Campbell

Glynnis Campbell – Publisher
P.O. Box 341144
Arleta, California 91331
Contact: glynnis@glynnis.net

Cover design by Richard Campbell
Formatting by Author E.M.S.

ISBN-10: 1-63480-048-6
ISBN-13: 978-1-63480-048-8

Published in the United States of America

BRIDE OF FIRE

The Warrior Daughters of Rivenloch, Book 1

DEDICATION

For all my beloved readers and reviewers
who raved over
The Warrior Maids of Rivenloch
and kept pestering me for a sequel.
Here you go!

OTHER BOOKS BY
GLYNNIS CAMPBELL

THE WARRIOR MAIDS OF RIVENLOCH
The Shipwreck (novella)
A Yuletide Kiss (short story)
Lady Danger
Captive Heart
Knight's Prize

THE WARRIOR DAUGHTER OF RIVENLOCH
The Storming (novella)
A Rivenloch Christmas (short story)
Bride of Fire
Bride of Ice
Bride of Mist

THE KNIGHTS OF DE WARE
The Handfasting (novella)
My Champion
My Warrior
My Hero

MEDIEVAL OUTLAWS
The Reiver (novella)
Danger's Kiss
Passion's Exile
Desire's Ransom

THE SCOTTISH LASSES
The Outcast (novella)
MacFarland's Lass
MacAdam's Lass
MacKenzie's Lass

THE CALIFORNIA LEGENDS
Native Gold
Native Wolf
Native Hawk

ACKNOWLEDGMENTS

A really big thank you to
the people who keep me on top of things:

Lauren Royal,
who told me even one hour a day was enough,

Mel Jolly,
who taught me to put Writing before The Internet,

Amy & Kirby,
who take the anxiety out of all the left-brain stuff,

Jill Glass,
who's always one step ahead of me,

&

The Jewels of Historical Romance,
who have fast answers when I panic.

CHAPTER 1

Rivenloch, The Borders, Scotland
Autumn, 1155

"This is war," Jenefer du Lac declared, clutching the grip of the longbow in her fist, drawing back the sinew, and firing.

"Is it?" her cousin Hallidis argued, lifting a skeptical blonde brow. "Because I distinctly remember our parents saying something about going to the king bearing honey, not vinegar."

"That was *your* mother," Jenefer said drily, eyeing the straw target. She'd hit it dead center. Again. Nodding in satisfaction, she gestured for Hallie to take her shot. "*My* mother would never stand for—"

"*Your* mother," Hallie bit out, nocking her arrow and raising herself to her full height, two infuriating inches taller than Jenefer, "isn't the Laird of Rivenloch."

Her bow twanged, and the shaft hit three full inches to the left of Jenefer's.

Jenefer smiled in self-assurance and tossed her tawny braid over her shoulder. "Deirdre may be laird," she scoffed, plucking another arrow from her quiver, "but when it comes to battle, she doesn't have half the ballocks that *my*—"

"My mother saved Rivenloch from the English," Hallie reminded her.

"Which would have been impossible," Jenefer fired back, loading her bow, "without *my* mother Helena commanding the—"

"Oh, for the love of Freya! Will you two stop your bloody squabbling?"

The reprimand, coming from their heretofore quiet cousin, Feiyan, rang out across Rivenloch's deserted archery range and startled them to silence.

Feiyan tucked her dark hair behind her ear and checked for witnesses before continuing in softly urgent tones. "We've no time to waste, cousins. We need to act before that scheming Highlander settles in and it becomes impossible to get rid of him. But Hallie's right. This may call for stealth instead of warfare."

"Stealth?" That got Jenefer's attention. Forgetting their argument, she gasped and seized Hallie's arm. "Oh, Hallie, please tell me you've dug a secret tunnel." She drew scheming brows together. "One that leads straight from Rivenloch to that High-and-mighty-lander's courtyard."

"A tunnel, Jen?" Hallie rolled her ice-blue eyes. "When would I have had time to dig a tunnel?"

"'Twould have to be miles long," Feiyan said.

"And we've known about the Highlander for less than a sennight," Hallie said with a superior smirk.

Jenefer frowned. Her cousins didn't have to look at her like she was daft.

Jenefer du Lac was a full-fledged warrior maid.

The granddaughter of a Viking, as they all were, and the firstborn of the renowned Helena of Rivenloch.

Seasoned in combat.

Fearless and feared.

Her cousin Hallidis might be the spawn of a Cameliard knight and Deirdre of Rivenloch. But Jenefer could match

Hallie's skill with a blade. And with a longbow, as proved by this morn's match, Jenefer could best her.

As for Feiyan, all that whelp had to show for herself were a few dancing, prancing battle maneuvers that her mother Miriel's servant from the Orient had taught her.

Aggravated, Jenefer drew and fired three arrows in quick succession. All of them landed within half an inch of the bull's-eye. "I refuse to sit idle while my future stands upon the edge of a sword."

"I know," Hallie said, clapping a patronizing hand on Jenefer's shoulder, "and I agree we need to act quickly, now that we know the Highlander's on his way. But we dare not endanger our parents' diplomatic efforts."

"Easy for you to say," Jenefer said, shaking off Hallie's hand. She set down her bow and stalked off toward the target, calling back, "'Tisn't *your* land in question."

"'Tisn't yours either," Hallie retorted. "Not exactly."

"But 'tis *meant* to be." She plucked the shafts from the target and returned to her cousins. "By Thor, *'twill* be."

Jenefer said that mostly to convince herself. In her heart of hearts, she doubted their parents could persuade the king to reverse his decision.

No matter how sensible it had always seemed to bestow the land adjoining Rivenloch to a Rivenloch heir.

No matter how convenient it would be for Jenefer to become laird of the keep next to her cousin Hallidis.

Unfortunately, the newly crowned King Malcolm had already offered the title to some heathen from the Highlands. And Malcolm was unlikely to change his mind, considering how much trouble the fourteen-year-old king was having, holding on to his *own* land.

As for the Highlander, word was he hadn't even waited for official documents to be drawn up. The greedy sot was on his way to claim the castle even now. Due to arrive any day, he might well be settled in before the cousins' parents returned from their futile mission.

But Jenefer was determined to keep a barbarian from laying claim to her land.

"Creagor will be mine," she swore, "even if I have to seize it myself."

Feiyan turned to Hallie. "See? I told you."

Hallie nodded.

Jenefer scowled at them. "Told her what?" she snapped. Were her cousins conspiring against her?

"Jen," Hallie said, "you're not doing this alone."

Jenefer narrowed her gaze. Sometimes Hallidis Cameliard could be so domineering. Aye, her oldest cousin had been left in charge of Rivenloch in her parents' absence. But that didn't mean she was the laird proper. Not yet.

"If you think I'm going to sit on my hands," Jenefer said, "while you try to woo a thickheaded Highlander out of his property—"

"Who said anything about wooing him?" Feiyan arched a dark brow and plucked a sinister-looking steel star from beneath her cloak.

Hallie glowered in disapproval, confiscating the star.

Feiyan gasped as Hallie hurled it at the wattle fence, lodging two of its sharp points in the wood.

"Violence is a last resort," Hallie said. "We're far more clever than that. But whatever course of action we take, I want your oath. We do it together."

She offered her hands to her reluctant cousins to confirm the pact they'd made when they were young lasses.

Jenefer didn't appreciate Hallie's overly cautious attitude. But she had to admit it would be good to have allies in this fight. So with a resigned sigh, she clasped first Hallie's hand, then Feiyan's.

"Amor vincit omnia," Hallie intoned.

Feiyan and Jenefer echoed the Latin words, which were inscribed on the Laird of Rivenloch's sword.

Love conquers all.

Jenefer wasn't sure about that.

She'd heard about Highlanders. They were filthy, half-wild creatures with mad eyes and tangled beards, who supped on raw lambs and carried shields decorated with the ribs of their enemies.

Shuddering in disgust, she shouldered her quiver.

She wouldn't break her oath to her cousins. But when Hallie's reasonable negotiations ultimately failed, Jenefer intended to have her weapons close at hand.

CHAPTER 2

Morgan Mor mac Giric could not endure another day in his Highland home.

"You mean Miriel?" the younger knight asked.

It had been three months. But the pain was still fresh. His grief was raw. His guilt was crippling.

It struck him most when he lifted gritty eyes to the gray-green pines, the stark rock mountains, and the silvery waterfalls trickling down the face of the cliff like tears.

Everything here reminded him of Alicia, his innocent wife.

The wife he'd given a bairn.

A bairn who'd killed her.

Godit the midwife had said it wasn't Morgan's fault. But he knew better. If only he hadn't taken Alicia to his bed, if only he hadn't planted his seed in her, she'd be alive now.

It was wrong to blame the bairn. He knew that. But he couldn't bear to hold his son. He hadn't yet named him. He could hardly look at the child without being filled with bitter resentment.

So when, only three months after his wife's death, Morgan received word he'd inherited his uncle's faraway holding—the place where his father, Giric mac Leod, had spent his childhood—he didn't hesitate for a moment.

He'd packed to flee the Highlands...forever.

He would have left his son behind as well. But his mother Hilaire tearfully insisted he take the bairn, along with two nurses to care for it. And his father gave him a score of servants for his household and a dozen warriors for his protection.

Morgan didn't have the strength to argue. He hardly had the strength to place one foot in front of the other for the long journey to the Borders.

He only hoped, with every mile forward, his memory of Alicia would fade. Dwelling on the past was futile. He had to look to the future.

There would be time later to acquire the documents declaring him rightful Laird of Creagor.

For now, it was enough to know there *was* a future for Morgan Mor mac Giric. Standing over his beloved Alicia's coffin, he'd thought his life was over. His chest had felt as cold and empty as the grave. He'd wanted nothing more than to climb into that deep hole beside his wife.

Even now, his eyes welled up at the agonizing, indelible memories preceding her death.

The horrid screams.

The bloody bedlinens.

The squalling infant.

The midwife's sorry face.

The sharp stab in his heart when Godit told him the bad tidings, wisely refusing to let him see the torn wreckage of his wife's body.

Then later...the deep, dark, silent grave carved into the peat.

The soft sniffles of his clan.

The rough wooden box lowered into the earth.

The soil pressed carefully down over his young wife, reminding him of a crofter planting a tree.

Except this tree would never sprout.

It was dead.

Alicia was *dead.*

Morgan clenched his jaw to stem the tide of his tears.

He should have known. The poor lass from sunny Catalonia had never been hale enough for the Highlands. Homesick and always cold, she'd spoken with longing about returning home. But he hadn't listened. He'd been so sure she could grow to love his home and his clan.

He was wrong.

God, his throat ached.

His heart ached.

The worst part was the feeling that he'd failed her. A man was supposed to protect his wife. Now proof of his failure lay buried in the earth forever.

The long trek over the misty, muddy heath was silent but for the creak of wooden cart wheels and leather tack, the hushed murmurs of his men, and the occasional lowing of the livestock they'd brought.

Now and then the bairn would whimper, jarring Morgan. The wet nurse was quick to silence the infant, jostling him, cooing to him, giving him suckle.

Then Morgan would resume the numbing trudge forward.

He had no idea how many hours he passed in that mindless journey. Only when his loyal companion, Colban, seized his arm to halt him, did he notice how late the day had grown.

"We'll camp here." Colban grunted, making the decision Morgan could not. With a nod, he indicated a streamside clearing bordered by a copse of trees.

The soldiers and servants quickly and quietly set up camp.

The barley pottage the cook served an hour later held no allure for Morgan. He had no appetite. But Colban insisted he eat, telling him he needed to keep up his strength if they wished to reach Creagor within a fortnight.

So he forced it past his lips, tasting nothing. He washed it down with a full cup of ale. Still it sat like a lump in his belly.

Later, bedded down under the dark, featureless sky, where no one could witness his weakness, he let his eyes fill. The thick wool of his plaid swallowed his tears, just as the cold earth had swallowed his wife.

CHAPTER 3

"**G**hosts," Feiyan breathed. Her pale face lit up. She set her ale cup on the floor, where she sat cross-legged in a surcoat of soft gray.

Jenefer, perched on one of the oak chests, choked on a piece of oatcake. "What?"

This morn, the three cousins had assembled in a storage room beneath Rivenloch's great hall to break their fast. It was the infamous spot where Jenefer's mother had once taken her father hostage, the perfect place to plot in secrecy.

Hallie stopped pacing the small chamber and turned. Her skirts, which were the same woad blue color as her eyes, swirled around her.

"Ghosts," she echoed, taking a thoughtful bite of cheese and nodding. "Maybe."

"Wait," Jenefer said. "Ghosts? What ghosts?"

Feiyan gave her a sly smile. "The ghosts that haunt Creagor."

Hallie grinned, clapping the crumbs from her hands.

Jenefer scowled in disgust. "Don't tell me you two believe in ghosts."

"*We* don't..." Feiyan began.

"But Highlanders are a superstitious lot," Hallie said, her eyes twinkling like ice crystals.

"Aye," Feiyan said, hopping to her feet. "And once the Highlander learns that Creagor is haunted..."

"He'll hie himself back to the Highlands," Hallie finished.

Jenefer rolled her eyes. "Look, I don't wish to darken your sunny skies, but that's the most ridiculous idea I've ever heard. How will you make him believe Creagor is haunted?" She shook her head and took a swig of ale.

"*'Twill* be haunted," Feiyan said, grinning.

"By us," Hallie said.

Jenefer almost spewed her ale. "Us?" she squeaked.

"Aye," Hallie replied, motioning Jenefer off the oak chest.

Jenefer gathered her five remaining oatcakes and half-finished ale and slid down from her perch. This she had to see.

Hallie threw open the lid of the chest and began pawing through the contents. "What does a ghost look like?" She flung rags of clothing, scraps of leather, and bits of fabric here and there.

"How should I know?" Jenefer smirked, taking another bite of oatcake. "Only fools believe in ghosts."

Feiyan winked. "Fools and Highlanders."

"What about these?" Hallie asked, showing them a couple of torn plaids of mud-colored wool.

"Nay," Feiyan said. "Those aren't otherworldly at all. We'd look like beggars."

Hallie tossed the plaids aside and continued rummaging.

Jenefer sighed and bit off another morsel of oatcake. This was pointless. The whole plan seemed far too complex. When it came to battle, she preferred direct confrontation. A face-to-face challenge. Hand-to-hand combat. A straightforward attack. And a clear victory.

Even if they were capable of pulling off some sort of deception to make the Highlander believe that Creagor was haunted, they were never going to find a garment in that chest that looked like it belonged to a ghost.

"Maybe?" Hallie asked, pulling out a huge threadbare cloak of black velvet. "If we tear it into three pieces?"

Feiyan twisted her lips in indecision. "I fear 'twill be invisible. We'll do the haunting at night, aye? Black garb will only vanish into the shadows."

Feiyan should know. As a lass, her mother Miriel had worn black clothing to steal invisibly through the woods.

Hallie nodded and cast the cloak atop a growing pile of rejected garments.

"This is a waste of time," Jenefer said. "Unless you have angel's wings tucked away in that chest—"

"This?" Hallie asked, holding up a length of wispy white cloth.

"That?" Feiyan cocked her head. "'Tis a veil, aye? Won't we be mistaken for nuns?"

Hallie wrinkled her nose and lowered the cloth. "You're right. It *does* look like a nun's veil."

But suddenly Jenefer saw something entirely different. She gulped down the oatcake and snatched the veil from Hallie. She draped it over the shoulder of her nut-brown surcoat, then twirled. The silky fabric caressed her in sheer, wraithlike folds.

"I can make this work," she decided with a wry smile. "And I promise you I won't look at all like a nun."

CHAPTER 4

Morgan ran a hand back through the dark tangle of his hair. He knew he should be pleased. In just under a fortnight, the company had finally crested the brae and caught their first glimpse of Creagor.

True to its name, the sandstone castle resembled a gold jewel, set on a low hill of green velvet grass. Unlike his rugged Highland home with its majestic peaks and towering waterfalls, the Borders featured gentle glens and bubbling burns. The land here was fertile, the weather mild. Life would be easy in such hospitable surroundings.

So his father had told him. His English mother, of course, had less pleasant memories of the Borders. Content in the Highlands, Hilaire didn't miss the battles between the English and the Scots, where loyalties were constantly shifting. And she had no interest in returning to the stormed castle where she'd nearly lost her life.

But despite the gasps of wonder and enthusiasm around him, Morgan felt nothing. He might be past the crushing sorrow of losing his wife. But he could take no joy in the world, no matter how beautiful. What he suffered now was a sort of numb resignation.

Beside him, his old maidservant Bethac murmured, "I think your son likes it here, m'laird."

He glanced down at the bairn, who gurgled and waved his fists. But he still felt nothing.

Bethac's face fell.

Morgan sighed.

"We've much to do," Colban announced in a strong, confident voice. "'Tis already midday. The sunlight lasts a wee bit longer this far south, but if we want to be settled in by nightfall, we'll need to make haste."

He looked expectantly at Morgan.

Morgan had nothing to say. He didn't know where to begin. Colban expected him to take command. But he couldn't even summon the spirit to respond.

Colban's gray eyes flattened in disapproval. With a disappointed scowl, he motioned the rest of the retinue forward.

The others descended the brae at an eager pace, exchanging cheerful expressions and excited whispers, while Colban marched beside Morgan in a cold silence so impenetrable a claymore couldn't cut through it.

Once they entered through the palisade gates, Colban remarked to the others with satisfaction, "At least the keep is in good repair. Until we find out if the neighbors are friend or foe, 'tis good to have strong walls between us."

While Morgan stood in the midst of the courtyard, activity commenced around him under Colban's expert direction. The clan began the process of moving in—assessing the outbuildings and unloading the carts.

"Perhaps ye should inspect the hall, m'laird," Colban suggested.

With a resigned sigh, Morgan made his way to the stone keep and hauled open the heavy doors to the great hall.

The shutters were open, and light came in through three tall windows, reflecting off the bare, polished wooden floor. The great hearth had been scrubbed recently, but slabs of dry peat were stacked beside it, ready to serve as fuel. Iron sconces were set into the plaster walls. Some still held remnants of beeswax candles.

His uncle had left no progeny of his own. Because of the castle's strategic location near the English border, the king had wanted it occupied as soon as possible. His uncle's few remaining servants had departed, taking most of the provender and supplies. But the keep was livable.

Morgan headed toward the stone stairs that spiraled up one corner of the hall. Despite the early hour, he wanted nothing more than to seek out his new bedchamber and sleep the rest of the day. Even if it was on the bare floor.

Before he could take the first stair, Colban entered the hall.

"Morgan!"

Morgan hesitated, but didn't turn.

"We need to talk," Colban said.

Morgan didn't need to talk.

He didn't want to talk.

He wanted to continue upstairs. Fall asleep. And never wake up.

But that was not to be.

Colban loped up beside him and set a firm palm on his shoulder. His gray gaze was stern and unrelenting. "We've known each other for—what—twenty years?"

Morgan lowered his brows. This sounded like the beginning of a lecture. He didn't need a lecture. Not from Colban, who'd never borne the responsibility of a lairdship or a wife.

"And in all that time," Colban continued, "I've ne'er spoken a word against ye. Ne'er questioned your good sense. Not once doubted your judgment."

"But?" Morgan bit out.

"But..." Colban hesitated, as if the words were painful to say. "Ye're not yourself, Morgan. Not since she died."

Morgan had thought he was beyond feeling. But Colban's words hit like a hammer. They struck a fiery spark from his heart, immediately inflaming his ire.

"God's bones, what do ye expect?" he hissed, knocking aside Colban's hand. "She was my wife, Colban. My... everything."

"I know." Colban looked truly sorry. "I know that. But she's gone now. And ye can't bring her back. Ye've had time to grieve. Now ye have to think about the future."

Morgan didn't want to hear about the future. Any future without Alicia was bleak. Empty. Hopeless.

"Ye have a chance to start anew here," Colban continued. "Ye have a fine keep, a substantial holdin', and a hale son who—"

"Who killed my wife," Morgan snarled.

Colban's gasp told Morgan he'd been too frank. Colban might know him better than anyone. But he had yet to witness the dark side of Morgan's raw grief.

Colban's shock didn't last long. He wrenched Morgan about by the arm and pinned him with flashing silver eyes.

"Don't ye ever say that. Don't ye believe it. That is an innocent bairn. He's flesh o' your flesh and blood o' your blood, heir to all this." He waved his arm at the great hall. "'Tis sorrowful enough the poor lad will ne'er know his ma. But for his own da to blame him for her death..."

Morgan knew Colban was right. But the spark in his heart had grown into a burning coal. And anger felt so much better than melancholy.

"Stay out o' my affairs!" he barked. "What would ye know about fatherhood anyway?" He regretted his next words even before they spilled off his bitter tongue. "Ye don't even know who your da *is.*"

Colban growled and gave him a hard shove.

Morgan shoved him back.

What followed was a brawl more befitting beardless lads than grown men.

Colban gave him a well-deserved punch in the jaw, hard enough to rock back his head.

Morgan cursed and clamped an arm around Colban's neck, pulling him off-balance.

Colban gained release by pummeling Morgan in the gut, bending him in half. While he clutched his bruised stomach, Colban tackled him to the ground.

They scrambled across the polished planks, kicking and clouting, wrenching at each other's garments, grimacing and cursing, scratching and spitting like wildcats.

As foolish as the grappling was, the rage was cathartic. For the first time since Alicia's death, Morgan felt...capable. What he was capable *of,* of course, was senseless violence. But the fury flowing through him melted the ice in his veins.

He might not be able to defeat death. But he could damn well leave Colban begging for mercy.

If only he could catch hold of the slippery bastard.

Colban escaped him and headed up the stairs.

"Coward!" Morgan yelled, thinking he was fleeing.

But when he charged forward in pursuit, Colban turned suddenly, using the advantage of height to leap down upon Morgan.

Morgan collapsed under the attack, twisting his ankle and striking his brow on the stone wall as he went down. Stars floated before his eyes. His fingers found blood dripping from his forehead.

Colban didn't escape unscathed by the fall either. He rolled away, groaning and clutching at his knee.

Morgan gave his head a hard shake to dispel the dizziness and struggled to his feet.

Colban regained his footing as well, though he favored his injured leg. He limped before Morgan, taunting him with a smoldering glare.

Morgan outweighed Colban by a wee bit in muscle and might. Unfortunately, Colban was the faster man.

His quick punch caught Morgan's left eye, blurring his vision.

Morgan barreled blindly forward. Catching Colban about the waist, he slammed him into the stone wall.

Colban grunted.

Morgan reared back and drove his fist toward Colban's fair face. But Colban dropped down in that instant, and Morgan's knuckles crunched against the hard sandstone.

Grimacing and cradling his injured hand, Morgan staggered back a step.

Colban seized the advantage, lunging toward Morgan's shins and knocking him backward.

The great hall careened upside down at lightning speed. Then the planks of the floor collided with the back of Morgan's head.

The last thing he heard was his old maidservant Bethac asking what in the hell the two of them were doing.

The last thing he saw was a black fog rushing in to eclipse his vision and render him senseless.

CHAPTER 5

Jenefer pulled her cloak tighter around her throat and peered out from the shadows of the trees. The castle below, lit by the last rays of the setting sun, truly did glow like gold.

She meant to lay claim to that gold. And even though she'd sworn an oath of solidarity to her cousins, she'd always known this fight was hers alone.

Besides, she wasn't exactly acting on her own. The three of them had agreed on their strategy. They'd decided to make the Highlander believe that Creagor was haunted. And since they'd learned from a passing merchant that the Highlander's household had arrived earlier today, they'd planned to begin the haunting tomorrow eve.

Jenefer didn't intend to veer from their objective. But she wasn't about to wait for the morrow. It was better to strike while the iron was hot and the moon was full, before the enemy had time to prepare.

Before supper, she'd feigned an aching head as an excuse to retire to her chamber. There she'd gathered her ghostly attire and stolen from Rivenloch by way of her Aunt Miriel's secret tunnel into the woods.

Jenefer already knew the way to Creagor. Years ago, when she'd first learned the castle might one day be hers, she'd sneaked over on her own to explore. She knew there was a wooden palisade surrounding the keep and a stone wall enclosing the courtyard. She even knew the exact location of the laird's bedchamber. Now all she needed to do was to wait until dark and move into place below the window.

Staying hidden at the edge of the forest in sight of the bedchamber, she perched on a lichen-covered boulder to keep watch from the trees. Then she opened the satchel she'd brought with her.

Knowing she was settling in for a long night, she'd procured supplies from the buttery. She pulled out a chunk of hard cheese, a dozen oatcakes, three veal pasties, four bannocks, two apple coffyns, a slab of butter, and a full skin of ale. That should last her till morn.

From this vantage point, she spied a guardsman occasionally popping his head above the palisade of timbers that fenced the keep. The Highlander had doubtless brought men-at-arms with him, but he either didn't have enough to post permanent lookouts at the four corners, or he was unconcerned about intruders.

While she waited for the inhabitants of the castle to retire for the night, she chewed on a buttered bannock and considered what improvements she would make to the keep, once it was hers.

The first thing she'd do was replace and expand the timber palisade with sturdy stone. Timbers could be put to the torch. But it would take a giant siege engine like a catapult or a trebuchet to fell a stone wall.

As long as she was enlarging the palisade, she thought, taking a swig of ale, she might as well expand the interior wall. There was plenty of usable land to enclose a much larger courtyard. It was always best to protect as many of the outbuildings as possible, considering how tempting a jewel like Creagor was to the invading English along the border.

The current palisade was far too close to the keep, and the towers didn't even have narrowed arrow-slit windows for defense. She could have easily fired an arrow over the timbers and shot the Highlander while he stood at his open window.

She arched a sardonic brow. That was still a possibility if her current plan failed. She'd brought her longbow with her. She never went anywhere without it.

She washed down the bannock with a swallow of ale and resumed plans for improving Creagor. In addition to the usual kitchens, dovecot, orchard, gardens, and shops that filled the courtyard, a larger space could house some rather appealing amenities...

A grand archery range.

A splendidly appointed tiltyard.

An impressive practice field.

A generously furnished armorer's forge.

And a stable large enough to provide for the mounts of knights who came to participate in the illustrious tournaments she intended to host.

Imagining the fluttering pennons and the clash of claymores sent a thrill through her. Her Aunt Deirdre hosted some of Scotland's most distinguished tournaments every spring at Rivenloch. But Jenefer was sure she could rival Rivenloch's events at Creagor in the autumn, once she put builders to work on the additions.

She shivered. She told herself it was from excitement. Not the cold. But the weather had definitely taken a turn today. Fog no longer blanketed the ground. A chill breeze stirred the crisp leaves of the trees.

Still, Jenefer was accustomed to cold. She'd be fine. Besides, what was a little bitter wind when men would shed blood for a holding as magnificent as Creagor?

Two veal pasties, seven oatcakes, and one apple coffyn later, Jenefer had begun shivering in earnest. But she forgot all about the cold when she suddenly spied light in the window of the laird's bedchamber.

She sat up straight, her gaze locked on the window.

That would be him.

The Highlander.

The savage who thought he could usurp her castle.

Quickly stuffing the remnants of her supper into the satchel, she felt the fire of battle enter her heart. She prepared to give the performance of her life.

Paying no heed to the icy wind, she threw off her cloak and began untying the laces of her surcoat. Once she'd loosened and hauled off the garment, the wind began to whip at her linen kirtle, wrapping it around her legs.

Leaning against an oak for balance, she tugged off her boots and stockings, tucking them under the boulder. She untied her braid and ran her fingers through her hair, separating the long tresses.

With a bracing, determined breath, she swept the kirtle off over her head...and lost it to the wind. She cursed as it flew across the sward, skipping away like a naughty child, alternately snagging on bushes, then blowing free. Figuring the garment was lost for good, she drew out the filmy white veil she'd packed.

It rippled in the breeze as well, but she managed to drag the veil over her naked body, anchoring it atop her windblown curls with a circlet of silver.

No one would mistake her for a nun now. The sheer veil afforded her no modesty. And no warmth.

But this was war.

Whatever discomfort she had to suffer, it would be worth it. She planned to win this battle. Her future and the title of Laird of Creagor depended upon it.

Clenching her teeth against the biting wind, she emerged from the trees and made her way toward the candle glow in the window. The light of the full moon glistened on the grass, where frost crunched under her feet. The translucent veil, lifting and fluttering on the currents, looked even more ethereal and eerie than she'd hoped.

As she positioned herself in view of the laird's window, she was tempted to yell out to get his attention. But that wouldn't have been ghostly. She had to have patience. Still, if he didn't look out soon, she supposed she'd have to resort to some sort of eerie emanation. Perhaps a low moan or a high keening wail.

Meanwhile, she'd simply stand in silence, stare up at the window, and shiver. The chill wind danced with her veil and gave her icy kisses while she waited.

And waited.

CHAPTER 6

It had been a long while since Morgan had done something so foolish as to engage in a brawl. Grappling was a behavior hardly befitting a laird, especially when it was with one's oldest and dearest friend.

After Morgan blacked out, Colban had entreated his maidservant Bethac to see to Morgan's welfare, in spite of that cruel insult about his birth. Then again, he supposed that was the least Colban could do after knocking the new laird of the clan out cold.

At Bethac's prompting, they'd both made the proper apologies. And in the end, Morgan had to admit Colban was right. He hadn't been himself. Not for weeks.

As it turned out, their fight might have been for the best. Engaging in combat had jarred Morgan out of the numbness that had paralyzed him of late. He wasn't mended. But at least he felt human again.

No longer interested in escaping into slumber, he'd returned to the great hall after addressing his injuries. There, he'd supervised the laying of the rushes, the stocking of the buttery, and the assembly of the trestle tables.

He'd ventured below to the armory, where his men-at-arms were already stockpiling weapons.

He'd wandered out to the stables, where a lad was busy wiping down the weary horses with straw.

The sheep had been securely penned, the coos were in the field, and the fowl nested in the doocot.

The tradesmen had chosen their shops and were setting up shelves and tools.

The cooks had raided the overgrown herb garden and fired up the clay ovens for the evening meal.

By nightfall, the clan proudly hoisted the mac Giric pennon, officially inhabiting the castle.

Of course, on the morrow Morgan would need to seek out more supplies. He'd have to trade for more cattle, purchase additional fowl, see what could be fished from the nearby streams, and evaluate the orchards to determine what they would bear.

Now that the house had been put in order and he'd supped on smoked bream and bannocks, Morgan went upstairs to retire for the night.

The servants had worked hard to make a home for him here. In his bedchamber, a modest peat fire already burned on the hearth. His chair sat beside it, fitted with a feather pillow embroidered with his initials. His personal things were arranged on the table against the wall—his whale bone comb, a pen and parchment, a pitcher of water with a basin, a candle, a cake of soap, a mirror of polished steel.

He picked up the mirror and winced at the bruised and battered face looking back at him. His swollen eye had a black ring around it. His lip was cut. His stubbled jaw was red and abraded. And at the top of his brow, near the hairline, swelled the lump of a bruise.

He hadn't looked so fearsome and pathetic at the same time since he'd engaged in his first tournament melee as a youth.

He'd meant to introduce himself to his neighbors on the morrow. But that seemed unwise now. He was a mess. He didn't relish turning up at the neighbors' doors, looking like a wildcat that had lost a fight with a wolf.

He replaced the mirror and went to stir the fire to life. Then he lit the candle from the flames, bringing the rest of the chamber to light.

The bed was assembled and made up with linens, bolsters, an embroidered wool coverlet, and sheepskins.

But as he looked at the pair of pillows gracing the bed, he felt a sudden, sharp, unexpected pang, like a dagger stabbed in his heart.

This bed—this chamber—was meant for the laird and his *lady.* It was too imposing and extravagant for one man alone.

She should have been here.

Alicia should have been here.

Sleeping beside him.

Sharing his chamber. His castle. His life.

Choking down his grief, he crossed the room to place the candle in the wall sconce. As he passed by the open window, his eye caught on something outside.

The image was so fleeting, he was sure he'd imagined it.

Just past the window, he stopped in his tracks.

The candle flickered in his trembling hand.

For one terrible instant, he would have sworn he'd seen her standing beyond the fence. Alicia. His dead wife.

Emotions coursed through him as swiftly as lightning. Shock. Disbelief. Wonder. Relief. Longing. Anguish. Misgiving. Dread.

His heart pounded as he continued to stare blankly at the empty black sconce on the white plaster wall, trying to make sense of what he'd just glimpsed.

His eyes must be playing cruel tricks on him. What he'd seen couldn't be Alicia. Alicia was dead. He'd laid her in earth himself. And only fools believed the dead returned as ghosts.

Nay, what he'd seen was likely only a sapling blowing in the wind.

Taking a steadying breath, he slowly backed to the window again and peered out.

Alarm sucked the spit from his mouth.

It wasn't his imagination.

It wasn't a sapling.

It was a lass.

The sight of her challenged his grasp on reality. Her veil swirled around her like a misty aura, glowing from the light of the full moon.

He'd never believed in ghosts. But he had to admit he'd never seen anything look so ghostly.

If he'd seen the figure more clearly the first time, he would have recognized at once it wasn't Alicia. The lass might be enveloped in a filmy white shroud, but beneath the sheer veil her naked body was quite visible.

Unlike slim Alicia, this lass possessed voluptuous curves. Unlike Alicia with her tightly braided black hair, this lass had gold-burnished waves that cascaded down her shoulders. And there was no way shy Alicia, even as a ghost, would have stood naked in the middle of a field.

He narrowed his eyes and studied her.

She stared back at him, unmoving. A gust of wind teased at her veil, revealing long, shapely legs and a delicate dark patch where they joined her body.

The sight caused an unwelcome twinge in his trews.

Still she didn't move.

He lowered a dubious brow.

Perhaps the lass was frozen solid.

Another breeze lifted the veil higher, exposing full breasts tipped by nipples as tempting as cherries. A groan caught in his throat as the twinge grew into a definite swelling.

Then guilt struck him like a blacksmith's hammer, overriding his desire. How could he be aroused when he'd just lost his wife? How could he even *look* at another lass?

Self-disgust tested his temper.

He wanted the lass gone. Now.

"What do ye want?" he yelled down impatiently.

She slowly raised a straight arm to point at him and intoned in a husky moan, "Yooouuu. Muuuuust. Gooooooooooo."

Her sinister directive would have sent chills up the spine of a lesser man. But he knew very well she was mortal. And when she delivered her message, he quickly recognized her ploy for what it was. The mischievous imp had decided to badger her new, unwelcome neighbor.

He supposed it could be worse. She could have thrown rocks at the windows or hung a dead cat on the fence.

As he continued to stare down at the beautiful, hostile lass, he almost wished she *were* a ghost. It was unsettling to have a naked lass cavorting beneath his window. And he didn't much care for her issuing demands.

He crossed his arms over his chest, unwilling to bend to her beauty or her intimidation.

"I must go?" he called out in unimpressed tones. "Is that so?"

"Aaaaaaaaaaayyyyyyyyeeeeeee," she wailed, making a slow and graceful turn that gave him an inviting glimpse of her tempting backside.

He didn't want to think about it. "Who says so?"

"Iiiiiiiiii d-d-d-ooooooooo."

He could hear the shiver of the cold in her voice. He wondered if someone else had put her up to this. Perhaps a gang of local whelps had wagered on who would do the badgering, and she'd lost.

The lass must be half-frozen. Surely she couldn't keep this up for long. Sooner or later, she'd decide pestering the new neighbor wasn't worth the price of becoming an icicle.

"Ye do?" he asked. "And just who do ye think ye are?"

"A ghoooooooooooooost."

As she lifted her arms, a gust of wind plastered the veil to her body, outlining the seductive curve of her waist.

Desire made him lose his words for a moment. Finally he managed to shout back, "Nobody warned me Creagor was haunted."

"Ohhhh, aaaayyyeee," she cried, waving one arm toward the forest. "Byyyyyyyyyy maaaaaaaaaany ghoooooosts."

If he weren't so tired...and battered...and inappropriately aroused, he might have found her performance amusing.

She lowered an accusing finger at him again. "Yooouuu. Muuuuust. Go—"

"I heard ye the first time," he bellowed back, closing one of the shutters. "Well then, carry on! Just see ye don't freeze to death. I don't want to wake in the mornin' to the sight o'—"

A wail interrupted him.

This time it wasn't the lass.

It was his bairn.

For some unfathomable reason, the nursemaids had decided to keep his son in the chamber adjoining his.

He grimaced. No doubt his shouting and the lass's moans had awakened the child.

He muttered a curse under his breath. Then he opened the shutter again and snarled at the lass, "See what ye've done, ye whelp? Off with ye now! Go!" He shooed her with a gesture.

She didn't shoo. Instead, she planted her hands on her hips and shouted back at him in a decidedly unghostly voice.

"Me? You're the horse's arse bellowing out the window!"

Her insult added fuel to the fire of his ire. How dared she call him names? And in his own home?

"Och, that's a bonnie thing!" he yelled. "Cursin' in front of a bairn!"

"Is that what that wailing is?" she challenged, flipping the veil back to reveal her lovely, smirking face...and her infuriatingly breathtaking naked body. "I thought 'twas one of your soldiers, crying for his ma."

It took a moment for the slight to sink in, so distracted was he by the lass's unabashed beauty.

But when her words registered, accentuated by the heightened screaming of his son next door, such fury boiled up in him that he swore steam hissed from his ears.

He wasn't worried about the bairn. Bethac would see to his needs.

But someone had to put that wicked-tongued lass in her place.

He slammed the shutters, snatched up his claymore, and headed for the door.

With any luck, she'd be gone by the time he got downstairs.

If she was foolish enough to stand her ground, she'd flee once she caught sight of Morgan Mor mac Giric charging toward her with his sword. There was a reason for the "Mor" title. Aside from the golden giant Colban, no one in the clan matched Morgan for height, might, and muscle.

One glimpse of him, and she'd scurry off like a frightened coney.

CHAPTER 7

"**S**hite," Jenefer bit out as the Highlander slammed the shutters and disappeared from the window.

Now she'd done it. The brute was coming downstairs. Which would have been fine if she were closer to her longbow.

But she'd left it in the trees. After all, what ghost carried a bow and arrows? Now it would take her too long to fetch.

Damn her cousins! She never should have listened to them. She'd always said this should be a battle of arms, not of wits. The Highlander hadn't been convinced for one moment that she was a ghost.

What she wouldn't give to have her bow—nocked and primed—in her hands right now.

Of course, bow or not, she wasn't about to run. Only cowards ran away from a fight. So she tossed off the veil, which would only get in the way. Then she blew into her icy hands and bounced up and down on her toes, hoping to warm up her blood enough to put up a good fight.

The babe upstairs was still carrying on. Its wails of woe sailed on the wind, almost as piercing as the cold. She wondered why its mother wasn't seeing to it. Then again, knowing the barbaric Highlanders, they probably toughened up their babes by letting them cry.

Sooner than she expected—had the Highlander *flown* down the stairs?—the timber gates burst open. What emerged was the biggest warrior she'd ever seen.

The breath deserted her lungs. Her eyes went wide. Every instinct told her to flee.

But she swallowed down her fear and braced her knees for impact, even though the fists she made seemed suddenly puny in the face of the beast coming toward her.

He was a good fifty yards away. But his long strides were swallowing up the ground at a rapid pace.

In a flash, all the gruesome rumors she'd heard about Highlanders streamed through her brain.

They ate live mice.

They slept in the snow.

They fought wolves barehanded.

They drank the blood of their enemies.

Twenty yards away.

Like a thunderhead, he boiled toward her with savage intent and the dark threat of violence.

A dozen yards.

Icy sweat covered her now. She was badly mismatched. But she refused to surrender. Better that she should die bravely on her two feet than cower in fear.

Six yards.

This close, she could see his face contorted with murderous rage and hear his feral growl of warning.

Her heart pounded. But she challenged him with an unwavering scowl.

Three yards.

He swept his claymore up in one massive arm, as if he planned to lop off her head then and there.

Still she held her ground and stared death in the eyes.

A yard away, really too close to strike, he finally stopped before her.

She held her breath.

His blade hung over her head. But his furious face was now marked by puzzlement. It was also marked by signs of a recent fight.

He could have killed her. But he hadn't. And that meant he *wouldn't.*

For an extended moment, they only stared at each other, like fire and ice, at an impasse.

Then he suddenly snarled, towering over her and shaking his blade in an attempt to scare her.

All she had left was the element of surprise. While he held his sword aloft, she drove her fist forward, punching him in the nose as hard as she could. Hard enough to make him stagger backward in pain and shock. Hard enough that she knew, once the thrill of triumph wore off, her knuckles would hurt like the devil.

His alarm didn't last long. With a curse, he dropped the sword and came at her with his bare arms.

Normally, she could slip out of a man's grasp with ease. She might be tall for a lass, but she was quick and agile. Especially when she was unhindered by clothing.

But with this giant, there was nowhere to slip to. She dodged left, and his right arm blocked her way. She dodged right, and his left arm corralled her back in. Her only satisfaction as they engaged in a back-and-forth combat dance was that his nose had begun to bleed.

Finally, deciding the only way to defeat a giant was to bring him to the ground, she dove toward his knees.

Her plan was to bowl him over.

She might as well have tried to bowl over an oak tree. All she managed to do was stop herself short. Worse, she ended up in the humiliating position of groveling at his feet.

But she needn't have worried. She didn't stay there long. In the next instant, he swept his right arm down and hoisted her up by the waist, settling her on his hip.

She fought for her freedom like a thrashing wildcat.

"Put me down!" she screamed.

"Nay," he bit out.

She pounded on his thighs. They were as hard as iron.

"Let me go!"

"Nay!" he barked. "I might have a moment ago. But that was ere ye bloodied my nose."

She twisted in his viselike grasp.

"You came at me with a sword," she spat, "and you're crying over a bloody nose?"

"I'm not cryin'," he growled, "and I wouldn't have harmed ye." Then he added, as if she should have known as much, "Bloody hell, ye're a lass."

That almost made her laugh. The Highlander had obviously never heard of The Warrior Maids of Rivenloch.

"That's right," she cooed. "I'm only a lass."

Then she drove her fist toward his ballocks.

CHAPTER 8

What instinct warned Morgan the lass was about to clout him, he didn't know. But he managed to twist just enough to make the blow land on the inside of his thigh rather than its intended target.

It still hurt like hell. For a wench, she packed a powerful punch. But at least he'd saved himself from debilitating damage. He quickly trapped her lethal arm against his side.

He probably deserved that punch.

First, it was completely against his code of honor to brandish his claymore at a woman, let alone one unclothed and unarmed.

And second, a good clout might have put an end to the unnatural craving he was experiencing, a craving exacerbated by holding a naked, squirming lass against his body.

Now what was he going to do?

He certainly didn't intend to give her a second opportunity to strike him.

Could he just put her down and let her go? She must realize by now she was no match for him.

On the other hand, she seemed curiously fearless. She didn't respond to violence. Maybe chivalry and reason would convince her to return to wherever she'd come from.

He was about to offer her the leine off his back, so she could at least be decent for the journey home, when two more lasses suddenly emerged from the trees into the moonlight.

It was an unpleasant surprise. But at least these two were clothed.

"Unhand her!" ordered the tall blonde. She spoke with an authority he'd never heard before in a woman, striding across the field with a regal bearing, as if he should obey her command without question. He didn't much care for her tone, particularly since she didn't know whom she was addressing.

A dark-haired lass followed the blonde like a smaller shadow, dressed in black, slipping silently through the grass.

These must be the naked lass's cohorts.

Great, he thought as his nose began to throb. Now what?

"I'd advise you do as she bids, before 'tis too late," the shadowy lass chimed in. "We don't want to hurt you."

The scoff burst out of him involuntarily. "Hurt...me?" His statement would have been more effective had blood not been dripping from his nose.

"Put me down," the naked lass muttered. "You have no idea who you're dealing with."

That amused him even more. He might not know their names. But it was clear he was dealing with three lasses. *Lasses.* Aye, he'd been caught off guard with that punch to his nose. But it wouldn't happen again.

Now, however, there was no way he was going to let them just go on their merry way. He wasn't about to let them walk away, thinking they'd bested him.

He was new here. He had yet to make a name for himself. A man's reputation was critical. If they started spreading gossip about how the three of them—three *lasses*—had subdued the new Laird of Creagor, he'd never live it down.

Perhaps he could call them on their empty threats.

"Fine," he said. "Then tell me, lassie, who exactly am I dealin' with?"

The blonde straightened with pride. To his surprise, she was almost as tall as his man Colban.

"I'm Hallidis Cameliard. This is my cousin Feiyan la Nuit. And Jenefer du Lac is the one you've got in a death grip. We're the Warrior Daughters of Rivenloch."

He resisted a snicker. He'd heard his father speak of Rivenloch. It was the property adjoining Creagor. But Warrior Daughters? They had to be jesting.

"Och aye," he drawled, "and I'm the Lion o' Scotland."

"I knew he wouldn't believe us," dark-haired Feiyan said, shaking her head.

Hallidis held up her hands in peace. "We mean you no harm. But you must put our cousin down."

"Or what?"

Jenefer strained in his grip and bit out, "Or they'll run you through before you can say 'Lucifer's ballocks'."

"Don't be ridiculous, Jen," Hallidis scolded, then turned to him. "We'll do no such thing."

Jenefer stiffened in outrage. "What do you mean?"

"I told you before," Hallidis explained. "We're on a mission of diplomacy."

Morgan's brows popped up. Diplomacy? They had a strange way of showing it.

"Thor's rod, Hallie! Does he look diplomatic to you?" Jenefer demanded.

"Besides," Hallidis added, "we're unarmed."

"What!" Jenefer exploded. "You're unarmed? You mean to say you followed me here and brought no weapons? Then why did you bother coming at all?"

Morgan was beginning to wonder if he should drop the lass to the ground and let the three work out their differences on their own when he spied a dark figure out of the corner of his eye. Someone else was stealing through the shadows behind the lasses.

For an instant, he feared he might be outnumbered.

Then moonlight glinted off the intruder's golden hair.

Colban.

He'd probably heard the noise and come down to lend aid.

Meanwhile, the Warrior Daughters bickered on, unaware they were being stalked.

"We *had* to come, Jen," Hallidis said pointedly, "because *you* broke the pact."

"I didn't break it. I followed the plan. I just...acted independently."

"You ran off. We were supposed to do this together."

Morgan could hardly keep up. What were they supposed to do together?

The one called Feiyan tried to intervene. "Honestly, sir," she said politely, "'twould be best if you let our cousin go now."

Colban was sneaking up behind the dark-haired lass. Morgan could see him, but he gave no indication.

"If I let her go," he said, "what assurances do I have she won't attack me again?"

"She'll give you her word," Feiyan said. "Isn't that right, Jen?"

"The devil I will!" Jenefer declared, struggling anew. "The bastard came at me with a claymore!"

"Ye see?" Morgan said as he saw Colban inch closer.

"I do," Feiyan said, lowering her brows and giving him a curious look of regret. "But don't say I didn't give you fair warning."

Just as Colban loomed over the lass, about to spring, Feiyan suddenly bent forward and spun round. She swung her leg in a powerful arc, clipping Colban's chiseled jaw with surprising accuracy and force.

So unexpected was the violent outburst that Morgan almost dropped Jenefer.

"Feiyan, nay!" Hallidis shouted.

But demure Feiyan paid no heed. No sooner did Colban recoil from the blow than the lass dropped to the ground and swept both legs forward toward Morgan, catching the back of his calves and bowling him over like a wooden pin.

Chivalry was ingrained in Morgan, even in circumstances like these. As he fell, he took care not to crush the naked lass in his arms. But he needn't have worried. As soon as he hit the sod, Jenefer sprang loose from his grip with a cry of victory.

Now he *definitely* couldn't let them escape. Three lasses besting Morgan was bad enough. But three lasses making fools of Morgan *and* his right hand man...

That was insufferable.

With a roar, he righted himself and lunged toward Feiyan. But she was lightning fast. She dodged out of the way. Twice.

"Feiyan!" Hallidis barked again.

Colban gave his head a shake to restore his senses and then brought his arms together, attempting to grab the elusive Feiyan. She seemed to disappear into the darkness. Colban's arms crossed, empty.

Before Morgan could comprehend what had happened, Feiyan stepped in and elbowed him in the stomach. His padded cotun absorbed most of the blow. But he was knocked enough off-balance that she managed to get in a jab with the heel of her hand, this one to the point of his chin.

Tiny lights burst in his vision like stars streaking across the heavens, fading into the black sky. He had one brief instant to wonder what the hell was happening.

Then, several yards away, he spied Jenefer swooping up his claymore. In the next moment, she came barreling toward him with the gleaming sword held aloft, like a naked avenging angel.

"Jen!" the other two lasses screamed.

But Jenefer wasn't listening. She had fire in her eyes and vengeance in her heart. She clearly meant to slay him.

In a tiny, dark corner of his soul, he almost wished she would.

Then that bitter thought vanished, and his survival instincts kicked in.

CHAPTER 9

Jenefer didn't intend to kill the Highlander. Of course she didn't.

She might be hotheaded. Short-tempered. Impulsive. Likely to act first and explain later.

But she was no murderer.

She only meant to frighten the brute, the way he'd frightened her.

The problem was her cousins didn't believe that. They didn't trust her. They thought she intended to cut down an unarmed man.

Their doubt troubled and distracted her. So much so that when she charged forward, wielding his claymore, she didn't notice the Highlander's fair-haired clansman bolting to intercept her.

Feiyan noticed. She reached into her bodice and pulled out one of her wicked steel stars. With a flick of her wrist, she fired it at the man.

Time seemed to slow as the star whirred through the air, catching the light of the full moon on its sharp points. Jen watched in breathless horror as it sailed straight for the man's heart.

With an audible thunk, it lodged in its target.

Time stopped then. The wind silenced. The stars froze. The moon hung motionless. Fate balanced on a dagger's edge. For a long moment, there was no sound. No movement.

Then the man looked down, puzzled.

The deadly star protruded from his chest. But it hadn't pierced his cotun. It was stuck fast in the padding.

The gears of time slowly ground to life again.

With cautious fingers and a grimace of fury, the man plucked the star out and dropped it on the frozen ground.

That moment of distraction, however, proved to be Jenefer's downfall. She hesitated just long enough to allow the Highlander to lunge forward and seize her wrist. He gave her arm a hard shake, making her drop the claymore. Then he caught her around the waist, heaving her up in one powerful arm while she spat oaths at him and struggled for freedom.

In turn, Feiyan, distracted by Jenefer's disarming, was late to notice the advance of the second man. He was large, but he was fast. Before Feiyan could dance away, he upended her, slinging the wee lass over one massive shoulder like a bag of barley.

"Nay!" Jenefer screamed, enraged that they'd both been so easily bested.

Now it was up to Hallie.

Surely she'd pick up his sword. It was her weapon of choice. Though Jenefer hated to admit it, Hallie's skill with a blade rivaled her own. All she had to do was sweep it up from the ground and…

"Feiyan!" Hallie chided. "We were supposed to be unarmed!"

Jenefer choked on astonishment. Why was Hallie scolding Feiyan? Why wasn't she taking action? Wasn't she going to defend them? Wasn't she going to snatch up the claymore and make a stand against the Highlanders? Would she actually betray her own cousins?

Feiyan's reply was muffled by the padding of the man's cotun. "Fie, Hallie, you know I never go anywhere without a weapon."

Hallie let out a disappointed sigh. But she couldn't possibly have been as disappointed as Jenefer felt.

Hallie addressed the men in a taut voice. "Let's be civil about this," she said. "I want no trouble. These two are under my command. I'll see they do you no further harm if you free them."

Jenefer, who had plenty of further harm in mind, bit back a retort. How dared Hallie make promises on her behalf—promises she had no intention of keeping?

Apparently, the men didn't believe Hallie or trust Jenefer either.

"Free them?" the one holding Feiyan barked.

"'Tis too late for that," the Highlander growled.

"I see." Hallie let out a long sigh. "Then you'll have to take me captive as well."

Feiyan gasped.

"Nay!" Jenefer protested. "You can't do that, Hallie! This is *my* battle! I won't let you sacrifice yourself!"

"Can't you see you've given me no choice?" Hallie muttered.

Jenefer twisted in the Highlander's grasp until she could see her cousin. "Go, Hallie! Run! Go to Rivenloch and bring back..." She stopped herself. It might be unwise to alert the Highlander to the fact they had a whole army at their command.

"I warned you, Jen," Hallie said. "I told you 'twas not a battle."

Jenefer gave her a black look. What the devil was Hallie thinking? Was she mad? She could have returned to Rivenloch for reinforcements, then come back and launched a proper attack on the castle.

With all three of them held captive, they were helpless to do anything until...until their parents returned.

The last thing Jenefer wanted was for her parents to find out she'd challenged the Highlander and *lost*. They might think twice about giving her command of Creagor.

Loki's bones! She never should have let go of the claymore. She never should have trusted Hallie to take up her cause. Hallie was a stubborn wench. And she always thought she was right.

"You know I'm right," Hallie stated, proving her point. "But never fear, cousin. I won't abandon you."

Hallie and her self-sacrificing, self-righteous ways always made Jenefer feel like a child.

She swore under her breath. Now, if she managed to escape, Hallie would brand her a deserter.

Damn her cousin. Hallie had effectively left them all at the Highlanders' mercy.

She shuddered once, hoping it was from cold and not fear. But these were challenges she'd never faced before.

She'd never encountered men as massive as these. She'd never seen agile Feiyan so swiftly dispatched by an opponent. And she'd never felt as defenseless as she did now, dangling from the Highlander's powerful arm like a sacrificial lamb.

Jenefer hated to confess it, but for the first time in her life, she felt a frisson of dread. Who knew what grisly punishments these barbarians practiced on their enemies? She'd heard tales about the brutes who dwelt in the Highlands...

They sharpened their teeth on grinding stones.

They marked their servants with burning brands.

They butchered cows by tearing them limb from limb.

And by the loud wailing that began again from the upstairs window, they hardened their offspring by ignoring their cries.

CHAPTER 10

Morgan scowled. Why were the nurses letting his bairn cry? If they didn't calm the lad soon, the whole household would wake. And if that happened, his clan would witness their laird wrestling with three lasses in the moonlight, one of them as naked as a newborn.

The idea was horrifying.

Just as horrifying was the thought of taking them captive. What was he to do with three bloodthirsty lasses? He'd barely moved into the castle. Did the keep even have a place to hold prisoners?

To be honest, he didn't want to bring them inside the gates, where they could endanger his clan. Nor did he want to see what manner of sword-wielding, axe-brandishing, vengeance-seeking Rivenloch warriors would march to Creagor on the morrow to reclaim their missing daughters.

This was no way to meet his new neighbors.

Yet what other choice did he have? He dared not let the murderous women go. Not after what they'd attempted.

For one terrible moment, he'd feared Colban had been mortally wounded. He had no idea what gruesome weapon that dark-haired witch had thrown. But he was grateful she was only a wee lass with limited strength in her arm.

Fortunately, Colban was clever enough not to take any chances with the slippery whelp. God only knew what other armaments were hidden on her person. Righting the wench again, Colban clamped her against his chest and set a dagger at her throat.

As for the fiery temptress still thrashing about in Morgan's grip, he had just about lost patience with her. The combination of her vulnerable nudity and violent savagery were creating confusion and conflict—in his mind and in his body. And he hated to be confused.

The blonde, Hallidis, might be overbearing. But at least she was reasonable. She didn't seem to possess her cousins' lust for blood. And she had the good sense to know when she was beaten.

Her voice was cool, somber with resignation, and she clasped her hands humbly before her as if she wore shackles. "What do you mean to do with us?"

What indeed?

Morgan was tired. He was aching. His body was bruised and battered. His soul was weary and dispirited. All he wanted to do was return to his chamber and go to sleep.

At that instant, the bairn let out a piercing scream, as if to say there would be no sleep for Morgan this night.

He let out a long-suffering sigh.

Then an insidious idea entered his mind.

Maybe he *did* know where to stash the wayward lasses.

All he needed was to ensure they wouldn't escape. They'd be safe enough. Duly punished, but unhurt.

On the morrow, when everyone was thinking more rationally, Morgan could greet the Rivenloch soldiers—who'd surely come for the lasses—with a clear conscience and the diplomacy to settle things peaceably.

First, however, he had to take a few precautions.

"Colban," he said, "search her for weapons."

"Nay!" Hallidis said sharply, vexing Morgan. But before he could rebuke the lass, she volunteered, "Please. Allow me."

Morgan glanced at Colban. By his worried expression, Colban likewise found the task of searching a woman at the point of a dagger distasteful. No matter that the woman had meant to slay him.

Then Morgan narrowed his eyes at the blonde, gauging her intent. She seemed sincere. He blew out a long breath. Hoping to God he wasn't being gulled by her forthright gaze, he gave her a slight nod.

"Feiyan," she bade the dark-haired lass. "I command you to surrender your arms." Then, as if she suspected her cousin's devious nature, she added, "All of them."

Feiyan's lips formed a disappointed pout. "Fine."

Colban cautiously removed the dagger from her throat and loosened his grip on her. He stepped backed, keeping his weapon at the ready.

While Morgan watched, she reached into her bodice with her finger and thumb, withdrawing another steel star, which she released onto the sod. Then she crossed her arms and drew two narrow-bladed knives from the waist of her surcoat. With a sharp flick of her wrists, she flipped the blades, driving them point-first into the ground.

From hidden pockets in her skirt, she pulled two small cylinders of wood. They were attached to the ends of the girdle of silver links circling her hips. Releasing one cylinder, she whipped the chain through the air in a whistling spiral. The force was lethal enough to knock a man cold. Instead, she caught the cylinder easily in her other hand and dropped the weapon harmlessly onto the grass.

It was the most curious assortment of arms he'd ever seen.

With a stubborn jut of her chin, Feiyan crossed her arms over her chest.

"And the rest?" Hallie said in a warning tone.

The rest? There were more?

Feiyan snorted in disgust. Then she lifted one corner of her skirt to pull something out of her boot. It looked like a folded silk fan. But when she snapped it open, the moon reflected off spines of metal embedded in the silk.

Finally, with a heavy exhale of regret, she swirled back her skirts to reveal a long leather sheath hidden on a belt between her surcoat and black linen kirtle.

When she unsheathed the weapon, Colban audibly gasped. The sword was unlike anything either of them had seen before. Long, narrow, curved, and impossibly sharp.

Feiyan gave Colban a smug smirk as she drew the dull side of the blade slowly against her upraised palm. Then she placed the sword with reverence on the ground before her.

"Feiyan," Hallie said, nodding her chin upward.

Feiyan's brow puckered for an instant. Then she remembered her last weapon. It was a wicked pair of long pearl-topped pins stuck into the nest of braids atop her head.

Now that Feiyan was disarmed, all eyes went to the naked lass Morgan held captive against his hip.

"Well, don't look at me," she snapped. "Where would I be hiding a bloody weapon?"

CHAPTER 11

Unlike her cousins, Jenefer had no intention of going quietly into captivity. She planned to force the Highlander to carry her, kicking and screaming, all the way.

He had other plans.

"Ye can wear my leine," he said.

His offer surprised her. She expected no mercy from him. But it was tempting to take him up on it. The sweat of battle was upon her, making the cold wind even more chilling.

Still, that would be surrendering. She didn't want to give him the pleasure.

"I don't want your filthy leine," she said stubbornly, half hoping his entire clan would witness the travesty of their laird forcing a helpless, naked lass into captivity against her will.

"I'm not givin' ye a choice," he said.

"I won't wear it."

"Ye will."

"Nay, I won't."

"Aye. Ye will."

"Nay, I w—"

Before she could finish the word, he dropped to the ground with her, pressing her back onto the icy grass and straddling her.

Holding her fast between his knees to prevent her escape, he tore off his cotun and hauled his pale saffron leine off over his head.

Jenefer lay stunned. She told herself that he'd knocked the wind out of her. That she was too cold to move.

But the truth was she was rattled by the impressive sight of him. Highlanders were as massive as the rumors purported. His shoulders seemed impossibly wide. His arms were well-muscled. His chest was as broad as a bull's. Yet for all the tales she'd heard about the furry, bearlike men of the north, his torso had only a light dusting of dark hair.

Only when he tried to sit her up did she remember to fight back.

It was a bad decision. In his efforts to wrench the leine down over her, his hands brushed her intimately more than once. Alternately gasping and cursing, batting ineffectually at his arms, she did more harm than good.

In the end, he had to settle the weight of his hips atop hers to anchor her to the ground. And all her shrieks of protest did nothing to prevent him from dressing her in his leine.

When he was done, and he set her on her feet again, her cousins' silence was damning. Jenefer's defiance had gained her nothing and only embarrassed them.

But she didn't care. In her opinion, her cousins had surrendered too easily. It was more proof she was the better warrior.

Worse than weathering their disapproval, however, was being forced to wear the Highlander's leine. The despised garment hung down past her knees, enveloping her as if to claim her. It was still warm from his body, and it smelled of spice, sweat, and smug triumph.

Still, that was the least of her troubles. If he was able to subdue her so easily, what might he do to her later, in the privacy of his chamber? What would happen to her cousins? Both of these men's faces bore numerous cuts and bruises, marks of violence. Would they try to beat her and her cousins into submission?

She cast another quick glance at the battle-hardened Highlander, who was slipping back into his discarded cotun and retrieving his claymore. Her heart pounded at the sight of his rolling shoulders and rippling back. Even if she could make a break for it, she couldn't leave her cousins in the arms of these powerful beasts. She had to protect them.

But she'd do it on her own terms.

When he made a move to pick her up in his free arm, she stepped back.

"I can walk on my own, Highlander."

"I'm sure ye can," he muttered. "But will ye?"

She chose not to answer. Instead, she let willfulness replace trepidation. She tossed her head and strode brazenly through the palisade gates and toward the castle. If her courage held, she could imagine she was *attacking* the keep rather than marching to her own imprisonment within its walls.

The others fell in. The tall fair-haired man still had a firm grip on Feiyan. Hallie came of her own accord.

It went against all Jenefer's instincts to surrender. But perhaps that was for the best. Perhaps they *should* go willingly and wait until the Highlanders had their guard down to make their move.

Once they were inside the walls, she and her cousins could take account of their resources, look for weaknesses in the castle defenses, and combine their strengths to figure a way out of this.

Jenefer shivered as a rogue breeze whipped the linen of his leine against her thighs. She only hoped the three of them could escape before the men decided to prove their manliness.

When they pushed through the door and entered the courtyard, she was dismayed to see how quickly the

Highlanders had made themselves at home. The once abandoned outbuildings were now filled with goods and tools. One pen was full of sheep. Another held half a dozen coos. And from the tower above, where her colors of du Lac and Rivenloch should have flown, waved the arrogant pennon of an unfamiliar clan.

A guard stood at one of the towers of the keep. Jenefer shot him a hateful glare, and he scrambled back, probably to alert the castlefolk.

Moments later, the doors to the great hall suddenly flung open to make way for them.

"Och shite," her captor muttered, getting a firm grip on her arm.

Apparently he'd hoped to enter the castle quietly, unseen, not in front of a crowd of curious clansmen.

She couldn't blame him. After all, marching through the hall with three unarmed lasses—one of them not even decently clad—was the act of a coward.

Naturally, she decided to make the most of it.

Coloring her voice with desperate fear, she cried out, "Please, m'laird, do not murder us!"

CHAPTER 12

Morgan's eyes closed to slits. It was bad enough that about a dozen of his clan lingered in the great hall. But this wicked-tongued lass was inciting them with her words.

Her ploy worked. Already they turned to him in askance.

Before he could explain, she spoke again, addressing his clan.

"I beg you," she entreated, blinking back tears from her enormous green eyes. "We mean you no harm. Don't let him slay us."

There was a collective gasp.

"Is it true, m'laird?" Symon the cook asked. "Do ye mean to kill these lasses?"

"O' course not," he snapped. How could his own clan doubt him? Did they believe a Lowland whelp over their own laird?

The lass, who'd been fearless enough outside the castle walls, now cowered as if in fright.

Colban tried to clarify. "We ne'er said we were goin' to kill them."

The lass somehow managed to blush as she lowered her voice to a murmure. "But you can see...he's already tried to ravish me."

The clan fell silent in shock.

Morgan shook his head. "I did no such thing, lass, and ye know it."

She sniffled. Twice. And tugged down the hem of his leine with her free hand.

Whispers of speculation circled the hall.

If Morgan weren't so vexed and tired, he would have laughed at the maid's cleverness. She'd made them think he'd taken her clothes. And now that he saw her by the firelight of the great hall, he could see why she'd gained his clan's sympathy.

For all her devilish wiles, she had the face of an angel. Her eyes were like deep emerald pools. Her trembling mouth was rosy and voluptuous. Her hair fell in soft and tempting dark honey-colored waves over her shoulders. And despite her uncommonly tall frame, she was dwarfed by his leine, which made her seem frail, delicate, fragile.

She'd managed to earn their compassion and cast doubt on him.

But he'd show the lass that two could play at that game.

To her, he said, "I'm no ravisher, and my clan knows that. They can see whose leine ye're wearin'." Then he announced to the clan, "I brought these lasses out o' the cold to warm their bones by our fire." He shook his head in pity and confided, "This poor creature was runnin' naked through the grass, like a madwoman. Lendin' her my clothin' was the least I could do."

When he glanced at Jenefer, her eyes had gone flat and were fast filling with ire. The meek, fearful victim had vanished. He'd spoiled her plot. And the minx apparently had a hot temper when she was foiled.

"Madwoman?" she said through clenched teeth. "I'm no madwoman."

"Why else would ye be skulkin' about in the middle o' the wintry night without a stitch on?"

"I wasn't...skulking," she argued, obviously grasping at straws for an explanation. "My cousins and I often go for...for strolls in the dark."

"Indeed? And are ye in the habit o' strollin' onto others' property?"

Fire flared in her eyes. "Others' property?" she choked out.

"Ye see?" he whispered to the clan. "I fear she's not right in the head."

"I'll tell you who's not right in the head," she snapped. "You, Highlander, if you think you can lay claim to *my* castle!"

Everyone gasped at that, including her cousins, as her words sank in.

In the long silence that followed, Morgan asked the obvious question. "What do ye mean, *your* castle?"

Hallidis rushed to intercede. "My cousin misspoke, m'laird. I fear she's in her cups."

"I'm not in my—" Jenefer blurted.

"The cold's affected her mind," added Feiyan, trying to help out.

"What?" Jenefer demanded.

"Aye," Hallie said, "or the full moon."

Feiyan nodded. "Aye, the full moon."

But Morgan knew she was neither drunk nor mad. He held up his hand for silence and repeated his question to Jenefer in measured tones. "What do ye mean, *your* castle?"

Jenefer ignored her cousins' attempts to silence her and drew herself up proudly. "Castle Creagor rightly belongs to me, and—"

"Jen!" Hallie said sharply.

"Bloody fool," Feiyan muttered.

"Nay," Morgan said, "let her finish." This he wanted to hear.

She obliged him. "And I've come to claim it."

Morgan was suddenly wide awake. "Is that so?"

"Aye," she said.

He stroked his chin, wondering if she *was* mad. How could she believe that possible? "By what right do ye claim this castle as yours?"

He saw an instant of hesitation in her eyes before she answered. "By the right of the king."

Morgan narrowed his eyes. The wench was lying. Surely she knew the king had decreed that Creagor should go to Morgan Mor mac Giric. The documents so decreeing were on their way even now.

"Is that so?" he asked. "And if ye're so certain o' that, then why did ye feel the need to dress like a ghost to frighten me away?"

"A ghost?" Colban asked. "Is that what ye were supposed to be?"

"'Twasn't my idea," Jenefer declared. She added proudly, "If 'twere up to me, I'd have besieged the keep."

Colban made the mistake of snickering then, which only fueled the blaze of her rage.

"Or declared war," she announced, "and sent the lot of you scurrying back to the Highlands!"

"Are ye threatenin' me?" Morgan asked, incredulous.

He could feel the tension in the hall as his clan waited for her answer.

Jenefer's eyes took on a wicked gleam. "'Tisn't a threat. 'tis a pro—"

"Nay!" Hallie interrupted. With icy calm, she decreed, "This is not the time or place for threats."

Jenefer countered, "If not now—"

"Hist!" Hallie scolded. "You've wreaked enough havoc already, Jenefer."

Jenefer blushed hotly at the reprimand, but she bit her tongue.

Hallie continued. "'Twas kind of you to offer us a warm fire, m'laird. We are grateful. Perhaps on the morrow we can discuss terms of our return to Rivenloch."

He drew his brows together. Return? He thought not.

Colban might have scoffed at Jenefer's attempt at intimidation, but Morgan knew it was more than an idle threat. He'd seen the ferocity of the lasses. If the women were that well-trained in battle, what were the men like?

He didn't know how soon his title would arrive, but until he had the document in his hands, his claim was in question.

If what Jenefer said was true, if there were those who believed the castle belonged to Rivenloch, he might indeed have a skirmish with the neighbors on his hands.

Morgan sighed. As much as he wished to be rid of the troublesome lasses, they had just become his only leverage against war.

CHAPTER 13

If Jenefer didn't know better, she'd think Hallie was plotting against her. Since when did her battle-seasoned cousin back down from a fight? Hallie had not only surrendered to the Highlander. She'd practically apologized to him for the inconvenience.

Jenefer's blood was so hot now that she scarcely felt the autumn chill. A hundred curses perched on the tip of her tongue.

Of course, she'd utter not a one. She might be short-tempered and impatient. But she was also a good soldier. Like it or not, Hallie was her commander.

"Do we have a cup o' refreshment for our guests?" the Highlander called out.

She didn't miss the subtle edge he put on the word "guests."

"Aye, m'laird," a woman answered, hurrying to do his bidding.

Jenefer had to admit a drink *would* be welcome. Perhaps a healthy swig would cool her boiling blood.

Hell. She dreaded the idea of staying at Creagor while the Highlanders were still in residence. She'd planned to frighten them away tonight, then return to claim the empty keep on the morrow.

She'd hoped to surprise her parents on their return by moving their household into Creagor.

Hallie had ruined everything.

And Feiyan hadn't helped.

If the two of them hadn't intervened in Jenefer's affairs...

The Highlander addressed the others. "Return to your beds. There is much to do on the morrow." Then, as if to rub salt in her wounds, he added, "We'll need to purchase more livestock and provender for the winter ahead."

When the drink arrived, Jenefer snatched her cup with a vengeance and tossed it back all at once. But whatever devil's fire the Highlanders put in their strong brew, it proved her undoing. Her bold gesture ended in a humiliating bout of eye-watering coughs and choking.

Feiyan smacked her on the back, which didn't help at all and only increased her anger. Hallie's knowing sigh made Jenefer feel like a disappointing child.

In the midst of the embarrassment, the Highlander's fair-haired friend leaned toward him and murmured, "Where will ye store them, m'laird?"

Jenefer glared at the rude man. He had a black eye, and she was suddenly glad that someone had given him a good drubbing. How dared he insinuate the Warrior Daughters of Rivenloch were to be "stored" like goods?

"Upstairs," the Highlander replied. "In my chamber."

Jenefer exchanged dark glances with her cousins. Of *course* the savage would want them taken to his chamber. He no doubt intended to take turns upon them.

She wasn't going to let that happen.

Hallie might have submitted to the enemy. Feiyan might have yielded all her weapons. But Jenefer wasn't about to give in to the Highlander. Not as long as there was breath in her body. And she'd make sure he didn't lay a finger on her cousins either.

As it turned out, she needn't have worried.

After leading them upstairs and into his chamber, he stirred the fire and opened the wooden chest at the foot of the bed to haul out a thick fleece coverlet. He quickly assessed the room and, apparently satisfied with its contents, headed toward the door again.

"Leap from the window, and ye'll break upon the stones below," he warned. "Come through the door, and I'll be waitin' on the other side with four feet o' steel. Ye're welcome to try scalin' down the garderobe chute, but I'd not advise it." With a curt nod, he added, "Sleep well."

Then, to her amazement, he closed the door behind him, leaving them alone in the chamber. Apparently, he intended to treat them with courtesy.

"Interesting," Feiyan remarked.

"The fool," Jenefer scoffed, amused at the idea anyone could keep the Warrior Daughters of Rivenloch prisoner. "He has no idea who he's dealing with."

She knew there was a way out. There was *always* a way out.

"Nay, Jen," Hallie said, sinking down onto the edge of the bed.

Jenefer gave her an innocent blink. "Nay? Nay what?"

"Nay, we're not going to try to escape."

"The hell we're not," Jenefer huffed. "He may have left us alone tonight, but make no mistake, once he's rested from his journey—"

"He won't harm us," Hallie said.

"You don't know that."

Hallie pulled off her boots. "He's an honorable man."

"What!" Jenefer exploded. "You know as well as I do—the words 'honorable' and 'Highlander' cannot be uttered in the same breath."

Feiyan shrugged. "He did give us drink and..." She bounced onto the bed, testing it. "A decent enough pallet."

Jenefer shuddered. "Are you going to *sleep* in it? The bed of a flea-riddled Highlander?"

"Don't be absurd," Hallie said, pulling back the coverlet. "'Tis clean enough." She climbed in, punching the bolster into a softer shape. "Besides, I'm going to need all the sleep I can get to untangle the coil you've put us in."

"*Me? You're* the ones who got in my way."

Feiyan shot to her feet. "In your way? My best weapons lie rusting out there on the sod, you ungrateful cur. Besides, as I recall, you were already caught fast in the villain's clutches when we arrived."

"I would have found a way free." In fact, she was sure of it. Just as she was sure she'd find a way out of this chamber.

Feiyan clucked her tongue. "That's the point, though, isn't it? You always have to insist on using brute force. You have no sense of finesse. You can't use brute force against a giant like the Highlander. By the Rood, Jen, did you get a good look at him?"

She *had* gotten a good look at him. He was not only incredibly large and strong. He was also, despite the nasty cuts and bruises marring his face, a maddeningly handsome figure of a man.

The fact that she'd noticed that irritated her greatly and made her snap at Feiyan. "Your precious finesse got you disarmed by *your* foe!"

"I could have killed him if I wanted to," Feiyan boasted.

"Ha!" Jenefer mocked Feiyan's delicate swishing moves. "All that polishing of your grace has left you with the strength of a child!"

"Oh ho!" Feiyan roared. "Would you like to challenge this child to a—"

"Quiet!" Hallie hissed from beneath the coverlet. "You'll wake the—"

It was too late. A renewed wail interrupted her, proving they'd already awakened the infant.

CHAPTER 14

"**B**loody hell, did he put us next to that babe?"

Jenefer could hear the crying as if the child were in the room with her. She made a mental note to relocate the nursery once she was laird here.

Hallie shook her head at the sound. "Get some sleep, Jen. And I forbid either of you to attempt escape." Then she burrowed farther under the bedsheets.

Feiyan arched a slim brow at Jenefer, as if to say this was all her fault, then fell back upon the pallet beside Hallie. She snatched a bolster from the bed and folded it over her ears with a smile of mockery.

Jenefer fired back a smoldering scowl.

Forbidden to escape? This was a travesty. How else was she going to raise an army to claim Creagor?

She bit back a curse and sat in simmering silence.

Meanwhile, the babe continued to wail—long, shuddering cries.

How anyone could ignore the sound, she didn't know. It felt like an insistent grating on her soul. Her two cousins, however, snuggled together, as content as a pair of hens in a warm coop.

Impatient with them, Jenefer got up and paced past the fire. She wrung her hands at the relentless howling.

Where was the child's mother? she wondered. Where was its nurse? Did the hardhearted Highlanders truly believe it spoiled an infant to answer its cries?

It was disgusting. And it only proved what horrible creatures these people were. Once Jenefer took over the castle, she swore she'd send the lot of them back to the Highlands.

To Jenefer's further annoyance, despite the persistent wails, in another few moments, her cousins had fallen asleep. Their slow, relaxed breathing made a stark contrast to the miserable cries.

Stopping beside the fire, Jenefer scowled intently at the wall, willing someone on the other side of it to come to the babe's aid.

After a long moment, the weeping finally subsided, as if someone had at last picked up the child.

Relieved of one source of exasperation, Jenefer turned to glare at the other—the two lumps of her cousins, snug and snoring in the bed.

They might sleep on the watch, but Jenefer would take no rest, not while a usurper inhabited her keep. Even if Hallie had commanded her not to escape, she would keep vigil. Someone had to be ready for an opportunity to overcome their captors or coerce the brutes into letting them go.

An oversized, cross-legged, leather-seated chair stood beside the hearth. A large bolster cushioned the seat. She narrowed her eyes at the embroidered letters on its face—M m G—and wondered what they stood for.

Maggot Mouthed Giant.

Miserable Meddling Goat.

Motherless Midge-witted Glutton.

With a sigh, she sank down upon the chair. It proved surprisingly comfortable. So comfortable that her eyes drifted shut and she slipped into slumber.

The serenity was broken a little while later when the babe started up again at full volume.

Startled out of a dead sleep, Jenefer instinctively shot to her feet and reached for her bow. Of course, it wasn't there. Two confused blinks later, she remembered where she was and what had happened.

She glanced at the bed. Her cousins were still sleeping peacefully, sawing planks with their breathing. The fire had burned low.

While the babe wailed away, Jenefer got up and poked at the fire, stirring the coals to life. She added another lump of peat. Ordinarily she wouldn't waste fuel like this, but it was cold in the room with no coverlet, wearing only a linen leine. Besides, she rather liked the idea of wasting the Highlander's resources and making him pay for the trouble he'd caused her.

On and on the babe cried, mewling and bawling, then gasping in a quick breath, only to howl again.

Jenefer scowled once more at the wall, silently cursing the occupants on the other side.

Once she secured the castle, she swore she'd take that babe away from its cruel owners and give it to a milkmaid or serving lass to raise. Hell, even that gruff old knight in her uncle's company, Sir Rauve, had better mothering instincts than whoever was caring for the child at the moment.

After an agonizing interlude, the cries took on a rhythmic sound, as if someone had finally picked up the babe and was bouncing it on a knee. It didn't help much, but at least Jenefer knew the infant hadn't been completely abandoned.

It took a long while to calm the child. But by the time its cries turned to soft whimpers, Jenefer was worn thin with irritation.

How long the peace lasted, she wasn't sure. It seemed she'd just lapsed into slumber once more when the air was split by new wailing and she was jolted awake yet again.

She squeezed her eyes shut, determined to ignore the sound. After all, if her cousins could sleep through the racket, so could she.

This time, however, the cries seemed far more piercing and insistent. Even the rhythmic bouncing didn't stop them. On and on they continued, driving Jenefer mad.

"Shite!" she hissed.

The fire had burned low again, but she was too distracted to bother reviving the flame. She paced briskly before the hearth, wondering what ailed the infant and why its nurse couldn't stop its infernal cries. How hard could it be?

Jenefer could stop them.

And she would, if only she could get to that chamber.

The Highlander had posted himself on the other side of the door, so that wasn't an option.

She glanced at the shuttered window. He'd warned them not to leap from the ledge. But what if she could climb out and make her way to the adjoining window?

It was risky. But risk had never stopped her before. Besides, she was getting no sleep. It would be worth the risk if she could stop the babe from crying and close her eyes for more than a few moments at a time.

She carefully unlatched and cracked the shutters, wincing as the volume of the babe's wails increased through the opening. But when she looked over her shoulder at her cousins, they dozed on. She poked her head out and peered at the adjacent ledge, perhaps a dozen feet away.

Pulling her head back in, she tugged hard on the shutter to test its strength. It didn't budge. If she could tie a rope to the latch, she could swing over to the second window.

Stirring the fire for light, she scoured the room for rope. There was none.

Then she narrowed her eyes at the bedlinens. Those she could use.

Disgusted by the way her cousins were still snoring through the heartbroken laments of the babe, she was tempted to yank the sheets out from under the lasses and dump them on the floor.

But she knew Hallie wouldn't approve of her daring plan. So she eased the linens out from around them, inch by cautious inch.

The babe was still wailing when she managed to tie two of the sheets together. She knotted one end and secured the other to the shutter latch. Then she payed the linens out over the ledge.

Casting one backward glance at her cousins, who were blissfully unaware of her machinations, she heaved herself up onto the ledge.

The air was still icy, and the Highlander's leine provided scant comfort from the chill wind. But she would be swift.

Giving one last testing tug on the sheets, she carefully lowered herself out the window. Bracing her bare feet on the stone wall, she made her descent, hand over hand, until she reached the end of the cloth, gripping it just above the knot.

It was tempting to drop the several yards to the ground. It was a long drop, but she was fairly sure she could manage it without breaking her ankle.

Still, she'd given her word to Hallie she wouldn't try to escape. And she was a lass of her word. Besides, she wouldn't leave her cousins defenseless against the Highlanders.

With a determined breath, she began swinging her legs forcefully, moving the rope of sheets back and forth along the ledge. She couldn't make too many passes, lest the fabric tear on the stone.

Fortunately, though it took half a dozen swings and cost her a few scrapes on the rough sandstone, she finally managed to swing close enough to hook her foot on the ledge of the second window.

For one awful moment, she hung suspended between her fists on the taut linen and one straining ankle. Then she managed to work her second foot onto the ledge. From there, she inched forward until she could balance on the ledge with both feet.

The window was shuttered and latched. Of course. There was no graceful way to steal into the room. She would have to knock on the shutters and hope someone came to open them.

Shivering as a gust of wind blew under her leine, she pounded on the wood with the back of her fist.

No one came to the window. The babe wailed on. Perhaps she couldn't be heard above its cries.

Again she pounded for entrance, a bit harder.

No one replied.

She got the fleeting impression that perhaps the nurse had deserted the babe.

Which meant no one was going to open the shutters.

Jenefer was going to freeze to death on this ledge, fall to the ground, and shatter like an icicle into a thousand pieces.

Out of desperation, wondering if she could splinter the wood with her hand, she reared back a fist to bang as hard as she could on the shutter.

Just as she punched forward, the shutter was snatched open. Momentum made her spill awkwardly into the room, landing in a heap on the floor with the leine bunched up around her waist.

Towering over her was the scowling Highlander.

CHAPTER 15

organ was dumbfounded.

It took a lot to leave him speechless. But the beautiful lass sprawled bare-arsed at his feet did just that.

The bawling bairn had been shocked silent as well.

Beside him, his maidservant Bethac, holding the red-faced infant close to her bosom, suffered no such affliction. She blurted out, "Who are *ye?* Where did ye come from?"

The wild-eyed lass didn't answer. She scrambled to her feet and tugged down the hem of her leine. *His* leine, he amended.

"What the devil?" he barked.

Startled, the bairn resumed its wailing, filling the chamber with a long-winded lament.

Morgan's plot to antagonize his captives by imprisoning them next to a loud and restless infant had proved a double-edged sword. The soul-piercing cries had kept Morgan awake as well. So in frustration, he'd charged in to the chamber to insist that if the nurses couldn't stop the infernal keening, they should take the bairn downstairs.

When he first heard the banging at the window, he assumed it was a loose shutter stirred by the wind. The last thing he expected to see when he snatched open the shutter was Jenefer, the comely lass he'd imprisoned...in the chamber *next door.*

She looked feral and breathless in the firelight, her eyes crackling with life, her hair dripping like honey over her tempting shoulders. One of those shoulders was dangerously bare where his oversized leine hung off the side.

But more dangerous than her beauty was the fact she was standing close to his son and his heir. *Too* close.

"How did ye get in here?" he demanded.

The bairn arched his back and let out a particularly shrill cry. Bethac handed him off to the wet nurse, Cicilia. She tried to quiet him, encouraging him to take suckle at her breast, to no avail. The infant turned his head away and screamed all the louder.

Then, before Morgan could send the servants and bairn from the chamber for their own safety, the warrior lass reached out and seized the child from the mortified nurse's hands.

The breath caught in Morgan's chest. His heart hammered at his ribs. He froze. He didn't want to incite the lass to some unspeakable act. But his gaze drifted to the open window behind her. For one horrifying moment, he imagined...

His mouth opened and closed, but he could find no words to prevent her.

He'd thought his son meant nothing to him.

He'd blamed the infant for his wife's death.

But now that the bairn's life hung in the balance...

The lass didn't seem to notice his panic. She was holding the bairn, *his* bairn, awkwardly before her in her two hands.

"What ails you?" she demanded, scowling down at the child. "You've got food and drink, aye?"

To his surprise, the infant stared back at her, as if he were listening.

"There's a roof o'er your head," she pointed out, "and you're bundled against the cold."

Relief came gradually as Morgan realized Jenefer meant the bairn no harm. Soon, to everyone's astonishment, as the lass continued speaking to him in words an infant couldn't possibly understand, the lad's whimpers softened.

Morgan glanced at Bethac, who looked just as puzzled as he. But as he continued listening, he realized, despite Jenefer's sweet and tender tones, her words were as sharp as Spanish steel. The wicked firebrand was speaking ill of him...to his own son.

"Never mind that nasty brute's bellowing," she confided to the bairn. "He's a horse's arse who thinks shouting makes a man of him."

"What?" Morgan demanded, almost certain he heard Bethac choke back a laugh.

The bairn had quieted now and was focusing intently on Jenefer as she clucked her tongue. "'Tis what comes when you're raised by barbarians and dunderheaded fools."

"What the—"

"There," she said with a nod of satisfaction as the bairn studied her. "All you needed was a kind word from a good Lowland lass, wasn't it? You come home with me, and I'll see you get the care you deser—"

"Nay!" Morgan shouted, suddenly possessed of a strange possessiveness.

The bairn fussed at Morgan's outburst, then quickly settled back down in Jenefer's hands.

"Why should *you* care?" Jenefer asked, giving him a black look. "You Highlanders clearly don't mind letting babes wail at all hours of the night."

Bethac gasped.

"That's absurd," Morgan said in his defense, angry that he felt he had to defend himself. "I came in to send them downstairs."

"Oh aye," she sneered, "send them away so the noise won't disturb your precious sleep. But the babe is clearly upset. Didn't you wonder why? Maybe it's swaddled too tightly. Or hungry. Or soiled. Or maybe," she added cagily, "it doesn't like being in a castle where it doesn't belong."

"Enough!" Morgan erupted, then glanced at Bethac. "Take him back."

Bethac stepped forward. Jenefer shrugged and passed the bairn into the older woman's arms. In the next instant, the whimpering resumed.

Morgan scowled at Bethac. "Can ye not keep the bairn quiet?"

Bethac tried jostling him, stroking his back, and even holding him out in front of her as Jenefer had, to no avail.

She passed him to the wet nurse, who tried once again to offer him her breast. The bairn's cries only grew in strength and volume, making the nurse more and more distressed.

"Oh, for the love of Freya. Give him to me," Jenefer said in disgust, holding out her hands.

The nurse looked up at Morgan with uncertainty.

Morgan fumed. It was aggravating to give the cocky Lowland lass the satisfaction of being right. And it was foolhardy to put his heir into the hands of the enemy.

Still, what choice did he have? He couldn't even hear himself think over the wailing. Besides, if she attempted some foul deed, he could snatch up the fireplace poker in the blink of an eye and do her significant harm.

"Fine," he decided.

To his chagrin, once Jenefer cradled the bairn in one arm against her waist, he silenced.

"He seems to like ye, Miss," the nurse ventured.

Jenefer frowned down at the bairn, as if she doubted the lad's good judgment.

Morgan doubted the lad's good judgment. The lass might have calmed the bairn, but she was clearly a bad sort. How the hell had she escaped his room? And how had she ended up on the ledge?

"How came ye to this chamber?" he growled.

Jenefer gave him a smoky-eyed, one-sided smile. "Maybe I *am* a ghost, after all," she slyly murmured, "and I floated through the air."

He knew better. But rather than ask her questions she'd answer with lies, he swept past her to the window and peered out. A rope of knotted bedsheets flapped in the wind from the adjoining window.

He was so astonished, he almost hit his head on the window when he pulled it back in.

"Ye climbed o'er from the other window," he guessed.

She gave him a cocky smile as she nodded.

"Are ye daft, lass?"

She shrugged one shoulder. "I made it, didn't I?"

Suddenly, he looked at the beautiful, fiery maid with new eyes. He'd already experienced her hotheadedness and strong will. But now he saw she was clever. Brave. Daring. And brilliant. The combination made her a formidable adversary indeed.

"Someone had to do something about the infernal noise," she explained. Glancing down at the bairn, who stared back at her with inquisitive eyes, she murmured, "What's its name?"

"What?" he grunted.

"The babe. What's its name?"

Morgan stared blankly at his son.

When he didn't answer, Jenefer turned to Bethac.

Bethac worried her hands together and knitted her brows. "He hasn't got a name yet, Miss."

"What? Hasn't he been baptized?" Jenefer glanced back at Morgan. "Whose babe is it?"

Guilt and shame tied Morgan's tongue.

Cicilia began to answer. "Why, Miss, do ye not know? 'Tis the son o' the lai—"

"The Lady Alicia!" he broke in before she could finish. He didn't dare give Jenefer any more leverage over him. The lass might appear to have a way with infants. But if she found out this one was his son, he had no doubt she'd bargain with the bairn's life to gain her freedom.

Jenefer smirked in disgust. "And where is this Lady Alicia, that she makes no effort to pacify her own babe?"

His eyes flattened. He'd tell her the brutal truth. That should shut her up. "Lady Alicia is d—" To his consternation, his voice caught on the word. It was too difficult to say.

Jenefer's brow creased, and she turned to Bethac for an answer.

Bethac's face fell. She murmured, "I'm afraid she's no longer with us, Miss. She died givin' birth to this wee lad."

CHAPTER 16

Jenefer furrowed her brow. That made up her mind. She was definitely going to take the babe.

The wee thing was clearly too much work for the old maidservant. And the laird knew less than Jenefer did about dealing with infants.

She'd take him off their hands and find a wet nurse at Rivenloch to care for the child.

"You should at least name him," she said, peering down at the newborn. Now that his face had paled from an angry, wrinkled red to a calm cream, she saw he was rather comely—for an infant. He had a sweet mouth, long lashes, and a fine dusting of dark hair covering his shapely head.

The maidservant exchanged a curious glance with her laird.

The Highlander scowled in irritation. "He'll get a name in due time."

Jenefer scowled back. It was ridiculous to put it off. And since she intended to take the lad with her anyway, she decided to name him herself.

"Well, if *you* won't do it..." She tipped her head down to ask the babe, "What about Miles, lad? Do you like the sound o' that?"

The babe waved his fists. She decided to take that as his approval.

"Then Miles 'tis," she proclaimed.

The maidservant beamed and gushed, "Och aye, 'tis a brilliant name!"

"Nay!" the Highlander boomed.

The babe stiffened. His lower lip quivered as if he might cry again. Jenefer scalded the Highlander with a look.

"What's twisted *your* trews?" she demanded. "'Tis a fine Scots name."

"I'm the laird," he told her, crossing his considerable arms over his considerable chest. "I'll be the one namin' the bairn."

She let her gaze course over the Highlander. Was that how they did things in the Highlands? Did the laird name all the babes of his clan? It seemed unfair.

But she wasn't going to argue with him now. Standing like that, he looked quite imposing and formidable. He had the confidence of a man who believed his word was law. And he probably thought he could squash her like a flea.

But all men had weaknesses. She'd find his—eventually.

Meanwhile, she arched a brow. "Do what you will. But *I'm* going to call him Miles."

She could see the Highlander wanted to gainsay her. But unless he was willing to cut out her tongue, he couldn't very well prevent her from calling the babe whatever she wished, whether it was Miles or Methuselah the Miserable.

Just to provoke him, she ignored him to address the babe. "You like your new name, don't you, Miles? And I'm sure Lady Aelfeva would have liked it as well."

"Not Aelfeva," the man groused. "Alicia."

"Is it now?" For someone who wasn't in a hurry to name things, it was curious he cared whether she got the mother's name right. She bowed her head in salute to the babe. "Well, Miles, good even to you. My name is Jenefer du Lac." She added under her breath, "Soon to be Laird Jenefer of Creagor."

"What was that?" the Highlander demanded.

"Just telling him my name."

He lowered his brows in disapproval. "Why? He's a bairn. He can't understand ye."

"'Tis the proper thing to do." She gave him a scornful glance. Apparently, it was true what they said—Highlanders had no grasp of common manners. "'Tis ne'er too early to learn courtesy."

Slowly the babe's eyes drifted shut, and Jenefer handed the drowsy Miles off to the maidservant. The woman settled the babe into his low crib by the hearth and tucked blankets in around him.

Then Jenefer faced the Highlander, mirroring his menacing posture—crossing her arms over her chest—and muttered, "Methinks *you* could have benefited from early lessons in courtesy."

He looked daggers at her. "Ye dare to insult me?" he challenged. "Do ye know who I am?"

"Nay, I don't," she replied, "which is my point. You have yet to properly introduce yourself."

"Ye don't know who I am?" He blinked in disbelief. "Do ye mean to say ye've decided this land doesn't belong to me, yet ye don't even know who I am?"

It *did* sound rather odd when he put it that way.

"I know who you *think* you are. You think you're the Laird of Creagor."

His arms unfolded. He clenched his fists and moved to loom over her. This close, he looked as if he might swallow her whole at any moment.

"I *am* the Laird o' Creagor," he bit out.

His quiet words were far more chilling than a shout. Despite her usually indomitable courage, in the shadow of the Highlander, she gulped and felt her fingertips dig into her arms. She'd poked the beast one too many times. And there was something menacing in his intense gaze that made her want to keep her distance.

Nonetheless, it wouldn't do to let him know she was anxious. So her tone was flippant when she said, "If you won't introduce yourself properly, perhaps I shall make up a name for you as well. Let me see... William the Weak? Olifard mac Awful? Marmaduke the Malevo—"

"Morgan!" he thundered in impatience, making her jump.

She cast a swift glance toward Miles, hoping the laird's shout wouldn't wake him.

Morgan's eyes were steely and his teeth clenched as he lowered his voice to say, *"Laird* Morgan Mor mac Giric."

Mor. It meant "big." An apt description, she thought as she peered up at him, mere inches away from his glowering countenance, close enough to feel the heat of his anger.

Her voice came out on a breathy wisp of air, but she forced herself to meet his stare with steadfast courage. "Pleased to meet you...Morgan," intentionally omitting the "Laird."

His eyes blazed into hers at the obvious slight. But she refused to look away. Showing vulnerability would have been a tactical mistake.

They locked gazes, her green eyes gleaming with feigned confidence beneath the scorching heat of his...what were they? Brown? Green? Golden? It was hard to tell.

As the moment drew longer and longer, neither of them willing to surrender in their silent contest of wills, a curious thing happened. The heat in his regard slowly cooled, like a coal diminishing from a riotous flame to a smoldering glow. The crease between his brows softened.

To her astonishment, a twinkle began to spark at the outer edges of his eyes. One corner of his lip curved up into the merest hint of a smile. Finally, he shook his head and let out a single chuckle.

"Are ye?" he asked.

"Am I what?"

"Are ye *pleased* to meet me?"

Her lips twitched. Those *had* been her words. Spoken out of habit, they hardly described the sentiment of a woman kept prisoner against her will.

Despite her best efforts, she couldn't help but be amused. An answering glint of mischief entered her eyes.

"I'd be pleased to meet you," she replied, "on the battlefield."

This time, his eyes danced with laughter, and he almost showed her an actual smile.

Her heart tripped. Despite her distaste for Highlanders, she had to admit, when he wasn't vexed and threatening, Morgan was dangerously attractive. Though it was flawed by injuries at the moment, his face was finely sculpted, with an angled jaw, prominent cheekbones, and a nose that was strong, if not quite straight.

"Ah, lass," he admitted with a sigh, "I'm far too weary to do further battle this eve, even a battle o' wits."

She wasn't surprised. He'd probably traveled a long way, spent the entire day installing his household—a household she intended to dismantle as soon as possible—and wanted nothing more than to get a good night's sleep, free from the sound of a babe crying.

But she couldn't forget what Hallie had said. It would be far more difficult to oust the invader if he had time to settle in.

"What about the morrow then?" she proposed. "I'll fight you for Creagor at dawn."

The maidservants gasped.

"Ye aren't serious?" He seemed genuinely surprised. He shook his head. "I won't fight a lass, no matter what combat skills ye claim to have."

"*Claim* to have?" She could feel her blood starting to simmer, as it always did when a man doubted her worth. "I've bested bigger warriors than you."

That was absolutely not true. But she had no doubt she *could* best bigger men than him.

"I doubt ye've *seen* a bigger warrior than me," he said, exposing her lie. He softened the blow by adding, "But I'm sure ye could send a grown man limpin' from the battlefield...if not from the keen side o' your sword, then from the sharp edge o' your tongue."

The younger servant giggled behind her hand.

Jenefer opened her mouth to reply and couldn't. Every response she thought of would only prove his point.

Flustered, she finally snapped, "Be ready at first light. I'll need to beg a sword and shield, as chivalry allows." Before he could refuse her, she jabbed a finger at his chest. "And know this, sirrah. If you do not accept my challenge, I shall brand you coward and spread that name far and wide."

CHAPTER 17

Morgan felt steam building in his ears. He lowered his gaze pointedly at the finger prodding him in the chest. The lass might look as appealing as a warm hearth, with her eyes blazing and her cheeks aflame. But like a poker, her insolent finger stirred the coals of his anger.

He reached up and curled his fist tightly around her offending digit, trapping her.

"Ye'll do no such thing, lass," he said. "This is my keep and my land. If ye're civil and honorable, ye may stay as a guest."

She clamped her lips and tried to jerk away, to no avail.

"If not, ye'll remain a prisoner."

"I can't be a prisoner in my own castle."

"'Tisn't yours, lass."

"The hell 'tisn't!"

Morgan hadn't been jesting when he'd said he was weary. He was brain-drained and bone-tired. He had no desire to engage the lass, either this eve in a battle of words or on the morrow in a clash of swords. So he cast her finger back at her.

"Ye'll go back to my chamber now...and stay."

"Oh, aye, I'll stay," she bit out, "but only because I vowed to my cousins I wouldn't leave them in the hands of savage

Highlanders." She sneered the words, "Not because you're commanding me like a hound."

Deep in his throat came an impatient sound that was half-sigh, half-growl.

She headed toward the window.

"Not that way," he said. "Through the door."

She turned and raised her chin. "Fine."

Striding past, she pointedly snatched her hem aside so it wouldn't touch him.

He shook his head in chagrin. The lass was wearing *his* leine, after all.

He followed at her heels, giving a farewell nod to the maidservants. He hoped he could trust them to be discreet about what had happened here. The last thing he needed was a crowd of his clansmen gathered at dawn, wagering on a match rumored between the new Laird of Creagor and a helpless, pesky flea of a wee lass.

He steered Jenefer back into his bedchamber. He was tempted to slam the door after her, just to emphasize the seriousness of his order.

But he didn't wish to wake Miles again. So he closed it gently and sighed as he looked down at his makeshift bed of fleece just outside the door.

Miles.

Now the pushy wench had *him* calling the lad Miles.

He had to admit it wasn't a bad name. When the bairn was grown, his full title would be Laird Miles mac Morgan. It was a good name, a strong name.

Still, it rankled at him that the lass had brazenly attached a name to the bairn, not even knowing whose it was.

He'd change it, he decided as he stretched out on the fleece. There were plenty of good names that would suit the son of Morgan Mor mac Giric. Maybe he'd christen the lad Allison, in honor of Alicia. Whatever he chose, he'd be damned if he'd let a headstrong warrior lass name his firstborn.

Yet to his annoyance, after several hours of blissfully undisturbed sleep, his first thought upon waking the next morn was gratitude that wee "Miles" had slept through the night.

With a self-mocking grimace, he rose up on one elbow. He yawned and raked his hair back from his brow.

As he blinked the cobwebs of sleep from his eyes, he heard stirring on the other side of the door. At first it was just the scraping of coals on the hearth and the patter of feet on the floor. Then he heard a flurry of female whispering.

He sat up with a sniff, stretching his arms carefully over his head. Yesterday's fight with Colban had left his ribs bruised and his shoulders aching. And his nose was still tender from the wench's punch.

The whispers were increasing in volume and agitation, though the words were too muffled to understand.

He'd have to sort everything out soon. He'd never taken hostages before. He was not in the habit of dealing with lasses much at all. Especially lasses as hostile, outspoken, and prone to squabbling as these Warrior Daughters of Rivenloch.

He didn't want to hold them any longer than necessary. With any luck, the documents from the king would arrive today, proving his claim. By afternoon, he could return the maids to their proper home and put all this behind him.

Then he could proceed with settling in to his new keep—exploring the land, purchasing provisions, finding a more suitable chamber for Miles, where his cries wouldn't disturb Morgan's sleep.

He frowned. It seemed the name Jenefer had given the bairn was going to stick.

He didn't care. Not really. The bawling bairn could be called Jehoshaphat, as far as he was concerned. He just didn't like the self-satisfied lass who believed she was the Laird of Creagor to think she could issue commands in *his* household.

From the other side of the door, he heard the self-important lass now.

"Aye, 'tis my handiwork. But you can see I'm still here," Jenefer was insisting. "Don't try to blame *me* for this!"

He couldn't hear her cousin's reply.

But Jenefer's response was, "I hope her da's knights *do* come. I told you from the beginning, we should have used force. *Now* maybe we'll get somewhere."

That brought Morgan to his feet.

He flung open the door.

The dark lass called Feiyan was standing beside the open window. In one hand was looped the rope of bedsheets Jenefer had made.

Jenefer wheeled toward him, her arms akimbo, her gaze defiant. Despite her rebellious expression, by day, she was even more captivating. The light of dawn filtered through the pale saffron of the leine, outlining her body in tempting relief. Her tawny tresses looked as inviting as sunshine.

Then he noticed the enticing flash in her emerald eyes. A flash that told him she kept a fatal secret.

"What have ye done?" he asked, afraid of the answer.

"*I* haven't done a thing," she said smugly.

He turned to Feiyan. "What's happened?"

Before Feiyan could reply, Jenefer responded with a silky, self-assured smile. "Exactly what I warned you about."

"Jen," Feiyan scolded.

Jenefer clucked her tongue. "You shouldn't have taken what wasn't yours...Morgan."

She'd omitted the "Laird" just to annoy him again. But he wasn't going to take the bait.

He turned to Feiyan again. She might at least give him a straight answer. "What are ye two up—"

He stopped abruptly as a swift perusal of the room told him what was wrong.

He narrowed his eyes. "Where's the third?"

CHAPTER 18

Jenefer had to give Hallie credit. She knew her cousin was clever. But she hadn't expected such ingenuity from her. Though Hallie had commanded Feiyan and Jenefer not to flee, she'd never said anything about making her *own* escape.

Apparently, sometime in the night, she'd done just that.

Using the rope of sheets Jenefer had conveniently left, it seemed Hallie had climbed out the window, dropped to the ground, and, if Jenefer's suspicions were accurate, lit out for Rivenloch.

Her domineering cousin must have finally seen the wisdom of summoning troops to take Creagor by force.

Jenefer felt like crowing with glee. Reinforcements would likely arrive within the hour. And once that swaggering Morgan Mor mac Giric glimpsed the magnificence of the Rivenloch knights, he'd pack up his clan and cattle and scurry back to the Highlands. Triumphant, Jenefer would claim Creagor for her own.

At least that was what she'd thought before the Highlander burst in, all might and muscle, looking more dangerous than she remembered.

Now, standing in arm's reach of the great beast of a man who somehow managed to loom even larger by the light of day, she had second thoughts.

Fearless and fearsome, he looked as if he might take on an entire army himself.

The contained fury in his eyes seared her. His nostrils flared with aggression. His jaw clenched. His chest swelled with rage.

Jenefer was sorely tempted to take a judicious step backward.

It took great restraint not to budge. But she managed, addressing him in a voice that was more confident than she felt.

"Did you think, Morgan Mor—just because we're wee lasses and you're a big man—we'd sit, and stay, like a pack of whipped hounds?"

To her dismay, her carefully aimed arrow went wide of its mark.

"Nay, Jenefer du Lac," he snarled. "I trusted—since ye claimed to be seasoned warrior maids—ye'd have a sense of honor and keep your word."

He glanced past her, toward Feiyan, branding them both with shame.

"Where has she gone?" he demanded.

"I don't know," Feiyan replied.

He glared at Jenefer.

She wasn't about to give the Highlander advance notice of an assault on Creagor. But she didn't need to lie to him. "She didn't tell us. We woke up, and she was gone."

Jenefer could see the gears grinding in his head as he imagined where she might go. She supposed it wouldn't hurt to give him a little unsolicited help.

She furrowed her brow with feigned concern. "I hope she isn't lost in the forest. There are wolves in the wood. And unarmed as she was..."

She hoped Feiyan wouldn't ruin her ploy with laughter. If there *were* wolves in the wood, Hallie had probably brought them all to heel long ago. And she could navigate the forests surrounding Rivenloch with her eyes closed.

Fortunately, Feiyan had her back. "Do you think something may have happened to her?" she asked, turning wide, watery eyes toward Morgan. "Our uncle will never forgive us if we've lost her."

Morgan glanced back and forth between the two of them, probably trying to decide whether to believe them. In the end, caution forced him to play into their hands.

"I'll send out a tracker." He sighed unhappily. No doubt he had few men to spare. "Are ye sure ye don't know where she's gone?"

Feiyan shrugged. Jenefer sadly shook her head.

Morgan wasn't fooled for an instant by the lasses' pitiful semblance of worry. And he was certain they knew exactly where Hallie had gone, especially since he'd overheard Jenefer mentioning her da's knights.

Hallie had obviously returned home to fetch her father's army.

Nothing could be worse.

He'd hoped to avoid a conflict with the neighbors.

Now he was heading towards all-out war. Short-handed. Ill-prepared. Without the means to withstand an attack or a siege.

God's bones. He hadn't even been in residence one full day, and all chaos was breaking out.

Muttering a curse, he wheeled away from Jenefer. It was hard to think with the winsome and wily beauty staring at him like that. Especially when he knew he might have to use the lovely lass as a hostage.

He grimaced. The thought of holding a dagger to her bonnie throat sickened him.

In frustration, he pounded the door with the back of his fist.

How much time did he have before the army of Rivenloch arrived at his gates? An hour? Two?

What was he to do?

The castle's defenses were his first concern.

He'd have to muster the few soldiers he had and station them along the curtain wall. He'd send servants out to gather the livestock and quickly harvest what remained in the fields to prepare in the event of a siege. Maids could haul up buckets of water from the courtyard well as a defense against fire. Young lads could set them at strategic points inside the palisade timbers.

His best defense, of course, was his possession of the lasses. Unless the Laird of Rivenloch deemed the Warrior Daughters expendable—and he didn't believe that for a moment, considering their marriageable beauty—battle could be avoided with that simple leverage.

But what about Hallie? What if she *hadn't* returned to Rivenloch? What if she *was* lost in the forest? Set upon by outlaws? Eaten by wolves?

His leverage was worthless without the third cousin. Hallie was the commander. She was the laird's daughter. If the Rivenloch knights appeared, and Morgan couldn't prove she was safe and unharmed...

He shuddered. He had no desire to face the army of a vengeful father.

He had to send someone after Hallie. Someone who could find her quickly.

His best tracker was Colban.

With any luck, his clever right hand man would find her before her clansmen could set foot on Creagor soil.

"So, Highlander, do you plan on starving us?" Jenefer suddenly asked, jarring him from his thoughts.

Food was the least of his worries. He would think it would be the least of hers as well. After all, she was about to become a pawn in a clan battle.

Feiyan chided her. "How can you think about breakfast at a time like this, Jen?"

Jenefer lifted a proud chin. "Unlike you, dwarf, I need sustenance to keep in fighting form."

Feiyan shook her head, then arched a judgmental brow. "You eat like an ox."

"I do not."

"A *pregnant* ox."

Jenefer's eyes flashed. "You spawn of a goblin! How dare you—"

"Enough!" he thundered.

Next door, awakened by all the noise, the bairn began to wail. Morgan growled deep in his throat.

"I'll send the maid up with breakfast," he grumbled.

"I won't eat live mice," Jenefer warned.

Morgan scowled. "What?"

Feiyan gave her an elbow. "Ignore her."

Jenefer elbowed her back.

Morgan shook his head. "Do ye think ye can keep from killin' each other till then?"

They exchanged smoky, slit-eyed glares full of malice, but nodded.

Feiyan got out of his way when he strode to the window. He unknotted the rope of sheets and hauled it in. For good measure, he took the coverlet as well, leaving only the sheepskins on the bed. He drew the line at confiscating the lasses' garments, though he wouldn't put it past the brash wenches to flee naked down a rope of their own clothing.

"I'm postin' a guard just outside," he said, opening the door, "so don't get any wild notions about takin' your leave."

"Taking my leave?" The fiery Jenefer couldn't resist adding, "Oh, I have no intention of leaving Creagor. Ever."

He answered her with a steely stare. He'd never raised his hand to a lass. And he never would. No matter how tempting it was to smack the smirk off her smug face.

And yet, as the willful wench continued to meet his gaze, he had to admit he was amused by her boldness. No lass had ever confronted him as directly, as unflinchingly, as this one did.

Even his own wife Alicia had shyly lowered her gaze in his presence.

Finally, realizing he was wasting precious time, he gave Jenefer a nod of farewell and left to prepare the keep for battle.

CHAPTER 19

The instant Morgan left, Feiyan turned to Jenefer. "Do you really think Hallie is bringing her da's army?"

It took a moment for Jenefer to comprehend the question. She was still rattled. No man had ever failed to back down under Jenefer's challenging stare. Until now.

The Highlander's gaze had been unyielding. Unsettling. Unnerving. And something else. Something that made her heart beat unsteadily.

"Well?" Feiyan insisted. "Do you?"

Jenefer, distracted, tried to recall what her cousin had asked. "Believe that Hallie is bringing the army? Aye, of course. Why else would she have left?"

Feiyan looked doubtful. "'Tis so unlike her."

"You don't think Hallie is truly lost in the forest and devoured by wolves, do you?" she scoffed.

"Nay, but..."

"Then she'll be here soon."

"You should know, when we left Rivenloch, she commanded the knights not to follow us. She said 'twas to be a mission of peace."

Jenefer bit her lip. Unfortunately, that *did* sound like Hallie. "But once we were taken captive," Jenefer reasoned, "she must have realized peace is impossible."

Feiyan gave her a quizzical look. "Is it though?"

"Aye," Jenefer groused, irritated that Feiyan seemed to disagree. "He plans to hold us hostage. He hopes to negotiate with Rivenloch for our release. And he'll demand Creagor as payment."

"Maybe. But 'twasn't what Hallie thought."

"Indeed?" Between the babe's incessant wailing and Feiyan's contrariness, Jenefer was feeling testy. "And just what did Hallie think?"

"She thought he meant to return us. She said he was a man of honor."

"Honor?" She rolled her eyes. "He's a Highlander, Feiy. You know they trade their children for cattle, aye?"

"Children for... Where did you hear that?"

"'Tis common knowledge. They're uncivilized." She waved toward the next chamber. "That's probably why the babe is upset. He knows he's going to be traded for a coo."

Feiyan shook her head and returned to gaze out the window. The wind had died down this morn. Fog softened the landscape.

Then she sighed. "My *dao* is out there somewhere, turning to shite in this weather."

Jenefer would have empathized, except she'd seen Feiyan's wall of weapons. Her cousin owned dozens of blades, axes, sticks, and stars. Daggers of all shapes. Some as small as sewing needles. Some as large as lances. Some looked as innocent as hairpins and ladies' fans. All of them were deadly.

She could hardly miss the few that lay strewn on the sod.

Besides, Jenefer's bow and arrows were out there as well. Worse, her satchel of food had been left to scavenging animals. It had contained a veal pasty, oatcakes, bannocks and butter, hard cheese, and an apple coffyn.

Her stomach growled in complaint. Of course it could hardly be heard over the babe's loud wailing.

She joined Feiyan at the window and leaned out over the ledge.

"Miles!" she shouted toward the adjoining window. "Quiet down now!"

By some miracle, he stopped. She and Feiyan exchanged looks of amused surprise. But in the next moment, he resumed his cries, even more piercing than before.

Jenefer shrugged and pulled her head back in. "I'm going to give that babe to someone who won't trade it for a coo."

Feiyan rolled her eyes.

Jenefer scowled as her stomach rumbled again. "Thor's beard! I'm starving."

Feiyan folded her arms in disapproval. "If our uncle's forces are indeed on their way, and if the Highlander intends to hold us for ransom, then we should be preparing for battle, don't you think?"

"I *can't* think," Jenefer said, "not on an empty stomach."

It was true. And Jenefer had given up trying to explain her voracious appetite, especially to Feiyan. She ate what she ate. Besides, despite her feasting, she was still rather lean for a lass.

Miles' cries grew muffled then and finally ceased. The nurse must have put the babe to her breast.

Jenefer sighed. At least *one* of them was getting fed.

"If I only had my *sais*," Feiyan said wistfully as she gazed into the mist.

Jenefer didn't know which weapon that was. But she understood. She longed for her bow as well. If the two of them were forced to face battle together, they needed to be armed. Even more, they needed confidence.

As much as she mocked her cousin for her whirling and prancing, she knew Feiyan's fighting methods could be effective indeed.

"You don't need weapons, Feiy," Jenefer said, giving her a wink and a sly grin. "You *are* a weapon."

Feiyan's wry mouth slowly turned up, and her eyes glittered with deadly threat. "That I am."

CHAPTER 20

Morgan scoured the armory as his warriors dutifully prepared for battle. They laced up their cotuns and buckled on claymores, donned helms and took down targes from the wall. All but one.

"Where's Colban?"

"He was on watch last night, m'laird," someone called out.

But no one knew where Colban was this morn.

Morgan searched the bedchambers, the courtyard, the great hall. He was nowhere to be found.

More often than not, Colban spent the night between the thighs of a lovely maid. His comely face and convincing grin assured him he seldom bedded down alone. And the black eye and split lip Morgan had given him had probably won him the sympathy of a willing wench.

But damn his hide! Morgan needed him right now. They were about to face a formidable force of knights bent on rescuing their precious clanswomen. And Colban was the only man he trusted to seek out and find the one that was missing.

Which reminded him… He'd promised to feed the two lasses in his bedchamber.

He stole several warm oatcakes from a kitchen maid's tray as she passed and grabbed a skin of ale off a trestle table. That would have to do.

Most of the servants were too busy stockpiling food and gathering livestock to tend to captives. So he decided to take it upstairs himself.

As he crossed the great hall, young Danald ran up to him.

"M'laird! I found these in the wood."

The lad had a quiver full of arrows and a longbow looped over one shoulder. He held up a satchel and what looked like a bundle of rags. Could they belong to the missing warrior maid?

Nay, she'd claimed to have come unarmed.

Tucking the wineskin under his arm, Morgan plucked out a length of sheer white linen and held it up.

When he realized what it was—a lady's leine—he quickly wadded it against his chest.

"Good work, Danald," he said. "I'll take them."

Once the lad scurried off, he set everything on a table to examine it more thoroughly. The bow was light but well-made, the arrows crafted by a master fletcher. There was a leather bracer tucked into the quiver. But neither it nor the quiver had identifying marks. There was no way to determine the weapon's owner.

Rummaging through the rest of the garments, however, it didn't take long to realize they belonged to Jenefer. He recognized the soft, earthy scent wafting off of them. Spicy. Sweet. Musky.

He blushed to think he'd been fondling her under-garment.

Clearing his throat, he moved on to the satchel. There were no weapons inside, just crumbs of whatever food she'd packed and a half-full aleskin.

Gathering everything but the bow and arrows, he bounded up the stairs.

Thankfully, Miles had ceased crying. Maybe he'd see if Bethac could slip downstairs to help with siege preparations.

First, however, he'd deliver the lasses' breakfast and clothing.

When he opened the door, Jenefer was sitting innocently enough on his pallet. But dressed only in his leine, she presented a compelling sight.

Her long, shapely legs dangled over the edge of the bed. Her delicate toes brushed the floor as Morgan entered. And where her knees were slightly parted, shadows hid the treasure he knew was there between them.

She didn't seem to notice that the breath had been stolen from him.

He used a moment to close the door behind him and gather his wits. Finally he dropped his burden onto the table.

"Breakfast," he announced. Then he frowned. "Where's Feiyan?"

"In the garderobe," she said, jumping up to see what he'd brought.

Apparently she wasn't going to wait for her cousin. She immediately pounced on the food like a wolf on a coney. She devoured the first oatcake at once. By the way she closed her eyes and licked her fingers, one would have thought she hadn't eaten for days and was dining on the finest swan.

She washed it down with a swig of ale, then began to demolish a second oatcake. He wondered if she intended to save any for Feiyan.

Feiyan was right. Jenefer did eat like an ox.

But it certainly didn't show. He'd held her, naked and squirming, against his side last night, and she hadn't seemed overstuffed in the least.

That memory made him uncomfortably warm, and it reminded him of what else he'd brought.

"Your clothin', I believe," he said, offering it to her. "A lad found it in the wood."

CHAPTER 21

Jenefer glanced down at the bundle of her clothes. She couldn't decide which she'd rather do. Refuse the clothing, thus denying him his own leine? Or tear his garment from her at once, telling him it stank of the Highlands?

In the end, she was too grateful for the warm breakfast to be rude. So she simply took the bundle and placed it on the bed. Then, swallowing down the last bite of her second oatcake, she whipped the borrowed leine off over her head and held it out to him.

The flash of shock in his eyes was amusing. Was this the same man who'd picked her up and carried her naked on his hip, then straddled her to force her into his leine? He looked as if he'd never seen an unclad lass before.

A merciful woman might have lowered her gaze and modestly covered herself.

But she wasn't feeling particularly merciful toward the man who'd usurped her castle. Besides, she found his discomfiture highly entertaining. So she challenged him with a half-grin and a steadfast gaze, observing his unease, waiting for him to claim his leine.

His jaw tensed. His nostrils flared. He compressed his lips.

But to her surprise, as uncomfortable as he appeared, he eventually met her gaze and held it. Resisting the urge to feast his eyes on her womanly attributes, he instead pinned her with a steely stare.

How he then turned the tables on her and made her suddenly feel ill-at-ease was a mystery. But as the moments dragged on, it began to take all her strength of will to stay focused on his smoky, unwavering gaze.

As he continued to lock eyes with her, she felt a curious warmth rush over her body, as if he'd set fire to her flesh. Her ears burned. Her cheeks turned to flame.

Then the stony-eyed devil reached up and loosened the laces of his cotun.

Her smile froze.

Never breaking eye contact, he hauled off the cotun and tossed it onto the bed, leaving his chest bare.

She gulped.

Surely he didn't mean to ravage her. Not now. Not when her uncle was on his way with an army.

Though she didn't let her eyes dip, she was all too aware of his powerful shoulders.

His broad chest.

The arms that could hold her down and bend her to his will.

He tormented her a moment longer. And then, with a knowing twinkle in his eyes, he snatched his leine from her and slipped it over his head.

He donned his cotun over the leine and fastened the ties.

Jenefer, however, was still naked when Feiyan returned from the garderobe.

Feiyan gave her a cursory and unsurprised glance and proceeded to the table. "Oatcakes!" she cried. "Did you leave any for me?"

Jenefer was too rattled to reply as she began fumbling into her own clothes with shaking hands.

Suddenly, her appetite was gone. She felt flustered. Unsteady. Off-kilter. She could hardly tie her laces.

To all appearances, Morgan suffered no such affliction, which made her even more vexed.

"I'm postin' a guard at the door," he warned them, "but I'm sure ye think ye can somehow outwit or outfight him. Ye told me ye were women of honor. Prove that. Swear to me ye'll not flee, and I'll do my best to find your cousin."

"I swear," Feiyan said readily, taking a sip of ale as if in salute.

Jenefer wasn't so sure. She didn't want Hallie to be found. But she didn't want to reveal that Rivenloch's army was on its way either.

"Fine," she said. "I swear."

She couldn't take a proper breath until Morgan was out of the room. And it didn't help her mood when Feiyan pointed out the laces of her surcoat were tied wrong.

But her appetite did return. She managed to consume the four oatcakes Feiyan left her.

Once her hunger was sated, she was more eager than ever to come up with a battle strategy. She needed to get rid of Morgan Mor mac Giric as soon as possible. He was dangerous.

"We only swore we wouldn't flee," she said to Feiyan, who was currently gazing out the window. "We didn't say anything about leaving this particular bedchamber."

"You know that's what he meant," she said, arching a brow at Jenefer. "He posted a guard outside the door."

"A guard we could dispatch easily."

"And then what?" Feiyan returned her attention to something on the ground outside the window.

Jenefer crossed her arms. "I thought you agreed we should be preparing for battle."

Feiyan bit her lip. "Aye, well, about that..."

"What is it?"

Feiyan motioned her over and nodded to the far end of the curtain wall, which enclosed a small practice field.

Jenefer peered down at the men on the field. There were only a dozen, but every one of them looked like a great beast, almost as large as Morgan. They were doing drills. Their feet pounded the sod as they advanced with their targes before them. In their powerful arms, the huge and heavy claymores sliced through the air as easily as a swallow's wing. The blades flashed in the morning sunlight. A collective rumble rolled like thunder as they grunted and lunged, roared and thrust.

They might be lacking in number, and there was little coordination in their fighting. But they resembled a formidable pack of wild wolves. Capable of intimidating by sheer size and aggression. Brutal and bloodthirsty. Eager to tear their prey limb from limb.

Even bold Jenefer was taken aback by the sight. One warrior that size she could handle. With Feiyan's help, she might cope with three. But even her expert swordsmanship and Feiyan's clever agility were no match for this monstrous horde.

Still, she wasn't about to admit defeat. She knew winning Creagor wouldn't be easy.

"They don't even have proper armor," she scoffed. They fought in padded cotuns and trews, without armor plate or chain mail. "Besides, Hallie is going to bring the entire force of Rivenloch. No one can stand against Uncle Pagan's army."

"An army will be useless if the Highlander holds us hostage."

"Then we'll have to make sure he can't."

"And how do you propose we do that?" she said, gesturing again to the massive warriors below.

"You tell *me*. You're always saying 'tis a matter of mind o'er muscle."

Feiyan gave her an icy glare and backed away from the window. "I'll have to ponder on it. Now, if you'll excuse me, I must do my *taijiquan*."

107

Jenefer sighed. The strange exercises Feiyan did every morning seemed utterly useless to her. As far as she could see, they neither strengthened her body nor improved her aim. Sometimes Jenefer wondered if Feiyan's old teacher from the Orient made her do them just for amusement.

She half-watched while Feiyan flexed her knees and swept her arms in wide arcs, turned slowly to draw strange shapes in the air and then sank into a lunge. But mostly Jenefer was intrigued by the practice going on in the yard below.

It was wise to know one's enemy. And what better way than to observe that enemy as they trained for battle?

Of course, the Highlanders had no idea how soon they'd need those skills. Only she and Feiyan were aware that the men of Rivenloch were on their way.

She lowered her brows. At least, she *hoped* they were on their way. It seemed like they should have been here by now.

She wondered how long ago Hallie had left. She trusted her cousin had made it to Rivenloch. She wouldn't have let herself be waylaid by outlaws. And no matter who Morgan had sent to hunt for her, if Hallie didn't wish to be found, she wouldn't be.

Still, it troubled Jenefer not to be in control of the situation. Hallie was missing. Morgan was out of her sight. She was confined to this chamber. Worst of all, she had no bow, no sword, not even a dagger to face the oncoming threat.

She sighed.

Feiyan, focused on her movement, slowly separated her arms as if she were swimming through a bowl of pottage. Then she seemed to draw an invisible bow.

Suddenly the babe next door began to cry. Feiyan, startled by the sound, jolted out of her pose, making it look like she'd fired an invisible bolt from her invisible bow.

Jenefer couldn't help but snicker. The babe must have finished his breakfast and was ready to begin his duties of disturbing the household.

Feiyan didn't find it amusing in the least. Her exercises disrupted, she reacted by cuffing Jenefer on the shoulder with the heel of her hand.

Jenefer was surprised at the power behind Feiyan's small fist.

"Hey!" she yelled, thwacking her cousin on the back of the head in return.

Faster than lightning, Feiyan seized Jenefer's hand and gave it a painful twist.

Then, before Jenefer could clout Feiyan with her free hand, Feiyan squeezed the knuckle of Jenefer's little finger. Jenefer gasped as the sharp twinge brought her to her knees.

Miles had begun to cry in earnest now. His wails came in through the open shutters as Jenefer knelt in pain and frustration, at Feiyan's mercy.

But Feiyan's cunning tricks were no match for Jenefer's might. Ignoring the agony in her finger, bent to its breaking point, she heaved her weight forward and bowled Feiyan over onto the bed.

Then she sprang up, shaking the ache from her abused finger, and glared down in triumph at her cousin.

Feiyan, not to be outdone, propelled her feet forward with great speed and force into Jenefer's belly.

Jenefer, folded in half by the blow, staggered back. She clutched her aching stomach, fearing for a moment she might lose the breakfast she'd just eaten.

Then, driven mad with frustration that she couldn't vanquish her pesky mite of a cousin, she barreled forward, intending to flatten Feiyan on the pallet.

But as she lunged forward, Feiyan rolled aside and Jenefer got a face full of fleece. And while she lay on her belly, Feiyan pinioned Jenefer's arm behind her.

Jenefer grimaced in pain as her shoulder began to throb. Levering up on her free hand, with one great heave, she pushed Feiyan off of her, then scrambled to pin her to the pallet, holding her there by the throat.

While Feiyan's eyes went wide, Jenefer cocked back her fist, threatening to plow it into Feiyan's bonnie face.

A knock at the door made them both freeze.

CHAPTER 22

The babe was wailing just outside the door now.

The knock came again.

Once interrupted, their quarrel was quickly forgotten. She and Feiyan hopped up from the bed.

Feiyan smoothed back her hair.

Jenefer straightened her skirts.

Cracking the door open an inch, Jenefer spied Bethac standing outside with red-faced Miles, who was screaming as if someone had dipped him in boiling oil.

Beyond them was the lanky lad Morgan had apparently set to guard the door. He looked uneasy about the door being opened on his watch. But he looked more uneasy about the screaming infant.

"Please, Miss," Bethac said, struggling to be heard above the din. "Do ye think ye could hold the wee one just for a bit? He's cryin' like his heart's about to burst, and he seems to like ye."

Jenefer glanced at the young guard. The maidservant's authority apparently exceeded his, for he looked away, disinterested.

Jenefer frowned in consternation. Just because she'd been able to stop the babe's cries a few times before didn't mean she had magical, infant-soothing powers. She wasn't even that fond of the wee, helpless creatures.

Nonetheless, she'd try. It was better than listening to the earsplitting sound all day long. And it was better than continuing the ugly, pointless battle with Feiyan.

She opened the door wider.

The maidservant gave a nod of greeting to Feiyan, who closed the door behind her. Then she handed the wailing babe to Jenefer.

Jenefer held Miles up before her, studying his misery-distorted face.

"What is it *now,* lad?" she asked. "Did a spider bite you? Did you have a nightmare? Drink sour milk?"

Miles seemed to recognize her voice. His crying softened, and he blinked his eyes.

"Or did your laird force you to come here when you'd rather be in the Highlands where you belong?"

Bethac made a moue of disapproval. But the babe stared at Jenefer, fascinated.

"How did you do that?" Feiyan asked in wonder.

Jenefer shrugged. She hadn't done anything.

"The bairn is clearly drawn to ye," Bethac gushed. "'Tisn't that way with anyone else, not even..." She stopped short. "'Tis quite wondrous."

"Wondrous?" Jenefer raised her brows. "'Tis quite inconvenient, I would think. Surely there's some woman in your own household who can calm the lad."

Bethac shook her head.

"Let me try," Feiyan said.

Jenefer passed Miles to her cousin. Feiyan cradled the infant against her chest, cooing down at him. But after a moment, his face crumpled, he arched his back, and he began squalling again.

Feiyan handed him back.

Jenefer lifted him up once more, narrowing her eyes. "If you keep crying like that, soon you'll have no tears left. Then what will you do when a faithless wench breaks your heart, eh?"

Miles' cries turned to sniffles.

"If you use up all your tears, what will you do when your favorite hound falls down dead?"

The babe quieted. His mouth made a perfect O as he listened intently.

"What will you do when your master sells you for a coo?"

"Miss!" Bethac chided.

"Oh, I know all about Highlanders," Jenefer assured her, clucking her tongue, "trading babes for coos."

"What?" Bethac exclaimed. "That's not true! We'd ne'er—"

The maidservant's outrage was interrupted by a soft, sweet sound from Miles that turned all three ladies' heads.

"What did he say?" Feiyan whispered.

Jenefer snorted. "'Twasn't a real word, Feiy."

But Bethac had other ideas. "It sounded like…" Her old, wrinkled face melted. "Da."

Feiyan giggled. "He thinks you're his da, Jen."

Jenefer shot her a scathing glance.

Miles made the sound again, sending Feiyan into another spate of giggles.

Jenefer scoffed. It didn't sound at all like "Da." The babe was only making a random noise.

"He does seem to be fond o' ye, Miss," Bethac said.

Jenefer neglected to tell the maidservant that was a good thing, since she intended to take the lad with her at the end of the day. Instead, she gave her a fleeting smile.

Bethac, encouraged by her silence, asked her, "Have ye always had a way with wee ones?"

Feiyan nearly choked on laughter.

Jenefer clamped her lips, tempted to smack her unruly cousin.

But Feiyan wisely stepped out of reach, stifling her amusement, and returned to staring out the window.

"Do ye have a bairn o' your own?" Bethac asked.

Jenefer could hear her cousin snickering at the window.

"Nay," Jenefer said politely. "I do not."

"Ye'll make a good mother one day," Bethac told her.

Jenefer arched a dubious brow at Miles. She would have sworn the babe returned her doubtful glower.

From the window, Feiyan, distracted by something outside, murmured, "They're preparing for siege."

Jenefer stiffened. "What?"

She unceremoniously tucked the babe under one arm, disregarding Bethac's gasp of horror as she did so, and strode to the window.

Young lads were placing buckets of water along the palisade. There was only one reason for that—to extinguish fire in the event of an attack.

In the distance, she could see sheep being driven through the palisade gates.

And from an embrasure atop the castle wall, an archer stood at the ready, his gaze fixed in the direction of Rivenloch.

They knew. They *knew.*

"Shite."

"Is somethin' amiss?" Bethac asked. Her concern for the babe was etched in her brow.

Shifting Miles to hold him in one arm against her shoulder, Jenefer confronted the maidservant. "Why are you preparing for siege?"

"I don't know, Miss. I only do what the laird commands."

"And what exactly has he commanded?"

The old woman blinked, startled by Jenefer's demanding question.

Jenefer realized, as Hallie was fond of saying, she might get further with honey than with vinegar. So she gentled her voice and asked a different question. "What are my cousin and I meant to do? Are we in danger?"

Bethac straightened with pride. "Oh nay, Miss, not with Laird Morgan in command. He knows what to do. And he's brought some o' the finest warriors in the Highlands. We'll be safe and sound. Ye'll see."

Jenefer's mood soured at once. Apparently the element of surprise wasn't on her side after all. How Morgan had learned about the approaching army, she didn't know. But it seemed he was expecting them.

At least she knew Rivenloch's numbers were greater. Besides, the "finest warriors in the Highlands" surely couldn't compare to her uncle's knights, who were undoubtedly the finest warriors in all of *Scotland.*

Crafty Feiyan decided to mine what information she could out of the maidservant. She feigned casual interest in the activities taking place in the courtyard.

"The warriors look fierce. How many are they?"

"A dozen so far," Bethac admitted. "The laird brought half his father's men and planned to hire more here. But they're braw lads and fine fighters." Then she beamed. "My grandson, William, fights for the clan as well."

Feiyan's eyes softened, and only Jenefer could detect the spark of cunning in their depths. "Is he a proper knight with a claymore and a targe, your William?"

"Oh, nay. He's an archer."

"My brother is an archer," Feiyan lied, "one of thirty in my father's company."

"Thirty!" Bethac exclaimed. "My William is one of eight who came with us."

"Only eight? He must be skilled indeed," Feiyan said.

Jenefer had to admire her cousin's shrewdness. Sometimes Feiyan was right. Brains *were* more effective than brawn. With only a few innocent words, she'd discovered their enemy had a dozen knights and eight archers.

"Do you think we'll have enough food for a siege?" Feiyan asked.

"Oh, aye," Bethac assured her. "The laird has ordered the crops harvested, and we've got cattle and sheep enough for the winter, if need be."

"The winter?" Feiyan exclaimed.

Jenefer pursed her lips. It had better not take that long for Creagor's fate to be decided. She had no interest in being confined to this bedchamber for weeks on end, sparring with Feiyan and looking after a…

She glanced down at Miles. His head was turned toward her, and his eyes were closed in slumber. His soft, pink mouth made a perfect bow, and his tiny fist rested on her breast.

She supposed looking after Miles wasn't so bad.

"Who do you think is attacking?" Feiyan asked. "Do you think it might be…" She clasped a trembling hand to her bosom. "…the English?" Damn, she was good. There wasn't anything Feiyan feared. But the worried lines of her brow would have fooled even her parents.

"I don't know," Bethac admitted.

"But you're sure they can't get in? There are no gaps in the wall or…or hidden passageways or…"

Jenefer held her breath. If Feiyan could find a secret passageway, they could make their way out of the castle. Morgan would lose his leverage over Rivenloch. And Rivenloch could easily take Creagor.

"Oh nay, Miss," Bethac said. "The keep is sealed tight as a beer cask. The laird himself inspected every inch."

Jenefer feared as much. *She'd* inspected every inch and hadn't found so much as a crack for a mouse to fit through.

"What about the archers?" Jenefer asked, attempting Feiyan's more subtle approach. "Do they always sink their points into the butt, or is it mostly fishtailers and bouncers?"

Bethac only stared at her with an open mouth.

"What my cousin means to say is," Feiyan interjected, widening her eyes at Jenefer in horror, "are they skilled enough to protect us?"

"Och aye," Bethac replied.

Jenefer scowled. Wasn't that what she'd asked?

Feiyan continued with her cagey interrogation.

"Do you know," she asked, pressing her fingertips to her lips as if she feared the answer, "if they've found our cousin yet?"

"Your cousin?"

Jenefer nodded, but she let Feiyan speak. Feiyan was clearly more practiced at deceit.

"She was lost in the wood last night," Feiyan blurted out, blinking back fake tears.

"Lost in the wood?" Bethac's eyes went round.

"Aye, and the laird promised us—"

She didn't get the chance to reveal what Morgan had promised. At that moment, the door burst open. There stood the man himself, wild-eyed and full of fury.

CHAPTER 23

Siege preparations had been well underway when Morgan finally received confirmation of Colban's whereabouts. The watchman who'd relieved him last night said Colban had rushed off, claiming he'd seen a suspicious figure heading into the forest. According to the man, Colban had followed the figure and never returned.

Morgan was fairly certain that figure had been Hallie. And since his best tracker was already on her trail, Morgan could rest assured she'd be found, unless...

Unless she'd lured him all the way back to Rivenloch.

If that had happened, Colban would be trapped in enemy country. Alone and defenseless, it wouldn't be long before he found himself at the mercy of the Laird of Rivenloch.

Once the laird found out his nieces were being held hostage at Creagor, he'd not only send his entire army to lay siege. He'd likely try to hold Colban as counter ransom for the Warrior Daughters.

For Morgan, Colban was not a pawn to be sacrificed. So if Rivenloch captured him, Morgan would no longer have leverage. And without the king's decree in his hands, he stood to lose Creagor.

But there was little more he could do at this point. The castle was as well-defended as it could be. There was nothing to do but wait. Either Colban would show up with Hallie in tow, or the army of Rivenloch would arrive to storm the gates.

In the meantime, he needed Bethac to supervise the maids who were stockpiling the harvested crops.

Bounding up the stairs, he approached the nursery with stealth. All was quiet, so he eased open the door. The wet nurse was slumped in a chair, fast asleep. Miles was nowhere to be seen.

Softly closing the door behind him, he scanned the chamber again, sure he'd missed something. The bairn had to be here somewhere.

His brow furrowed as he peered cautiously under the coverlet. Nothing.

His breath grew thin as he searched every inch of the rush-covered floor. Nothing.

His heart was pounding as he opened the wooden chest at the foot of the bed. Nothing.

The wet nurse awoke with a gasp. "Oh! M'laird!" She staggered to her feet and bobbed a curtsey.

"Where is he?" Morgan asked, lowering the lid of the chest with trembling fingers, astonished at the raw edge of fear in his voice.

"Who?"

"My s-," he breathed. "The bairn."

She looked around the room in confusion.

"Where *is* he?" he demanded, fast losing his patience and his sanity.

She blinked, and then shook her head as if clearing the cobwebs from her brain. "Ah, I remember now. Bethac has him."

Relief softened his rage. Nonetheless, his temper was tested as he bit out, "And where is Bethac?"

"In your bedchamber."

"My bedchamber? *My* bedchamber? With the prisoners?"

"Wee Miles wouldn't stop cryin'," she explained, "and Bethac said that the Lowland lass was the only—"

His growl silenced the nurse.

For God's sake! Didn't he have enough to fret about? Losing his wife. Leaving his home. Holding onto his castle. Protecting his clan. Now he had to worry that his son had fallen into enemy hands.

He wheeled and left the nursery. Five angry strides brought him to his bedchamber. His dark glower convinced the young guard to stand aside.

When he barreled in through the door, it was as he'd feared.

The three women stood in clear defiance of his wishes, consorting together.

The scheming Jenefer had taken possession of his son. The innocent, trusting infant dozed against her breast.

And as loyal a maidservant as old Bethac was, the dreamy expression on her face told him she'd been gulled by the Lowland lass as well.

"What are ye doin' here?" he demanded of Bethac.

He almost saw the hackles rise on her neck as she straightened in challenge. He should have remembered that though old Bethac was a trusty servant, she'd also known Morgan when he was a suckling bairn. She wasn't easily intimidated by him, even with "laird" attached to his name.

She told him in no uncertain terms, "The bairn was quite distraught, m'laird. Since ye were busy with the siege, I took matters into my own hands." She gave Jenefer a smile. "The lass seems to have a way with wee Miles, as if the two o' them are—"

"Enough!"

Morgan didn't want to know about the lass's way with the lad. The bairn was Alicia's child. *Alicia's.* And he'd settle that, once and for aye.

"Give him back," he commanded Jenefer, nodding toward Bethac.

She shrugged and surrendered the bairn, who fussed at being disturbed.

"From now on," he told Bethac, "ye'll call him Allison, after his mother."

Bethac didn't respond, probably because she was occupied, trying to keep the bairn from waking.

"Go back to the nursery," he told her, "and don't come here again."

She left without a word or a glance, and he faced the two cousins with a scowl. "And *ye...*"

"What have *we* done?" Jenefer challenged, her hands on her hips. "We've stayed here like good little hostages all day. We haven't tried to escape. We haven't so much as fired a wicked word at the guard."

Feiyan decided to take the offense. She was direct and demanding. "What about our cousin? Have you found her yet?"

In the tumult of preparing for siege, Morgan had forgotten he'd promised to search for their cousin. But Colban was already following Hallie. So he didn't have to lie.

"Not yet," he grumbled. "But my best tracker is on her trail."

"Just one?" Feiyan seemed disappointed.

He scowled. "'Tisn't as if I can spare an entire army for the task."

He was irritated with the lasses.

Vexed with Bethac.

Impatient with the bairn, who had started crying again.

And he needed his man Colban by his side for the fight ahead.

Unable to control any of those things, he headed downstairs to take care of something he *could* control— quenching his thirst and sharpening his claymore.

CHAPTER 24

"**j**ust one tracker," Feiyan repeated when Morgan was gone, this time with a sly smile. "You know what that means."

Jenefer wasn't listening.

"He can't just change the babe's name," she said in annoyance. "I'm going to keep calling him Miles."

"What? What are you talking about?"

"Miles. I can call him whatever the hell I want."

"Why do you care?" Feiyan asked. "The babe's not yours."

Jenefer knew that. But she *did* intend to take him.

Eventually, she'd find him a suitable home at Rivenloch. Maybe she'd invite Bethac along. The charming old maidservant would probably be glad to leave her hot-tempered, dominating brute of a master.

"Allison," she sneered.

"Honestly, Jen, let it be. We need to make a plan."

Jenefer had a plan. She intended to send Morgan Mor mac Giric packing to the Highlands. The sooner, the better.

The man was infuriating. For one moment, she'd thought he might actually have a heart beating in his chest. Now she knew he was as cold as chain mail.

"As I was trying to say," Feiyan continued, "if he only sent one tracker, then Hallie likely wasn't found."

That *was* good news. "I suppose we'll know soon enough if she made it to Rivenloch."

"Aye, and now we know the Highlanders' strength."

"That *was* quite clever, Feiy," she had to admit, "getting all that out of the maidservant."

Feiyan smiled with pride.

Jenefer sighed. "I hope Bethac's grandson doesn't become a casualty of the siege."

Feiyan shrugged. "He's a soldier. He knows the risks."

"Aye, but 'twill be hard to convince her to stay here if the knights kill her kin."

"Stay here? Jen, what are you talking about?"

"I'm taking the babe."

"What?" Feiyan's eyes were as round as an owl's.

"And 'twould be good to have a maidservant who knows a thing or two about babes."

"You can't just take the babe!" Feiyan hissed.

"Why not?"

"For one thing, the laird would tear Rivenloch apart looking for him."

Jenefer gave her a puzzled laugh. "Why would he do that? He doesn't even like the child."

"The hell he doesn't. Why do you think he stormed in the way he did?"

Jenefer flinched in surprise. Then she bit the corner of her lip. Morgan *had* seemed excessively upset that Bethac had brought the lad here. She assumed it was because he hated being disobeyed.

"Besides," Feiyan added, "I think the babe's mother might have something to say about that."

"That's just it. He doesn't have a mother. She's dead."

"Wait." Feiyan stared at her for a long while and then bit back a smile. "You don't think *you* are going to be his mother, Jen?"

"Of course not."

Still, the scornful, mocking look Feiyan gave her and the cruel laughter afterward felt like a kick in the gut.

Why Feiyan's words should bother her, she didn't know. But ire suddenly blazed in her like fire on a hot forge.

Before Feiyan knew what was coming, Jenefer gave her a shove that made her tumble back onto the bed.

"What the..." Feiyan began.

Another skirmish might have started then, but from outside the window came a distant cry. "Aim! Draw! Loose!"

The familiar commands made them forget their quarrel and rush to the window.

In the courtyard, a row of four archers were shooting at a straw target. Morgan yelled out the orders again, and they let their arrows fly.

"Are they any good?" Feiyan murmured.

Jenefer watched with a critical eye. While Feiyan could be classified as a weapon in and of herself, and Hallie was deadly with a blade, Jenefer's weapon of choice was the longbow. Neither of her cousins could come close to her skill.

"'Tis hard to gauge their marksmanship at this distance," she said. "But two of them missed the target completely."

"Aye? That bodes well for our uncle then."

Jenefer wasn't so sure. "Bethac said there were eight, aye? Their best archers may already be posted atop the wall."

"Ah. Right."

They shot again. Their form was flawed. One of them jerked as he released the bowstring. Another pulled to the left. And one of them didn't even have the strength to draw the bow back fully.

"Again!" Morgan yelled.

She narrowed her eyes at the Highlander. He might have a loud bellow and a firm hand. But he didn't know the first thing about archery.

"If I were in charge," she mused, "I'd have those archers hitting the target every time."

Feiyan grew bored and left the window.

Jenefer watched for another hour, longing all the while to feel her own bow in her hands. She wondered if anyone had yet retrieved her weapon from the woods.

Soon her stomach began complaining again. How long would it be, she mused, before someone brought food to them?

She glanced over her shoulder at Feiyan, who was lying on the bed, staring up at the ceiling. She looked like she was daydreaming. But Jenefer knew Feiyan was probably devising a plan of attack. Though her cousin could be bothersome sometimes, there was no one Jenefer would rather have by her side in a battle.

But it had begun to look like there wasn't going to be a battle today. The sun had moved halfway across the cloud-strewn sky, and there was still no sign of Rivenloch.

Finally, Feiyan voiced what they both were thinking.

"Damn it, they should have been here by now."

CHAPTER 25

Several hours later, Morgan was fairly confident the army of Rivenloch was not coming—at least not today. He entered the crowded great hall for supper after a long day of drilling the archers.

The clan had performed admirably. His knights were ready for war. His servants had followed instructions swiftly and with efficiency, despite Bethac's absence. Even the children had helped prepare for siege.

A siege that had never come. Which was for the best. He didn't want war with the neighbors.

If the king's messenger arrived on the morrow, there would be no need for a confrontation at all. He could substantiate his claim and return the Warrior Daughters to their laird. That would be the end of it.

He washed his hands in the basin of water near the screened end of the hall, drying them on the linen cloth one of the maidservants offered.

There was still one complication. Where the devil was Colban? And where was the lass he'd gone after? Without her, any encounter with the Laird of Rivenloch would be volatile indeed, for the laird was sure to blame Morgan for her disappearance.

He didn't relish breaking the news to the fiery lass upstairs. Indeed, he'd half hoped Rivenloch *would* come today so he could banish the winsome, troublesome hellion from his household. Even if purging her from his mind might take a bit longer.

Finding his seat at the high table, he looked down at his cup of ale and smirked. Jenefer had half choked on their strong brew. Like everything else here, the Lowland ale was probably a diluted version of the Highland's, with all the roughness smoothed away.

Except for Jenefer. She definitely had jagged edges. Like a thistle, she was a lovely flower above with thorny spikes beneath.

He glowered into his cup. Why the lass haunted his thoughts, he didn't know. But he felt it wasn't right.

Alicia had been gone for but a quarter of a year. Yet even now, he was beginning to have trouble recalling her face.

Instead, his thoughts were full of images of flashing green eyes and a sultry smile, waves of bronze-colored hair and a body to put a goddess to shame.

The way the lass had held Miles...Allison, he corrected... seemed so natural, as if the bairn belonged in her arms.

With a silent curse, he shook the feckless thought from his head. The child had belonged to sweet and gentle Alicia, he reminded himself. Not a sword-toting warrior wench who would sooner hold the bairn up as a human shield than rock him to sleep.

Morgan sighed. The beguiling lass was trouble. He had to be rid of her as soon as possible.

Once the meal was over, he took a platter of food upstairs and sent the guard down to fetch more peat for their fire. Then he knocked on the door, realizing as he did how ludicrous it was to knock on the door of one's own bedchamber.

"Finally!" Jenefer exclaimed as she threw open the door in dubious welcome. "I thought perhaps you *were* going to starve us."

He gathered his brows. "Didn't a maidservant bring ye a midday meal?"

"Aye," she said, "but that was hours ago."

She practically mauled the platter out of his hands and dove into the roasted chicken as if she hadn't eaten for days.

"Leave some for me, brat," Feiyan said.

Morgan was fascinated, watching Jenefer. There was something raw and sensuous about the way she ate. She closed her eyes, savoring every morsel and licking her fingers with élan.

Alicia had never eaten like that. She'd always picked at her food with mild distaste, more so when she was carrying their child.

But it was foolish of him to make such comparisons. They were two different creatures, Alicia and Jenefer. Alicia had been like a prize falcon, requiring gentle treatment and careful coddling. Jenefer? She reminded him of a woodland wildcat.

He cleared his throat. "I thought you'd wish to know about your cousin."

"Oh. Aye." Jenefer honestly seemed more interested in the coffyns than in her cousin. "What of her?"

Feiyan appeared slightly more concerned. "Did your man find her?"

He shook his head. "He hasn't returned."

He caught a quick glimpse of Jenefer. He would have sworn she smiled at that.

"I hope she's all right," Feiyan murmured.

Jenefer mumbled cryptically, "I hope your man is all right."

"If they're not back on the morrow by midday, I'll send another man."

Those were his words. But he wasn't entirely sure he wanted to do that. They needed every man they could spare if a siege was to take place. And the last thing he wanted was to give the Laird of Rivenloch another hostage to use.

He just hoped the king's messenger would arrive before then to relieve him of all this complicated intrigue.

The guard knocked on the door to deliver a bucket of extra peat.

Morgan stirred the fire and added several thick black chunks. "Ye seem to go through a great deal o' fuel."

"No doubt we'll go through a great deal more," Feiyan said sardonically, "now that we have no coverlets."

With that, she brushed past him to visit the garderobe.

Once she was gone, Jenefer confided, "I was watching your soldiers from the window."

"Aye?" He hunkered down to poke at the glowing coals.

"The knights are quite good," Jenefer she told him between bites of chicken.

"They're the best in the Highlands," he said. It wasn't a boast. It was the truth.

"That may be," she said, "but they haven't faced the knights of the Lowlands."

"Not yet," he admitted. But if Lowlanders couldn't handle Highland ale, they probably couldn't defend against Highland knights.

The peat caught fire. He leaned the poker against the hearth, dusted off his hands, and came to his feet.

"Your archers, however," Jenefer said, wagging a chicken bone to emphasize her point, "need improvement."

Morgan stared at her for a moment, dumbfounded and amused. He folded his arms over his chest.

"Is that so?"

How the wee lass could possibly think he would take military advice from her, he didn't know.

"The small one needs a lighter bow," she said, smacking her lips. "He's not drawing it all the way back."

That was true. Robert had left his own longbow for his younger brother in the Highlands, and there had been no time to make him a new one. So he was borrowing Colban's bow, which was far too heavy for the lad.

"Also, that stocky one is flinching when he fires." She licked her lips. "That's what's making his arrows go astray."

Morgan blinked. How would she know that?

"And the one who keeps shooting to the left of the target? I'd wager he's squeezing his right eye shut."

"And ye know this because..."

She tossed the chicken bone down on the platter just as Feiyan was returning from the garderobe. "I'm a master archer."

His lips twitched, but he forced himself not to smile. "I see."

"Oh aye, she is," Feiyan confirmed. "She's better than all the men in her father's retinue."

"And *your* father's retinue," Jenefer said.

"And *my* father's retinue," Feiyan agreed.

Morgan gave them an indulgent smile. The Rivenloch archers must be poor indeed if they could be outshot by a lass.

On the other hand, she did seem to know a great deal about longbows. The weapon Danald had found beside her clothing in the wood seemed well-crafted and well-used.

Still, he couldn't let her get any ideas about usurping his command. She was already trying to usurp his castle.

"Perhaps I shall call upon your counsel then, *master archer,* when I fill out my army at Creagor."

That he'd audaciously claimed Creagor as his own didn't escape her. Green fire flared in her eyes. She was still sputtering when he inclined his head in farewell and made his exit.

CHAPTER 26

Lying on a pile of sheepskins outside his own bedchamber door—particularly when his bed had been appropriated by two Lowland lasses—was a travesty of his authority.

Morgan, however, was used to sleeping on the hard ground. Despite the unwelcome circumstances, he might have spent a perfectly comfortable night where he was.

Instead, he lay on his back, unable to sleep.

Staring up at the dark beams of the ceiling.

Listening to his son cry.

And cry.

And cry.

He knew the maidservants were doing all they could.

He could hear the change in the bairn's cries when Bethac jostled him or the wet nurse tried to give him suckle.

He could see the subtle shift of shadows leaking beneath the door as they passed back and forth in endless pacing.

He even heard a faint melody between the sobs as Bethac tried to lull the bairn to sleep.

They all knew what would stop the cries.

But Morgan had forbidden it.

At the time, it had seemed like the right idea. Jenefer was his captive, after all. He didn't dare give her an opportunity to use the child as a hostage.

Besides, no matter how strenuously the wench proclaimed she was never leaving Creagor, she would eventually return to Rivenloch. Somehow, the maid-servants were going to have to figure out how to calm the bairn without her.

In the light of day, his decision to wean the lad away from Jenefer had seemed practical.

But now, in the middle of the night—with his eyes gritty from sleeplessness and a painful pulsing in his temples—Morgan reconsidered.

As much as it irked him to yield to the demands of an infant and the whims of wenches, he knew it was foolish stubbornness on his own part to refuse the one thing that would solve the problem.

So with a sigh of defeat, he came to his feet and rapped softly on the bedchamber door.

It startled him how quickly it was snatched open. Peering through the crack was Jenefer, looking as lovely as ever, even with sleep-mussed hair and weary eyes. Had she been standing behind the door, waiting?

"Aye?" she asked.

He gave her a black look. She must know why he'd come. The bairn's cries echoed down the hallway like the clang of cathedral bells.

"What can I do for you?" she asked, as if she were deaf to the noise.

He narrowed sleepy eyes at her. She was going to make him beg. He could see that now. It was on the tip of his tongue to tell her to never mind, to go back to bed, to have a restful sleep.

But just then the bairn let out a particularly melancholy cry. Morgan couldn't let his pride keep him from comforting the poor child, giving the maidservants a reprieve, and getting a good night's rest himself.

So with a sigh of humility, he murmured, "If ye'd be so kind..."

"Aye?" She winced only slightly when the bairn started up with a piercing wail.

"To give a wee bit o' comfort to Allison..."

"You mean Miles?" she inserted with a raised brow.

He bit back a retort. "I mean the bairn—whatever ye're goin' to call him—so we can all get some rest."

She clearly didn't intend to do his bidding so readily. "I thought 'twas forbidden."

He was too tired to argue. Instead, he gave her a drowsy smile. "I un-forbid it."

At that, she opened the door with a knowing smirk. "Then stand aside."

Even acting smug and superior, Jenefer was one of the most beautiful lasses he'd ever seen. Her proud chin tipped upward, displaying lips as ripe and succulent as cherries. The firelight kissed her unbound curls and danced in her eyes. He retreated to let her pass, and he couldn't help but breathe in her scent—the womanly, sweet, spicy fragrance all her own.

As she moved toward the nursery, he thought again about how different she was from Alicia. Neither meek nor mincing, Jenefer strode with confidence and purpose. And when Bethac opened the door to let her in—glancing toward Morgan for his approval—Jenefer didn't wring her hands in indecision or uncertainty. She took the bairn in capable arms, trusting she could resolve his troubles.

To Morgan's amazement, the bairn grew quiet almost at once. With the sound of her voice and the power of her touch, Jenefer convinced him there was nothing to cry about, that all was right with the world.

Indeed, there *was* something compelling about her reassurances. Morgan himself was almost ready to believe her.

Almost.

And then he remembered he'd lost his wife.

Nothing was right with the world.

Nothing would be easy from now on. Not with the clan. Not with the keep. Not with this child.

Especially when the child's father could be so easily distracted by a green-eyed, golden-haired Lowlander and so easily dismiss the woman who had given the child life.

No longer kept awake by the bairn's cries, he could only blame his sleeplessness on guilt. And that guilt was compounded by the fact that he couldn't remember the exact color of Alicia's eyes or the sound of her voice.

CHAPTER 27

"Nay!" Feiyan screamed, jolting Jenefer out of her peaceful nap.

Jenefer sat bolt upright and fumbled in panic for the bow that wasn't there.

But Feiyan's face wasn't marked by fear as she glared out the window. It was full of outrage.

Jenefer sighed in exasperation. Her cousin wasn't being killed after all. She slumped back onto the bed.

She'd spent half the night awake in the nursery, coaxing Miles out of tears. Every time she'd put him in his wee bed, he'd cry to be held. In the end, she'd curled up on the nursery floor near the hearth and fallen asleep with him in her arms.

Now, back in Morgan's bedchamber, satiated from a breakfast of oatcakes, ruayn cheese, and watered ale, she'd hoped to garner a few hours of serene slumber.

Feiyan, however, seemed determined to destroy that serenity.

"Fool!" she was yelling at someone in the courtyard.

Jenefer groaned. "Feiyan, must you?"

"Nay!" Feiyan cried again at some unseen enemy. "Oh, nay!" This time she sounded truly distressed, as if someone were drowning a kitten in the castle well.

Jenefer edged up onto her elbows. It was useless to try to sleep.

"Odin's blood, Feiy, what is it?" she grumbled.

But Feiyan's attention was riveted to whatever was happening in the courtyard. Her fists were clenched on the sill, and she chewed at her lip.

"Feiyan," she repeated, "what's wrong?"

Feiyan cringed. Her jaw dropped in outrage. She angrily ground her teeth.

With a resigned, impatient sigh, Jenefer got up and joined her cousin at the window.

"Look!" Feiyan snarled, stabbing a finger toward the activity on the ground below. "Just look!"

Jenefer rubbed her eye with the heel of her hand and followed Feiyan's gaze. Then she drew her brows together. "That looks just like *your* sword."

"'*Tis* my sword."

Of course. It was inevitable someone would retrieve Feiyan's curious abandoned weapons from outside the keep. Four burly men-at-arms were currently taking turns, swinging the strange, narrow blade around, examining its curved edge, hacking at a straw target.

"What are they doing with it?" Jenefer asked.

"Exactly!" Feiyan huffed. Then she cupped her hands around her mouth and yelled down, "Halfwits!"

That finally got the men's attention.

"Bloody fools!" she added.

They stared in silence.

"Dunderheaded clods!"

At last, the one wielding her sword took offense. "Hey now, lassie! There's no need to—"

"You're doing it all wrong!" Feiyan shouted.

"What?" he yelled back.

"I said, you're doing it. All. Wrong!"

"Am I now?"

Predictably, the knights elbowed each other, snickering at the idea of a wee lass daring to tell a pack of seasoned warriors how to fight.

"Well, lassie," the man jeered suggestively, "why don't ye come down and show me what ye know about handlin' three feet o' steel?"

The others laughed uproariously at his crude humor.

Feiyan ignored their crassness. "First of all, you don't swing it like that. You have to use it like a blade, not a bloody sickle."

The men stared, dumbfounded.

She continued. "And you don't hack haphazardly at your target. You only waste motion that way. Watch." She leaned out the window and, as if holding her sword, made a slow, smooth, slicing motion in the air. "'Tisn't a claymore. 'tis a fine, sharp *dao* that cuts with ease. It requires finesse, not brutishness."

To Jenefer's surprise, though the men around him were chuckling, the knight holding the sword attempted to imitate Feiyan's movements.

"Aye, like that," Feiyan said. "You see? It takes very little force."

The man repeated the movement.

"Keep your elbows close in," Feiyan said.

He did.

"Now try it on the target."

He brought the sword down in a graceful arc, easily slicing through the corner of the straw.

The others oohed and ahhed.

Another man held up one of her steel stars. "What about this?"

"That's a *shuriken*. You throw it like a dagger," she called down. "Pinch it between your thumb and first finger. Aim at the target, and give your wrist a quick flick."

He flung the star forward, vertically.

Unfortunately, he missed the target.

Fortunately, he missed the other men-at-arms.

"Sideways," Feiyan said, "a *sideways* flick, like you're casting grain to hens." She flicked her wrist sideways, parallel to the ground, to demonstrate.

The man nodded, retrieved the star, and tried again. This time, the star stuck in the lower corner of the target. The others cheered.

"That's it," Feiyan said with satisfaction.

Jenefer looked at Feiyan in wonder. She thought her cousin would be upset that her beloved weapons were in enemy hands. But the daft lass was more concerned that they were using them improperly.

Continuing to observe, Jenefer could see these Highlanders were skilled indeed. They might be wild, ferocious, unruly. God only knew how Morgan managed to mold them into a disciplined fighting force. But they were eager to train and fast to learn. Though at first they'd laughed at Feiyan, they listened to her now with as much respect as they would a commander.

But it seemed careless on Feiyan's part. Jenefer wondered how her cousin would feel if one of these men used her weapons to kill a Rivenloch knight.

On the other hand, the knights of Rivenloch were formidable foes. And once the Highlander saw he was outnumbered, he'd probably choose to negotiate rather than wage battle.

Besides, Feiyan seemed to be enjoying herself. Though she'd no doubt rather train on the ground with her newfound apprentices, at least shouting directions down to them from the window relieved her boredom.

Unfortunately, it also awakened Miles next door, who began whimpering.

Jenefer suspected Bethac would come calling soon.

Feiyan beckoned the men closer to the window so she could teach them to use her spined fan.

Jenefer shook her head and crossed the room. When she cracked open the bedchamber door to peer into the hallway, the young guard posted there nodded toward the nursery. Apparently, Morgan had granted permission for her to tend to the babe.

Bethac answered the nursery door with the bleating child in one arm. "Thank ye for comin', Miss. I fear wee Miles won't have anyone but ye."

CHAPTER 28

t wasn't lost on Jenefer that Bethac had called the babe Miles. She smiled in approval and reached out for the lad.

"He's been fed," Bethac said as she handed Miles over to her. She ushered Jenefer in and closed the door. "And Cicilia's gone downstairs to sup."

Jenefer lifted the squirming babe to peer into his distraught face.

"So, lad, what's got your trews in a bunch today? Aside from my noisy cousin trying to command your laird's army."

"Is that what the fuss is about?" Bethac asked, wide-eyed.

"Oh, aye. She's a bossy wee minx, my cousin."

The old woman whispered in awe, "Is what they say true then? Are ye both...warrior maids?"

"Aye." She cocked her head at Miles. He was still crying, but he'd stopped writhing about. "My cousin Feiyan is a master of fighting skills from the Orient. And I can outshoot anyone with a longbow."

This time her boast wasn't empty. It was true.

"Indeed?" Bethac clasped a hand to her breast. "By my faith! A woman-at-arms. 'Tis remarkable." Then she worried one corner of her lip with her teeth. "But ye haven't...killed anyone, have ye?"

"Nay." She smiled in grim recollection. "Though I have maimed a few amorous knaves who refused to heed my younger sister's refusals."

Bethac gasped.

Jenefer squinted at Miles. "You'd never do that, would you, lad—try to take a lass against her will?"

Miles stopped crying and peered at her intently, as if he were trying to decipher what she was saying.

"Nay, you're a good lad," she told him.

Bethac shook her head in awe. "'Tis marvelous the way the bairn has grown attached to ye, Miss. God's truth, 'twill be a shame when ye go. I don't know what we'll do."

Jenefer glanced sideways at the maidservant. It was too early to broach the subject of Bethac remaining with her when Morgan was sent home. But she was encouraged by the fact the woman liked and appreciated her. And unlike her disparaging cousin, Bethac seemed to be of the opinion that Jenefer had good mothering skills.

As long as they were exchanging pleasantries, Jenefer thought, she might as well try to get some useful information from Bethac.

Resting Miles' head against her shoulder, she strolled slowly around the room.

"So tell me about this laird of yours," she said casually. "Is *he* the kind to take a lass against her will?"

"Laird Morgan? Oh nay!" Bethac's conviction was emphatic. "He's a good man. Decent. Fair. And honorable."

"Yet he keeps my cousin and me prisoner." Jenefer looked at her with calculation, adding the half-truth, "And we don't know why."

Bethac blinked in surprise. "Prisoner? Oh nay, Miss. He keeps ye here for your own protection. He dares not set ye loose when a hostile army may be near. 'Twould be unthinkable."

Jenefer gave her a sharp glance. "Is it?"

"Aye, o' course. Ye may be warrior maids. But ye're also innocent lasses who—"

"Nay, I mean...is a hostile army near?" She tried to hide her keen interest in hearing the answer.

"Ah. None has been spotted yet. But..." Bethac leaned forward to confide, "The young lad who's guardin' ye? He told me his cousin overheard a knight tellin' his father that this army might very well attack in the middle o' the night."

Jenefer's eyes dulled. Rumors. In her experience, a man's armory spawned just as many rumors as a lady's solar. Rivenloch would never be so unchivalrous as to attack a castle in the middle of the night.

"So ye see?" Bethac assured her. "The laird is doin' his best to keep ye safe. Ye're not prisoners. Ye're guests. Indeed, that's his own bedchamber ye're stayin' in while he sleeps on the floor."

Jenefer nodded. She had to admit that was a noble gesture. But it might have more to do with the fact that Creagor had no proper dungeon or even doors on the storage rooms.

She shifted Miles in her arms.

That was another thing she'd add when she moved in. The storage rooms should be more secure.

Then she smirked. Her mother might disagree, since her father had locked her in one such storage room at Rivenloch.

"Are ye not comfortable in his bedchamber?" Bethac asked.

"Oh aye." Now that she'd discovered the bed was *not* flea-ridden after all, she found the well-stuffed mattress quite to her liking.

"And he's feedin' ye well?"

She was already impatient for her next meal. But he couldn't be blamed for that. "As well as can be expected."

Bethac nodded. "The stores were depleted when we arrived. We haven't had time to stock the pantry."

Depleted stores meant a short siege and a quick surrender. That was good. Jenefer was willing to face the Highlanders in battle. But she didn't relish letting them die of hunger.

Besides, if anyone was going to starve within the castle walls, Jenefer supposed she'd be one of the first to go.

And what of Miles? she thought, running a palm over his soft, warm head. How long would a wee babe survive a siege?

"What will happen if they lay siege?" Jenefer asked.

"Don't ye fret, Miss. Laird Morgan will take good care o' the clan...and the two o' ye as well. He won't let anyone starve."

Jenefer raised a brow. "So he'll negotiate?"

"If the demands are reasonable."

She tried not to sound too hopeful. "He'll relinquish Creagor?"

"Oh nay," Bethac said with a chuckle. "He's come a long way to claim his rightful place as Laird o' Creagor. He won't surrender his inheritance."

Jenefer's jaw tensed, but she hid her disappointment. "Then I hope he's a good fighter." For his own sake, she silently added.

"Oh, aye," Bethac gushed. "He's a great champion. No one is fiercer with a claymore."

That was the last thing she wanted to hear. But she supposed it was little surprise, considering his massive size.

Bethac continued. "I remember the first time Morgan held a sword. He was a lad o' three years, and the sword was a wee thing his father made out o' wood. But he waved it around with such ferocity that he knocked his da in the knee." She laughed. "To this day, Laird Giric bears a scar from the blow."

Jenefer lifted her brows. "Three years old? Have you known him so long?"

"I was with Lady Hilaire when she gave birth to him," she said with pride. "I've watched him grow from a mischievous lad to a magnificent laird."

Magnificent. Jenefer had to admit he *was* that. Tall, handsome, and arresting. With a natural air of command. He would set any foe's heart to quivering.

But she felt a sinking in her chest. She'd never imagined Bethac might be loyal to the snarling Highlander. If she cared so much for the man, it would be difficult, if not impossible, to convince her to stay behind.

"And what about ye, Miss?" the maid asked.

"Me?"

"When did ye first learn to fight?"

She shrugged. "I can't remember *not* knowing how to fight."

At that moment, one of Miles' flailing hands smacked her jaw.

"Oh ho!" She chuckled. "So you're a fighter as well, aye?"

Bethac beamed. "He'll be a fine warrior like his da."

Jenefer caught Miles' fist in hers and gave it a shake. "Is that so, Miles?" Then she turned to Bethac. "And who *is* his da?"

The color drained from the old woman's face. For an instant, Jenefer would have sworn she glimpsed panic in Bethac's eyes.

But just as quickly, it was gone. Bethac turned her attention to Miles, giving him a fond smile and patting him on the back.

"Oh, he's a braw swordsman, he is."

"So he's alive?"

"Oh, aye." Bethac cleared her throat. "Very much so."

She frowned. "Then why does he not visit his son?"

Bethac hesitated. "He...does."

"But how? I've never seen him."

The maidservant seemed suddenly fixated on the hem of Miles' gown. "Are ye certain?" she asked, smoothing the edges between her fingers as she spoke. "Because he comes most every day."

"When?" Jenefer had stayed up with Miles half the night and a good part of the day. The only men she'd seen were Morgan and the guard.

"Oh, at different hours. He may have come when ye were sleepin'."

Jenefer didn't think so. She'd hardly slept at all.

Bethac moved away to tend to the hearth, speaking over her shoulder. "He's...he's in mournin', as ye might imagine. 'Tis difficult for him to look at the bairn. 'Tis why the poor wee lad has gone so long without a name."

Jenefer nodded. That made sense. The man had just buried his wife.

"Does Miles look like his mother?"

Bethac dusted off her hands. "A bit. Lady Alicia came from Catalonia. She had a frail, fey look about her, peat black hair and eyes and fair skin. Miles is far bonnier, to my mind, and more hale, thank God, but he has the heartlike shape o' her face."

"That must be difficult for his father."

"Aye, I think 'tis."

If Miles was a painful reminder of his father's lost love, was it possible that when the Highlanders were forced to return home, he'd be grateful to be rid of the child?

The thought pleased her.

For the first time, she tried to imagine herself as a mother. What would it be like to raise a babe like Miles to manhood? To mold him into a warrior without peer? An able commander? A leader of men?

She envisioned teaching the lad knightly courtesy. And archery. And how to wield a sword.

Telling him the Norse legends of her forefathers. Sharing the stories of her clan. Teaching him how to read and write and keep accounts.

She smiled and lowered her head to breathe in Miles' unique sweet scent. It seemed she may have found a way to not only win a holding for herself, but also to avoid the pesky business of taking a husband to get an heir.

CHAPTER 29

organ scowled and scratched at the back of his neck. Where were the Campbell brothers? The last time he'd seen his four knights, they were patrolling the perimeter of the woods, searching for signs of the missing Colban while keeping an eye out for Rivenloch scouts.

He checked the armory. Twice.

He scanned the great hall, where tables were being assembled for the final meal of the day.

He scoured the stables.

On his second turn through the courtyard, he heard the clash of steel. Following the sound, he found the Campbells sparring on the sward beneath his bedchamber window. They were wielding strange implements. A slender, curved sword. A pair of pointed daggers. A lady's fan.

Feiyan's weapons.

Ordinarily, he would have no qualms with his men confiscating the weapons of fallen foes. But the lasses were neither fallen nor foes. Not exactly. He might not be quite ready to *return* their arms to them yet. But neither would he condone his men stealing them.

He marched toward the Campbells. But before he could demand they turn the scavenged weapons over to him, to his amazement, he heard the lass herself shouting down commands from his window.

"Aye, Davey, that's it! Sweep the fan beneath your elbow. But take care not to—"

"What the bloody hell is goin' on?" Morgan bellowed.

His knights froze, looking as guilty as priests in a brothel. No one spoke.

"Ye," he barked, stabbing a finger at the dark-haired sprite at the window. "What do ye think ye're doin', orderin' my men about?" Before she could answer, he glared at his men, adding, "And ye. Why are ye takin' orders from a lass?"

The Campbells looked shamefaced.

"M'laird, I can explain," Davey, the oldest, said.

Before Feiyan could reply, Jenefer appeared at the nursery window to defend her cousin. "'That lass' happens to know how to wield those weapons, you big oaf."

Morgan's blood boiled at the insult.

She added, "They might well have chopped off a hand without her instruction."

"My men need no instruction," he ground out. "Men, return these weapons to the armory. And ye two," he said, skewering the lasses with a hard stare, "get away from the win—"

The two lasses simultaneously slammed their respective shutters before he could finish.

The men began gathering Feiyan's weapons.

"Our apologies, m'laird," Davey mumbled.

Morgan blew out a vexed breath. To be honest, he wasn't all that upset that his men were learning a new skill. He wasn't even that bothered that they were taking direction from a lass, who probably did know a great deal about the curious weapons.

What worried him was that the Campbells had neglected to report back to him after their search.

"What news do ye bring o' Colban?" he asked them.

"Naught, m'laird," Davey said. "We scoured the forest for hours. We can see where Colban entered the wood. But there's no visible trail."

He rubbed his jaw. With leaves littering the autumn ground and hours since he'd left, that was to be expected. "Ye encountered no Rivenloch scouts?"

"Not a soul in the wood but us."

He nodded and dismissed them with a wave of his hand.

It was late enough that Morgan could be fairly certain Rivenloch was not planning to attack today. But they might have sent spies ahead to do surveillance.

As he wheeled to return to the armory, from the nursery above, he heard his bairn's sorrowful cry.

The sound reminded him of his own grief over the loss of his wife. Thin. Hollow. Relentless. He wondered if the torment of Alicia's death would ever end.

And then, not long after, the whimpers softened into cooing.

There could be only one reason for that. Jenefer. Despite her angry outburst, she'd been willing to attend to the bairn. Morgan was glad, for everyone's sake, he'd relented and given the guard orders to allow her to care for his son as long as Bethac was there.

What kind of magical sway the lass held over the child, he couldn't fathom. Even Bethac was mystified.

But what troubled him was wondering what he was going to do when she left.

He made his way back to the armory. There, he calmed his disquiet over Colban by inspecting the weapons hanging on the wall.

Though the Campbells could sometimes be wild-mannered, all of his knights were well disciplined. The soldiers kept their gear in good repair. The lances were sharp, and the axes had a keen edge.

As for Colban, he was a clever tracker. He'd find the lass.

Morgan took each longbow down, flexing the wood between his hands to test its strength.

From what he'd seen of Hallidis, she was a sensible woman. The most levelheaded of the three cousins, she seemed the least likely to make trouble.

Morgan made a cursory inspection of the quivers. The arrows were straight and neatly fletched.

If Colban had intercepted Hallie, Morgan reasoned, he'd assure her that her cousins were safe. He'd tell her that the king's messenger was on his way to settle the matter of the ownership of Creagor. He'd let her know there was no need for war.

And because peaceable Hallie hadn't wanted a siege in the first place, she'd agree to wait for the messenger's arrival.

Unless she didn't trust Colban.

Still, Colban had the upper hand. He was a seasoned warrior. She was a vulnerable lass. Colban no doubt had everything under control.

His mind eased, Morgan examined the claymores, one by one. Freshly polished, they gleamed like the surface of a still loch. Into each hilt was carved the mark of its owner.

Davey Campbell's hilt bore a cross.

John mac Dougal's symbol was a circle.

The X belonged to Ian Clare.

Colban's sign was...

The pit of Morgan's heart suddenly went cold. Colban's claymore still hung on the wall. Which meant he'd gone into the wood unarmed.

CHAPTER 30

"Oon't ye fret, Morgan." Standing before the buttery, Bethac actually patted Morgan on the arm, whispering to him as if he were a child. "The lass was up there with us most o' the afternoon. She was only feelin' peckish. So Cicilia and I came down to fetch her a wee crumb."

Cicilia smiled in innocent agreement.

Morgan couldn't breathe. The shadows cast by the torches in the great hall wavered ominously over his dozing clansmen as apprehension snaked through his veins. Did the maids not understand the peril?

Nay, of course not. To Bethac, the lasses were guests, not prisoners. But he'd given specific orders for Bethac to remain in Jenefer's presence if she was caring for his son.

Under his breath, he said, "Ye left the warrior maid *alone* with my bairn?"

Cicilia's smile faltered.

"O' course," Bethac said, oblivious to his concern. "Ye've seen how she is with Miles. The bairn loves—"

"His name is Allison," Morgan choked out, casting an alarmed gaze toward the nursery.

In a dozen strides, he crossed the great hall. He took the stairs two steps at a time. By the time he passed his bedchamber guard, who snapped to attention, his heart was pounding.

With no knock of warning, he pushed open the nursery door.

The flames on the hearth flickered wildly in the silent room, illuminating the honey-haired beauty curled atop the bed, fast asleep.

Cradled in her arms was the wee bairn. His eyes were closed in slumber. One tiny fist was tucked under his chin.

Morgan let out a shuddering breath and closed the door softly behind him.

Why he'd been so full of dread, he didn't know. He should have realized Jenefer would never hurt a child. Particularly this one. As Bethac had noted more than once, the lad had a curious affinity for the warrior maid. No doubt the feeling was mutual.

Besides, Jenefer was as yet unaware that the lad was his. Morgan had sworn the maidservants to secrecy. The lass from Rivenloch would have no reason to think the bairn could be used as a hostage.

He narrowed his eyes at the child and took a few cautious steps forward.

Morgan was accustomed to seeing a screaming infant with his features contorted in rage. Now that the bairn was at peace, Morgan saw he was a handsome lad. His hair was as fine as silk thread. His skin was flawless. Dark brows arched over his eyes like drawn bows. And the lashes below them rested upon rounded cheeks. His mouth was set in a drowsy pout, as perfect as the bud of a rose. And the shape of his face...

It was *hers*. He had Alicia's heart-shaped face.

Of course he did.

He probably had Morgan's features as well.

Morgan had never thought about it. In fact, he'd hardly given the lad a second glance. No matter how irrational it was, lost in his own anguish, he'd always secretly blamed the bairn for Alicia's death.

Now, gazing at the helpless, innocent, angelic child—*his* child, *their* child—his eyes filled. How could he blame the wee bairn? He'd not asked to be born. Why should the poor lad suffer from the unfortunate circumstances of his birth, when he'd had no say in the matter?

As Morgan stared down at the motherless infant left in his care, his vision blurred. How would he ever replace what he'd lost, what both of them had lost? Would Morgan marry again? Was he even capable of feeling affection for another woman?

Regret and love and grief tangled into a knot in his throat.

Jenefer always slept with one eye open. She might be wandering deep in the land of Nod, but if a wee beetle entered her bedchamber, she'd know it instantly.

So, though she gave no sign, she sensed at once that someone had come into the nursery. It wasn't Bethac or Cicilia. They wouldn't have opened the door with such speed and force.

Maintaining measured breaths and closed eyes, she silently calculated the path she'd have to take to get to the fireplace poker, bearing in mind she'd have to sweep Miles up safely in one arm.

The door closed, and she heard the intruder steal toward the bed. Every muscle in her body was primed, ready to spring.

But then, there was a long silence.

She waited.

And waited.

Finally, unable to endure the suspense, Jenefer lifted her lids just enough to peer through her lashes.

It was Morgan.

He was standing by the bed, staring down at the babe.

His head was tilted, and his eyes shimmered. She'd never seen a man look upon an infant with such tenderness, such fondness. Indeed, the way he was gazing at the lad made her hair stand up on the back of her neck.

This was not just any clan child.

Not just the son of a common soldier and a lady who'd died in childbirth.

Her eyes widened in surprise as the truth struck her like lightning.

Morgan, seeing she was awake, inhaled sharply. Caught off guard, he sniffed and blurted, "Bethac will be here soon with food."

But for once in her life, she wasn't hungry. Her thoughts were reeling.

This was no ordinary babe.

She nodded stiffly.

Their attention was drawn then to Miles, whose brow creased as he squirmed in his sleep.

"I didn't mean to...to wake the bairn," Morgan whispered.

What was it Bethac had said? That the babe's father visited him most every day. That he was in mourning. That was why he hadn't named the lad.

Was it possible? Was Morgan the lad's father?

He'd insisted the infant be called Allison. After the lady who'd borne him.

Had Lady Alicia from Catalonia been more than just his clanswoman?

Had she been his wife?

The idea filled her heart with simultaneous wonder and sorrow.

"My thanks to ye," he murmured, "for lookin' after him." He looked contrite, as if he were sorry for his earlier rudeness.

"He's a good lad," she said.

As if to prove her point, Miles blinked open his eyes and peered up at Morgan. His mouth opened into a perfect O, and then the corners curved into a smile.

Jenefer glanced at Morgan, who was transfixed.

He swallowed down some emotion and then, unable to resist the babe's sweet grin, smiled back. His delight was palpable. And yet it was guarded somehow by bittersweet caution.

She said carefully, "He has your smile."

She expected him to deny his relationship to the babe. He clearly wouldn't want her to know Miles was his, lest she try to ransom the child.

But Morgan was too enrapt with Miles' expression to even realize he'd revealed himself with his silence.

Fortunately for him, she had a well-developed sense of chivalry. It was unconscionable for her to put a babe in harm's way, no matter what could be gained from it. Children were weak and vulnerable, not to be preyed upon.

But a Highlander probably didn't know much about chivalry. All he knew was that Bethac and Cicilia had left his captive alone with his son. That explained why he'd rushed in the way he did.

She levered up on one elbow to look down at the babe. "He likes you, I think."

Morgan couldn't hide the joy in his face. He straightened with pride. "Aye?"

She nodded. His pleasure melted her heart at once.

And just as swiftly broke it.

If Miles was the laird's son and heir, there was no way he was going to leave the lad behind when he returned to the Highlands.

"May I?" he asked, indicating the bed.

She nodded, and he sat on the edge.

"He's quiet now," he remarked.

"When the mood suits him," she quipped.

Now that she could get a closer look at both of them in calm tempers, she was amazed she'd overlooked the resemblance. Miles' eyes were the same elusive color as Morgan's. His hair was a similar shade. And it hadn't been flattery to say they shared the same smile. It was a beaming, brilliant thing that felt like it illuminated the whole chamber.

"He's always quiet when he's in your arms," Morgan observed.

He couldn't know how his gentle words shot like a bolt into her chest.

A part of her had known it was folly, mentally creating a destiny for herself with the babe. She now realized that destiny was impossible.

The Highlanders might indeed be forced to leave.

She might win command of Creagor.

But she was never going to raise Miles to manhood.

She'd never teach him honor and chivalry and loyalty.

Never watch him become a capable knight.

Never see him grow into the role of the Laird du Lac.

She had only herself to blame for the sinking pain in her chest. She should never have begun daydreaming about the future.

In the end, she might have the will to battle a whole army of Highlanders. But she didn't have the heart to steal the son from their laird.

ChAPTER 31

j enefer was drowsing on the bed, only half-awake, when she remembered where she was. How much time had passed since she'd come to the nursery, she didn't know. The fire had burned low, but it was still dark in the room.

Feeling Miles, soft and warm and nestled against her in the bed, made her smile. He smelled like a bowl of fresh blancmange. Or maybe it was only hunger that made her think that.

She was lying on her left side with her left arm stretched out above Miles' head and her right arm curled around him.

But a strange, heavy weight pressed down on her right hip. The fingers of her left hand were tangled in hair that was too thick to be Miles'. And the back of her right hand rested against someone's body.

Bethac? She didn't think so.

Cicilia? Nay.

She opened her eyes to peer into the shadows and froze as she realized who it was.

Morgan.

They were lying face to face with the babe between them. She didn't dare move, for fear she'd awaken him. But his hand, resting with brazen possessiveness on her hip, the fingers grazing the skirts over her buttocks, alarmed her.

She couldn't accuse him of overstepping his bounds. After all, those were *his* locks into which she'd so boldly insinuated her fingers.

So she continued to remain still, listening as Miles' shallow breathing contrasted with the slower exhales of Morgan. His father, she reminded herself.

It wasn't unpleasant, she decided, lying here with the two Highlanders. There was something calming about their trust. Even Morgan's palm upon her hip—which she was sure was as unintentional as her hand curled against his stomach—felt reassuring and protective.

In contrast to the oak-hard muscles of his body, the hair crowning Morgan's head was soft. Curling over his ear, it twined around her fingers like a caress. She closed her eyes again, enjoying its texture.

Miles stirred then, and she stiffened.

He only made a few smacking sounds and a quick sigh, returning immediately to sleep.

But Morgan was roused as well, though he didn't fully wake. His hand drew her bottom closer. With a satisfied growl, he pressed his hips forward against her fist, which was trapped between the two of them.

To her horror, the back of that fist came into contact with something long and hard and unmistakable beneath his trews.

A shriek stuck in her throat. A hundred courses of action collided in her brain.

She should slap the Highlander for his impertinence.

She should remain still and wait for him to move away.

She should snatch her hand back.

Drive a knee into his ballocks.

Give his hair a good yank.

Feign sleep and roll away from him.

Wake Miles and let his cries awaken his father.

In the end, she did nothing. Holding her breath, she waited to see what would happen next.

She bit her lip as she felt his member pulse reflexively against her hand. But her horror turned quickly to fascination.

His fingers dangled low on her buttocks now. And even though her skirts separated their flesh, she could feel the light heat and pressure of his fingertips, resting there as if he owned her.

Yet as she continued to endure his touch in the darkness, she realized she didn't feel so much owned as she felt...protected.

It was a heady feeling.

After all, she was in control of the situation. Morgan was as sound asleep as a hibernating bear. Completely vulnerable. At her mercy.

If she chose, she could easily overpower him. Push him off the bed. Run him through with his own dagger.

It was quite an interesting predicament.

Eventually, while he snored on in oblivious innocence, Jenefer grew curious about what it would take to stir him. She liked nothing so much as a good risk. And she couldn't resist poking this sleeping bear.

With stealthy daring, she moved her fingers through his hair.

He didn't waken.

With a fingertip, she traced the rim of his ear.

Still he didn't waken.

With the back of her other hand, she applied increasing pressure, watching his face carefully for any response.

Finally, his brow creased, and he made an erotic murmur deep in his throat.

It was only a small sound, but it seemed to rouse a wild beast inside her. That beast came to life with a sensuous purr that resonated through every fiber of her being. Its fiery tongue licked at her nerves with a strange and powerful craving. And she sensed at once this was the deadliest animal she'd ever summoned.

Her breath quickened. Her heart pounded like an armorer's hammer. Her skin flushed with heat.

Then, just as she was trying to understand this maelstrom of emotions, the nursery door suddenly opened a crack.

Jenefer's breath caught.

Peering in cautiously, her face illuminated by candlelight, was Cicilia.

Jenefer held her breath, wary of moving a muscle, and stared mutely at the nurse.

But as soon as she slipped through the door, Cicilia skidded to a halt. Spying the couple lying there with limbs entwined, her mouth went round with shock.

Thankfully, she made no outcry. The last thing Jenefer wanted was for Morgan to wake up and see the mischief she was perpetrating.

Cicilia stammered in a whisper, "Och! Oh! I didn't know ye… Beggin' your pa-…I…I…"

Miles, as if sensing his breakfast was nearby, woke up with a hungry whimper.

Jenefer felt the blood rush to her face. She could think of nothing to say. She was just grateful Morgan was snoring away, oblivious to her shame.

Cicilia wrung her hands and spoke under her breath, trying to explain. "I'm so sorry, but 'tis midnight. The bairn's goin' to need feedin', and—"

She was interrupted by Bethac plowing into the back of her as she came through the nursery door. In an instant, the older maidservant took in the situation. She rushed forward and smoothly scooped Miles up from the bed.

"Come on, now, lad," she quietly cooed. "Let's tend to ye in the laird's bedchamber."

While Jenefer looked on, slack-jawed, Bethac hooked an arm around Cicilia's waist to drag her out, calling softly over her shoulder. "Ye go back to sleep now. We've got things well in hand."

Then she gently closed the door.

Jenefer let out a shuddering breath. There was no way she was going to go back to sleep. Not after that humiliating episode. She'd been caught by the servants, compromising their laird while he slept.

Shouldn't they be concerned?

Would they blather the gossip all over the keep?

Or perhaps, she thought sourly, this sort of clandestine affair was commonplace for the Highland laird.

Before she could become disgruntled by that idea, Morgan drew in a long, rasping breath and shifted on the bed.

Afraid to move lest she wake him, Jenefer closed her eyes and feigned sleep.

But it took all her willpower not to cry out when he buried his face in her hair and drew her hips firmly against his. And when he made that growling murmur in his throat again, she sighed as desire blew through her soul. Desire as warm and arousing as his breath upon her brow.

An erotic shiver coursed through every part of her body, converging in a brilliant burst of lust between her thighs, at the precise spot where his male hardness pressed against her.

Never had she felt so awake, so alive.

But she yearned for something else. Something more. Something closer. Something that could never be.

She was his captive. He was her enemy.

She was a noble warrior maid. He was a crude Highlander.

She was a virgin. He was a widowed father.

And yet none of that mattered when her flesh felt on fire and every sense was attuned to his slightest movement.

How long she languished, listening to his deep breaths, feeling them rasp across her skin, melting beneath the searing pleasure of his touch, she didn't know.

Eventually, fatigue overcame her. And then, the sleep she enjoyed was deep and untroubled by dreams.

CHAPTER 32

Before Morgan opened his eyes, he smiled in contentment. There was nothing as peaceful and satisfying as lying with a woman drawn back against his chest, enfolded in his arms. For a few moments, he enjoyed that serenity.

Her soft hair tickled his nose.

Her breast rested like a pillow in his hand.

Her buttocks cradled him where he swelled against her.

And her scent...

Nay. That wasn't right.

Alicia always smelled like roses.

This was a spicy, musky scent.

He cracked open his eyelids a fraction of an inch.

His face was nuzzled, not in Alicia's black braid, but in loose curls of dark golden honey.

Heartache stabbed him first. For a few precious moments, he'd been with Alicia again. But now that pleasant dream had been ripped from him.

Then the woman in his arms stirred. She made a soft, sleepy moan and snuggled closer. Her arm hugged his hand tighter to her breast. Her buttocks nestled, warm and inviting, against his cock.

He sucked in a ragged breath.

It had been months since he'd exercised the beast between his legs. While Alicia was breeding, she'd had no interest in sharing his bed. He'd been patient, knowing the birth of their child was momentous, more important than satisfying carnal hungers.

But that abstinence had served to increase his need to a fever pitch. He was as hard as a lance. And there was a dull throbbing in his ballocks that only one thing could relieve.

He knew it was wrong. Alicia had been gone but a few months. It was too soon. And he was ashamed. He'd never been a man to be commanded by such base needs.

And yet, lying here in the dawn's pale light, their limbs entangled, their breath mingling, her scent so intoxicating, it was hard to believe that his desire for her was so unnatural, so terrible.

Alicia was dead, after all.

Nothing he did or did not do would ever change that.

He was certain he'd never love again. The loss of a wife was too painful to endure a second time. And to be honest, now that he had a healthy heir, there was no need to remarry. Despite Colban's urging that he move on with his life and Bethac's incessant search for a mate for him.

Swiving, on the other hand...

This morn, his body was completely in agreement with the idea. He squeezed his eyes shut against a wave of intense lust.

At the moment, it was easy to imagine burrowing under the lass's skirts and plunging himself ballocks-deep into her warm, womanly recesses.

None would blame him.

He was widowed. And a man had his needs.

Indeed, most lasses would be happy to bed with a considerate, gentle lover like Morgan.

Not *this* lass, of course.

She would sooner lie with a wild dog than a Highlander.

Indeed, she'd be mortified at their current situation. No doubt she'd run him through, if she had a weapon at hand. The only reason she was pressed so intimately against him this morn was that she was fast asleep.

Jenefer was wide awake. How could she not be, with Morgan's breath ruffling her hair, his palm brazenly cupping her breast, and the rock-hard proof of his desire poking at the crevice of her arse?

She hadn't meant to sleep here all night. She'd intended to leave and slip into bed with Feiyan in the laird's bedchamber once Bethac and Cicilia returned with Miles.

But the maids never returned.

And to her chagrin, Morgan never left.

So here they were, in an embarrassing snarl of limbs and emotions, and Jenefer couldn't begin to imagine how to extricate herself.

It was daybreak. Soon Bethac would come to stoke the fire. Cicilia would come to fetch fresh linens for Miles. Someone would come to bring breakfast.

If news of the laird sleeping with his captive hadn't circulated the keep already, the rumors would fly fast and furiously the instant someone walked in.

It wasn't the wagging tongues that bothered her. Or even the notion that her reputation might be sullied. A lass willing to masquerade as a half-naked ghost didn't attach much importance to reputation.

What bothered her was that they hadn't actually done anything. If gossip was to be spread around the castle, at least it should be based on real scandal and not conjecture. Nothing was quite as annoying as being charged with a crime one hadn't committed.

And yet, would she rather he *had* ravished her?

Such a thing was unthinkable.

He was her enemy. A feral Highlander. A lawless giant. The usurper of her castle.

And yet...

He was also a man. An appealing, virile, tempting one. That couldn't have been made any clearer to her as he nestled close with his staff wedged against her bottom.

And if she forgot all the details about who he was, if she focused only on the way he made her feel, her thoughts went in a completely different—and dangerous—direction.

His arm surrounded her like a cozy cloak, protecting her from the elements. His legs, tucked behind her knees, formed a comfortable chair. His chest rose and fell with every breath, pressing against her back. And each exhale sent a new shiver of warm desire down her spine that added to the last. Soon she felt lost in a sultry haze of longing.

And it wasn't unpleasant. Not at all.

But it was useless to be hungry when no food had been offered.

Unless Morgan woke up with a complete change of heart and uncontrollable lust in his eyes, he wasn't going to satisfy her appetite.

So she needed to shake off her lingering desire and his grip on her before someone could catch them in the throes of... She mentally sighed. The throes of nothing.

Feigning sleep, she shifted under his arm and rolled onto her back, sure her movement would wake him.

It didn't. He was still dozing. And she'd only made things worse. His arm was now slung diagonally across her chest. His hand curved beneath her breast, and his thumb rested with brazen grace upon her nipple.

She ventured a cautious sideways glance.

He continued to breathe heavily. His nostrils quivered with every breath. His hair fell in unruly tendrils along his corded neck and over his brow, not quite reaching his closed eyes. Fine, dark stubble covered his jaw. But it was upon his lips her gaze fastened.

Not quite like his son's perfect, pouting bow, his mouth looked similarly soft and slightly swollen from sleep. It was hard to imagine harsh words coming from those lips. Easier to dream of whispers of affection, murmurs of passion, groans of desire.

She bit the inside of her cheek as irresistible yearning swelled through her body, entering through the aching spot between her thighs, flowing deep inside through her abdomen, and bursting out at the tingling tip of her breast, where his thumb rested.

Transfixed by the sight of his mouth, Jenefer continued to stare, licking her lips, wondering how it would feel on her flesh. What he would taste like. What it would be like to kiss him.

Then he suddenly parted his lips, and she caught her breath.

With his eyes still closed, he mumbled, "Do not torment me with starin', lass. If ye're goin' to strike, do it."

Shocked by his invitation, encouraged by her lust, and unfettered by caution, Jenefer took him at his word. She pitched forward, angling her head, and planted her lips on his surprised mouth.

CHAPTER 33

Morgan could not have been more startled. He had braced himself for a slap of outrage. At worst, she might deliver a punch to his jaw.

He figured he deserved as much. And he'd given her permission. He was well aware he should have found a way to judiciously separate from the lass before she awakened.

But he hadn't. And the reason was simple. He liked the way she felt in his arms.

Her hair was fragrant. Her body was supple. Her breast sat perfectly in his hand. And her hips were inviting as hell.

That she didn't clout him for his intimate transgression was astonishing.

And what she *did* do was so unexpected that he froze in stunned wonder. At first.

Then, of course, his masculine instincts took over.

He answered her kiss, drawing her velvety lips against his and pressing tentatively forward.

She sighed into his mouth, a sigh full of wonder and pleasure. Like a bellows, her breath instantly inflamed his desire.

Weaving his fingers through her curls, he pulled her closer, kissing her with desperate haste.

She responded with a sort of breathless enthusiasm he'd never before experienced. Her fingers raked through his hair to seize him by the back of the neck. With her other hand, she clenched the front of his leine in her demanding fist. Gasping and ravenous, she kissed him again and again.

Her kiss was like ale splashed on the flames of his passion, driving the blaze high and out of control. The beast in his trews roared like a wild inferno. Morgan's brain deserted him, and his body acted on instinct alone.

He slid his palm over her lovely bottom and hauled her hips against him. He groaned as his cock, squeezed between the two of them, throbbed in anticipation.

She answered his groan with a sensuous purr, born deep in her throat, driving him to even greater heights of desire.

Without thought of the consequences, he turned with her then, rising above her, trapping her between his legs and pressing her down into the mattress. He rained kisses all over her beautiful, enraptured face and then returned to her mouth, delving with his tongue to slurp up every drop of her lust.

Wrapping her arms around his neck, she arched up against him, urging him to continue.

He let one hand delve beneath the neck of her kirtle to find the peach-soft flesh of her breast.

She rasped in a quick breath of welcome shock as he plucked her nipple to a firm point.

It had been so long since he'd touched a woman, he feared he was proceeding too quickly. His head swam with yearning. His heart drummed at a feverish pace. Already the pressure was building in his loins.

He felt like a runaway cart, careening with reckless haste down a steep mountain. He wasn't sure he could stop. He sure as hell didn't want to.

Jenefer had never been touched like this before.

But she'd never been afraid of the unknown.

Kissing him was more exciting than she'd imagined. His lips were succulent and inviting, like the most delicious sweetmeats, and she couldn't get enough of them.

Despite his willful strength, his touch was surprisingly gentle. It made her skin tingle and warmed her blood. Where his fingers grazed her, she felt awakened and alive.

His ragged breath—upon her face, along her throat, beside her ear—made her shiver in delight. Her head swirled in a lovely fog of lust as she writhed beneath him.

His trespass beneath her kirtle to caress her breast stole her breath and her senses. But when she responded to his touch against her will, she knew an instant of panic.

She was as helpless as an overturned beetle, flat on her back. Why had she let him render her so vulnerable? Especially when he commanded her body with such precision?

In alarm, she fought back. Hooking one leg around him, she heaved upward with all her might and at last managed to roll him onto his back beneath her.

But rather than exerting her will and proving her domination, she'd only fed his lust. He was just as content to have *her* conquer *him.*

She thrust her tongue deep into his mouth in victory. She clasped his thighs between her knees, holding him captive. She ran her palm boldly over his trews, relishing the blade-hard proof of his craving.

Not once did he object to her subjugation.

Not once did he fight for his freedom.

Though by virtue of his superior strength and size, he might have thrown her over again, not once did he try to master her.

Instead, he sucked in a sharp breath between his teeth when she squeezed the hardening in his trews, arching up against her in need. His face was a study in torment, and his fists contained a powerful fury that longed to be unleashed.

His surrender was intoxicating, almost as intoxicating as her own desire. Her heart raced at the signs of his raw yearning—his deeply creased brow, his tightly closed eyes, his flaring nostrils. Her nipples tensed, and the ache between her legs increased from a painful throbbing to an excruciating need that demanded relief.

Overcome with longing and uncertain what to do next, she lowered her mouth to his again, gorging on his fervor with unabashed greed. For one incredible moment, drunk on desire, lost in lust, Jenefer believed she could happily remain here for the rest of her life.

When the door burst open, Morgan had no time to think. He only did what came naturally to him—the chivalrous thing. At the first creak, he rolled Jenefer back beneath him, protecting her with his body and hiding her from view.

Unfortunately, Jenefer didn't see it that way. She blustered in outrage and tried to thrust him off of her. She probably would have spat a few choice curses as well, except Bethac spoke first.

"Oh!" the maidservant exclaimed from the doorway. "Beggin' your... M'laird, I... I didn't know ye still had compa-... I'll come back late-..."

"Wait!" Jenefer cried.

Morgan lowered his brows. What was the lass doing? He meant to shield her, to protect her honor. After all, Bethac couldn't report what she couldn't see. As far as she knew, Morgan's consort could well be a serving lass. Why would Jenefer betray her presence?

To his consternation, Jenefer called out, "We weren't swiving. I want that to be clear. I won't have you bandying

171

about that you saw the laird swiving me, because we weren't. Not yet at least."

Morgan tried not to laugh. She sounded mildly irritated. They may not have been swiving. But they'd been close to it. And what difference did it make anyway?

"Oh, Miss," Bethac said with great dignity, "I would ne'er say such a thing, not me."

"Because if you do, I'll put frogs in your bed, I swear."

"My lips are sealed," Bethac promised.

Then, to his utter amazement, Jenefer confided, "And I don't want you to think poorly of Morgan. 'Twasn't his idea. 'Twas mine. You were right. Your laird is not the kind of man to ravish a captive against her will."

"Aye, Miss."

Though Jenefer didn't meet his eyes, Morgan's heart melted as he gazed down at the blushing lass.

She'd stood up for *him.*

That was a rare and touching thing. And in that amazing moment, he realized what he felt for her was more than mere lust or admiration. It was something far more perilous. Genuine respect and affection.

"One more thing," she said.

"Aye, Miss?"

"Did you bring breakfast?"

CHAPTER 34

Morgan figured Bethac's interruption had been for the best.

Jenefer was right. He'd never take a woman against her will. But given enough temptation, he might take a willing woman against his better judgment.

So, with as little comment as possible, he left her to her breakfast and headed to the practice field, hoping to work off his frustrations with a claymore.

There was still no sign of Rivenloch, though he kept his archers posted on the wall and his knights armed and ready for war.

By midday, he was dusty from bouts and dripping with sweat. But he was no closer to forgetting the winsome wench who'd fired his blood this morn.

He couldn't stop thinking about her irresistible scent. Her lush curls and silky skin. Her glazed and sparkling eyes. The evocative pressure of her lips. Her supple, voluptuous breasts. The feral, feminine sounds she made as she helped herself to his body.

Even now, the memory made him grow hard.

Raising his claymore, he hacked at the stuffed dummy in the midst of the practice field until he chopped it into bits of straw.

He wished he could beat his emotions into submission so easily.

But visions of Jenefer kept intruding.

And to his shame, he kept comparing her to his wife.

They were worlds apart.

Alicia had been sweet and reserved. Too timid to hold his hand or kiss him in front of the clan, she'd blushed if he so much as whispered in her ear. Because she was modest, their swiving had been done in the dark and under the coverlet. She'd never gasped or cried out, but merely endured his fondling and thrashing in compliant silence. Never would she have dreamed of initiating lovemaking.

He smiled as he recalled Jenefer climbing atop him with brazen command, pinning him to the bed with voracious kisses.

Then he sighed.

Surely that was his long forced chastity speaking and not reason.

It was only that he missed trysting. That was all. Jenefer was like a brimming cup of ale to a thirsty traveler.

Still, he couldn't forget how flattering her bold advances were. How unabashed she'd been at being discovered by the maid. And most touching, the way she'd attempted to salvage his honor.

He'd never imagined he'd grow fond of another woman. He'd thought himself incapable of ever loving again. And it still felt wrong to feel tenderness toward Jenefer, as if he were somehow being disloyal to Alicia.

If Colban were here, he would tell Morgan that he was being ridiculous. Alicia was gone.

In his head, Morgan knew that. But in his heart? His heart wasn't so easy to convince.

"What's wrong, Jen? Don't you want some of this?" Feiyan asked in disbelief.

From the window, Jenefer glanced briefly over her shoulder. The guard had brought in a platter of smoked haddock, hard cheese, bread, and ale. But it didn't look half as appetizing as what was charging across the practice field below.

"In a bit," she replied, returning to gaze out the window.

Even at this distance, she was drawn to Morgan like iron to a lodestone. The mere sight of him made her burn.

What devilry affected her, she didn't know. But her heart throbbed as she watched him wield his claymore with passion and power. The violent ring of steel on steel as he faced his challengers, defeating them with a roar of victory, called to her warrior's blood. And the memory of lying atop his magnificent body, feasting on his lips while his fingers swept with gentle restraint across her flesh, left her breathless.

She wished she *had* swived him while she had the chance. Maybe then she wouldn't be tormented by *imagining* what it would have been like.

But that opportunity wouldn't arise again. Not before the Rivenloch knights arrived to banish Morgan Mor mac Giric and his clan to the Highlands.

She narrowed her eyes at the laird sparring with his men below, studying him as sparks flew from his great blade. She'd been watching for nearly an hour when a crafty, devious idea began to coil its way into her brain.

What if she *didn't* banish him?

She bit the corner of her lip as she watched him destroy the stuffed dummy in the midst of the field.

What if she refused to *let* him go back?

What if she forced him to stay...as her husband?

Her heart skittered as she considered the rash possibility.

It made practical sense.

Marrying him would eliminate the conflict over the possession of Creagor. No matter what the missive from the king declared or what her parents reported, the holding would remain in her hands. At least *half* of it would remain anyway.

If they wedded, she wouldn't have to bother with stealing Miles or convincing Bethac to stay on to care for the babe, since Jenefer would perforce become his mother.

Best of all, there would be no war or siege. Morgan's fighting force of Highland giants would make the combined armies of Rivenloch and Creagor undefeatable. The Scots border would be impenetrable.

Of course, what made her pulse race at the idea of marrying Morgan was far more primal. It was desire.

As mad as it was, she was attracted to the wild Highlander, like a bee to a thistle. Not only to his magnificent body and inspiring prowess, but also to his good heart, his clan loyalty, his sense of honor.

Whether Morgan was attracted to her, she didn't much consider. Marriage among nobles was a matter of political alliance, not sentiment.

Besides, how could he say nay? Once he glimpsed the might of the Rivenloch knights, his choice would be simple. Either wed her and remain at Creagor or refuse her and be banished to the Highlands forever.

Bethac pinched her nose between her thumb and finger as she accompanied Morgan through the great hall after supper.

"I insist, m'laird," she chided under her breath.

Morgan didn't think he smelled that bad. But he *had* worked up a sweat on the field today. He'd also taken several strategic dives into the dirt.

"I'll fill a tub for ye upstairs," she said, refusing to take nay for an answer.

"Fine." Then, remembering who was in his bedchamber, he added, "I'll bathe in the nursery."

She seemed disappointed. "The nursery?"

"I'm not goin' to feed the gossipmongers by bathin' with the two lasses in my bedchamber."

Offended, Bethac gave him a pout. "No one's mongerin' any gossip."

"And I want to keep it that way."

She sighed. "Very well. I'll send Cicilia up to feed the bairn and put him down for a wee nap while I have your bath prepared."

As she bobbed in farewell and scurried off, Morgan shook his head. Why would the old maidservant care how he smelled? She hadn't reminded him to bathe since he was a young lad. Maybe, now that he was a laird in his own right, she thought he should answer to a higher standard of cleanliness.

Whatever her purpose, he was glad enough of a good soak a half-hour later when Bethac had him summoned to the nursery.

His son was asleep in his cradle near the hearth. The wooden tub, which he'd had built specially to accommodate the larger men of his clan, stood in the middle of the chamber.

But instead of his usual tepid water with a few rags thrown in for scrubbing, the tub was carefully lined with cushioning linens, surrounded by candles, and half-filled with steaming water into which Bethac was sprinkling some sort of dried herb.

"What the devil?"

Casting a quick glance toward the bairn, she hushed Morgan with a frown and a finger to her lips. Then she explained in a whisper, "The hot water will ease your achin' muscles and bruised bones."

He whispered back, "And the...what are those? Leaves?"

"Woodruff. 'Twill make ye smell sweet."

He scowled. He wasn't sure he wanted to smell sweet. And all those candles seemed like a waste of beeswax.

But once he undressed and slipped into the warm and fragrant water, he closed his eyes and felt his tensions begin to melt away.

Bethac gathered up his discarded clothes.

"I'll be back anon with fresh trews and hose and a clean leine." She clucked her tongue as she held up his filthy cotun. "I'll see if I can find a servant lad to beat the dust from this."

"What about the bairn?" He was uneasy about being left in charge of a creature about which he knew nothing.

"Oh, he's sleepin'." She gave him a twinkly smile before she left. "Take your time, and enjoy your bath, m'laird."

He *did* enjoy it. The water was soothing. The flickering candles calmed him. And there was something about the scent of the woodruff...

Jenefer.

His eyes flashed open.

It was Jenefer's scent. Sweet. Spicy. Musky.

He inhaled the fragrant steam, and when he closed his eyes again, he saw her. Her cascading tawny hair. Her glittering emerald eyes. Her soft, rosy, delicious lips.

Beneath the water, he stirred to life. Since he was alone, he didn't bother to hide his arousal.

Instead, he sank further into the water, resting his neck on the padded edge of the tub, and dreamed of an impossible future.

A future where he could begin again. Forget about the love he'd lost. Move past the memory of his beloved, departed wife.

CHAPTER 35

Jenefer spread out the napkin she'd pilfered from supper on the bedchamber table. Then she fished a cooled piece of charcoal from the hearth. By holding the cloth taut and carefully dragging the sharp edge of the charcoal along the surface, she could draw black lines on the white linen.

"What are you doing?" Feiyan asked.

"Making plans."

"Plans for what?" Feiyan leaned over her shoulder. "An escape tunnel?"

"Improvements."

She began rendering the curtain wall, moving it out a considerable distance from where it was now.

"Improvements to what?"

"To Creagor."

"You haven't even won the keep yet," Feiyan pointed out.

"I have a plan for that as well." Jenefer gave her a cryptic smile.

Feiyan arched a sardonic brow. "Does it involve eating them out of house and home? Because that's the only plan you seem to be employing at the moment."

Jenefer gave her a simmering glare. "Well, at least I'm not training their soldiers."

Feiyan colored.

Jenefer worked in silence after that.

Meanwhile, Feiyan salvaged her pride by punching and kicking at the air in the strange fighting style she'd learned from her mother's servant.

"So, Feiy," she said casually, "what do you know about seducing men?"

Feiyan was so startled by the question, she stumbled in the middle of a lunge and almost kicked herself right off her feet. "Wha-what?" Then she planted indignant fists on her hips. "What makes you think I would know anything about seducing men?"

"Don't you?"

Feiyan's jaw dropped in disbelief.

Jenefer shrugged. "I figured you had lots of experience."

"What the hell is that supposed to mean?"

Jenefer didn't know why her cousin was so upset. "'Tis a simple question. Aye or nay? Do you or do you not know how to seduce men?"

"What kind of a strumpet do you think I am?" Feiyan demanded.

"So you don't know?"

Feiyan answered with a growl, then bit out, "Nay, Jenefer. No doubt *you* have swived your way through the ranks of your father's knights. But I..." She halted, narrowed her eyes, and cocked her head. "Wait. Why are you asking me that?"

Jenefer shrugged. "Just...curious."

But Feiyan was as perceptive as a hunting hound when it came to sniffing out answers. "Are you planning to seduce someone?"

Jenefer didn't care for Feiyan's amused tone. "Nay."

"You are, aren't you?" Then she inhaled sharply. "Thor's ballocks! Don't tell me you're going to try to seduce the Highlander?"

Before Jenefer could deny it, Feiyan erupted into peals of laughter.

Though Jenefer would never admit it, her cousin's mirth made her suddenly uncertain of her plan. What if she didn't have the charm or wit or wiles to seduce Morgan?

But she couldn't afford self-doubt. Turning hurt into fury, Jenefer wheeled and gave Feiyan a hard shove.

Unprepared, Feiyan plopped onto her arse on the floor. Her laughter was cut short, and revenge flared in her eyes.

"If *that's* your idea of seduction," Feiyan sneered, nodding to the drawing Jenefer had made, "then you might as well toss those plans onto the fire."

Jenefer was saved from having to think of a cutting retort. A thin, sad cry leaked through the wall from the nursery.

Miles.

She clenched her jaw. If Miles hadn't been wailing, Jenefer would have stayed to settle things between her caustic cousin and her, once and for all, with her fists.

But the babe's cries were growing louder. If she didn't go to the nursery of her own accord, Bethac would come knocking. And she didn't want the maid to witness her beating Feiyan to a bloody pulp.

So she threw the piece of charcoal at Feiyan, making her flinch out of the way, and left, slamming the door behind her. With a curt nod to the guard, she stalked down the hallway.

Taking a deep, calming breath, she swung open the nursery door, expecting to see Bethac pacing in frustration.

What she saw instead made her freeze in stunned amazement. Before her was the most magnificent embodiment of a warrior she'd ever seen.

Morgan stood in all his naked glory.

Wet and dripping from his bath.

Gleaming from the light of a dozen candles.

Holding a babe that was squalling loud enough to summon the dead.

Her gaze involuntarily raced from the top of the man's freshly washed head, down his perfectly sculpted body, to his sturdy bare feet, and back up again.

She'd seen plenty of nude men before. Spending as much time as she did in the armory ensured that. But this one took her breath away.

Before she could make a stammering fool of herself, she turned to secure the door behind her and catch her breath.

When she turned back, Morgan's confused expression had grown to complete discomfiture.

Suddenly, despite her fascination with the Highlander's godlike contours, she thought the spectacle before her might be the most hilarious and awkward thing she'd seen in a long time.

Morgan—completely naked, vulnerable, and alone—was holding Miles in his outstretched arms as if the babe were a feral, raging wildcat that he feared might deliver a lethal bite.

She clapped her hand over her twitching mouth, furrowing her brow and trying not to smile.

She was unsuccessful.

"Lass, will ye not..." he started, wincing every time Miles let out a particularly piercing scream. "Can't ye... What the... Are ye goin' to just stand there, or..."

If it weren't for Miles' distress, Jenefer would have *loved* to have just stood there watching Morgan struggle with the infant and squirm in naked discomfort.

But she had a heart. And the sight of Morgan was doing strange, uncontrollable things to her. So she took mercy on the babe and his incredibly splendid father.

Sweeping past his oversized tub, she caught a whiff of woodruff—her favorite scent. She smiled in approval. Morgan must have sprinkled it in his bath, just as she always did.

Advancing, she plucked Miles from Morgan's hands and settled him against her shoulder.

To her disappointment, Morgan immediately snatched up a linen square and tied it around his hips. Not so quickly that she didn't catch a glimpse of his well-muscled buttocks. And not before she stole a last peek at the manly treasure nestled in his crop of dark hair.

"My thanks," he mumbled, running an embarrassed hand through his wet locks. "Bethac said he was sleepin'. She said he'd be fine. And then she left and... She said she'd come back, but she hasn't and..."

"He *is* fine." It was amusing how inept this brave, bold warrior was when it came to his son. She would have thought he'd know more about his own flesh and blood.

Perhaps he'd taken little interest in the babe since he'd lost Miles' mother.

She thoughtfully pursed her lips. If that were so, Jenefer could use that to her advantage in her plans to seduce the Highlander.

She placed a tender kiss on Miles' head. "He's only wailing because he misses his dear Jen, don't you, lad?"

Morgan sat on the edge of the bed. While she sauntered around the chamber, she felt him studying her, as if he meant to memorize her infant-soothing tactics.

She rubbed Miles' back and murmured to him, loud enough for Morgan to hear. "Ah, don't you fret, Miles. I'm here now. I'll keep you safe and warm. And I vow I won't trade you for a beastie."

Miles let out a pathetic, shuddering cry.

"Oh, I know," Jenefer told him. "I know you lost your ma. How hard it must be for you." She gave Morgan a brief sidelong glance. "But I can be your ma for a wee while, can't I? At least until the laird says I have to go."

Out of the corner of her eye, Jenefer saw Morgan open his mouth to say something. But Miles interrupted with a wail.

"Ah, sweet wee child, I'll miss you as well. But what are we to do?"

After a few more circles around the nursery, Miles' cries diminished. His face relaxed, and his eyes drifted shut. Jenefer slowly and carefully lowered him back into his cradle, tucking the sheepskin in around him.

When she turned to face Morgan, she saw gratitude in his eyes.

She saw something else as well.

Attraction. And speculation.

Perhaps Feiyan was right. Perhaps Jenefer didn't have the skills to seduce a man. Perhaps she couldn't tempt the Highlander.

But she could maneuver him. She could make herself seem indispensible to his son. And she believed she'd just planted that seed.

"He should sleep well now," she whispered, "at least until Bethac returns."

He nodded.

She gazed at the oversized tub surrounded by candles. Was that water actually steaming?

Jenefer rarely got a hot bath. And never one in such an enormous tub. Water took so long to heat, and the tubs at home were pitifully small. Thanks to a good measure of Viking blood, she'd grown accustomed to bathing in the loch most of the year. Still, that warm, fragrant, spacious bath looked inviting indeed.

She looked away to feast her eyes on the handsome warrior one last time. Then she smiled and swept her arm toward his luxurious, linen-lined tub. "Enjoy the rest of your bath."

Chapter 36

There was no way Morgan was getting back in that tub.

Not while Jenefer was here.

Not in his present state.

While she'd been busy allaying his bairn's woes, he'd watched her with growing interest and admiration. And to his dismay, that interest had begun to manifest in a conspicuous way beneath his targe of thin linen.

No matter what his brain told him, at least part of him quite clearly wanted the lass to remain here with him.

He cleared his throat, deciding, "I'm done bathin'."

She cocked her head. "Are you sure?"

"Aye."

"You can't have spent more than a few moments in the tub," she argued. "'Tis still steaming."

Morgan wished she'd leave. "'Twas enough."

When she made no immediate move to depart, he stood up, carefully clasping his hands before him to cover his arousal.

She shrugged. "Well, if you're sure you're done with it..."

"I am." He turned away to collect his clothing, hoping she'd be headed for the door when he turned back. "Thank ye for comin' to tend to the bairn." He scanned the bed, trying to locate his trews and leine. "I hope 'twasn't too much trouble." Where the hell was his cotun? "He seems to cry at all hours o' the..."

Suddenly he remembered Bethac had taken his clothing, promising to bring him a fresh leine and trews. He had nothing to wear but the scrap of linen tied around his hips.

"...night." He grimaced. "Good night then," he improvised, turning to bid her farewell.

But the bold lass apparently had her own ideas about that. She'd slipped out of her surcoat and flung it to the floor. Now she was kicking off her boots and wriggling out of her kirtle.

"What are ye..." he choked out.

"'Tis a shame to let good hot water go to waste," she said.

Before he could take a breath or turn away, she pulled the kirtle over her head and tossed it on top of her discarded surcoat.

Before he could object, she stepped with brash entitlement into the bath. *His* bath.

His mouth went dry as his gaze traveled up her long legs to her soft nest of downy amber curls.

He couldn't breathe, letting his eyes trace the womanly contours of her body. The sensuous curve of her hips. The slope of her narrow waist. The perfection of her generous breasts.

A lusty jolt of lightning struck between his thighs. He pressed down hard against it with his clasped hands, trying to will it away.

"Ohh," she sighed in wonder as she sank slowly into the water. "This is heavenly." The deep tub allowed her to submerge up to her shoulders.

Heavenly, he thought. Aye, that was one word to describe the lass.

"'Tis the biggest tub I've ever seen," she said.

"Is it?" His voice was not his own. The words came out as taut as a drawn bow.

"Mmmm." She teased the surface of the water with her fingers. "And woodruff is my favorite."

Yesterday, Morgan didn't know what woodruff was. Now it was his favorite as well. He'd never again be able to smell it without envisioning the tempting lass as she was now. Leaning her head back against the edge of the tub. Sluicing water up over her arms. Sighing with delight.

Morgan couldn't tear his eyes away. No matter how unwise it was to hunger after a sweetmeat he couldn't have, it didn't stop him from doing it.

When she held her breath and immersed her head, his breath caught as well until she emerged again. Her golden hair was now dark amber and dripping. Her face was bedewed with droplets that caught the light of the candles.

She cast about for a moment in the water and then looked up at him. "Do you have a rag for washing?"

He gulped. He did. He was wearing it.

But certainly he could find something else. There was a stack of rags on the table beside his son.

Wary of both waking the bairn and exposing his arousal, he cautiously made his way to retrieve a rag for her. The wise thing would have been to wad it up and throw it to her. But that would have been discourteous. Besides, as weak as he was feeling, he would be lucky to clear the bed.

So he bit the inside of his cheek and conveyed the rag into her hand with a stiff bow.

He tried, and failed, to overlook what lay beneath the surface of the water. Rose-tipped breasts, lapped by the warm waves. Impossibly long, lean, and shapely legs. Gently wafting curls at the juncture of those legs.

Closing his eyes against temptation, he swung around and tried to find something, anything, to distract him from the beauty bathing before him.

From the moment Jenefer melted into the fragrant water, she thought she'd never felt such warmth. The waves seemed to permeate her skin, filling her with heat that eased her muscles and penetrated her bones.

Gone were her cares. Gone were her defenses.

But then Morgan brought her the rag, and she glimpsed the naked lust in his eyes.

Instantly, her blood surged like molten iron through her veins. Tongues of flame lapped at her womanly core. The drops of water clinging to her face felt like beads of sweat.

When he turned away, her gaze followed him, drifting down the captivating wet locks of his hair, the beautiful hollow of his back, locking on his lean, firm buttocks, defined by the linen drawn tightly across them.

She swallowed hard.

He wanted her.

And she wanted him.

"Morgan," she breathed.

He didn't turn around. "Aye?"

She cast about in her mind for an excuse to bring him close. "I can't...reach my back."

She saw his shoulders rise and fall, as if he prepared for battle. At last, with a grim countenance and clenched fists, he came to the tub to oblige her.

Her heart thrummed like a hummingbird's wings when she handed him the wet rag. She leaned forward to clasp her knees and grant him access to her back.

At first, his motions were minimal and pragmatic.

Kneeling beside the tub, he moved her hair to one side.

Then he scrubbed lightly at the place between her shoulder blades, working his way gradually down her spine to the middle of her back. Moving a few inches to the left, he repeated his movements.

But when he shifted again, his circles with the cloth slowed, and Jenefer could feel his hot breath on her shoulder.

His breath kindled something inside her. Something that made her blood flow hot. Something that made her bones as liquid as honey.

She closed her eyes, resting her forehead on her knees.

He lowered the rag into the water again, then pressed it against the blade of her shoulder, letting the water drizzle down her spine.

The only sounds in the chamber were the soft plashing of the bath, the quiet crackle of the fire, and her sigh of passion.

Slowly, gently, he swept the sopping rag across her skin, awakening every inch. Then he delved beneath the water, letting the rag trespass across her lower back and farther, along the curve of her buttocks.

She hardly dared to breathe. She bit her lip as an intense twinge sparked between her thighs, heating her entire body like a glowing coal.

The sensation of his breath on the back of her neck made every hair stand on end. And when he placed a tender kiss there, her sigh was almost a moan.

Releasing the rag, he tangled his hand gently in her hair and pulled her head back until she turned her face up to his. The smoldering need she saw in his eyes reflected her own.

She licked her lips, waiting for him to extinguish the fire there.

CHAPTER 37

Morgan knew he was walking straight into the fires of Hell.

The lass was his captive, not his consort.

What if she was a virgin?

If he did anything to compromise her virtue, there would be no forgiveness from her clan.

And yet the sight of her—wet and hot and eager, licking her lips in anticipation, looking up at him with smoky lust—made him forget reason.

Just one kiss, he told himself. Yet even as he articulated that lie, he was already engaging in a second kiss. And a third.

Her lips were not only welcoming. They were demanding.

Every kiss became more and more insistent, until he lost count of them.

She threaded her fingers through the wet strands of his hair, drawing him closer. She slanted her mouth across his again and again, feasting on him with ravenous hunger.

Before he could catch his breath, she locked her arms around his neck, clinging to him with a desperation born of desire.

She arched up toward him, and the sensation of her supple breasts sliding over his chest, her tight nipples grazing his skin, wrenched a groan from him.

Casting caution to the winds and damning himself for a fool, he plunged his arms into the water, delved his hands beneath her bottom, and scooped her out of the bath.

The divine, slippery curve of her buttocks and the sleek legs she immediately wrapped around him did nothing to dissuade him from his purpose.

Nor did the trail of water he left as he carried his beautiful, dripping prize to the bed.

He laid her atop the coverlet. A fierce swelling of lust left him breathless as he gazed down at the beautiful lass. Her mouth was open in awe. Her breast heaved with passion.

He'd never wanted a woman more.

And yet enough chivalry remained to give him pause. He clenched his fists, fighting his inner beast. He closed his eyes, hoping—robbed of the sight of her—he might see reason more clearly and change his mind.

He never guessed she would seize the reins of his desire. Nor did he anticipate the frenzied pace at which she intended to compel him.

But in the next instant, she tugged off his linen covering with a soft gasp of wonder. Then there was no hiding his ardor now. No denying what he craved.

And when he dared to open his eyes, he saw a thirst in her gaze that was undisguised and unabashed, brash and demanding.

He knew then that he was completely wrong about her. The lass had definitely done this before.

There was no hesitation in her manner. Not a shred of modesty. Not even a pretense of maidenly shyness.

And that, more than anything else, convinced him to plunge headlong into the waters of temptation.

Jenefer's head was spinning.

She had no idea what she was doing.

Instinct made her race headlong toward the seduction she'd intended. And she didn't dare stop, lest her plans be undone.

But her heart was pounding at the prospect. Coursing through her veins was a thrill of excitement and desire and fear. Fear, because she'd never done such a thing before.

Once, she'd caught a pair of servants coupling in the stables. And she'd overheard tales of conquest from knights in the armory. But what she knew of lovemaking wouldn't fill a thimble.

Besides, this felt so much more real. More present. More compelling.

She was no longer master of her body. She could hardly catch her breath. Every nerve was quivering with life.

And yet, instead of feeling panic, the rush of sensation and emotion exhilarated her.

She felt like an arrow shot from a bow, arcing with precision and purpose toward its target. Once released, it couldn't be recalled. And she wouldn't know for certain whether she'd sailed true until she met her mark.

So she ventured onward, following her heart's desire and her body's cravings.

Freeing him from the linen, she was startled for an instant at the size of him. Perhaps he was no larger than other men. But considering what she was about to do, that part of him seemed enormous and foreign and forbidding.

Then he swept down upon her, branding her as they met, skin to skin, and blotting out her thoughts.

Now there was only want and need. A primal urgency to mate that went beyond the two of them. A drive as old as nature. As inevitable as time.

With every fiber of her being, she welcomed him. Already clasping her arms around his neck, she arched up and locked her legs around his buttocks.

He groaned against her ear.

A primitive vibration shivered through her.

He rasped his chest against her bosom.

Her nipples stiffened, sending fiery current racing to the spot where her legs joined.

She pressed hard against him, hoping to ease the suffering there.

He growled in answer, pressing back.

Yet it wasn't enough.

Somehow he knew it wasn't enough.

Slipping his hand down between their bodies, he combed through her woman's curls with gentle fingers. Resting his brow against hers, he carefully parted her nether lips.

She caught her breath, feeling suddenly too exposed, too vulnerable.

But it was too late. Already he trespassed with his fingers, awakening her with a tender touch.

Squeezing her eyes shut and biting her lip, she moved against his hand, writhing in a sensual dance that was both familiar and unknown to her.

But as engaged as she was in her own rising sensations, she felt him journeying beside her. His labored breathing, blowing across her ear, summoned her to new heights of passion.

He kissed her, and she answered with a deeper exploration, longing to taste every recess of his mouth.

And then a strange thing happened. The arrow of her lust mysteriously changed course. It had been racing with ever increasing haste, heading for the bull's-eye at the speed of lightning. Then, as wave after wave of sensation surged through her body, the arrow arced up at a steeper angle until she wasn't sure where it was headed.

Just when she felt it had veered completely off course, the quarrel halted at the top of its arc. Her body went rigid, frozen in time. For a wondrous, terrible, divine instant, desire hovered at the breathless point of no return.

Then, plunging faster than a bolt from a bow, she shot earthward with deadly speed. As she caught her breath in awe, shaken by shuddering flutters of release, he drove into her.

She gasped, startled more than wounded by the sudden sting of his invasion and his thick presence within her.

He gasped as well and went instantly still.

His brows collided as he stared down at her.

She knew a moment of dread. Had she done something displeasing? Would he withdraw now? Were her plans going to go awry?

"What is it?" she whispered, afraid of the answer. When he didn't reply, she muttered, "You don't want this? You don't want me?"

"Nay, 'tisn't that," he was quick to answer.

"You're certain?" Despite his assurances, she felt her throat thicken.

"Bloody hell, Jenefer," he blurted, "I want ye more than I've ever wanted a woman. 'Tis only..."

She braced herself for the worst.

"Did I hurt ye?" he asked, his brows gathered in concern.

"What?"

"I didn't mean to hurt ye."

She blinked. Surely he wasn't that ignorant. Even *she* knew losing one's virginity came with a bit of pain.

But it wasn't as bad as thwacking your forearm using a bow without a bracer. And he looked sincerely full of remorse. So she told him, "It doesn't hurt. Not really."

He looked deeply into her eyes, as if to measure the truth of her words. "I didn't know ye were a maiden."

That made her scowl. "Wait. You thought I *wasn't* a maiden?"

CHAPTER 38

Morgan opened his mouth, closed it, opened it again, and closed it. There was no way he could answer without insulting her.

He'd made up his mind that Jenefer couldn't be a maiden. No maiden, he'd reasoned, could be so fearless and assertive. She'd been flirtatious and demanding, as expert in her seductive manipulations as a harlot.

To realize with such immediate clarity that he was wrong—by stealing her maidenhood—was mortifying.

Courtesy had made him cater to her desires first. It was always his way. But then he'd claimed her with all the grace of a barbarian, taking no special care to be gentle with her.

She should despise him.

But when he looked at her, it wasn't hate he saw. Aye, she was vexed at him for believing she wasn't a virgin. And he was sure she'd not been truthful about the pain. But a glaze of desire lingered in her eyes.

Still, he'd already guessed wrong once. He wouldn't do it again.

No matter how much he craved the lass.

No matter how beautiful and tempting and desirable she looked with her damp hair spilled across the coverlet and her glorious body naked beneath him.

No matter how he throbbed in the irresistible grip of her womb.

No matter how painful it would be to withdraw from her now.

"Tell me the truth," he breathed. "Do ye desire this?"

She didn't answer him at first, only gazing up at him with her smoky green eyes, as if she stared into his soul. After a moment, a soft sparkle glistened there, joined by the upward curve of one corner of her lip in a coy smile. "Oh aye."

Relief flooded his veins. But he still intended to be careful. "If ye like, we can…"

Before he could finish, she arched up against him with a smug look of triumph.

He gulped. "If 'tis less painful, I can lie…"

She angled her hips backward, easing him halfway out, and then thrust forward again, sheathing him completely.

The sensation left him speechless. It had been so long since he'd lain with a woman, it was almost like starting anew. And to couple with a lass so direct and unashamed was intoxicating.

He'd intended to let her sit astride him, to allow her to set the pace, to slow, to stop if she wished. But she never paused long enough in her amorous pursuits for him to make the offer.

Even from beneath him, she became mistress of her own passion. She retreated to draw back the bow of her arousal. And surged up to impale herself on the shaft of his desire.

Again and again, she fired with ever-increasing swiftness and precision, until his heart was pounding and he forgot how to breathe.

The roar that erupted as he shuddered on his arms and exploded into her was deep and loud and fulfilling.

It was also loud enough to wake the next town.

But by some miracle, as their gasps collided in the room, making the candlelight flicker wildly...as they covered each other with grateful kisses and collapsed in a tangle in the sheets...as they drifted off to deep, untroubled slumber...the bairn never stirred in his crib.

By the time Jenefer woke, the candles had guttered out. The fire was burning low. The bath water was no longer steaming. The light of the waning moon filtered in through the crack of the shutters. But there was still no sign of Cicilia or Bethac.

Miles slept in his cradle. She could hear his shallow breaths.

She bit her lip. As much as she was enjoying lying beside the Highlander—savoring the heat of him, feeling his hot breath on the back of her neck and his warm flesh against hers—she wondered why the maidservants hadn't returned.

Soon Cicilia would come to feed Miles.

More importantly, someone had to catch Jenefer in bed with Miles' father. After all, how else would she snare Morgan for her husband?

Her husband.

The words made her smile.

As heir to the du Lac title, she'd always expected her marriage would be one of political strategy. She'd be wedded to a wealthy but landless man. Or a landed man with whom an alliance needed to be forged.

Never had she considered she might arrange her own strategic match. Not in her wildest dreams did she imagine she'd actually be attracted to her husband.

But she was. Every inch of him.

From the soft brown waves of his silk-fine hair to his oversized feet, currently entangled with hers.

From his broad and powerful shoulders to his lean, thrusting hips.

From the twinkling humor in his eyes to the feather-light touch of his fingers upon her skin.

And the way he'd made love to her—with his hands, with his lips, with his body—made her long to join with him again.

But there was something else.

Something that went deeper than the mere joys of trysting.

Something warm. Touching. And treacherous.

It wasn't only attraction she felt.

For so long, she'd heard Highlanders were cruel beasts, crude and uncivilized. She'd believed the stories. That they filed their teeth to sharp points. Enslaved the children of their enemies. Hacked their servants to death in war games.

But she could see now the tales must be completely untrue.

Morgan Mor mac Giric had qualities she'd never expected to find in a savage Highlander. Qualities she'd treasure in a husband.

A strong sense of honor.

A rough-hewn nobility.

The admiration of his servants.

An even hand when it came to justice.

A sweet and caring tenderness.

A respect for her wants and needs.

Could it be she'd...fallen in love with him?

Surely that was impossible. She'd known him only a few days.

But even her own parents had started out as bitter enemies. Sometimes love took root in strange ground.

She coiled a lock of his hair around her finger. Then she frowned, letting it unravel and withdrawing her hand.

What did it matter whether she did or didn't care for the Highlander?

Love had no place in marriage. Not when you were destined to be a laird. Besides, emotions could be as fickle as the moon.

She'd made a plan. She meant to stick to it.

She'd managed to seduce him into swiving her.

Now she had to coerce him into marrying her.

And then she'd force him to bestow the stewardship of Creagor upon her.

Her gaze followed a moonbeam down to where it bathed sweet Miles in its gentle light, and she sighed.

If she was so certain of her plan, why then was she racked with guilt over the idea of manipulating Morgan, preying upon him at his weakest, while he was still mourning Lady Alicia, his dead wife?

As mad as it was, Jenefer couldn't get past the feeling she was stealing the husband of a much better woman than herself.

Morgan awoke briefly as Jenefer stole out of the nursery, just enough to miss her warmth and feel a hollow ache in his chest.

He'd been so sure he'd never love again. So certain the fracture in his heart was beyond repair.

Yet what he'd had before with Alicia paled in comparison to the way he felt now.

This was an entirely new emotion.

It wasn't only because Jenefer was engaged and interested in him. Expressive of her desires. Free with her passions.

It wasn't only because her appetite for swiving rivaled that of her appetite for food.

Not as impulsive and bloodthirsty as she pretended, Jenefer was honest and honorable. Generous and kind. And whether she was defending his reputation to his maid or stubbornly insisting on calling his son "Miles," her strength of character and outspoken ways were refreshing.

She was an uncommon lass, full of fire and wit. He found himself drawn to her, wishing to be consumed in her lusty flames. And he was chagrined to admit he might be falling in love with the fiery maid.

He could guess why she'd sneaked out of the nursery.

She didn't wish for Bethac or Cicilia to find their laird in a compromising position.

He grinned. The same lass who had once claimed ravishment at his hands was now protecting his honor.

Her concern was completely unnecessary. He intended to make things right. He'd never been more certain of a decision in his life.

As much as he'd resisted her temptation, he realized now that Jenefer held the key to his future.

He meant to marry her.

It was the natural solution. She could be a mother to his son. They could share the castle. And the two properties of Rivenloch and Creagor could become powerful border allies against invasion.

Content that the matter was settled, he drifted back to sleep, dreaming of sharing his bed, his clan, his fortune with the desirable Scots lass.

CHAPTER 39

Jenefer sighed as she stole past the snoring guard and into the laird's bedchamber. The decision was the most painful she'd ever made. But she knew she'd made the right choice.

In the end, her conscience had gotten the best of her.

Gazing at the sweet, sleeping babe in the moonlight and remembering Morgan's adoring face as he looked down at his son, her heart had cracked, and she'd realized she couldn't do it.

She couldn't trick the trusting Highlander into wedding her.

Morgan Mor mac Giric was decent.

He would have done the right thing.

He would have willingly accepted the consequences of his actions.

And he would have thrown away his entire future to pay for one night of reckless passion.

But she couldn't bear to think that his heart wasn't in it. That he'd only be agreeing to marry her out of duty. The knowledge that she'd tricked the laird into wedding her would haunt her for the rest of her life.

Nay, she decided, if she couldn't win his affections honestly, she'd rather win the keep in battle than betray him in bed. So she'd slipped out of Morgan's arms, dressed, and left the nursery before the maids could return.

"Where have you been?" Feiyan whispered when Jenefer climbed into bed beside her.

"In the nursery." She didn't intend to confide in Feiyan, not after the argument they'd had.

"Listen, Jen, I'm sorry for laughing before." Feiyan sounded truly contrite. "'Tis only that I've always seen you as a brilliant warrior, not a lover. The thought of my fierce cousin seducing a man...well..."

Jenefer couldn't help herself. She wanted to prove to Feiyan, once and for all, that she was deserving of a man's affections. "But I did."

Feiyan sat up on her elbows. "What?"

"I did seduce him."

"The Highlander?" Feiyan almost strangled on the words. "But how? What...?"

Feiyan's amazement was almost enough to lift Jenefer's spirits.

"Too sleepy." Jenefer yawned. "I'll tell you in the morn."

"The devil you will!" Feiyan replied, giving her shoulder a rousing shake. "I want the whole story. Now."

"There's nothing to tell. I just used my natural feminine wiles and..." She shrugged.

By Feiyan's long silence, Jenefer could tell her cousin didn't believe her.

"You actually swived him?"

"Aye."

"I mean, you...you spread your legs for him."

"Aye."

"And you let him put his cod—"

"I know what swiving is, Feiyan."

Feiyan let out a low whistle. Then she quietly cheered, "This is perfect! Now you'll make him wed you. And then you can lay claim to Creagor."

Jenefer sighed. It sounded so uncomplicated, the way she said it. That was how it had sounded to her as well. But that was before she'd fallen in love with Morgan. "Nay."

"Nay?" Feiyan tossed back the covers and shot to her feet beside the bed. "What do you mean, nay?"

"I can't do it."

"What? Why? Didn't you just surrender your maidenhood to him?"

"Aye."

"It doesn't grow back, you know."

"I'm aware."

"But I don't understand. Why would you…"

"I just…I won't do it."

After a pensive moment, Feiyan gasped. "Because he's a savage? Is that it?" Her manner abruptly changed to fierce protector. "Did he hurt you? I swear, Jen, if he so much as raised a hand to—"

"Nay. Nay. 'Twasn't like that, only…"

"Only what?"

Jenefer could see she wasn't going to get any sleep until she explained. "'Tis one thing to best a man in battle when both of you are fully armed and evenly matched. But to slay a man in his sleep…"

"Lucifer's ballocks!" Feiyan quickly lowered her voice to a harsh whisper. "Did you slay him, Jen?"

"What?" She blinked. "Nay."

"Then what are you talking about?"

"He's a good man, Feiy. Decent and kind and noble. He deserves better than to be forced to wed a maid against his will."

"Surely you jest," Feiyan scoffed. "After all, nobody was forcing him to swi-…" She reconsidered. "You didn't swive him at the point of a dagger, did you?"

"Nay." The word soured on Jenefer's lips. Was it so hard for Feiyan to imagine a man actually desiring her?

"If he's so decent," Feiyan decided, "then he should be glad to marry you."

"I don't want him on those terms."

"How can you say that? Wasn't that your plan all along? What about all those sketches you made earlier? All the changes to the castle? Now you don't want him to wed you?"

"Not by force, nay."

"Yet you're willing to take the *castle* by force."

"Aye." Jenefer didn't have the words to explain to her cousin how that was different. But it was.

Feiyan threw up her hands in exasperation and flopped back into bed.

It was still dark, but nearing dawn when Morgan heard a rapid knocking on the nursery door, bringing him instantly awake. Assuming it was Cicilia coming to feed the bairn, he rose on his elbows and called out, "Come."

But it was Bethac who stuck her head in with a candle. She looked as pale as linen. Her brow was creased with worry.

"Where is she?" she whispered.

"Who?"

"Jenefer."

His heart dropped. Had the lass gone missing? Now that he'd decided to bare his heart and tie his fortunes to a woman, had she fled?

Bethac didn't wait for an answer. "Perhaps she returned to your bedchamber?" she suggested.

His shoulders dropped in relief. Of course that was where she'd gone.

But how the devil did Bethac know the lass had been here with him? Sometimes it seemed like the old maid was a touch fey, the way she could winnow out the truth. And now that she'd hinted at his indiscretion, it seemed pointless to deny it.

"I suppose so, aye," he said.

She nodded, then waved Cicilia into the nursery and shut the door behind them. The young maid rushed to the hearth to wake the bairn for his feeding.

Bethac set a bundle of Morgan's clothes atop the bed. Her expression was impossible to read. She looked simultaneously fretful and sorrowful, aghast and confused.

"What's amiss, Bethac?"

"Ye're needed below," she said urgently. "Please, m'laird, dress and come quickly."

He lowered his brows. Bethac never made idle demands.

"Is it Rivenloch?" he guessed. Perhaps her uncle's army had come to claim Jenefer after all.

"Nay."

"Colban?"

Morgan would never forgive himself if something dire had happened to his right hand man.

"Nay. Only...hurry."

With that vague directive, Bethac scurried out the door.

Morgan wasted no time. While Cicilia discreetly fed the bairn in one corner of the nursery, he threw on his clothes and hurtled down the stairs.

The clan was crowded into the great hall, most only half-dressed. A few guards held aloft flaming brands, illuminating something in their midst.

"There he is!" someone called out.

All heads swiveled to him. Their faces were full of wonder and nearly as pale as Bethac's had been. They quickly separated to make a path for him.

By the light of the brands, Morgan could see Bethac crouched beside what appeared to be a cloaked body. Only when he ventured forward did he see the blood staining the wool.

He prayed it wasn't the Rivenloch lass Colban had been tracking.

"'Tis a miracle, m'laird," a woman gushed as he passed.

"God's hand," someone agreed.

"The stars must be smilin' on ye," a young lass said.

None of their comments registered. As he drew nearer to the cloaked form, Morgan felt chilling recognition shiver along his spine.

He knew this body.

Bethac's baleful glance toward him confirmed it.

But his mind couldn't fully comprehend what he saw. Until a soft moan came from the ground.

He froze in his tracks.

'Twasn't possible.

He'd shoveled dirt over her grave himself.

And yet he'd wager his entire fortune that was Alicia.

CHAPTER 40

Morgan couldn't speak.

He couldn't breathe.

Alarm sucked the spit from him, leaving his mouth as dry and dusty as...as an empty grave.

The absurd thought almost made him laugh.

But laughing would have proved him mad. And he didn't dare lose his grasp on the few wits he had left.

She groaned again.

He swayed, dizzy from shock. It *was* her.

Half grateful, half fearful, he crept forward, cautious lest his hopes be dashed. After all, she was obviously in pain, and all that blood...

The hall had fallen so silent by the time he reached her that he could have heard a spider reeling down to the flagstones.

"Alicia?" he managed to croak out.

At the sound of his voice, her pale arm flailed out, and she whispered, "Morgan? Is it you?"

The familiar voice, her subtle Catalonian accent, made him fall to his knees beside her.

"'Tis me, my love," he whispered back. "But what trickery is this? How can this be? Are ye...?"

He meant to ask if she was hurt. But the sight of her face was answer enough. She looked as if she'd dug herself out of her own grave. Perhaps she had. Perhaps she hadn't been dead when...

The thought was too terrible to consider.

"I'm...alive," she said, clutching at his sleeve and trying to smile.

Her black braid was matted. Her lip was crusted with blood. One eye was swollen shut. And there was an ugly lump on her brow.

"What...? How...?"

Bethac intervened. "There will be time to talk later, m'laird. The physician should be summoned. Her hurts need to be seen to."

"Nay," Alicia gasped out. "First, I need to tell you what happened. You deserve to know."

It sickened him to see her like this—scraped, scabbed, her face bloated with her injuries. But she was alive. *Alive.* He couldn't fathom how that could possibly be.

He bent down to her. The clan kept a respectful distance, their voices hushed. Every ear strained to hear the explanation of how Alicia had come back from the dead.

"I was taken," she softly explained, "from childbed."

"But the midwife said ye...ye died."

She shook her head. "She deceived you."

Morgan creased his brow. The midwife's forlorn expression, delivering the sad news of Alicia's death, flashed through his memory. Had she only been feigning sorrow?

"But I buried..."

"An empty box," she told him.

Was it possible? Of *course* it was possible. The proof lay before him on the flagstones.

"Godit was a spy," she said. "She was working...for the English."

The word "English" started a soft rumble of disapproval among the clansfolk. Morgan was half English himself, but he had no love for the land his own mother had fled.

"An English lord...desired me," she continued, wincing and pressing the back of her hand to her bloodied lip.

Morgan clenched his jaw tightly enough to crack walnuts. If some foreign swine had not only beaten Alicia, but *bedded* her...

"Godit was working for him," she rasped out. "After our infant was born, she helped him to abduct me."

A dozen curses perched on Morgan's lips. *Him.* Who? Who had stolen her? What English brute had put filthy hands on his wife?

But he kept his fury in check. He didn't wish to upset Alicia any more than she already was.

Still it was guilt, not anger, that pressed like a heavy yoke on his shoulders. How could he have let his guard down? How could such a thing have happened on his watch? Right under his nose?

He silently swore he'd see the Englishman and that betraying shrew of a midwife dead before another sunset.

Alicia coughed—a pitiful, hacking cough that shook her frail ribs and made her grimace in pain.

Morgan's eyes watered in sympathy and rage and frustration. He took her wee hand between his, hoping to lend her his strength.

When the coughing ceased, she peered up at him with her one undamaged eye. Her brows rose in pained askance.

"Oh, *amor meu,* will you ever forgive me?"

His heart splintered at her words.

"Forgive ye? For what?"

She glanced at the faces gathered round and whispered so softly, he could scarcely hear her.

"For not finding my way to you sooner. For trusting Godit. For leaving you and the infant."

A lump clogged Morgan's throat. Alicia had always been so meek, humble, helpless. That she would somehow imagine he'd blame her for succumbing to abduction—especially when she was at her most vulnerable, having just given birth—tore at his heart. What kind of cur did she think he was?

He reached up to stroke her tangled hair. For one awful moment, he recalled honey-colored tresses, softer and silkier than Alicia's black locks. And then he put the disloyal thought aside.

He had to put that other lass out of his mind now. Forever.

"Oh darlin'," he murmured, "I could ne'er blame ye. How could ye even think that?"

Grateful tears squeezed from her black eyes.

Always careful with sensitive Alicia, he guarded his emotions and forced a smile of gentle reassurance to his lips.

"I'll go fetch the physician," Bethac mumbled, adding pointedly, "Shall I ready your bedchamber, m'laird?"

"Oh." He blinked, startled. He'd forgotten his bedchamber was already occupied. "Aye. Can ye take care o' things there?"

"I'll do my best, m'laird." She gave him a nod and hurried off.

He had no idea where Bethac would put his two guests. Certainly it wouldn't be as secure—or as comfortable—as where they were now. But he trusted Bethac. And he believed the lasses would keep their word not to flee.

He then addressed the clan. "The rest o' ye, return to your beds. Your mistress is weary. And there's naught more ye can do here."

Morgan needed his men well-rested. He wouldn't press poor Alicia for a name tonight. But on the morrow, he intended to hunt down the English bastard who'd abducted his wife. He'd cut out the man's black heart and bring his head home on a spike.

Jenefer bolted awake as Bethac burst into the bedchamber.

"Wake up!" Bethac hissed. Her arms were full of bedsheets. "Make haste!"

"What is it?" Jenefer gasped. "Is it Rivenloch? Has my uncle come?"

For the first time, she feared her kin might attack first and negotiate later. Two days ago, she would have been fine with that. But now she wanted as few casualties as possible.

Sleeping with Morgan had changed her. Changed the way she felt about him. She saw now he wasn't a usurper to be ousted. He could be a friend and an ally.

Maybe even, she dared to hope, a husband.

But only by his own choice. She wouldn't have it any other way. If she couldn't earn him by virtue of her qualities as a wife, she didn't want him at all.

Bethac didn't answer. She charged into the room with her candle flickering wildly. She dumped the bedsheets on the end of the bed and yanked the sheepskins off the cousins.

"Come! Now!"

Feiyan, groggy and disoriented, groaned as she was abruptly uncovered. "What the...?"

But Bethac's agitation troubled Jenefer. She shot to her feet. "What's happened?"

"No time," Bethac muttered. "Gather your things and come with me to the nursery."

The nursery? Jenefer's heart dropped. "Miles." Had something happened to the babe?

Her fear must have shown in her face, for Bethac hastened to assure her, "He's fine. Just hurry."

Jenefer swept up her boots and snagged her cloak from the hook.

The guard was gone when they shuffled down the hall to the nursery. They entered quietly so as not to wake the babe.

Cicilia was asleep on the floor beside Miles' cradle.

The bath was still there. The water had grown cold. The melted remains of the candles surrounded the tub. But the memory of warmth and light was fresh in Jenefer's mind.

The sight of the rumpled bedsheets heated her blood. The only thing missing was the irresistible Highlander. And she didn't dare ask Bethac where he'd gone, lest she reveal their indiscretion.

"Ye'll be safe here," Bethac whispered.

Jenefer frowned. "Safe? From what?"

For an instant, Bethac looked as if she might confide in her. Then she shook her head. "'Tisn't my place to say."

Jenefer grabbed the old maid by her sleeve. "If there's danger, my cousin and I can be of use."

Feiyan nodded in agreement.

But Bethac only gave her a sad, sweet smile. "'Tisn't the kind o' danger that can be battled with a blade."

With those cryptic words, she hurried from the room, leaving Jenefer and Feiyan to exchange baffled glances.

"Do you think Hallie has returned?" Jenefer wondered.

Feiyan shook her head. "There would be no reason to separate the three of us."

"Maybe he has a new batch of captives and nowhere else to imprison them."

Feiyan smirked. "The laird is probably just tired of sleeping on straw while we take his downy bed." Then she eyed the pallet. "At least this one looks reasonably comfortable." She sat down to test the mattress and almost immediately popped back up. "Oh! Is that the spot where you...?"

Jenefer was glad her cousin couldn't see her blush. "Aye."

Feiyan wrinkled her nose and crept into the opposite side of the bed. "God knows how I'll sleep, knowing that."

She was snoring within moments.

Jenefer, however, couldn't quiet her thoughts. What kind of danger couldn't be battled with a blade? And why had Bethac moved them out of the bedchamber in such haste?

She winnowed down the possibilities until only one remained. Maybe the king's messengers had finally arrived, and the chamber was needed to house them.

Jenefer was mulling over this probability and what it might signify when she heard activity on the other side of the wall. There were muffled voices and the sound of the door opening and closing.

She stole to the window and cracked open the shutters. If she leaned out over the sill, she could hear better—not enough to make out words, but enough to tell who was speaking.

She recognized the lilt of Bethac's voice. There was a gruff male grumble she didn't recognize. Then she heard a voice she knew all too well.

Morgan.

The deep, smooth timber warmed her against her will. The familiar cadence penetrated her bones, turning them to custard. Melting her into a pathetic puddle of desire.

Until she heard a woman answer him.

Her voice was light and sweet. Soft and vulnerable. Not menacing in the least.

Yet Jenefer suddenly felt more threatened than if she'd heard a boar letting loose with a hellish roar.

She strained to hear.

A sound of disgust came from behind her. "Jen, close the shutters," Feiyan hissed from the bed. "You'll freeze everyone."

Jenefer ignored her. Feiyan let out a loud sigh, then flounced over in the bed, pilfering all the furs.

Jenefer resumed listening. She heard Bethac leave. Then she heard the gruff-voiced man bid Morgan farewell. Now there were only Morgan and the woman. Alone.

Every tender syllable that dropped from his lips was like the sharp cut of a dagger. Whoever the woman was, Morgan clearly cared for her.

And by the faint melody of the woman's responses, that affection was returned.

Jenefer felt sick with betrayal.

How could Morgan have forsaken her? And so quickly?

Mere hours had passed since they'd trysted.

She thought their joining had *meant* something.

Morgan may not have lost his virginity. But he'd given her something of himself. His ecstasy. His passion. His soul.

And she'd given him all of her.

She thought he was just as affected by the experience as she was.

She thought they'd shared something unique and special and intimate.

Apparently, she was wrong.

It meant nothing to him.

She meant nothing to him.

CHAPTER 41

In her heart of hearts, Jenefer knew she had no right to feel like a victim. After all, it was *she* who had seduced *Morgan*. She glanced at the bed, still rumpled from what they'd done. None of what had happened there had been his idea.

But knowing he'd practically leaped into another woman's arms while his seed was still warm inside her...

Her eyes welled. Her throat ached.

But she refused to shed a single tear for the rutting stag of a man.

Instead, she swallowed down her hurt and banged a fist on the stone ledge, turning her sorrow to ire.

It was just as she'd always heard, she decided. Highlanders were faithless beasts who sowed their seed like wild thistles. Unfeeling, uncaring brutes who took what they wanted and left a trail of destruction behind.

How could she have forgotten that?

How could she have believed otherwise?

She'd been a lovesick fool.

Unwilling to subject herself to any more of the soft, crooning exchanges taking place in his bedchamber, Jenefer closed the shutters and jabbed at the fire.

There was no point in trying to sleep. She'd only toss and turn and annoy her cousin.

Instead, she paced the nursery in an angry swirl of skirts. She clenched and unclenched her fists. She muttered curses under her breath. She scowled at the wall between the chambers with enough hatred to scorch the plaster.

On one pass, she ventured too near the tub. Striding forward, she caught her bare toe on the hard oak. Sharp pain shot up her foot, wringing a gasp from her.

"Bloody shite!" she hissed, clutching her throbbing toe and hopping on her good foot.

Her oath woke Miles. Which made her utter another.

Cicilia roused to Miles' whimpers. She sleepily patted him, hoping it was only a bad dream.

But when the young nurse suddenly spied Jenefer in the room, she gave a squeak of surprise, bringing Miles fully awake.

After that, even Cicilia's cooing and patting couldn't calm him. His whimpers rose to a high-pitched wail. Feiyan, half-buried in sheepskins, dug her way out to complain.

"Odin's eye, Jen, can't you quiet him?"

She bit her lip. She *could* quiet him. And it was becoming second nature to her to console the crying lad.

But if she didn't, if she let him cry, Morgan wouldn't be able to sleep. Neither would his soft-voiced concubine. The philandering Highlander would be forced to come to the nursery to look after his son. And she'd get the chance to show him just what fury a woman scorned could deliver.

Ignoring Miles wasn't easy. His sobs grew more plaintive and miserable by the moment. Jenefer's heart ached for him. Cicilia looked over at her with pleading eyes. And if Feiyan's glares had been daggers, Jenefer would be dead by now.

Finally, just before Jenefer was about to yield to her maternal instincts and comfort the crying babe, the door swung open under Morgan's hand.

She faced the Highlander with her chin held high and her arms crossed in challenge. Her heart knifed sideways at the sight of him, adorably disheveled from sleep, and her resolve almost crumbled.

But she steeled herself against the heartbreak. She refused to give him the satisfaction of seeing her suffer. By God, she would confront him with his duplicity.

He looked weary, drained, and somewhat startled to see her. "Ye're here."

"Aye, I'm here," she snapped. "Why? Were you hoping Bethac tossed me out on my arse?"

"Nay, but..." He glanced at Miles, screaming in Cicilia's arms.

"Ah, that's right," she said bitterly. "You couldn't throw me out. Then you'd have no one to keep the babe quiet."

"Listen, Jenefer..."

She stiffened, hating how the sound of her name on his lips made her heart catch.

"There's somethin' I need to tell ye," he said. "If ye can quiet the bairn..."

Hurt and fuming, she bit out, "If you mean to tell me our tryst meant nothing, don't waste your breath."

Shocked at her candor in front of Cicilia and Feiyan, he judiciously closed the door. "Naught could be further—"

"'Tis clear you scarcely waited for the linens to cool ere you sought out another lass's bed."

Cicilia gasped and covered Miles' ears.

"What?" Feiyan exploded, outraged on Jenefer's behalf.

Morgan gave her a sullen look. His fatigue was gradually diminishing, being replaced by growing ire. "'Tisn't what it seems."

She should have known he would make excuses. "Oh, tisn't?" She raised her voice to a shout. "I wonder how the lady lying in yonder bedchamber feels about that."

"What lady?" Feiyan demanded.

217

Morgan grimaced, raising his hands to bid them be quiet. "I can explain."

"Can you?" Jenefer doubted that.

Feiyan skewered him with a glare. "This I'd like to hear."

"No one can hear anythin' with..." Morgan gestured in frustration toward the bairn, who was now screaming at the top of his lungs.

Unable to endure any more of Miles' forlorn crying, Jenefer lifted him from Cicilia's arms.

Jostling him against her bosom, she confided in the lad, loud enough to be heard over his wailing. "You see, Miles, what a fiend your laird is. Like a fickle bee, stealing nectar from one blossom and hastening on to the next."

Morgan's brows collided in aggravation. "'Tisn't like that at all."

"And then denying it," Jenefer added, raising her voice again so the woman in his bedchamber would be sure to hear, "even though his paramour is right next door."

"Will ye keep your voice down?" he pleaded between clenched teeth.

She took his request as a challenge. "Why? Are you afraid your doxy will hear the truth from me?"

"Damn it! Ye don't understand," he growled.

"Oh, I understand. Like all Highland heathens, you simply seize what you want."

"Not true," he argued.

She gave him a smoky glare and resumed addressing Miles. "But you'll be raised in the Lowlands, won't you, Miles? And Lowlanders are faithful."

"Now hold on," Morgan said, indignant.

She wasn't in the mood to hold on. "Lowlanders don't flit from bed to bed, stealing lasses' virtues and breaking lasses' hearts."

"Stealing?" He arched a brow.

She ignored his parsing of words, cooing, "And you, sweet Miles, you'd never use a lass as you see fit and cast her aside like offal, would you?"

"Och, for the love o'..." Morgan muttered.

The babe was beginning to settle down. And it seemed as if he were paying heed to her words.

"I know you can't help being born in the despicable Highlands, but maybe there's time to save you from your da's bad habits."

She knew she was prodding at a dangerous beast. Belittling Morgan's beloved Highlands was like yanking a tooth from a sleeping wolf.

Morgan straightened to his full, impressive height. Stabbing a finger down at her, he snarled, "Don't ye ever insult my home and the place o' Miles'..." He bit out an oath at his mistake. "Allison...Allison's birth. 'Tis a fine piece o' land belongin' to my clan for generations. And as far as my habits, I hope he..."

He broke off, blanching. For a long moment, he only stared at her.

Feiyan's mouth went round with surprise.

Miles silenced as well, sucking on his fist and gazing at Morgan.

Morgan spoke softly. "How...how did ye know the bairn was..."

"Yours?" She smirked. "'Tis plain to see."

"How long have ye known?"

"What does it matter?"

"Give him to me."

"He'll cry again," she warned.

"Give him to me." His eyes had lost their sheen. He was deadly serious.

"Wait." She lowered her brows. "You don't think I would hurt him?"

"Now," he commanded.

His mistrust was almost as hurtful as his infidelity.

"Fine."

She held out the babe to him. As predicted, Miles began to wail as soon as Morgan took him. Racked by new pain, she wanted to wound Morgan.

She sneered, "I'm sure your mistress will be delighted to share your bed with a squalling infant."

Morgan leveled his gaze at her. "She's not my mistress." He took a deep breath and let it out on a sigh. "She's Allison's mother. My wife."

CHAPTER 42

As Alicia snuggled in welcome solitude beneath the coverlet, her self-satisfied smile turned into an impatient growl.

What the devil was all that noise? What was going on next door?

After all she'd been through, she thought she deserved to sleep in peace.

No one could ever fathom what a rare and special gift for deception she had. Nor what a grueling, demanding business it was.

She'd had to employ that gift a lot lately.

Feigning her love for Morgan.

Faking her death.

Fabricating her abduction.

Inventing her harrowing escape.

And those were only the lies she'd told her husband.

It grieved her to admit that things had not gone as well as she'd liked.

But now that she'd successfully insinuated herself back into her husband's household, her fatiguing work to cover her tracks and her arduous midnight journey had caught up with her.

And the commotion on the other side of the wall was preventing her from getting a good night's rest.

Still, it was hard not to smile in self-congratulations after her brilliant victory. She'd made naïve Morgan believe her story. And she'd even had time to take sweet revenge on those who'd wronged her.

She closed her eyes, reliving the tumultuous events of the last several weeks.

Sick to death of the miserable and uncivilized Highlands and weary of carrying Morgan's heir in her belly, Alicia had been desperate to find an escape. Six months ago, she thought she'd finally found one.

The English knight, Sir Edward, with whom she'd had a brief affair in Catalonia, had recently become a lord in his own right. He'd acquired a castle at Firthgate, along the border with Scotland. A few fawning letters from her reignited his affections, guaranteeing that—should she find her way back to him—a home, a title, and all the comforts of civilization would be hers. Or so he'd promised.

His offer was too tempting to refuse. All Alicia had to do was rid herself of a husband and an infant. For that, she'd enlisted her midwife. Godit had arranged her childbed ruse, declaring Alicia dead and hiding her away. Once Alicia was hale enough to travel, they planned to abandon the wretched Highlands, journeying to Edward's holding. No one at Firthgate would ever know Alicia was once wed, and faithful Godit would guard her secret. Or so she'd vowed.

Alicia had expected Edward and Godit to keep their promises.

Their disloyalty in the form of a love affair had been an enormous disappointment.

But two days ago, fate had finally smiled on Alicia. She'd learned her estranged husband Morgan had left his dreary Highland home to inherit the holding at much more temperate Creagor. As luck would have it, Creagor was not far away, just on the opposite side of the border. Suddenly she found the prospect of life with him once again appealing.

Godit and Edward's betrayal had made her decision easy.

How Alicia had relished watching the life slowly drain out of the midwife's bulging eyes, holding Godit close so the young woman couldn't free herself from the dagger Alicia had shoved beneath her ribs.

Yet it was a shame things had had to end that way. Godit had been a skilled midwife. She'd delivered scores of babes in her short lifetime, including Alicia's own. Godit had been willing to lie for Alicia, telling Morgan she'd died in childbirth. And she'd shown Alicia how to halt the flow of milk that lingered in her breasts after she'd delivered.

The useless milk had still seeped from her for days, not unlike the blood that seeped from Godit's wound. The dark liquid had bathed Alicia's fingers where she gripped the hilt until Godit finally stopped scrabbling at the blade.

"You brought this upon yourself, you know," she'd whispered to the dying woman. "If only you'd kept your knees together and stayed away from Edward, none of this would have happened."

Godit had opened and closed her mouth like a hooked trout until her eyes began to glaze over. She'd tried, and failed, to suck in a few last, desperate breaths.

"But you couldn't do it, could you?" Alicia had told her, twisting the knife in Godit's bare abdomen with cruel vengeance and forcing a sickly gurgle from the woman's throat. "You couldn't keep your hands off of what was mine. And now you've spoiled everything."

But Godit's eyelids had already fluttered shut. The stupid wench was beyond hearing. Before she went completely limp, Alicia pushed her naked body back onto the garderobe seat.

When Alicia gazed down at the dagger protruding from the midwife's chest, she realized it was the same one Godit had used to cut the cord when Morgan's infant was born.

That had seemed like an age ago. It had been just over three months. That things could go so wrong in so short a time was maddening.

Yet, like a cat, Alicia always landed on her feet.

Receiving news about Morgan Mor mac Giric had shifted the winds of fate for her.

She'd disposed of the philandering midwife. Half of her problem had been solved. Once she took care of the rest of her unfinished business, she'd emerge untouched by the violence she'd wrought.

Taking a cleansing breath, she'd ripped the dagger out of the woman's body, oozing blood onto Alicia's saffron skirts. But that was fine. Soon she'd be able to afford a whole chest full of new gowns.

Besides, she knew her fickle Edward would never notice the stain. His thoughts always centered solely on what was between his legs, which had finally proved to be his downfall. Once Alicia had grabbed him by the ballocks, he was oblivious to all else.

Half an hour later, in the bedchamber they'd shared, Alicia was staring down at the second part of her gruesome handiwork, amazed by how well it had gone.

It was still hard to believe how much she'd sacrificed to be with Edward. A large inheritance. A handsome husband. The protection of the mightiest army in the Highlands. And now he'd forced her to murder him.

The English lord had never truly appreciated her. Not the way he should have.

Now things were back under her control. She'd left Edward dead on their bed, gawking blindly at the ceiling, with Godit's dagger protruding from his belly.

She didn't feel an ounce of remorse. The betraying bastard deserved every inch of the steel she'd thrust into him.

Of course, she'd never truly loved Edward in the first place. She was incapable of feeling love. The emotion had eluded her all her life.

But she'd made plans with him.

And she hated to have her plans ruined.

The deception after that wasn't difficult. Her bloody clothing lent credence to her story. And her injuries…

She winced now as she touched the stinging, bloody scratches Godit had raked down her cheek. Her bruised breasts and thighs ached from the hard pinches Alicia had administered herself. A convincing lump swelled where she'd intentionally bashed her brow against the bedpost.

She'd torn her skirt, drenched it in Edward's blood, and dragged it across the floor to the window, leaving the scrap on the sill.

Those who discovered the grisly trail would assume she'd been a victim. They'd believe that whoever had killed Edward and Godit must have kidnapped Alicia.

In all honesty, she didn't expect Edward's people to expend much effort to find her. After all, they'd known her only a few months. She'd been his lover, not yet his wife. Surely the carrion crows in his household would be too busy deciding who was to inherit Firthgate to concern themselves with a missing mistress.

The trek to Creagor had been several miles long. But the journey had been worthwhile. She'd managed to throw herself upon Morgan's mercy and into his grateful arms.

Now, however, she was exhausted from murder, sore from her injuries, and drained from having to play the meek, remorseful wife. All she wanted to do was lick her wounds and fall into a deep sleep.

The altercation in the next room was robbing her of that well-deserved rest.

The infant was screaming relentlessly. That was bad enough. But now she could hear the muffled voice of Morgan upbraiding the servants. Worse, one impertinent maid who didn't know her place was squawking back at him.

If Morgan were wise, he'd knock the maid across the room. Maintaining one's rank in the world required ruling with a fist of steel.

But beneath all that warrior muscle and bone, Morgan was cursed with a soft heart. It was why she'd always been able to manipulate him so easily.

That bloody infant, however, was going to be difficult.

Infants were selfish and needy. She despised the mewling creatures with their screaming demands and their sopping trews. If she had her way, she wouldn't lay eyes on her offspring until they were full-grown, useful, and capable of complete sentences.

A particularly piercing cry seeped through the wall, and Alicia cringed. Her head ached from her self-inflicted crack, and that cry was like a spike driven into her brain.

At least she didn't have to feed the shrieking beast. He'd probably love to suck the life from her and leave her with withered teats. Thankfully, she'd gone dry and had no milk to give.

Finally, the cries began to subside, though there was still much shouting and carrying on.

If only she weren't so weary... If only Morgan weren't there as a witness...

Alicia sighed. She would have enjoyed marching to the nursery, ripping that insolent maid's tongue out, and feeding it to the hounds.

But she supposed she had to stifle her temper while she was with Morgan.

At last the cacophony diminished, and Alicia was able to drift into a semblance of sleep. She wouldn't truly rest easy, however, until Morgan was by her side.

She'd been careful not to leave any evidence of her crime behind. But there was always the danger of a stray witness. Until she was in the clear, she'd have to be cautious.

With loyal Morgan Mor mac Giric beside her, she'd be safe. The gullible, able-bodied Highlander would march into the fires of Hell to protect her.

She only hoped that when he came to bed, he wouldn't bring that miserable infant back with him. On the morrow, she'd have to look in on the child for appearance's sake. But tonight she wasn't up to the farce of feigning affection for her squalling spawn.

CHAPTER 43

Morgan's revelation—that his wife was in his bed—made Feiyan and Cicilia gasp in unison. Jenefer, stunned, was struck silent. Even Miles quieted in his father's arms.

His wife? Lady Alicia? How could that possibly be? Wasn't Miles' mother dead?

Morgan explained as Jenefer listened with a tightly clenched jaw. Her knuckles were white where she clutched her skirts. She hoped no one could tell that beneath her stoic demeanor, her heart was breaking.

It seemed she was destiny's foe. By some cruel miracle, the one person in the world who could prevent Morgan from falling in love with Jenefer and making her his bride had managed to come back to life.

"Lady Alicia was..." Morgan hesitated, grinding his teeth in vengeful anger. "Imprisoned and viciously mistreated at the lord's hands."

Jenefer uttered not a word, for fear her voice would betray her selfish heartache.

It *was* selfish. She knew that. After all, the Highlander's true love, the mother of his son, had returned to him. She should be glad for Morgan.

And the poor woman in the room next door had suffered great harm. Torn from her infant and her husband. Forced into an Englishman's bed. Abused by her abductor.

But it was too difficult for Jenefer to get past her own misfortune at this fortunate turn of events. And it was pure torment to see Morgan's grief-haunted eyes shining with hope.

She swallowed the bitter taste of fate and said nothing.

"Lady Alicia is in no shape to care for the bairn," he continued. "I'm askin' ye to watch o'er him for the night. But I'll need your vow that ye won't harm the lad."

Jenefer's hurt was so profound that it curdled into anger.

"Bloody hell!" she spat. "How could you suggest such a thing? The Warrior Daughters of Rivenloch don't prey on helpless babes."

"Not e'en the bairns o' their enemies?" he asked with an arched brow.

Miles' chin quivered, and he began to whimper again. In disgust, Jenefer practically snatched him out of Morgan's hands.

"I've known Miles was your son for days now, Highlander," she snarled. "And I haven't harmed so much as a hair on his wee head."

He narrowed his eyes, as if gauging whether he should trust her, and finally gave her a stiff nod. He made his way to the door and, just before he closed it behind him, bit out a warning.

"I won't hesitate to do you harm if you hurt my son."

Incensed, she retrieved a wet rag from the tub and threw it at him. It smacked uselessly against the closing door.

The next morn, Jenefer rose with the sun and was pacing the floor by the time Cicilia gave Miles his first feeding of the day. She'd slept very little, troubled all night by the story of Lady Alicia.

Now, by the light of day, with her emotions locked away inside an armored heart, Jenefer began to question the details of the tale.

The story bothered her. Something about it wasn't quite right. It seemed too full of coincidence, too far-fetched and implausible. For many reasons. None of which Morgan would want to hear.

Feiyan, however, might be able to help her untangle the threads.

Once Cicilia was finished and took Miles downstairs to break her own fast, Jenefer roused her cousin by pulling off her coverlet.

Feiyan protested with a weary whine.

"Get up, Feiy," she said. "I need to talk to you."

Feiyan groaned.

"'Tis about Lady Alicia."

Feiyan growled and turned her back on Jenefer.

"Feiy!"

"What!"

"I need your help."

"Can't it wait?"

"Nay. Come on. If you get up, I'll let you teach me that dance you do every morn."

"'Tisn't a dance," Feiyan said in disgust.

"Isn't it? Hmm. See? You're already teaching me." Despite her grumbling, Jenefer knew Feiyan couldn't resist an eager student.

"Fine," she groaned.

They pushed the furnishings out of the way. Then, while Jenefer stood behind her, mirroring her movements, she reviewed the elements of Alicia's story.

"First," she wondered, "why would an English lord travel all the way to the Highlands to steal a lass? How would he even know about her?"

"Maybe he knew her from before, from when she lived in Catalonia." Feiyan peered over her shoulder. "Lift your arm higher."

Jenefer lifted her arm. "Maybe. But she'd been living in the Highlands long enough to wed and birth a child."

"Probably a year."

"At least a year. So an English lord is so infatuated with a maid he met in Catalonia that he waits for her while she marries another man and delivers that man's child. And then he kidnaps her on the very day she gives birth. 'Tis hard to believe."

"Nay, bend *both* knees. *Very* hard to believe."

Jenefer bent both knees. "Right?"

"Unless... Maybe he's been stalking her for years. Maybe she's so breathtakingly beautiful that no man can resist her."

That Jenefer didn't need to hear. She stiffened, losing her balance and stumbling sideways.

"Concentrate," Feiyan said.

Jenefer bit back a retort. She didn't want to think about how beautiful Morgan's wife might be.

"That English lord couldn't care for her all that much," she reasoned, "forcing her to travel so soon after childbirth."

"True."

Feiyan swept her right arm before her in a graceful arc. Jenefer mimicked her.

"And why would he not take the babe as well? 'Twould have made her much easier to manage."

"What's curious to me," Feiyan said, slowly lifting her knee, "is how she knew where to come."

Jenefer copied the movement. "What do you mean?"

"She claims to have escaped her captor, aye?"

"Aye."

Feiyan brought her left elbow in against her side, making a fist. So did Jenefer.

"How did she know to come to Creagor?"

Feiyan lunged forward on her right leg.

Jenefer froze.

"How *did* she know to come here?" she wondered. "Morgan only arrived a few days ago."

"Exactly." Feiyan turned with a smug smile that vanished when she saw Jenefer had stopped doing the exercises. "If she was abducted and hidden away from the outside world, as she claims, with no way to get messages in or out, how did she learn that Morgan had come to the Lowlands?"

"Right." Jenefer looked at her cousin with new respect. "But she knew. She knew he was here."

Feiyan nodded and swept her right arm up while drawing back her left. Jenefer sat on the edge of the bed to think.

"'Tis highly suspect," Feiyan agreed, making a half-turn and a lunge. "And yet, there's no disputing the fact the woman is Morgan's wife and Miles' mother." She drew back, pressing her hands together, palm to palm. "Which means your latest plan will have to be abandoned."

Feiyan had been mercifully vague about Jenefer's plan to beguile the Highlander. But she was right.

In the end, it didn't really matter how improbable Lady Alicia's story seemed. Morgan's wife was alive. And well. And here.

Jenefer's heart might be fractured. But she had to look after her own best interests. If she couldn't win Creagor by marrying the Highlander, she'd just have to go back to her plans of taking it by force.

If Rivenloch ever arrived to lend aid.

And if the king's messengers didn't bring bad news.

Jenefer was still mulling over the troubling details when Bethac returned Miles to the nursery. A kitchen lad followed with a tray of food, accompanied by two brawny men who emptied the bathwater into the chute of the garderobe and carried the tub out of the chamber. Bethac collected the candles that had been burned to stubs, and followed the men downstairs.

While Miles slept, Jenefer nibbled on the rim of an oatcake. But she was too distraught to eat much more.

Gazing down at the sweet child with the soft brows and pouting lips, her heart sank. A flood of melancholy washed over her. How would she go on without the wee babe?

She'd spent a pathetic amount of time over the past day, imagining her life as Morgan's wife and Miles' mother. She'd dreamed about the things they'd do together. Uniting their clans at the wedding. Drawing up plans for the castle modifications. Training warriors for tournaments. Teaching Miles how to read and write, to ride and fight. Making more babes until they had a dynasty of Scots champions.

Now she was paying for her foolish dreams.

Her throat ached from choking back an unexpected sob.

She couldn't bear the thought of never seeing the babe wave his tiny fists again.

Never hearing him gurgle out words of his own making.

Never feeling him fall asleep in her arms.

Curse the gods. She hadn't been this close to tears since the time she'd accidentally jammed an arrow point into the heel of her hand. What was wrong with her?

Miles started fussing. Soon he'd be weeping all the tears she could not. And that would do neither of them any good.

So she sniffed back her sorrow and picked him up, trying not to think about how accustomed she'd become to holding him, how perfectly he fit into the hollow of her shoulder.

Feiyan murmured, "You aren't still thinking of stealing the babe, are you?"

"Maybe," she lied.

"Shite, Jen," Feiyan bit out. "You can't do that, now that you know he's Morgan's heir. You'll be branded an outlaw. Hunted as a fugitive."

Jenefer knew all that. Miles had two capable parents now. She could no longer justify taking him. And her destiny was to be a laird of her own keep, not an exile.

Still, she couldn't bear to accept that she was going to lose this battle.

Feiyan crossed her arms. "You can't always have your way, Jen."

She scowled at her chiding cousin. "I know."

But was that all it was? Was she only upset because she was accustomed to getting her way?

All her life, she'd taken what she wanted.

As a tot, she'd stolen arrows out of her father's quiver.

As a child, she'd proclaimed herself the owner of a newborn colt in the stables.

As a young lass, she'd secretly competed in an archery tournament.

And now she'd set her sights on Creagor.

Was she just vexed to be thwarted?

Whatever drove her, in this instance, she had to yield. She had to sacrifice personal victory for the sake of the child. The young lad's fate was at stake. As much as it pained her, she had to wean herself away from Miles. Or Allison. Or whatever the hell his mother intended to call him. And the sooner, the better.

Feiyan said gently, "You'll have babes of your own one day, Jen. I know it. And you'll be the best mother ever."

Jenefer gave her a fleeting smile. It was a kind thing to say. But at the moment, though she'd developed a new respect for babes, she couldn't imagine letting a man near her again.

She'd given Morgan her honor. Her trust. Her virginity. Her heart. To think it had all been for naught...

Her eyes misted, and she bit back bitter sorrow.

She wouldn't think about it. Not now. For now, she would do the right thing.

Straightening her shoulders by strength of will and preparing for a deed that was far more challenging than any bout with a blade she'd undertaken, she perched the babe on her hip and headed for the door.

"Be a good lad now, Miles. 'Tis time for us to meet your rightful mother."

CHAPTER 44

Morgan rose on one elbow. He stared down at his sleeping wife beside him in their bed.

He still had trouble believing she was alive. Only the gentle rise and fall of the coverlet proved she'd eluded death.

His throat closed with pity as he tried to imagine the horrors she'd been through.

Thank God she'd survived.

Thank God she'd managed to escape.

By the light of day, he could see bruises mottling her skin in ugly shades of purple, green, and yellow. Bloody trenches carved by her abuser's fingernails marred her pale cheek. There was a grotesque, misshapen lump near her hairline. And blood had collected and dried beneath her nails, proof she'd had to defend herself.

But more powerful than Morgan's pity for Alicia was his thirst for vengeance upon her abuser. His blood began to simmer. Foul air filled his lungs. And he ground his ire between his teeth.

None of his anger, however, would gain him the justice he sought. Not until he learned the name of Alicia's abductor.

And for that, he had to tread carefully.

"Alicia," he breathed.

Her forehead creased.

"Alicia," he whispered, brushing a stray wisp of ebony hair from her pale brow.

She woke with a start, slapping his hand away. Then she blinked, confused.

"'Tis all right now," he murmured. "Ye're safe."

Her features relaxed when she looked up at him. "Morgan. Oh, Morgan, *amor meu.*"

"How are ye feelin'?" he asked.

She pulled the bedlinens up to her chin and lowered her eyes. "Safe, thanks to you."

"And I intend to keep ye safe," he promised. "There's just one thing I need to know."

"I'm so thirsty."

"Oh," he said. "O' course."

He threw off his covers, eliciting a gasp from her. He'd forgotten how his nudity shocked and bothered her. It was strange how that had slipped his mind.

He swiftly donned his trews. Then he poured a cup of water from the ewer Bethac had left.

Alicia struggled to sit up, wincing in pain. Morgan swept in to lend assistance with an arm around her back and carefully pressed the cup to her swollen lips.

She took a few sips and gave him a meek and grateful smile. He set the cup down on the bedside table.

"Can ye tell me now," he ventured softly, "who did this to ye?"

"I... I..." She closed her eyes and shuddered. "I don't want to talk about it."

"I know, lass, I know. But if I'm to keep ye safe, I need to know who I'm up against."

"He won't know where I've gone," she said, her black eyes wide and naïve. "Can we not just abide here in peace?"

"Not until he's dead and gone," Morgan replied, with more than a little menace in his voice.

She shivered as she clutched the coverlet to her bosom. "You don't mean to challenge him?"

"I cannot suffer the bastard to live, m'lady." He clenched his fists. "Not after what he's done to ye."

Tears filled her eyes. "Nay! Please do not tangle with him," she cried. "You don't know how treacherous he is." Her face was contorted with anxiety. "I can't bear the thought of losing you to that monster."

Bothered by the fact she assumed her abductor could best him, he replied, "Ye won't lose me."

"You don't know that," she said, "and if I lose you, what will become of me?" She ended in stifled weeping, with her fist pressed against her mouth.

"I'll be fine," he assured her. "I'm a good swordsman. And I know how to watch my back. I need only his name."

He sulked, mildly insulted that he had to defend his abilities to her. She'd been his wife for two years. She'd seen him take up arms against dozens of formidable warriors. Did she have no faith in his skills?

She answered with a thin wail and more weeping, burrowing her face in her hands.

He flinched. Damn his callousness. What kind of brute was he to make demands of a lass who was clearly still suffering the anguish of abuse?

He wrapped a consoling arm around her quaking shoulders. "I'm sorry, Alicia. I shouldn't have asked."

He supposed revenge would have to wait. But for each instant her tormenter breathed, Morgan's need for revenge wound tighter. Soon it would reach its limit. Then he wouldn't be able to stop himself. He'd insist she give him the villain's name. And blood would be spilled.

He was still fantasizing about the form his retribution would take when someone knocked on the door.

Alicia sighed in irritation.

"Who is it?" Morgan called out.

"Jenefer."

At the sound of her voice, his mind suddenly roiled with a tempest of images.

The beautiful lass in the throes of passion. Her golden tresses lashing his ribs. Her skin glowing. Her eyes shimmering like sparks.

But then he remembered their last conversation. Her eyes blazing in rage. Her mouth twisting in mockery. Her arms tense with fury. Her voice hoarse with hurt and anger.

Warring emotions bombarded him as well. Love and regret. Lust and shame. Temptation and forbiddance. Desire and duty.

Before he could work out how he felt about her and how he should respond, she let herself into the chamber.

In the flesh, Jenefer was even more compelling and disturbing than he'd remembered. He'd been racked with guilt for comparing the spirited, vibrant lass to his muted, lackluster wife. But seeing them together, he couldn't deny the contrast.

Jenefer's demeanor this morn, however, was formal. Stiff. Cool. Polite.

"I thought Lady Alicia might wish to see her son."

She ducked through the door with Miles in her arms. Morgan imagined it couldn't have been easy for her.

"Who is this?" Alicia's voice was terse, guarded. He supposed it was only natural that she would be defensive, considering what she'd endured.

But how should he answer her?

He couldn't very well say Jenefer was his lover.

Nor could he confess that he'd let a hostage care for their bairn.

To her credit and his relief, Jenefer had a quick answer. "I'm the babe's nurse, m'lady."

She swept forward, and Morgan closed the door behind her.

"No doubt you're eager to see your son," she said.

But as Jenefer carried him toward her, Alicia appeared to shrink into the mattress. Her eyes grew round, and her fingers tensed in the bedlinens.

"I... I... I don't think I have the strength to..." She sank onto the pillow, turning her back to them. "Perhaps later."

Jenefer exchanged a look of bafflement with Morgan.

He didn't understand Alicia's reaction either. It seemed like she would want to see their son. He'd hoped that holding the bairn might distract her from her tribulations and make her whole again.

But maybe the shock was too much. Maybe she needed time to adjust to being a mother. Maybe bonding with him would help.

"I've named him Allison," he told her. "After you."

"I'd like to rest now," Alicia murmured over her shoulder.

Morgan was crestfallen. He'd expected that Alicia's return from the dead would change everything. That she would be so grateful to see him, she would embrace him and their child with all the love she'd held close to her chest before.

He was wrong.

He'd forgotten how Alicia could withdraw like a snail into its shell. How, with a word, she could cut off all conversation and retreat into solitude. How she could leave him with his mouth hanging open and no one to hear his thoughts.

In the ensuing awkward pause in the room, the bairn naturally chose to begin whimpering.

Jenefer looked expectantly at Morgan.

He swallowed, unsure of what to do or say.

She raised her brows in silent communication.

He frowned.

She indicated Alicia with a sharp nod of her head. Then she lifted the bairn as if she intended to leave him beside her in the bed.

He shook his head.

She compressed her lips in frustration.

He mouthed the word, "Nay."

She narrowed her eyes with smoking fury.

Alicia groaned from the bed. "Please take him away."

Jenefer's jaw dropped.

"She's goin', m'lady," he whispered, catching Jenefer by the shoulder and wheeling her around toward the door.

He should have known she'd resist. Her brows collided in disapproval, and she wrenched out of his grip. Of course, her violent movements upset the bairn, who began to wail in earnest.

Alicia flounced in the bed, biting out, "What kind of nurse can't keep a babe quiet?"

"What kind of mother—"

Morgan clapped a hand over Jenefer's mouth just in time. "Go on, now, please. Lady Alicia needs her rest. There will be time later to—" He sucked a sharp breath between his teeth as she clamped down on the tender flesh of his palm.

Forced to release her, he was grateful at least that she didn't finish what she'd started to say. Not that she needed to. Her expression said everything.

Jenefer was disgusted with Alicia. Disappointed in him. She might go along with his deception for now. But she wasn't going to play nursemaid forever.

Sucking at his injured flesh, he gave her a nod of understanding.

Then she exited with a final jab meant to bruise. "Come along, lad. We're not wanted here."

Morgan stared at the door long after she was gone. When his gaze returned to his wife, who had now shifted under the coverlet to commandeer the entire bed, he couldn't help wonder if the same could be said of him.

CHAPTER 45

"**S**omething's not right with that woman," Jenefer declared as soon as she returned to the nursery. Feiyan creased her brows. "She *wasn't* breathtakingly beautiful?"

"I didn't notice."

That was a lie. Jenefer *had* noticed. Beneath the cuts and bruises, Morgan's wife was lovely. She had cream-pale skin and coal-dark hair, enormous black eyes, and a delicate chin that made her look fey and frail. Next to her, Jenefer had felt like a sun-baked giant.

"So what's wrong with her?" Feiyan asked.

"She acted as if..." Even though she knew Miles wouldn't understand her words, it felt wrong speaking in front of him. She tucked the drowsy lad tenderly into his cradle. Then she whispered to Feiyan, "She acted as if she didn't want Miles."

"Are you sure 'tisn't just wishful thinking on your part?"

Jenefer's eyes went flat. "Nay." Then she shook her head in wonder. "She wouldn't even look at him—her own babe."

Feiyan's brows popped up. "Truly?"

"'Tis three months now. What mother wouldn't want to see her child after all that time?"

"Maybe she's just tired?" Feiyan shrugged. "The Highlander said she'd been treated badly by her captor."

"Maybe." But Jenefer thought it was more than that. The woman had seemed almost fearful of the lad.

"I've been thinking, Jen," Feiyan said in low tones, sitting on the edge of the bed. "The return of Lady Alicia may be a good thing."

"How?" She sat beside her cousin.

"Think about it," Feiyan confided. "The English lord who took her—he can't live very far from here, aye?"

She shrugged. "Aye."

Feiyan lifted a slim brow. "Would *you* want to live so close to the man who'd abducted you?"

Jenefer carefully considered the question before responding, "Absolutely."

"What?" It wasn't the answer Feiyan expected. "Why?"

Jenefer thought that was fairly obvious. "How else could I exact revenge?"

"Ah, of course." Then she leaned toward Jenefer to confide, "But you saw the lady. Did she look like the sort of woman to exact revenge?"

Jenefer scoffed. "She's half my size. Wispy. Weak. Trembling. Fearful."

"Not a warrior maid."

"Hardly. If an English lord had raised a hand like that to one of us, he wouldn't have lived to tell the tale."

"Exactly. So the last place this poor, abused lass will want to live is within easy reach of her abuser."

"True, though I doubt her abuser will live long. Not if Morgan Mor mac Giric has anything to say about it."

Feiyan held up a finger. "Ah, but the king may have sent Morgan here to secure the border and keep the peace. The Highlander wouldn't dare start a war."

Feiyan had a point.

But Jenefer scarcely had time to mull it over before Bethac and Cicilia entered the nursery.

Cicilia had brought cups of ale for them. Seeing that Miles was asleep, she quietly stirred the fire.

Bethac shooed them off the bed and began straightening the bedlinens.

Feiyan took a long swallow of ale and casually asked Bethac, "Now that Lady Alicia has been found, will your clan return to the Highlands?"

Jenefer held her breath.

"Nay," Bethac said, quashing her hopes. "Laird Morgan is the rightful heir to Creagor." The maidservant's gaze landed and lingered an extra moment on Jenefer, as if to challenge her claim to the keep. Then she lowered her eyes and resumed smoothing the sheets. "Besides, Lady Alicia will not wish to return."

"She won't?" Feiyan said.

Jenefer blinked. "Why not?"

Bethac opened her mouth, but didn't answer her at first. "Cicilia, take the bairn's soiled linens down to the laundress, will ye?"

"Aye." Satisfied that Miles was sleeping quietly, Cicilia left with the pail of laundry.

When she was gone, Jenefer repeated the question. "Why would Lady Alicia not wish to return?"

Bethac's lips were taut as she replied, "The lass never cared for the Highlands." She swatted at the coverlet, brushing away lint. "She was always pinin' for her home." She continued, aggressively fluffing the pillows. "Complainin' o' the cold. Weepin' that she was weary o' bein' kept among..." Her lips thinned. "Among savages."

Jenefer grimaced. Though she knew better now, that was the very word *she'd* once used for Highlanders.

Bethac pulled the linens as tight as her lips. "Morgan was too kind, sayin' her condition made her weepy. He said she was like a tender rose, too frail for the Highlands. But I think..." She stopped herself.

"What?" Jenefer asked. Her heart was pounding. "What do you think?"

Bethac wiped her hands on her skirts. "'Tisn't my place to say."

"Oh, go on," Feiyan urged. "We won't tell a soul."

Bethac glanced at them both, as if measuring whether she could trust them. Her desire to confess apparently outweighed her need to keep the secret. "I don't think she's half as frail as she claims to be."

"Why?" Jenefer asked.

Bethac skewered them again with her gaze. Then she beckoned them near and confided, "Lady Alicia may have skin like silk. But she's got a spine o' steel when it comes to gettin' her way. And she's got the laird on a tight lead." She clucked her tongue. "Morgan, bless his soul, is blind to it." Then her voice took on a tart edge. "O' course, now the lady's got what she wants. She's in a warmer clime and among civilized folk."

Feiyan lifted a brow. "Things couldn't have turned out better for her if she'd planned it."

Bethac didn't answer. But her eyes were hooded when she looked at Feiyan, and she said no more, returning to tidying the chamber.

Jenefer blinked. Planned it? That wild idea fired into her brain like a swift and impactful arrow.

Was it possible? Could Lady Alicia have traveled to England of her own free will? Had she had a hand in her abduction? Had there even *been* an abduction?

The idea was staggering.

"Are you suggesting," Jenefer asked, "she may have deceived Morgan, made him believe she was dead, and feigned her own kidnapping, abandoning her newborn child?"

"I'm suggestin' nothin'," Bethac declared. "'Tisn't my place. And ye'd best keep such notions to yourself."

With those elusive words of warning, Bethac left the nursery.

But just because Bethac hadn't suggested it didn't mean it wasn't true.

Still, the whole thing seemed unfathomable.

"What kind of woman could walk away from a wee, helpless infant?" she wondered aloud. Silently, she added, or from such a magnificent warrior of a husband.

Feiyan gave her a sly glance. "No doubt the same kind of woman who's not so grateful to be *reacquainted* with him."

Jenefer nodded. This put a coil in things.

She had to reconsider the entire notion of returning Miles to his birth mother. How could Jenefer hand an innocent babe over to the woman who had heartlessly abandoned him? How could she surrender Morgan to a wife who had ruthlessly betrayed him?

"I can't give him back now." Even she wasn't sure if she meant Miles or Morgan or both.

"'Tis decided then."

Jenefer lifted a brow in askance.

Feiyan closed her eyes to scheming slits. "This is war."

CHAPTER 46

Alicia didn't like the lass who'd come in this morn. Something about her was galling. The tawny wench was oversized and overbold. Too pretty for a servant. And she had a kind of fatal sensuality that only men and clever wives like Alicia could smell.

"I don't like that woman," she muttered, pouting.

"What woman?" Morgan asked.

Still claiming weakness from her ordeal, Alicia half-reclined against a bolster on Morgan's bed. He was hand-feeding her bites of trout pottage.

"That nurse."

"Bethac?"

"Not Bethac." To be honest, Alicia wasn't too fond of Bethac either. The old maidservant was always sticking her nose into Morgan's affairs. But that wasn't who she meant. "The other one." She picked at the corner of the coverlet. "The one who was trying to force the infant upon me this morn."

Morgan frowned. "I'm sure she meant well."

"I don't trust her."

Alicia was almost certain she was the same woman she'd overheard challenging Morgan in the nursery. There was something disturbing about her. She looked as fierce and forceful as her bellowing. But she was also beautiful in a wild and intrepid way.

"Our son seems to like her," he said.

Morgan was clearly trying to placate her. He lifted a spoonful of pottage to her lips. She wanted to spit it onto the floor. Instead, she gave him a coy smile.

"Infants always like the one who feeds them," she said, accepting the pottage and dutifully swallowing. But she didn't intend to be distracted. "Nay, I fear the woman doesn't know her place. She's bold and abrasive. Far too free with her words. And there's a conceit about her that..."

She glanced abruptly at Morgan. Was that a smile glimmering in his eyes? Her breath caught. By the devil, her suspicions were correct. "You," she breathed, narrowing her eyes perceptively, "you like her."

Morgan was quick to reply, "O' course I like her. I wouldn't let her tend to our son if I didn't."

Alicia wasn't fooled for an instant. There was more to it than that. The circumstances felt all too familiar. The tryst between Godit and Edward was still fresh in her mind.

Maybe things hadn't progressed that far between Morgan and this maidservant. But too much was at stake for her now. He couldn't be trusted. No man could be. She'd be damned if she'd let a man betray her again.

Rage bubbled inside her veins. But she dared not let Morgan see it. Gentle persuasion always worked best with him.

She lowered her head until her chin rested on her chest, hiding the livid glimmer in her eyes. When she spoke, it was in a trembling voice, one she hoped he'd mistake for fear, not fury. "Don't be angry with me, Morgan, but...well...'tis only that she makes a mockery of your command. She defies your orders and doesn't treat you with the proper respect." She slid her gaze up slightly to gauge his reaction. "I think, for your own good...and the good of the clan...you should dismiss her."

His brow clouded at once and his mouth turned down. "I fear that won't be possible."

She blinked. "Why not?"

"'Tis...complicated."

Her jaw tightened. Complicated. What did that mean? "Unfortunately," he explained, "she's the only one who can keep the bairn from wailin' all night long."

His answer surprised her. "Does he? Wail all night long?"

"Aye. He probably misses his mother," Morgan said, clearly trying to cajole her into a maternal role.

She refused to take the bait. "Can't Bethac make him quiet?"

He shook his head. "Nay. Only Jenefer seems to have the gift."

Alicia clenched her teeth. So the nurse had a name, did she? Jenefer. Alicia preferred to think of her as a nameless, disposable servant, easily replaced.

"But she'll be gone soon, aye?" she asked. "After all, he won't be a sniveling infant forever."

She saw Morgan flinch at her words, and she made a quick correction, giving her head a little shake and resting a hand lightly on his sleeve.

"Forgive me, Morgan. I'm not myself. I'm testy and ill-at-ease. To be honest, I fear my faith has been shaken. Having been away from you for so long, I find myself uncertain of your affections."

She thought she detected a telling hesitation in his reply.

"Ye're my wife, Alicia. O' course ye have my affections."

"But I fear that..." She stopped herself, then lowered her gaze, murmuring, "Nay, you'll think me a fool."

"Never."

"Just a silly lass."

"Nay. Just tell me. What is it?"

"I fear..." She bit her lip. "I fear that nurse has designs on you. The way she looks at you..."

"Looks at me?" He seemed sincerely surprised.

"Not that I can blame her. Who wouldn't wish to be with a man like you?" Before he could respond to her flattery, she tempered it with a pointed remark. "Especially a man with a title and a magnificent holding?"

Just as she'd predicted, doubt slowly formed a furrow in his brow.

"I'm sure ye're wrong about that," he said. His eyes, however, betrayed uncertainty.

"And she's already earned the trust of your infant." Watering the seeds of his misgiving with the elixir of shame, she amended, "*Our* infant."

She allowed herself a secret smile. She was in control again. She had Morgan back under her thumb. Penitent and malleable. Riddled with guilt.

Her blood cooled to a low simmer as she took another bite of the trout pottage. She might not be able to get rid of the troublemaking lass. But knowing Morgan, she could get him to do it himself.

Morgan couldn't possibly let Jenefer go. Not only because she kept the bairn's weeping at bay. But because, at the moment, she was his hostage, his leverage against war.

But he couldn't tell Alicia that. She'd never understand.

He didn't want to talk about it anymore. So he continued to feed her in silence.

It troubled him to think the attraction between himself and Jenefer was so obvious. Yet in their brief time together in this chamber, even his wife had sensed the connection between the two of them.

Morgan knew, if the clan found out about his indiscretion, none would blame him. Everyone had believed that Alicia was dead, that Morgan was a widower. It wasn't as if he'd been intentionally disloyal.

He could even forgive himself for falling in love with Jenefer. She'd seemed so devoted to his son, so forthright in her passions, so genuine in her affections.

But now Alicia had sown doubt in his mind. Her words haunted him.

Had he been plied by the warrior maid? Had she only charmed his son to make herself indispensable to Morgan? Had she only seduced Morgan to insinuate herself into his life? Had she only pretended to care for him in order to...

His eyes dimmed. The only thing Jenefer had ever claimed to want—nay, demanded to have—was Creagor. Were all her actions only a clever ploy to win his holding?

His heart caved at the thought.

Mostly because it had almost worked.

He'd been ready to marry her, to share his son with her, to bestow his wealth and land upon her.

And now?

Now his mind was filled with mistrust.

He steeled his jaw.

It didn't matter. None of it mattered. Whatever had happened between them was in the past. Alicia's return had sealed all their fates. There was no point in dwelling on the motivations behind anything. It served no purpose.

What he needed to focus on was taking vengeance on the brute who'd hurt his wife.

Alicia took one last bite of the pottage and refused the rest with a dismissive hand. She'd always been a light eater, nothing like...

He shuttered his mind against the thought and set the pottage aside.

"Alicia, sweetheart, I need to get that name from ye," he said gently.

"Name?"

"The man who did...this...to ye."

Alicia's face crumpled. "Can't it wait but a little while?" she begged. "I haven't seen you for weeks. I want to spend as much time as possible together."

She peered at him from under her lashes and ran a speculative fingertip across her collar bone. He knew that look, that gesture. It was Alicia's way of saying she would be amenable to his advances.

"I've returned from the dead," she said. "Is it not a time for celebration and not rancor?"

The plea in her wide eyes convinced him to defer his revenge again. But he knew better than to imagine Alicia wished to celebrate their reunion *now*. She would never accede to swiving him by the light of day. She was far too modest for that.

By nightfall, they would make a symbolic renewal of their wedlock, restoring the sanctity of their union. And that was exactly what he needed to forget Jenefer, the fiery temptress who had intruded upon his placid marriage as briefly and powerfully as a bright, destructive spark.

CHAPTER 47

"We're going to need weapons," Jenefer decided, pacing the nursery as she chewed on a piece of barley bread.

"Hold on," Feiyan said. "What?"

"You said it yourself. This is war."

"Not all wars are fought with arms. What happened to *amor vincit omnia?*"

Jenefer rolled her eyes. This again. "What's the point of knowing how to wield a blade and shoot a bow if you're not going to use them?"

Feiyan challenged her with crossed arms. "And how are you going to use them? Will you shoot Bethac and Cicilia? Will you threaten to cut Lady Alicia's throat?"

Jenefer scowled. That last suggestion held some appeal. But she supposed Feiyan was right.

"Nay," continued Feiyan, "we need a plan first."

"Fine. You plan. I'll collect the arms."

The situation might not require weapons. But for Jenefer, losing her bow felt like losing a limb. Under such uncertain circumstances, she wanted to be prepared. It was clear by now that Hallie wasn't bringing the army of Rivenloch to the rescue. Her cool-headed cousin was no doubt patiently waiting at the keep for their parents to return.

Jenefer couldn't hold off that long. Knowing now what cruelty Lady Alicia was capable of, she couldn't shake the feeling that the woman meant Morgan some harm.

What made things worse was that Jenefer was in love with the damned Highlander. Every hour that Morgan spent alone with his wife felt like a mortal blow to her heart.

Jenefer peered into the cradle, where Miles sighed in his sleep. She thanked the stars Lady Alicia had shown no interest in her son. At least Jenefer was able to keep the babe safe.

The sun had reached its zenith and only begun its afternoon descent when Jenefer started thinking about the evening to come, anticipating a new torment. She couldn't help but muse about the couple in the bedchamber next door.

Would they swive tonight?

Would Morgan touch his wife with the same gentle care and desperate need that he'd touched *her?*

Would she stroke his luxuriant hair? Kiss his supple mouth? Run her fingers across the warm, muscled contours of his chest?

Would their bodies come together like the smoothed feather of a well-fletched arrow?

The thought gnawed a hole in her heart.

She squeezed her eyes shut, willing away the painful images.

From the window, Feiyan called out softly, "Longbow practice again. Care to watch?"

Jenefer would welcome any distraction. And when she joined Feiyan, peering past the shutters to the ground below, she was relieved to see Morgan commanding his archers. After all, if he was on the field, he couldn't be in the room next door with Alicia.

As she observed the four archers, she had to smile. It seemed Morgan had taken her suggestions. At least the arrows were striking the target more often. The one lad still couldn't draw his string back far enough. But Morgan had him practice pulling the bow without shafts to strengthen his arm.

After half an hour, Bethac tiptoed in to bring them ale.

"What are ye lookin' at?" she whispered.

"The archers," Feiyan said, taking an ale.

Bethac handed a second ale to Jenefer. Her eyes lit up as she peeked out the window. "Och, that's my William down there."

"Where?" Jenefer asked.

"That's him," she said with a proud nod, "the handsome lad with the fiery red hair."

"Ah."

"He *is* handsome," Feiyan said, to be polite.

Jenefer had been watching the lad. He had decent form, but he always aimed too high. A few slight adjustments would fix that. If she had her bow...

Suddenly, an idea struck Jenefer.

She narrowed her eyes at the lad. "He's...*fairly* skilled."

"Fairly?" Bethac echoed in concern.

"Aye. He's young yet. Give him time." Jenefer wrinkled her nose. "Anyway, he wouldn't be fighting on the battlefield yet, right?"

Bethac's brow creased with worry. "I...I don't know."

Jenefer shrugged. "Well, as long as he's posted at a distant wall and not in the thick of things, I'm sure he'll be fine."

Bethac peered past her to the archery field. "What's wrong with him? Is something wrong with him?"

Feiyan caught on quickly. "Nothing's *wrong* with him. He's just, well, a novice."

Bethac blinked rapidly. "He's been an archer for two years now."

Jenefer and Feiyan exchanged a look of discomfiture.

"I see," Feiyan said. "Well, Jenefer is right. I'm sure the laird knows where his talents can best be used."

But Bethac was now neck-deep in fretting.

"What if he doesn't, though?" she said, half to herself, wringing her hands. "What if the laird sends him to battle?" She looked at Jenefer. "He's my only grandson."

Jenefer nodded and placed a consoling hand on Bethac's shoulder. "Listen. If you think you can keep a secret," she murmured, "I may be able to help."

"How?"

"I told you I was a master archer, aye?"

"Aye."

"I could give your William a few suggestions, a wee bit of guidance, enough to keep him safe."

"Ye could?"

"Jenefer is the best archer in her da's army," Feiyan chimed in. "Your William could have no better trainer."

Jenefer nodded to the field below. "We can practice right here, below this window, so you can keep an eye on him."

Bethac's face relaxed with hope. "Ye would do that?"

"Of course," Jenefer said. "There's just one wee problem. The laird took my bow and arrows."

She wasn't sure that was entirely true. But they'd been with the rest of her things in the forest, and he'd brought her clothing to her. He must have done something with her weapons.

"He did? Why?" Bethac asked, narrowing her eyes. The maidservant may have been easy to manipulate when it came to her grandson. But she was also observant and shrewd. She trusted Morgan's judgment. If he'd confiscated her weapons, he must have had a good reason.

Jenefer decided to tell her the truth. "I think he feared I'd use them against him."

Bethac nodded. "Would ye?" The question was blunt.

Jenefer hesitated. At one time she would have. "Nay. Not now."

The look they exchanged spoke volumes. The maidservant could not be unaware of what had passed between Morgan and Jenefer. Indeed, she'd practically sown the seeds of love herself—arranging that romantic candlelight bath and leaving them in bedded bliss together. Though the two of them might never allow that love to blossom, a bond still existed between them.

"I'll see what I can learn in the armory," Bethac promised her.

It took all afternoon. But the maid finally located her weapons. For Jenefer, the sight of her bow and arrows in Bethac's possession was more enticing than even the fish pottage she'd brought for supper.

She immediately inspected the bow. God knew what rough handling it had received from these undisciplined Highlanders.

But it appeared whole. Her score of shafts were all there and intact as well. Her bracer was still tucked into the pocket of her quiver.

The hour was too late and the day too dark to begin training tonight.

"On the morrow," Bethac said, "after William has finished his chores and while Morgan is busy with his midday meal, I'll help ye slip downstairs."

"Perfect."

Jenefer couldn't deny a pang of guilt over how easily she'd tricked the devoted grandmother into bringing her weapons. But she completely understood how Bethac felt. Jenefer wasalready keenly protective of Miles, and he wasn't even blood kin to her.

At least she'd be helping William. Her efforts might serve to save the lad's life one day.

It was plain to Alicia that Morgan expected to swive her tonight. He'd washed his face and combed his hair. He'd let the fire dwindle, leaving the room dimly lit by a single candle, just the way she preferred it. And he'd slid into the bed with such stealth that even the abbess of a convent wouldn't have detected him.

But she was no longer interested. Her earlier fear and jealousy, her worry that the scheming nursemaid was trying to insinuate herself into Morgan's household, had waned somewhat. She hadn't glimpsed the pesky wench all day. And every time she'd stolen from her bed to peer out the window, Alicia had seen Morgan engaged in the field with his soldiers.

Perhaps the seeds of doubt she'd planted in Morgan's mind had taken root after all, and he planned to keep the woman at arm's length. If so, she had nothing to worry about. Consequently, she felt less of a necessity to bed him.

When he sidled up next to her in the bed, she moaned, half in feigned pain, half in annoyance.

He froze. "Have I hurt ye?"

"Nay," she said, her voice tight. "'Tisn't anything *you've* done."

"What can I do to make ye feel better?" he murmured against her ear.

She squirmed away from him. "You've already made me feel better."

He snaked a hand beneath the coverlet and began inching up the fabric of her linen kirtle. "Perhaps I can help ye forget the pain."

She let out a shuddering sigh and pushed his hand away. "Oh, Morgan..."

"Aye, sweetheart?"

She tugged her kirtle back down. "I fear I may not be quite ready."

He nuzzled her neck. "I can help make ye ready, love."

She turned her head away and rolled her eyes.

How she hated swiving. She hated the sweat, the smell, the panting, the grunting. She hated the feeling of invasion when a man shoved his member inside her. Abhorred the beatific victory on his face when he pumped her full of his seed.

For her, swiving had always been a means to an end. A weapon to be wielded strategically. A way to make a man do her bidding.

At the moment, Morgan was already amenable to her wishes. She had no need to engage in the disgusting act.

"Oh, Morgan, *amor meu,*" she lied, "'twould be my greatest desire to oblige you. But after my ordeal, I fear..."

"Aye?" He stiffened.

"It may be some time before..." She left the words as she intended to leave Morgan—dangling and unfinished.

She felt his heavy sigh of disappointment.

Morgan cursed his body. It hadn't yet grasped that he wasn't going to swive anyone tonight. His skin still felt warm and alive. His heart was pumping with anticipation. And beneath the covers, he'd roused like a bear from its winter sleep, awake and ravenous.

But it wasn't to be.

He couldn't blame Alicia. The poor lass had endured much at the hands of the enemy. It might be more than her body that was injured. Her mind could be wounded as well. He'd have to have patience with her in their bed. More than ever before.

He'd always needed to take his time with Alicia. She was a fragile creature, not easy to please. Extremely modest, she never removed her kirtle, nor was he to remove his leine. She wasn't fond of kissing and insisted on trysting in the shadows. They coupled no more than once a week, less when she was suffering from her monthly courses.

As long as he followed her requirements, she was compliant enough to let him climb atop her. She would close her eyes while he made love to her, lying quietly beneath him, waiting for him to finish.

He supposed it was always thus for man and wife. Coupling was for making babes, after all. Whether they enjoyed it or not was irrelevant.

Still, tonight, as Alicia moved farther away from him, taking most of the coverlet with her, he couldn't help but remember how different it had been, making love to Jenefer.

While Alicia's breathing deepened into soft snores, Morgan stared at the ceiling, imagining the fiery, brazen lass who had ridden shamelessly atop him, demanding in her kisses and breathless with awe.

But even while his body stirred, that memory was tarnished by the nagging notion Alicia had slipped into his brain—that Jenefer was after him only for his title, his wealth, and his keep.

CHAPTER 48

By the time Alicia awoke, the day was half gone. Morgan, as usual, had arisen at dawn. A laird's life was a busy one.

That was fine with her. She preferred not having to play the role of the timid and dutiful wife every hour of the day. As long as she had servants to do her bidding and see to her needs, she had no need of Morgan.

To be honest, she required very little in life. Morgan should consider himself lucky she was so easily pleased.

She demanded only five things.

A loyal husband of good standing.

Enough coin to maintain her comfort.

The authority to command others.

Civilized company.

And a bearable climate.

For two years, she'd had to live without the last two. Now that Morgan had moved the clan to the Lowlands, she could be assured of all her needs.

Swiving him was the price she paid for that assurance. She wouldn't fool herself about that for a moment. She might have slipped through his lusty fingers last night. But Morgan would eventually insist on having his way with her. After all, as laird of a clan, he expected to sire more than one child.

For now, at least, she could use the excuse of her horrid ordeal to keep him at bay.

She picked up the steel mirror on the table beside her and examined her face. Already her cuts had begun to heal. Her black eye had turned yellow-green. The lump on her brow had diminished into a flat purple bruise.

She smiled in satisfaction. Her wounds were severe enough to be convincing, but not enough to scar. Of course, if that wretch Edward hadn't swived the midwife, she wouldn't have needed to inflict them at all.

Her face grew ugly as she sulked at the memory of the adulterous swine. She slammed the mirror back down on the table.

Then she forced her lips into a brilliant grin. There was no need to dwell on the past. She'd taken care of all that. Her husband would give her no cause to fret. Morgan wasn't Edward. He'd never prove disloyal.

The shutters were ajar, and Alicia suddenly heard voices coming from outside the window. Curious, she gathered her kirtle and crept from the bed to peer out to the ground below.

Standing on the sward and conversing with Bethac's redheaded grandson was that damned nursemaid.

Irritation crawled up Alicia's spine. What was the irksome woman scheming? Wasn't she supposed to be watching over Morgan's infant? And what was her business with his soldier?

Her earlier concerns about the wench immediately resurged. It was a small step from dallying with Morgan's men to pursuing Morgan himself. Alicia should know. She'd moved many a man to possessive jealousy by flirting with those around him.

She ground her teeth and dug her nails into her palms. Somehow she had to get rid of the tedious wench.

She hoped it wouldn't be necessary to kill her. Not that the prospect didn't hold some appeal. Alicia wouldn't have minded at least destroying the wench's face with a thorough beating. It would serve her right. The maid was too pretty for a servant and too cocky for her own good.

But murder would be far more difficult to pull off this time.

Reminded of her last victims, she wondered what was happening now at Edward's castle. Did anyone care who had disposed of the lord? Or were the scavengers of his household too busy fighting over the scraps?

As she pondered the odds of anyone tugging on the dangling threads of her crime, she noticed the nursemaid was doing more than just chatting with William.

She watched in bafflement as the wench loaded a longbow, drew back the string, and let an arrow fly. The movement seemed as natural as breathing. And when Alicia shifted to see where the arrow had landed, she spied a wee straw target at the far end of the wall, pierced in the dead center.

When William picked up his bow next, Alicia decided she must be mistaken about the target. The arrow in the bull's-eye no doubt belonged to him. Perhaps he was trying to impress the wench with his marksmanship.

He loosed his arrow. It lodged in the upper right corner of the target, far off the mark.

The two conversed for a moment, gesturing and flexing their bows.

Alicia scowled. Was William teaching the wench how to shoot?

That was highly irresponsible. The woman had been hired to care for Morgan's child. Not to waste her time on archery.

Besides, a bow in the hands of a woman was hazardous. A weapon in the hands of a serving maid was foolhardy. And if that maid had a rebellious nature and an insolent tongue...

Alicia lifted a calculating brow. No doubt Morgan would deem that a dismissible offense. And if not, she was certain she could convince him of it.

Only half-finished with his supper, Morgan nonetheless threw his napkin onto the table and stormed to his feet, scraping back the bench. The fact that Alicia had managed to limp her way downstairs to the great hall to deliver the message to him meant it was serious. And the news she whispered in his ear had the ring of truth to it.

A quick glance around the trestle table revealed she was right about one thing. William was noticeably absent.

Why the lad would be teaching Jenefer, a self-proclaimed master archer, how to shoot was a mystery. But that wasn't what concerned Morgan. He only cared about two things.

Jenefer had somehow managed to steal out of the keep.

And she was armed.

Bidding Alicia return to his chamber and the clan to return to their supper, he left the great hall with claymore in hand to deal with Jenefer's treachery.

His heart pounded as he stalked across the sward at the foot of the keep. But as he drew near his bedchamber, he slowed his step to observe the pair of archers beneath his window.

His wife's report had been partially accurate. William was indeed practicing his marksmanship, drawing his bow, taking aim at a target. But Alicia hadn't quite grasped the truth of the situation.

The lad wasn't teaching the warrior maid how to shoot. *She* was instructing *him*. And the amazing thing was, whatever she'd done, Morgan could see William's posture was much better, and his aim had improved. For a moment, Morgan watched in fascination.

Then, Jenefer took the lad's place. With no apparent effort, she nocked an arrow into her bow, drew back the sinew, and released the shaft. And the breath stopped in his chest.

She was magnificent. Her form, her strength, the ease with which she took aim, the grace with which she loosed her arrow—as if the bow were a natural extension of her arm—left him thunderstruck.

He looked beyond her to the target.

Her shaft had struck squarely in the center of the bull's-eye.

His mouth went dry. Jenefer du Lac's skills weren't just an amusing curiosity. The woman was formidable. Deadly. Dangerous.

Clenching his jaw and tightening his grip on the claymore, he strode forward.

"Hold your arrows!"

Before he could shout another command, in one fluid motion, the lass wheeled about, whipped an arrow from her quiver, nocked it, and took aim at his heart.

ChAPTER 49

Jenefer had simply acted on instinct.

She wouldn't have fired.

She knew the difference between a real threat and an imagined one. Even if that imagined threat was brandishing his claymore at her again.

He'd only startled her.

And she'd definitely startled him. His eyes widened, and he slid to a halt not five yards from her.

For a breathless instant, frozen in time, they stared at each other. Her three fingers, curled around the taut bowstring, were all that kept her from loosing the arrow and slaying him where he stood.

And he knew it.

Two days ago, she might have considered shooting him. This was war, after all. And one Highlander was a low price to pay for a prize like Creagor.

But two days ago, she hadn't known Morgan. Two days ago, she hadn't been in love with him.

From behind her, William suddenly squeaked with guilt. "M'laird!"

She heard the lad's bow clatter onto the grass. Without turning around, she knew he'd turned as red as a cherry.

They'd been caught. And now Morgan would confiscate her weapon.

She silently swore.

Defying Morgan would only make things worse. With a sigh of frustration, she lowered her longbow.

Morgan's fear vanished, replaced by anger and outrage.

"Where did ye get that weapon?" he demanded, indicating her longbow with the point of his sword.

Jenefer had intended to be reasonable. She'd intended to remain calm. But his question made her hackles rise.

"This? 'Tis mine," she declared. "I found *my* longbow in *your* armory. Where did *you* get it?"

Morgan's eyes narrowed, and she saw him muttering curses under his breath. To William he said, "Leave us."

"Aye, m'laird," William choked out.

"Wait!" Bethac's sharp bark, coming from the nursery window above them, surprised Jenefer as much as it did Morgan. "Ye stay right there, William."

The lad hesitated, unsure whether to obey his laird or his grandmother.

"M'laird," Bethac continued, "ye cannot blame the lad or the maid. 'Twas my idea."

"*Your* idea?" Morgan burst out. "Your idea to arm a lass who has a grievance against me?"

"Och, m'laird! She has no grievance against ye. Do ye, lass?"

To be honest, she had several. But Bethac didn't give her time to answer.

"Besides, I've been right here, keepin' an eye on her the whole time," the maid continued.

"She has," Feiyan confirmed, appearing at the window beside Bethac.

Jenefer didn't mention that she could have shot William, Morgan, and half the laird's army before the old maid could have done anything about it.

Morgan probably knew that as well. "So ye approved o' this? Ye approved o' your kin consortin' with the lass?"

"Consortin'?" Bethac scoffed. "I don't know what ye're talkin' about. The lass was only doin' me a kindness, trainin' my William so he'd not be killed in battle."

"Battle?" William yelped. "Is there to be battle?"

"Nay!" Morgan ground out in exasperation. "There will be no battle."

"But there *could* be," Bethac argued. "And ye can't deny his marksmanship has improved. Hasn't it, lad?"

"Och, aye," William said with a proud grin.

"He hasn't missed the target once," Feiyan said. "And he shot two bull's-eyes."

"The lass is remarkable, m'laird," Bethac gushed, "as skilfull as Flidhais."

Jenefer lifted her chin a notch. It wasn't the first time she'd been compared to the goddess of the hunt.

"Flidhais? Is that so?" Morgan asked, arching a sardonic brow. "So ye think I should put her in charge o' my army now?"

"Och, nay, o' course not," Bethac said, wrinkling her nose. "Just the archers."

Morgan pressed at his throbbing temple.

Jenefer bit her lip. Here was a tempting idea. If Morgan put her in charge of the archers, she'd get to keep her weapon.

"I'll do it," she blurted out.

"What?" he scoffed.

"I'll train your archers."

"Ye'll do no such thing."

"Why not?"

"Aye," said Bethac. "Why not?"

He glanced up at the maidservant. Jenefer knew he didn't wish to reveal the truth to her. That the warrior maids were not in fact guests, but prisoners. Not innocents to be protected, but foes to be feared.

"I can train them myself," Morgan said.

"Do you doubt my skills?" Jenefer said in bold challenge.

"Do ye doubt mine?"

She gave him a grim smile. She'd never seen him draw a bow. But she was confident she could outshoot any man.

"I'll make you a wager," she offered. "Three shots. Whoever wins gets command of the archers."

"Don't be ridiculous."

"A contest of arms!" Feiyan cheered from above.

"You can even fetch your own longbow to make it a fair match," Jenefer said. "I'll wait."

"I'm not goin' to shoot against ye," he told her.

"Why not? Are you afraid you'll lose?"

Young William stepped forward in his defense. "Laird Morgan isn't afraid of anythin'. Isn't that right, m'laird?"

Morgan's eyes narrowed, and his jaw ticked. He was trapped now. And he knew it.

"Very well. I'll shoot against ye," he said. "But only on one condition. If I win, your bow belongs to me."

Feiyan crowed with glee.

Jenefer shrugged. "Fine."

He stabbed his claymore into the ground and gestured to William. "Lend me your bow?"

Jenefer lifted her brows. "Don't you want your own weapon?"

William's bow was far too small and light for him. Unless he tempered his strength, he risked breaking it.

"'Twon't be necessary," he boasted, taking the bow and three arrows that William offered.

"You're sure?"

He answered her with a smug grin as he stabbed his three arrows into the ground. Then he indicated with a magnanimous sweep of his hand that she should shoot first.

She looked forward to wiping that grin off his face.

William quickly removed the arrows still stuck in the target and stood back to watch.

Jenefer gave Morgan a smoky smile as she slowly drew an arrow from her quiver. Then, just to unsettle him, she didn't bother turning toward the target. Fitting the arrow to her bow, she waited until the last moment, and in one continuous movement, swung around, drew, and released it.

It struck the target dead center.

CHAPTER 50

I t might have been a lucky shot. But Morgan didn't think so.

To say he was impressed by Jenefer's skill was an understatement. His jaw dropped. He blinked in disbelief. And when he met her self-satisfied gaze, he was forced to see her with new eyes.

Bethac hadn't exaggerated. Jenefer *was* as skilled as Flidhais. She was better than any of his men. Her shooting was smooth. Effortless. And deadly accurate.

Defeating her would be more of a challenge than he'd expected.

But he wasn't exactly a novice himself.

Bethac cheered from the window.

He gave her a withering glare. "Whose side are ye on, old woman?"

Her eyes twinkled, but she refused to reply.

Jenefer made an exaggerated sweep of her arm. "Your turn."

He nodded and flexed the light bow a few times. The weapon wasn't nearly as powerful as his own. If he drew it too forcefully, the ash would crack. But shooting at this distance didn't require power, only aim.

He plucked an arrow from the earth. From the corner of his eye, he saw Jenefer watching him.

Her longbow rested casually against her shoulder. Her arms were crossed in swaggering self-assurance. But it was her complacent yawn that pushed him over the edge and made him decide to provoke her.

"Ye know, the claymore is my weapon o' choice," he admitted. "I'm no archer."

She crinkled her eyes at him. "Do you wish to forfeit the match then?"

"Nay, nay," he said, nocking the arrow. "I agreed to your challenge, and I'm a man o' my word."

He lifted the bow, preparing to shoot. As he did, he intentionally hooked his first finger across the top to hold the shaft in place. It was a mistake common to beginners.

Jenefer's brow creased. She unfolded her arms. "Wait. Are you...?"

"Aye?"

"You aren't going to leave your left finger like that, are you?" she asked in disbelief.

He shrugged.

A tiny, troubled scowl flashed between her brows. "The feathers will catch. You'll be lucky if the shaft leaves the bow."

He smirked. "How else am I to hold the arrow in place?"

The dilemma in her expression was palpable. Should she help him? Or let him fail?

"Fine," she said tightly. "You've got three chances, after all, aye?"

He squinted hard at the target.

"You know you should keep both eyes..." she began.

"What's that?"

"Nothing. Never mind."

He slowly drew back the string, hugging his elbow close to his side.

"Lift...lift your..." she sputtered.

Between gritted teeth, he said, "Are ye goin' to keep interruptin' me or let me shoot?"

She let out an exasperated breath. "Go on."

As soon as she glanced away, shaking her head in pity, he opened his eyes, moved his finger, lifted his elbow, and released the arrow.

It landed with a thunk beside her shaft, in the middle of the target.

"What?" Jenefer exclaimed. The shock on her face was priceless. "How did you...?"

He gave her a one-sided smile. "Just lucky, I guess. Your turn."

She was still staring at him, baffled, when he backed away to let her shoot.

This time, he saw she wasn't taking any chances. Rather than risking a clever shot, she lined up carefully in front of the target, taking time to smooth the fletching on her arrow before setting it into the bow and resting it lightly on top of her left fist.

It was pure pleasure to see her shoot. Very quickly, he found himself watching her with more than mild interest.

There was something enticing about her flawless form as she lifted the longbow in one steady arm.

Something provocative about her slowly pulling the string back until it creaked and the way her fingers curled softly against her cheek.

Something intoxicating about the intensity with which she stared at the straw target.

By the time she let the arrow fly, he was too distracted, watching her, to see where her shot had landed.

And when she turned to him with a triumphant grin, he no longer cared. Her brilliant smile and her sparkling eyes took his breath away.

"Another bull's-eye!" William crowed. "Och, this is goin' to be a good contest."

William's cheer jarred him back to reality. He glanced down the field. Three arrows now crowded the center circle of the target.

Jenefer stepped back with a magnanimous gesture of invitation. "Morgan?"

On her lips, his name sounded like a purr. Pleasant. Sensual. Arousing.

But he couldn't let her unnerve him.

Damn her feminine temptations. He had to win.

Jenefer had been so sure she'd leave Morgan in the dust. Feiyan was right. She'd always been able to outshoot her father's men.

And once she'd seen Morgan's dreadful form—his hooked finger, his squinting aim, his dropped elbow— she'd almost pitied him. With such terrible technique and a bow that was the wrong size for him, he'd be fortunate to hit the target at all.

His first shot might have been luck. But she wasn't certain enough of that to let down her guard. This time she'd watch him carefully.

Sure enough, this time he didn't hook his finger. Or squint. Or clamp his elbow against his side.

But he did talk the entire time. Which was equally disturbing.

"So how long have ye been an archer, lassie?" he asked, cocking his head away from the bowstring to eye up the target.

Shouldn't he be focusing on his task? Didn't he need to concentrate? Hold his breath? Steady his aim?

"Ever since I can remember," she replied.

He sniffed, adjusting his stance. "Indeed? And who taught ye?"

"My ma."

"Your ma?" he said in surprise. He lowered the bow and shook his head in amusement. "Aye, o' course she did. Warrior maid, aye?"

Raising the bow again, he pulled back the bowstring until his knuckles rested against his cheek.

"And did she teach ye to fight with a sword?" he asked, eyeing up the target.

"Aye."

"And a dagger?"

"Aye."

"What about your fists?"

Now she was getting exasperated. "Lucifer's ballocks. Do you intend to shoot, or are you going to chatter at me all afternoon?"

To her utter annoyance, he chuckled. "Ye know, that temper o' yours," he said, unexpectedly releasing the arrow mid-sentence, "is your fatal flaw."

She scowled. Had he actually managed to wedge his arrow between two of the others? While he was carrying on a conversation?

William cheered.

"Bloody hell," she said.

How had he done it? How had he managed to shoot in the midst of rattling on about her temper?

Her *temper?* Her hackles rose. There was nothing that incited her to anger faster than someone mentioning her temper.

He gave her a taunting grin. "Your last shot, I believe?"

She shot him a scathing glare and wrenched an arrow out of her quiver with a vengeance. Fatal flaw? She didn't think so. Her fatal flaw was believing him when he said he was no archer.

She lined up sideways to the target.

"Watch carefully, William," Morgan said in a loud whisper. "Ye see how she lines up sideways to the target?"

She ignored him. She knew what he was doing. He was trying to distract her. She wasn't about to let him have the satisfaction.

She set her arrow atop the hand gripping the bow, twisting the shaft until the cock feather faced upward.

"See how she twists the shaft," he murmured, "until the cock feather faces upward."

She felt her blood start to simmer. But she was determined to pay him no heed. Drawing back the bowstring, she took aim.

"And here she holds her breath and... Ye do hold your breath, aye? Do ye take a breath before ye draw or after ye've got the target in your sights?"

What the devil was he yammering on about? Drawing a breath? Holding her breath? How was she supposed to know? She'd never thought about it before. And now that he'd planted the notion in her brain, suddenly she felt like she couldn't breathe. Worse, her arm was beginning to shake from holding the string taut.

Before the bow could wobble out of her control, she took her best shot. The arrow landed in the second ring.

"Shite!" she cried, turning on him. "Look what you made me do."

"Me? What did *I* do?"

"You know very well," she snarled. "Drawing your breath... Holding your breath..."

"I was only tryin' to help the lad," he claimed, "showin' him how a master archer does it." There was a mischievous twinkle in his eyes that belied his innocence.

"Cheating is what you were doing." She turned to William. "See, lad, the depths to which an inferior archer will sink to win?"

"And how easy 'tis to use a foe's weakness against them?" Morgan said to the lad. "A fatal flaw, that temper o' hers."

Her blood was boiling now. But saying any of the foul things that came to mind would only prove his point about her temper.

Instead, she took a deep breath, blowing out all her tension as she'd seen Feiyan do. While he was flexing the longbow, she considered what *his* fatal flaw might be.

For most men, it was lust.

Now that she'd tried her hand at seduction and succeeded, she was sure she could summon up enough womanly wiles to throw him off his game.

She snagged one of his arrows from the ground and sidled up to offer it to him.

Drawing his attention with her smoldering gaze, she murmured just loud enough for him to hear, "Make sure the *cock* feather is *upright* before you release it."

His nostrils flared briefly, but then he gave her a soft chuckle. "I always do."

She sauntered away then, swaying her hips in what she hoped was a provocative fashion until she was standing out of the line of fire, but well in his line of sight. She leaned back against the castle wall and used her finger to coyly tease the neckline of her kirtle, something she'd seen a milkmaid do once.

Unfortunately, the smile he gave her wasn't full of lust. It was sad and wistful. And in the end, her scheme only created unanticipated consequences.

From this angle, she could see every gesture he made. Every muscle he tensed. Every movement of his eyes. Every expression in his face. And it was painfully obvious to her now that he was no novice.

Before he shot, he examined the arrow itself, sighting down the length of it to make sure it was straight. Then he ran the fletching lightly across his lips to smooth the feathers.

She gulped. She'd never noticed before what an enticing gesture that was, almost like a kiss. She remembered the feel of those lips on hers.

When he fitted his arrow this time, it settled evenly on top of his fist without the awkward interference of his hooked finger.

He raised the bow and drew back the string in one smooth, practiced gesture.

Beneath his taut sleeves, she could glimpse his formidable, well-muscled arms. She was instantly reminded of the way those arms felt around her. Powerful. And protective.

Because the bow was light, he was able to hold the arc steady for a long while as he challenged the target with his gaze.

She'd seen that challenge in his eyes before. There was a penetrating force of will in his gray-green-golden gaze that would make any but the strongest adversary tremble.

His fingers, curved against his swarthy jaw, held the string with the perfect grip. Firm yet flexible.

Her breath caught as she realized the way he gripped the arrow reminded her of the way he held her when they'd made love. Tightly enough to maintain control, loosely enough to set her free at the right moment. A surge of desire rose up in her as the memory of her own passionate release assailed her.

Then her thoughts were abruptly interrupted by a bewildered cry drifting down from the bedchamber window. "Morgan?"

His wife.

CHAPTER 51

Startled, Jenefer gasped.

Alicia's voice apparently rattled Morgan as well. When his arrow sprang from the bow, it missed the target completely.

"What are you doing, *amor meu?*" Alicia asked in plaintive tones.

Jenefer saw the pleasure vanish instantly from his face, replaced by shame and defensiveness.

"I'm takin' care o' things," he assured her.

"Are you?" she asked. Her question was innocent enough, but Jenefer detected a sharp edge to her voice.

"Aye," Morgan said. "I've got the matter well in hand."

Jenefer scowled. Matter? What matter?

Alicia clasped a hand to her bosom as she leaned out the window. "I'm sorry, Morgan," she said in dulcet tones. "I'm afraid, since the kidnapping, my trust has been... damaged."

Morgan colored at her remark. His jaw tensed. He lowered his gaze.

As for Jenefer, righteous indignation boiled up in her like a cauldron of molten iron on the fire.

Lady Alicia knew very well the guilt Morgan must feel over what had happened. How he must blame himself for allowing her to be taken from him. Damaged trust? The woman was intentionally jabbing at his wounds.

Jenefer itched to tell the vile wench just what she thought about her treachery. She had the weapons in her verbal arsenal to send the woman recoiling from the window.

But her ire was tempered by pity for the Highlander.

So instead, she rose to defend him.

Pushing away from the wall, she shook her head in wonder. "Oh m'lady, be at ease. I'm certain you could have no more trustworthy a guardian than Morgan." She intentionally called him by his first name, knowing it would aggravate Alicia. "No kidnapper could slip past his keen eye a second time. Not without some *help.*"

Jenefer could feel the wave of rage Alicia sent her way. But in the next instant, the woman recovered, as if she'd donned a coat of chainmail that hid her malevolent underbelly.

Alicia affected a smile of sympathy, "No man is perfect. I'm sure *my husband,"* she said pointedly, "did the best he could."

"Morgan is a valiant warrior," Jenefer replied. "You couldn't hope for better." She didn't have to lie about that. It was the truth. Then she drew her brows into a puzzled frown. "'Tis perplexing how an abductor slipped past him the first time. Even more bewildering is how the villain knew the exact day of your labor."

Her remark unnerved Alicia, but only for a moment.

"I suppose he lay in wait nearby," she said.

"Indeed. But then, to have somehow made his way inside the keep," Jenefer mused, "hiding right under the noses of the mac Giric clan..."

Alicia gave Morgan a nervous glance, then replied with sweet condescension, "With all due respect, lass, you weren't there."

Jenefer ignored the comment, pacing pensively before the window. "Was it just the English lord by himself? Or did he have his men with him? How did he manage to steal you out of the castle while you were kicking and sceaming?"

Alicia's fury was palpable, but she gave Morgan a trembling smile. "I don't wish to talk about this now." She lifted quavering fingers to her brow. "I don't feel well. Will you come up soon, Morgan?"

"At once," he said.

With that, Alicia withdrew from the window.

Jenefer was unprepared for the venomous glare Morgan shot at her a moment later. He wasn't vexed with Alicia. His anger was aimed at *her*. Sharper than any arrow, his betrayal pierced her heart.

He stepped near, looming over her like a raging dragon, and spoke through clenched teeth. "How dare ye speak like that to my wife?"

"What?" For a moment, hurt left her speechless.

"Ye don't know what she's been through."

Her pain was quickly replaced by outrage. She narrowed her eyes at him, muttering, "Neither do you."

"What's that supposed to mean?" he hissed.

"It doesn't make sense, Morgan. None of it does. And you know it."

"I don't know what battle ye think ye're wagin', lass, but I won't allow ye to attack the woman I...my wife...in that way."

She met him, eye-to-eye, both of them aware of the subtle change he'd made in that statement. He'd meant to say "the woman I love." And he hadn't.

"Fine," she said.

She sensed it was time to leave the field of battle to recover for the next. Despite Morgan's stubborn defense of his traitorous wife, Jenefer knew her words would haunt him and make him question the truth. Meanwhile, she'd do everything in her power to protect him—and Miles—from Lady Alicia's treacherous ways.

"I won the match," she reminded him. "I'm keeping my longbow. And I'll be commanding your archers."

She could see he wasn't pleased by the outcome. But he was a man of his word.

"Ye'll be *trainin'* my archers. Command o' them is still mine."

Morgan trudged up the stairs to his bedchamber on leaden legs. He was displeased that Jenefer had upset his wife. He'd hoped to get Alicia to reveal the name of her abductor today. Now, because of Jenefer's prodding, his wife had likely taken a step backward in her recovery.

But that wasn't the only thing niggling at his brain.

Jenefer's questions had been sensible. If he'd felt anything but relief over seeing his wife alive again, he would have asked them himself. And now they gnawed at his sense of reason like a rat at grain.

Godit the midwife may have facilitated Alicia's abduction. True enough, she'd disappeared at roughly the same time. But she couldn't have carried her out of the castle. After all, Godit had been the one to inform Morgan that Alicia hadn't survived. She'd handed him their newborn infant. And she'd never allowed Morgan to see his dead wife. Which meant...

Someone else must have spirited Alicia away. Someone strong enough to silence her protests. Someone capable of conveying a new mother—desperate to save the bairn torn from her womb—out of the keep.

So how *had* her abductor managed to infiltrate his household? And how had he slipped out again?

Why had he left the bairn behind?

Surely whoever took Alicia must have known she'd be more compliant with her child in tow. The bairn was Morgan's firstborn son and heir. The abductor could have demanded a hefty ransom for the lad's return.

But he hadn't.

There was something Morgan wasn't seeing. But until he could get the name of the villain from Alicia, there wasn't much he could do.

Reaching the top of the stairs, he pushed the door open.

"Morgan," Alicia sighed from the bed, wiping stray locks of hair from her brow with the back of her hand. She wasted no breath. "Did you get rid of her?"

Morgan couldn't admit the truth. He turned around to close the door so he wouldn't have to meet her eyes. "She won't trouble ye anymore."

"Thank God. A woman like that with a longbow. I was afraid she might harm you, Morgan. Or our son." She shuddered. "She was too wild and unpredictable."

Wild and unpredictable were two of the things Morgan loved about Jenefer. But that was in the past. Now he had to make peace with his wife.

"Ye know, 'twould make things easier," he gently ventured, "if ye took your place as Allison's ma."

The smile she gave him was brittle. He knew it was a difficult step for her to take. She'd virtually never been the bairn's mother. Snatched from him at birth, she hadn't had a chance to bond with the lad.

But he was certain, once she saw how beautiful he was with his creamy skin and bright eyes, his bow of a mouth and his sweet, gurgling voice, she'd fall instantly in love.

"All right," she agreed. "I'll try." Then she muttered, "You know I can't feed him."

"O' course."

Her lips pursed nervously. "And I haven't held an infant before."

"Neither had I," he said with a smile of encouragement. "Shall I fetch him then?"

"Not if he's squalling. I won't be able to quiet him."

He grinned. "If he were squallin', ye'd hear him."

"What if he's asleep?"

"'Twill be worth wakin' him to meet his ma," he assured her.

He could see she was fretful. But the longer she waited, the harder it would be. And considering Alicia's feelings toward Jenefer, it would be best if she took over the bairn's care as soon as possible.

When he rapped softly on the nursery door, Bethac and Feiyan greeted him with cheeky smiles.

"I warned you my cousin was a master archer," Feiyan gloated.

He shook his head. "Ye know very well I wouldn't have missed that last shot."

Bethac shrugged. "Maybe. Maybe not."

"Is my son awake?"

Bethac opened the door wider and glanced over her shoulder. "He is now."

From his cradle, the wee lad waved his fists wildly. Morgan approached, and the bairn looked up at him. He cooed at once, then sighed, and his open mouth formed the most charming smile.

Morgan smiled back. Alicia was going to love Allison. He just needed to unite them and let maternal instincts do their magic.

"I want to take him to his mother," he said.

To his surprise, Bethac's brow wrinkled. "Are ye sure 'tis wise?"

"She's his ma, Bethac."

"Aye. But Lady Alicia is still sufferin' from her ordeal."

Feiyan scoffed.

Morgan scowled at her. "She *wants* to meet him."

"Does she?" Bethac asked.

"O' course. Why wouldn't she?"

Bethac had no answer for that. And to be honest, he was annoyed at the maid's distinct lack of enthusiasm.

Without another word, Bethac bundled up the lad and put him in Morgan's arms. "Good luck."

All the way back to his bedchamber, the bairn babbled softly at Morgan, looking up at him in wide-eyed wonder. Morgan couldn't help but smile down at the comely lad. Suddenly he longed for a whole keep full of sons and daughters. He hoped Alicia would feel the same.

CHAPTER 52

Alicia perched on the edge of the bed, hoping she could put on a convincing show of bonding with her son.

She shuddered at the thought. She truly had no use for infants. Holding one was as appealing to her as cuddling a gigantic, writhing slug.

But she'd delayed the meeting as long as she could. She had to lay claim to the lad now, to ensure the departure of that pesky nursemaid before she could whisper any more mischief into Morgan's ear. Mischief that might stir up investigation into Alicia's story.

Morgan entered, securing the door behind him, and lifted the bundle up to show her their son. "Isn't he handsome?"

There was nothing handsome about a pale, formless blob. But she gave Morgan a quick nod of agreement. Then she extended her arms, indicating her willingness to hold the infant. Her smile felt tense, and her arms felt clumsy.

He set the bundle carefully into her arms, propping the lad's head against her shoulder and guiding her other arm beneath him for support.

Then she stared down at the lad.

And felt nothing.

Not love. Not hate. Not pity.

Only vague repulsion.

But she managed a nervous grin.

The infant stared back at her uncertainly.

As the moments stretched on, her smile grew weary.

Slowly, the lad's forehead began to crumple.

"What is he doing?" she muttered anxiously.

Morgan peered down at the child, speaking softly. "'Tis all right, wee lad. This is your ma, the lady who gave ye life. Don't be afraid."

Morgan was talking to the infant. Why was Morgan talking to the infant?

"He can't understand you, can he?"

"In his way," he replied.

She continued to hold the squirming thing, counting the moments until she could give him back. The infant's chin started to shiver. Then he started to fuss.

"I can't..." Alicia began.

"Hush now, lad," Morgan said. "Be good for your ma."

But the infant had clearly had enough. So had Alicia.

When the lad arched his back, turned red, and began to wail, she felt every hair stand on end.

"Make him stop," Alicia said to Morgan. "Can't you make him stop?"

"Jostle him a wee bit," Morgan suggested.

She didn't want to jostle him. She didn't want to hold him an instant longer.

"Nay, you take him," she said, shoving him forward.

"Ye can do it, m'lady. I know ye can."

She fought the urge to fling the screaming infant onto the floor and let Morgan clean up the mess.

Instead she whimpered, "I don't want to do it, Morgan. Can you not get Bethac to take him?"

Morgan finally gave in and rescued her from the bawling babe. But she could see he was disappointed.

That was fine. She couldn't please him in everything. Morgan should be happy she'd come back at all.

Besides, raising infants was what servants were for. The lad had a nurse to feed and change him and a maid to rock him to sleep. What more did he require?

When the lad was seven years of age, she intended to send him to a neighboring clan to foster anyway. And she'd not see him again until he was grown.

After Morgan bounced the babe in his arms for a few moments, the lad quieted. She watched him interact with the child. He murmured words an infant couldn't possibly understand. He tenderly grazed the lad's cheek with the back of his knuckle. He gazed lovingly into his son's eyes.

Jealousy struck Alicia like jagged lightning, sending scalding current through her body.

How dared Morgan show the child the affection *she* was due?

The affection she'd been deprived of for so many weeks?

The affection that ensured Morgan would always provide for her?

All at once she saw the infant for what it was.

A threat.

Originally, she'd imagined a child would forge an unbreakable bond between the two of them, safeguarding their relationship as husband and wife. But now she realized it had only created an obstacle to Morgan's attachment to her.

She'd made a tactical mistake.

Instead of dangling the promise of fatherhood before him, keeping him in a constant state of longing, she'd simply handed Morgan what he prized most.

A son to carry on his name.

And now Morgan would have no use for *her*.

Curse her shortsightedness. She'd made herself superfluous. Unnecessary. Expendable.

But she could fix her mistake. She'd fixed her mistake with Godit and Edward, after all. She could do the same with the infant.

How difficult could it be? The thing was much smaller than Godit and completely helpless. She wouldn't even need a dagger. She could just smother it. Infants died mysteriously in their sleep all the time.

"Would ye like to try again," Morgan asked hopefully, "now that he's calm?"

This time when she reached out for the child, there was genuine warmth in her smile.

"Oh aye."

Jenefer dragged the archery target out of the way and gathered up her bow and quiver with haste. But by the time she raced up the stairs and burst into the nursery, her worst fears were confirmed.

"Miles?" she asked Bethac.

Bethac nodded toward Morgan's bedchamber.

"Shite."

Jenefer closed the door behind her and set her weapons against the nursery wall. She'd hoped to arrive before that viper of a woman could get her wretched hands on the babe. But Miles was already in her clutches.

Grimacing in frustration, she ran a restless hand through her hair.

"I'm sure the bairn's safe enough," Bethac said. "He's with his da. And once Miles starts fussin', she'll likely send him away."

Jenefer hoped Bethac was right. She began pacing, chewing on her thumbnail, obsessing over what could go wrong.

She'd faced villains before. Some were mean and brutal and some devilishly clever. Some were full of vengeful spite, others irreparably broken.

But she'd seen none quite as cold-blooded as Lady Alicia.

The woman's eyes were flat and unfeeling. Her smile was forced and cool. It was as if she wore a mask over an empty shell.

The worst part was that Morgan seemed blind to it.

He was obsessed with the idea that his dead wife had miraculously returned from the grave. He thought he'd been given a second chance. He thought he could repair what had been done to his poor, innocent, damaged Alicia.

Any narrative that challenged his version of events was unwelcome.

And that willful ignorance was *his* fatal flaw.

Through the wall, Jenefer heard Miles' faint wail. She halted in her tracks, listening.

The babe continued to cry for a long while. Finally Jenefer turned to Bethac in askance. "Should I go and...?"

Bethac shook her head. "After that interrogation ye gave Lady Alicia? Nay, lass, ye're the last person she wants to see. And ye'll only vex the laird. Besides, Morgan can calm the lad when he has a mind to."

Jenefer suspected as much, despite the persistent myth that only *she* could soothe the lad. Morgan was the babe's father, after all.

As for her interrogating Lady Alicia, *someone* had to challenge the woman's improbable story. Even if Morgan was too stubborn to hear it.

Eventually, Miles' crying diminished. Soon afterward, she heard the bedchamber door close and footfalls in the passageway. Morgan was returning to the nursery.

Jenefer braced herself. She intended to confront him with the truth. Give him a piece of her mind. And force him to listen.

But when Bethac opened the door under his soft knock, Morgan looked crestfallen. His shoulders sagged. The light in his eyes was dimmed by sorrow. And all of Jenefer's bullish intentions fell by the wayside.

Bethac took the babe from him, patting Morgan on the arm. "'Twill take time, m'laird. To Mi-, Allison...she's a stranger." She added, "And not all mothers take to motherhood naturally."

He looked up once at Jenefer. A tiny, troubled crease formed between his brows. But he said nothing.

"Go on back now," Bethac said. "I'll take care o' the lad."

After he left, Jenefer took it upon herself to inspect every inch of the babe, to be sure the wicked wench hadn't pinched him or scratched him or done him any harm.

She was only slightly less worried about Morgan. He might be a mighty Highland warrior. But she saw now that his heart was as soft as clay. Easy to bruise. And easy to break.

As the afternoon hours dragged on toward evening, Jenefer grew more restless. She bit her thumbnail down to the quick. She returned again and again to the window, troubled by how quickly the sky darkened. She only picked at the generous platter of food Feiyan offered her.

Later, as she watched the moon slip between wisps of cloud, she couldn't decide what troubled her more. The thought that Alicia might plot to kill Morgan. Or that she might plot to kiss him.

CHAPTER 53

Alicia couldn't put it off forever. Sooner or later, she was going to have to return to Morgan's bed. She needed to establish, once and for all, that he belonged to her. And she needed to show him that it was she, not his son, who held the most intimate claim on Morgan.

It wouldn't be easy. She wasn't exactly in the mood for trysting. Not after the rough week she'd had, fretting over whether she'd left any evidence of her crime behind. Tangling with that conniving, loose-tongued lass. Suffering through a less than ideal reunion with her wriggling, demanding infant.

At least, in some ways, Morgan was a better lover than Edward had been. He never tore her fine silk garments with clumsy hands. He never shoved his member into her while she was sleeping. He actually made an effort to please her.

Still, for Alicia, swiving was only a means to an end. She needed leverage to bend Morgan to her will.

When Morgan returned from the nursery, she'd be prepared to acquiesce to his seductive whims. She'd be timid and apologetic, in need of his reassurance. Though it could set a dangerous precedent, she might even allow him to swive her by the light of day.

That plan was propelled forward at full speed when Morgan entered the bedchamber.

He looked brooding and uncertain. More of a mind to engage in deep conversation than tryst with her.

She couldn't have that. Doubt had already reared its ugly head with Morgan. She couldn't have him poking his nose into the past, digging into the details of what, to her mind, was dead and done.

So she schooled her features to a sort of helpless dismay and let her kirtle slip strategically off of one shoulder.

"Morgan, I'm so sorry," she murmured. "I know I've disappointed you."

"Disappointed me? What do ye mean?"

She lowered her gaze and worried the coverlet between her fingers. "I know you wanted me to bond with wee Al-..." Shite. What had he called the infant? Alfred? Alisdair? She covered her faltering with a soft sob.

He fell neatly into her trap, venturing near to give her comfort. "I know 'twill take some time."

She sniffed and nodded shyly. "At least we have each other." She gave him a sidelong glance, gauging his response.

His expression wasn't what she expected. Or what she wanted. His brow creased, not in instinctive empathy, but in concerned contemplation.

She couldn't have that. She couldn't have him *thinking* about things.

"Unless you don't want me anymore," she said softly, "now that I'm...soiled."

He looked sharply at her. "What? Never. What happened wasn't your fault. Ye aren't to blame."

That was what she needed to hear. She looked up at him with wide, watery eyes. "Oh, Morgan, what did I ever do to deserve you?"

He sat beside her on the bed. To her chagrin, he reached out and slipped her kirtle back up, covering her shoulder.

But then that was Morgan. He was a gentleman. Almost too much of a gentleman.

Maybe that was what had attracted her to Edward. Besides being strategically located to give her the lifestyle she desired, Edward had always been forceful and demanding. She didn't have to play the meek mouse with him. He took what he wanted. So did she. They understood each other perfectly.

Swiving Edward was rough, urgent, and over with in moments.

With Morgan, she'd had to learn a complicated dance. He wanted caresses and kisses, whispers and whimpers, a breathless passion that was hard for her to emulate and sustain.

So she'd created strict rules for trysting that ensured he wouldn't discover her pretense. She feigned modesty to keep him at arm's length and in the dark. She made frequent claims of illness and infirmity to keep his desires at bay. When she did relent and allow him to come to her bed, it was with carefully modulated responses that eased his hunger while maintaining her aloofness.

Considering the infrequency of their trysts, she'd been astonished to discover she was with child. But she'd never let circumstances of fate interfere with her plans. Not then. And not now.

"Alicia," Morgan breathed, taking her hand between his two, "I don't wish to hurry ye."

She resisted the urge to smirk. Sometimes she wished he *would* hurry her. The quicker a thing was begun, the quicker it would be over with.

"You're so kind. So patient," she said.

Then the conversation took a nasty twist.

"But I do need to know the name o' your abductor," he said.

Fury flared in her, though she dared not show it. This was exactly the subject she'd hoped to avoid. She stared at her lap while her mind worked furiously.

"'Twill do no good to keep it secret," he said. "The longer the wound festers, the less likely 'twill be to heal."

There wasn't an icicle's chance in hell she was going to divulge the name of her lover.

There was only one way out of this discussion. She was going to have to seduce him for all she was worth.

Morgan couldn't allow Alicia to distract him. Finding and questioning her lover was the only way he'd settle the truth of her abduction once and for all. The only way he'd discover whether she'd been snatched forcibly from his castle as she claimed or if there was more to the tale.

He wanted to believe her story. That she'd been swept away by a cruel villain. That for weeks, she'd languished in his keep. That her return had been a miracle.

But Morgan didn't believe in miracles any more than he believed in ghosts. And now that he was thinking with his brain instead of his heart, he realized her version of what had happened was full of holes.

He couldn't question Alicia. She was still too feeble. He couldn't force her to relive what had happened.

But he could damn well interrogate the English lord who'd taken her. All he needed was a name.

"Will you hold me?" Alicia murmured.

Morgan blinked. It was a curious request, coming from her. But maybe the ordeal had changed her.

He folded his arms around her, tucking her against his chest. For once, she didn't stiffen. Despite the daylight filtering through the window, she nestled against him in perfect trust.

"I feel so safe when I'm with you, Morgan." She placed her palm over his heart. "So loved."

He curled his fingers around her hand. Something *had* altered Alicia's nature. She'd always cherished him in her own way. But now she seemed particularly thankful for his affection, welcoming his touch in a way she never had before.

He should have been relieved, grateful.

Instead, he felt guarded.

When her free hand slithered up his throat, lodging in the curls at the nape of his neck, his suspicions increased.

This aggressive woman was intriguing. But she was not the Alicia he'd married.

"'Tis been such a long time," she breathed. "I've missed you."

There was no mistaking her meaning. He replied with caution. "I've missed ye as well."

She raised her face to his. "Would you... Will you..." She blushed and blurted out, "Take me, Morgan."

"Here? Now?"

"Aye," she sighed.

His nostrils flared. Alicia had never made such a request. Not once.

He couldn't help but be moved. But he resisted his instinct to swoop down on her trembling lips, to kiss her in answer.

No matter how much he wanted this reunion—needed it to heal their marriage—he needed the truth more.

"'Tis my dearest desire," he said. "But I can't find peace until I have your villain's name."

In answer, she traced his ear with her fingertip. "I don't want to think about him, Morgan. I only want to think about you."

Her delicate touch sent a shiver of longing through him. But he refused to be diverted from his purpose. He captured that hand as well and clasped both between his, brushing her knuckles with his lips.

"And I only want to think o' ye, Alicia," he said. "But I can't stop dwellin' on what he did to ye. If I can only have his name, 'twill purge him from my mind."

A peevish glower flashed across her brow, so quickly he might have imagined it, before she spoke. "I've already purged him from mine. All I've been thinking about for weeks," she said, her eyes filming over with lust, "is returning to you, my beloved Morgan."

He couldn't deny that he was moved by her desire. He'd never seen such warmth in her gaze. And only now did he realize that was all he'd ever wanted from his wife. The knowledge that she wanted *him.*

As he stared down at her in wonder, she lowered her gaze to his mouth and wet her lips with the tip of her tongue.

Only a will of iron kept him from surrendering to her seduction.

Still, his voice cracked as he repeated his demand. "His name."

This time, unmistakable ire hardened her gaze. Her lips tightened into a thin line. She moderated her irritation, giving him an offended pout.

"If I tell you his name, will you let it go?" she pleaded. "Will you make love to me so I can forget him?"

"Aye."

"Very well." She pursed her lips and muttered, "Lionel. Lord Lionel."

Oddly, hearing a name attached to what had happened to Alicia made her abuse seem far more real. No matter the circumstances of her abduction, he now knew that the bruises on her face, the scratches on her neck had been

BRIDE OF FIRE

caused by a living, breathing brute by the name of... "Lionel what?"

She shook her head. "I don't know."

Morgan narrowed his eyes. He found that hard to believe. She'd been in his keep for three months. Had no one addressed the lord by his surname in all that time?

Alicia leaned in toward him again, resting her cheek against his chest and extricating her hands from his grip.

"Now can we make love?"

She let one hand drift up to caress his jaw. The other she placed brazenly upon his thigh, letting her thumb graze perilously close to the beast quickening in his trews.

He had the name now. At least half of it. He was sure he could find the culprit with that.

For now, he'd yield to her temptation.

After all, Alicia was his wife. He had every right to swive her. And now he had her invitation.

After weeks of guilt and longing, he was finally getting the absolution he needed. And for the first time, at her request and by the light of day, he was going to make love to his wife without regret.

Half an hour later, he sighed as he rolled off of her in shame.

She didn't seem to mind that he hadn't been able to fulfill their tryst. With a soft, sleepy murmur, she turned away to doze.

But he was mortified. Never in his life had his body betrayed him so completely.

It wasn't Alicia's fault. She'd been open and willing. Letting him feast his eyes on her slender, pale body. Allowing him to cup the small swell of her breasts. Encouraging his kisses.

Finally, clasping him in her cool hand, she'd guided him to the crevice between her legs.

Their coupling had been brief and unsatisfying.

After a few dozen thrusts, his interest flagged. Unfortunately, that wasn't all that flagged.

But what caused him to shrink wasn't Alicia's forwardness. Or knowing her abductor's name. It wasn't that he was out of practice. Or drunk. Or weary.

What caused him to wither was guilt over the intoxicating lass in the chamber next door.

All he could think about was Jenefer's fiery nature and fierce body, her honest, innocent, unfettered desire. And, curse the lass, that memory was ruining him for any other woman.

Even his own wife.

CҺAPϹƬЕR 54

It was well past dawn on the archery field when William struck his first bull's-eye of the day under Jenefer's guidance.

He grinned at the cheering onlookers while the other five archers grumbled.

"All it takes is practice," Jenefer told them as William loped toward the target to retrieve his arrows. "Soon you'll all be hitting bull's-eyes."

They'd been practicing for the good part of the morning. After a night of troubling dreams involving Lady Alicia, Jenefer had risen from her bed at first light, snatched up her weapon, and lit out alone for the archery field.

Shooting always relieved her anxious brain. Each successful launch of an arrow restored her sense of control. Centering her mind—on her form, her bow, the wind, the target—kept her thoughts from straying. There was nothing as satisfying as the thunk of an arrow lodging in the straw. Sending a shaft spiraling into the bull's-eye felt like a small victory.

She'd hit three bull's-eyes when a group of curious onlookers began to gather. William had spotted her and quickly collected his fellow archers so they could watch what he claimed was "a master at work."

But Jenefer had quickly tired of being a spectacle. She'd invited the archers to the field to begin giving them instruction. Now that she knew it was unlikely Morgan's men would be fighting against her uncle's forces, there was no reason not to mold them into the finest archers possible. After only a few hours, she could see improvement.

"That's enough for today," she decided. If they practiced too long, their arms would be useless on the morrow.

But that wasn't the only reason she wanted to leave the field.

The nightmares disturbing her slumber all night had centered on Lady Alicia and the harm she might do to Morgan. But she was more worried about Miles, who was small and helpless. She knew Bethac would protect the child with her life. And Feiyan could fend off an attacker. But neither of them could keep the lady from demanding that her own son be brought to her. And Jenefer feared what a neglectful mother might do with an unwanted child.

As the men collected their weapons, she slung her bow and quiver over her shoulder and made haste toward the nursery.

She could hear Miles' wails as she climbed the steps. But they weren't coming from the nursery. Her heart dropped. The babe was in Morgan's bedchamber.

Trying to stay calm, she lifted her hand to knock.

Then she hesitated at the door. What if Morgan was inside? She couldn't stomach seeing the reunited couple in bed together, with their beautiful child nestled intimately between them.

But something in Miles' voice sounded wrong. Not his usual plaintive wailing, his cries were full of distress, desperate screams that were suddenly muffled, as if someone had...had smothered them.

Her thoughts went wild with panic. Privacy be damned! She burst in the door.

Lady Alicia was bent over the bed with one knee on the pallet. She'd seized the coverlet in both fists and was pressing it down over the squirming bulge stop the bedsheets. She had a horrific expression on her face. An expression of cold, calculated drive. Without compassion. And utterly soulless.

For an instant, Jenefer was too shocked to move.

In the next instant, though Alicia never shifted her gaze from the bed, her features were transformed as if by magic. Her icy mask suddenly cracked into a fretful pout, and her eyes widened in childlike concern. Even the determined pressure of her hands became tender caresses as she slipped the coverlet down from Miles' red face.

"Morgan, I'm so glad y—"

"What are you doing?" Jenefer demanded, jarred from her daze.

Once Alicia realized it wasn't Morgan at the door, her innocent manner quickly turned to hostility. She picked up Miles and gripped him to her chest, almost like a shield. He arched his back and writhed in her arms.

"What are you doing here?" she snapped. "You're supposed to be gone."

Jenefer paid no heed to Alicia's words. She was more concerned about the babe's welfare and getting him out of the woman's grasp. What Jenefer had seen might have been her imagination, but she didn't think so. Miles' mother had been trying to suffocate him.

Jenefer's first urge was to attack, to forcibly snatch Miles away. But she was unnerved by the crazed unpredictability in Alicia's eyes, a look that said she wouldn't hesitate to toss the babe out the window before surrendering him to Jenefer.

So Jenefer subdued her warrior instincts and fought her impulse to fight, even though Miles' distraught wails were tearing at her heart. Instead she took a cautious step inside the room.

"Why don't you let me calm him?" she asked.

"Get out!" Alicia barked.

Startled, Miles screamed.

Jenefer gulped. Fear sent a cold shiver through her blood. She dared not leave the babe alone with this madwoman.

She tried reasoning with her. "Once he's quiet, we can talk," she said, managing a sympathetic smile. "Who can think while Miles is wailing like that?"

"Miles?" Alicia scowled.

Jenefer silently cursed herself for her slip. "Allison. I meant Allison."

Alicia squeezed the squealing babe closer to her. His arms waved in helpless protest. She was apparently deaf to his cries.

"You stay away from him," Alicia sneered. "And stay away from Morgan. I won't have you sharing your nasty lies with him."

Jenefer flushed. If Alicia knew what else they had shared, she'd be livid.

But that was in the past. Now Jenefer's only concern was keeping his son safe.

Alicia narrowed her eyes to glittering slits. "I know what you're trying to do. You're trying to steal the infant from me."

"Nay, I only—"

"You think by laying claim to the infant, you can have his father."

"'Tisn't true."

"You think if Morgan believes your filthy lies," Alicia bit out, "you can get rid of me and take my place."

Her grip tightened around Miles' chest as she spoke. Jenefer could hear him struggling, coughing between his wails, and she knew she was going to have to take action, regardless of the risk.

Alicia gave her an ugly, twisted grimace of a smile. "I'll see the babe dead before I let you get your conniving hands on him."

Jenefer's heart plunged into the pit of her stomach.

Left with no other choice, she was forced to resort to her warrior ways. She whipped an arrow from her quiver.

CHAPTER 55

Nothing could have prepared Morgan for the standoff he stumbled onto when he followed his son's cries, up the steps to his bedchamber.

His wife was clutching their screaming child tightly in her arms. Her eyes were wild and glittering.

The babe's face was ruddy. His fists shook in desperation. His anguished sobs were interspersed with sputtering as he gasped for breath.

As for Jenefer... She wasn't trying to comfort the child. To his horror, she had a loaded bow aimed at Alicia's throat.

His first mad thought was that his hostage had outwitted him. She might not threaten an innocent babe to gain her release. But she may have no such qualms about intimidating Alicia.

It wouldn't work, of course. One stride would put him within reach of Jenefer. One blow of his hand would disarm her.

But in the blink of an eye, Alicia made him see the situation in a completely different light.

"Morgan!" she screamed, her face dissolving into terror. "Help me!"

She pointed a trembling finger of accusation toward Jenefer, who was already lowering her bow.

"She tried to harm our son!" Alicia cried. "I-I found her in our bedchamber. Sh-sh-she was smothering him! She meant to kill him!"

"What?" Jenefer said, incredulous.

Alicia turned on her in dismay. "How could you do such a thing? To an innocent child?"

Jenefer's jaw dropped. Her weapon hung limp from her hands.

"Morgan!" Alicia barked. "You must send her away! This instant!"

Morgan narrowed his gaze at his wife. He felt like a film had been lifted from his eyes. He seemed to be seeing her clearly for the first time.

Alicia was mistaken. There was no way Jenefer had tried to kill his son. The lass had had plenty of opportunity to do so if she so desired while he was asleep in the nursery.

Besides, Jenefer loved the lad. She might not have intended to bond with him, but she had. She'd vowed no harm would come to him. And she'd proved to be a woman of her word.

Alicia, on the other hand, filled him with doubt. She made him question her loyalty.

"Morgan!" she screeched. "You can't let her near our child again! He's our son! Our firstborn!"

He held up his hand. "Alicia—"

"She's right," Jenefer answered before he could reply. "He should be in his parents' care. Not mine." Despite the strength of her voice, he could see the hurt plea in her wet eyes. "But you must believe me. I'd never do anything to hurt the wee lad."

He *did* believe her. In fact, he believed her over the woman he'd been wed to for two years.

Alicia must have seen the change in his eyes. She gasped. "She's lying! I saw her myself."

Jenefer had no answer. She only entreated him with her gaze to trust her.

Morgan decided to give Alicia one last chance, the benefit of the doubt. "Perhaps ye only *thought* she was tryin' to harm him. Perhaps she was tryin' to give him comfort."

Alicia hissed, "I know what I saw." She tempered her tone, and her voice quavered as she begged him, "Please, Morgan. I don't want her coming near our precious child. Ever again."

"I won't," Jenefer choked out. "I won't come near him. I swear. But Morgan, don't leave him alone with her. Please."

The sincere concern in her dewy eyes troubled him.

"How dare you!" Alicia shouted at her. "What are you insinuating?"

"I'm leaving," Jenefer murmured, making a hasty exit before she could burst into tears.

"Come, Alicia," Morgan said when she had gone. "Let me see if I can quiet him." He was eager to take his son out of the hands of the woman who had suddenly become a stranger to him.

Alicia readily surrendered the child. Too readily.

The tension left Morgan as he cradled his traumatized son in his arms. He murmured reassurances to the wee lad, soothing him with gentle touches.

"You don't believe that wench, do you?" Alicia asked. "Because she's only trying to steal you from me, Morgan."

"Steal me?" He shook his head. "And why would she do that, Alicia?"

"Why else?" she said, looking at him as if he were daft. "For your wealth, your position."

Under his tender care, the bairn's sobs softened. With a relieved shudder, the lad finally relaxed against his chest.

"Wealth and position." He lifted a brow at Alicia. "Is that why *ye* pursued me?"

"What?" She seemed surprised at the question. "Me? How could you think such a thing?"

A day ago, he wouldn't have imagined it. Now it seemed a painfully obvious assumption. What didn't make sense is why she had left.

"You know I don't mean us," she continued. "I mean that vile, wicked, scheming maidservant."

"The one who thinks she can steal me by killin' my son?"

She looked rattled, but only for a moment. She turned toward the window. "It seems mad, I know. But who knows how her depraved mind works?"

He'd been asking himself that very question about Alicia. Now that he had his son safely in his arms, he could press her for answers.

"What happened that day, Alicia?" he asked. "The day ye disappeared?"

Her voice was brittle. "Are *you* doubting me now?"

"Tell me the truth."

Even now, he wanted to believe the best of her. He could even find it in his heart to forgive her if she'd be honest with him. Perhaps the responsibility of a child had frightened her. Perhaps she'd run away out of fear. Perhaps she'd invented this abductor, "Lionel," because she was ashamed of the truth.

"I've told you the truth," she insisted. "I was taken by an English lord and held prisoner at his keep."

"Lionel?"

"Aye."

"And if I send someone to seek out this Lord Lionel?"

She shrugged. "You can do as you please."

"He's not real, is he?"

"Of course he's real!" Her expression dissolved into tears of anguish. "You don't believe me. How can you not believe me? I was abducted. I was held at an English keep. I escaped and came here. And that witch—the one who's put all these ideas into your head—was trying to kill our son!"

That last part he didn't believe for an instant. And if Alicia had lied about that, she'd probably lied about everything else.

"She'd never do that," he said.

There was an edge to her voice as she said, "I know what I saw, Morgan."

"What you *think* you saw. But what about the things one *doesn't* see? The things we only *assume* to be true?"

"I don't know what you mean."

He gazed down at his weary son, who was drifting off to sleep. He didn't think he'd ever loved anything as much as he loved this wee bairn. To think the lad's own mother might have abandoned him...

"I've been thinkin' lately about how easy 'tis to make a man believe a thing when his heart is vulnerable."

Misunderstanding him, she whipped around. There was a satisfied glimmer in her eyes. "Exactly! Which is what that wench has been doing. She's been poisoning your mind."

The blood curdled in his veins. He couldn't bear to listen to more lies falling from Alicia's lips. He couldn't believe he'd ever been fooled by her wide-eyed, scheming ways.

"That day ye disappeared," he mused, "I believed ye were dead. But I ne'er saw your body. And I believed ye were in that wooden box lowered into the grave, though I ne'er saw the proof."

"Godit was clever. She—"

"But what I keep askin' myself is how this Lionel managed to steal ye away while Godit was swaddlin' my bairn and deliverin' the bad news to me. He couldn't have managed it alone—infiltratin' the castle defenses, stealin' ye from the childbed, carryin' ye off while ye were carryin' on and fightin' for your life."

He saw her visibly gulp.

CHAPTER 56

Alicia seldom panicked. She had a quick answer for everything. And she could switch from innocent angel to avenging devil and back in the blink of an eye.

But she felt the walls rapidly closing in. Morgan was getting too close to the truth. And like a stubborn hound, he wouldn't let go of the bone between his teeth, the bone that cursed wench had handed him.

Morgan continued to pressure her. "So I'm guessin' Lionel had help. How many were there? One? Two? Three extra men?"

She licked her lips. "I...I don't remember."

He nodded, but she could see the doubt in his eyes.

She pressed her fingers to her brow. "I think...I think I may have fainted."

"But when ye roused... I mean, it must have taken a fortnight to travel all that way."

Damn Morgan! His dogged persistence sent a bolt of rage through her. He'd backed her into a corner. Even her usual attempts to elicit protectiveness in him weren't working.

But like a cornered cat, her best defense was a strong offense. It was time to unsheathe her claws and bare her teeth.

"I don't remember, Morgan!" she burst out tearfully. "And 'tis cruel of you to make me try. That wretched woman has turned you against me. Your own wife. The mother of your child. How could you?"

To her horror, not a muscle moved in Morgan's face. For the first time in her life, he was completely indifferent to her suffering. And that frightened her more than she cared to admit.

She wanted this life back. She wanted to be Morgan's wife again. She wanted the prestige. And the wealth. And the power.

But if she couldn't rely on his compassion and his protection, there was a chance she could get tangled in the web of her lies. And that meant there was a chance Morgan would uncover her two murders, despite her giving him a false name.

It was all that bloody wench's fault.

She turned her rage on Morgan. "You told me you'd sent that witch away. You lied to me."

Morgan's brows collided. "I said I'd taken care of it." Then his mouth twisted. "But I can't send her away."

She blinked. "What? Why?"

"'Tis a matter of honor," he said. "I vowed to keep her here, under my protection."

Her eyes flattened. Honor. Of course. It was his stupid honor that made Morgan so predictable. And so easy to play.

"And you won't break that vow? Even for me?"

She already knew the answer.

"I cannot."

"Cannot?" she asked. "Or will not?"

"Ye know they're the same thing."

Alicia felt her stomach coil as her best laid plans went rapidly awry. Nonetheless, she made one final, desperate effort to cling to what she had. Crossing her arms in challenge and proudly raising her chin, she delivered an ultimatum. "'Tis either her or me."

Morgan's face turned to stone. "Don't do this, Alicia."

She'd finally found a foothold. And she'd be damned if she was going to budge.

Morgan moved one hand up to hold the back of the infant's head. "If ye leave, I won't let ye take the bairn."

She'd never wanted the child in the first place. But she was sure Morgan was only bluffing. Trying to manipulate her. "Her. Or me."

"Ye'd leave your own child?"

"You're giving me no choice."

How Morgan could expect her to have pity on him when he wasn't willing to send away one pesky maidservant on her behalf was astonishing.

"I...we...lost ye once already," he said. The memory of suffering shadowed his eyes.

"'Tis your decision," she repeated with growing confidence. "The maidservant or me."

He stared at her a long while, weighing the consequences. His delay angered her. But Morgan was a practical man. She had no doubt he'd ultimately see reason. He had to realize how foolish it would appear to choose a common servant over his own wife, who'd been miraculously returned to him from the dead.

Finally, he nodded and let out a long sigh of surrender.

The melancholy in his eyes was like a balm for her wounded pride. She felt the pleasure of triumph, knowing she'd won at last.

Then he spoke.

"Go then, if ye must."

Alicia's look of utter shock gave Morgan no pleasure.

He didn't need her confession to figure out what had happened. Her guilt was obvious from the alarm in her eyes.

She hadn't been taken from her childbed by Lord Lionel.

She'd run away to him. Willingly.

It had been no secret that Alicia hated living in his home. The English lord must have promised her wealth, position, *and* an escape from the Highlands.

But even knowing she'd abandoned him to run off with her lover, he'd held out hope that she'd somehow be repentant. If not for his sake, at least for the sake of their child.

Unfortunately, she was not. Whatever shred of remorse might have slipped into her gaze was obliterated by fury. Her face, contorted by hatred, disfigured by rage, was that of a stranger.

She spat vile curses at him, words he'd never heard her utter before. Then, with a scream of outrage, she bolted past him, shoving him aside, and threw open the door to flee.

The slam of the door shook the whole keep and startled a whimper from Allison.

Miles, he corrected. He murmured reassurances against the bairn's soft, warm head. From now on, he'd call his son Miles.

He could stop Alicia, he thought. He could summon the guards to prevent her from leaving.

But he knew where she was going.

She was returning to her lover.

A day ago, Morgan had sent young Danald as a scout to locate Lord Lionel's keep. The lad would report back soon. Should he need to find Alicia, Morgan would know where to look.

At the moment, however, he had no desire to do so.

By right, he could punish her for her sins—adultery and desertion.

But he had no will to hurt the mother of his child. His thirst for justice was tempered by a deep melancholy for his poor abandoned son.

Self-preservation propelled Alicia forward as she crossed the courtyard. She didn't know if Morgan would have her stopped. But she didn't dare take the chance he might wish to seek vengeance for her crimes.

She couldn't afford to linger. She had to go—now—before things got any worse.

Before that evil wench could convince Morgan that she'd tried to kill their son.

Before he could find out about what she'd done to Edward.

Even if it meant leaving without a single possession to her name and not a morsel in her satchel.

Somehow she'd survive. She always had.

Scurrying past the workshops lining the walls, she ignored the guards at the gate who saluted her.

No one ordered her to halt.

Only when she slipped safely out the gate and into the thick of the woods was she able to consider her next move.

As she wended her way with breathless haste down the forest path, what finally came to her was as simple as it was devilishly clever.

There was no reason to fear Edward anymore, she realized. No one who knew the truth was alive. She'd been careful to leave behind no clues. So she'd march boldly up to the gates of Lord Edward's keep and give them a story they'd not only believe, but be *eager* to embrace.

Her lips curved into a smile as she congratulated herself on her brilliance.

As always, things had turned out for the best. Tossed by the cruel winds of fate, Alicia had once again managed to land on her feet.

CHAPTER 57

"Shall I stop her?" Jenefer called over her shoulder. As Lady Alicia stormed out of the gates toward the woods, Jenefer watched from the nursery window, her arrow trained on the fleeing woman. Even at this distance, she could kill the wench with one well-placed arrow or at least shoot a shaft into her arse to send her staggering to the ground.

"Nay! Don't shoot her," Bethac answered. "Morgan would ne'er forgive ye."

Beside her, Feiyan squinted down at Alicia. "Thank God, she doesn't have Miles."

"Where will she go?" Jenefer asked Bethac, keeping Alicia in her sights.

Feiyan smirked in disgust. "Probably to her lover."

"She won't be back," Bethac predicted.

Finally, as Alicia strode out of range, Jenefer lowered her bow. Though her aim had been steady enough, her hands were now shaking.

She'd never killed anyone. Never had to. But after witnessing the horror of what Alicia had tried to do—smothering poor wee Miles—she would have been glad to sink a shaft into the woman's black heart.

Earlier, the three of them, crowded together at the window ledge of the nursery, had been able to hear much of what transpired in Morgan's bedchamber. Still, Alicia's vile shrieking before she charged out of the room had sent a ripple of shock through all of them, making them recoil from the window.

For an agonizing space of time, until she'd seen Lady Alicia fleeing the keep, Jenefer had feared the worst—that the madwoman might have taken Miles with her.

"Poor Morgan," Bethac said, clucking her tongue. "He's had to lose his wife twice now."

Jenefer propped her bow against the wall and headed for the door. She needed to go to Morgan. To convince him that Lady Alicia's desertion was for the best. And to assure herself that Miles was safe and unharmed.

"Nay, lass," Bethac said, halting her with a hand on her forearm. "'Tisn't the time. He needs to work things out for himself."

A few days ago, Jenefer would have disregarded the maid's advice. Accustomed to acting on impulse, when she wanted to do a thing, she did it. She never let reason delay immediate action.

But she'd begun to learn the wisdom of patience and the power of using persuasion rather than force. Though she hated to admit it, her aunt Deirdre might be right about using honey instead of vinegar to get one's way.

So with a submissive sigh, she nodded in agreement and sank onto the edge of the bed.

"Morgan will come round," Bethac confided. "Ye'll see. And he'll realize the answer to his woes is standin' right in front o' him."

Jenefer looked up sharply. Was that approval in Bethac's eyes? Was it possible she not only forgave, but condoned what had happened between her and Morgan?

It was almost too much to wish for. At the moment, she only prayed the maidservant was right, that Alicia would never return.

Combat had always served to help Morgan work out his frustrations and center his mind. So when Cicilia came to feed Miles, he snatched up his claymore and headed to the practice field. With each slash of his sword, he felt his despair dwindle and his resolve return.

He'd already lost Alicia once, so his grief was spent. All he felt now was disappointment and emptiness.

Yet he wouldn't take her back for the world.

She'd betrayed him. She'd abandoned her newborn. And she'd revealed herself to be a monster.

What he would do now, he didn't know. He was still wed to Lady Alicia. And the only way he could remedy that was to formally accuse her of her crimes. For Miles' sake, he didn't want to do that.

But the lad needed a mother. And, despite believing at one time that he'd never love again, Morgan couldn't imagine living without a woman to share his life, warm his bed, and fill his heart.

He was in the midst of crossing swords with the Campbell brothers when young Danald came tearing across the practice field.

"My laird!" the lad cried breathlessly. "I bring news!"

Morgan lowered his claymore. "What is it?"

"I did as ye asked," he said. "I inquired at three o' the Scots keeps along the border. No one had heard of an English lord named Lionel."

Morgan nodded. As he suspected, Alicia had lied about her lover's name.

"But 'tis the oddest thing!" Danald's eyes were wide with excitement. "A few days ago, Lord Edward o' Firthgate was murdered in his sleep," the lad said, adding in a whisper, "along with his mistress, a lass by the name o' Godit."

The breath deserted Morgan in an icy rush. A cold blade of dread stabbed him through the gut. He braced himself on his claymore.

"M'laird?" Danald asked in concern. "Are ye all right?"

"Aye," he managed to croak out. "Thank ye, lad."

But he was not all right. His world was careening like a runaway cart.

Everything he'd believed in was a lie. His faith was in ruins. His trust was destroyed.

Was it possible?

Could the meek, mild lass he'd married be a cold-blooded killer?

The prospect was too painful to consider. And so he thought of a dozen other explanations.

Perhaps it wasn't the same Godit.

Or if it was, perhaps the murders had occurred after Alicia left.

Maybe Alicia had witnessed the murders and fled in fear.

But no matter how he tried to reason away the evidence staring him in the face, he couldn't stop thinking about the last he'd seen of Alicia. Her crazed eyes. Her twisted mouth. The vile oaths she'd screamed at him.

She must have done it. She must have killed her lover and her midwife, and then come to Morgan for safe haven.

He trembled as he thought about his precious wee son. How he'd left him alone with her. How, if not for Jenefer's warning, he might have never suspected what evil lurked beneath Alicia's guileless face.

Gossip traveled quickly through Morgan's clan. Before nightfall, Jenefer had heard the news from Bethac, who'd heard it from William, who'd overheard Danald tell it to Morgan. Alicia's English abductor and her midwife had been murdered.

Though there was no proof, Jenefer immediately assumed Alicia had done the deed. She would never forget the horrid, emotionless cast of Alicia's face as she tried to smother Miles. Only someone that indifferent and unfeeling could kill a man in his sleep.

She wished now she *had* shot the vicious wench when she had the opportunity. While she lived, the chance remained that Lady Alicia would return to do harm to Morgan and Miles.

As Jenefer lay in the nursery bed with Feiyan snoring beside her, it sent a chill through her to think that Miles had been in the clutches of a murderer. The horrifying thought kept her awake.

Suddenly, she craved the comfort of holding the babe in her arms.

She slipped out from under the coverlet, crept past Bethac and Cicilia, who were sleeping on pallets on the floor, and leaned over Miles' cradle. Gently lifting him against her breast, she carried him back to the bed. There, she stretched out on the bed, enfolding him in protective arms and letting her lips graze the top of his warm, downy head.

She felt more at peace now, holding him safely in her embrace. And yet a mix of unexpected emotions washed over her, squeezing tears from her eyes.

Deep love and deeper sorrow.

Sorrow for what would never be.

Though Alicia had fled, she was still Morgan's wife, still Miles' mother.

It wasn't fair.

Morgan deserved more than to be wed to a woman who would betray her husband, abandon her child, and commit murder.

Damn her eyes! *Jenefer* was the one who loved them. Who deserved them. *She* would have been a faithful wife and a loving mother...if only she'd had the chance.

Amor vincit omnia was a bloody empty promise.

Love conquered nothing.

For the first time in her life, fierce and fearless Jenefer du Lac wept herself to sleep.

CHAPTER 58

organ let a whole day go by. He peered out his bedchamber window this morn at the ominous iron-colored clouds. A brutal storm was coming.

As foolish as it was, even after two days, he kept expecting his wife to return. Not that he would have taken her back. She was no longer the Alicia he'd known.

A soft knock sounded at his door.

"Come," he replied.

It was Bethac. She'd wisely held her tongue for the past two days, as had Jenefer and Feiyan. This morn, the maidservant busied herself with silently straightening the bedlinens and stoking the fire.

"She's alone out there," he said, nodding toward the forest. "And a storm is on its way."

He'd been Alicia's husband for two years. In spite of everything that had happened, looking after her was second nature to him.

"She made her choice," Bethac replied.

"She didn't even take a cloak."

When he turned to her, he saw Bethac struggling with her ire. Though his faithful old maidservant had hidden it well, she'd never approved of Alicia. He understood why now. Apparently, Bethac had better instincts than he did.

"She'll be just fine," she answered through thinned lips. "She's a sly fox, that one, always findin' a way out."

He nodded. That was probably true, considering her gift for deception.

"Besides," she added, "from what I hear, she has much more to fret about than the rain."

Secrets were hard to keep in the mac Giric clan. By now everyone had likely heard about the murders. But he supposed it was just as well. His first priority was protecting his son. In her present state, and considering what she was capable of, he dared not let Alicia come anywhere near Miles.

Bethac answered the second knock on the door.

It was Jenefer. She had Miles. The wee lad looked at home in her arms, as if he had always belonged there. The bairn, blissfully unaware of the trauma that had unfolded around him, lit up when she transferred him to Morgan.

Morgan's heart melted as he gazed into the lad's innocent, smiling face.

He glanced at Jenefer, half-expecting the warrior maid to arch her brow, crowing that she'd *told* him his wife was a liar and a cheat and a traitor.

But she didn't. Instead, her fiery eyes were softened by compassion and shared sorrow. She said not a word. She didn't need to. And her silent empathy touched him more than words could say.

When she left the room, he felt her absence. More than ever, he wanted her beside him. But now that his circumstances had changed, he was at a loss about what to do with her.

He'd told Alicia that Jenefer was under his protection. Of course, that wasn't true. He'd been holding her as leverage against attack by her clan. But that attack hadn't come, and he wasn't sure it ever would.

He could no longer keep her here on the pretext of needing her to calm Miles, for Morgan was now capable of soothing his son's tears.

The king's messengers would arrive any day now to clear up ownership of Creagor once and for all. Yet he dreaded their coming, for he was in no hurry to be rid of Jenefer.

And unless he was mistaken, she was in no hurry to leave.

As if Bethac had read his thoughts, she said, "That lass is goin' to be heartbroken to leave the two o' ye."

Morgan replied carefully, "I fear Miles is goin' to miss her."

"And ye?"

He tensed his jaw and ignored her question. The woman could be as pushy as an ox-driver.

She continued. "She could stay on as your archery master. She's done wonders for my William."

Miles chose that moment to wave his fists wildly, making Morgan chuckle.

"Ye see?" she said. "Miles agrees."

A distant rumble of thunder served as a welcome interruption. But it made him think again of Alicia, alone and defenseless against the coming storm. Not only the one the thunder predicted, but the one she'd face if she returned to the English keep.

"You have to eat something," Feiyan insisted, chewing on whatever Bethac had brought to the nursery.

But Jenefer had no appetite. Her heart was breaking.

She'd always been able to get what she wanted. Whether it was procuring a new bow, secretly competing in an archery contest, or laying claim to the holding at Creagor, she'd always found a way to achieve her ends, usually by threat or force or simple stubbornness.

For the first time, she was unable to influence her destiny.

She couldn't take Miles by force.

She couldn't make Morgan love her.

She couldn't make Alicia disappear.

"I'm going to the archery field," she decided, seizing her bow from where it was propped against the wall.

There was nothing she could do to change the course of fate. So she'd vent her frustration with the one thing she *could* control.

In spite of the moody clouds, heavy with rain, and lightning on the horizon, the practice field was crowded with knights when she arrived. To Jenefer's consternation, Morgan was there too, crossing swords with his men. Even here, it appeared she couldn't purge herself of the Highlander.

She paused beside the yard-high wattle fence that divided the fields to watch him. His aggressive blows took her breath away.

His fighting was fierce and brutal, and he wielded the heavy claymore as if it weighed nothing. His bellows as he charged forward, plunging his sword violently against his opponent's targe, sent a primal shiver through her bones.

His scowl of concentration as he cast off blade after blade with powerful swipes of his shield was as magnificent as it was intimidating, and she found her heart pounding from the thrill.

Even in this cold weather, he was dripping. His hair fell in damp locks over his brow, and his cheek was smudged where he'd wiped away sweat with a grimy gauntlet.

His was the face of a champion, brave and noble and steadfast.

A face that demanded respect and admiration.

A face Jenefer had grown to love.

Swallowing back maudlin tears, she hefted up her weapon again and strode to the archery field. Once she had a drawn bow in her hands and began hitting bull's-eyes, she was sure she'd forget all about the laird she couldn't have.

Davey Campbell advanced on Morgan, pressing him back against the wattle fence. Their blades ground together, making sparks. Morgan gave him a hard shove with his targe, and Davey retreated a step.

"Aim!" Morgan suddenly heard from the archery field. He blinked. Jenefer. Her voice was unmistakable.

In that instant of inattention, Davey almost lopped off his sword arm at the shoulder.

"Draw!" Jenefer cried.

Annoyed at himself for his slip, Morgan lunged forward with a vengeance, forcing Davey back with successive slashes of his claymore until the lad tumbled back into the dust.

"Loose!" she called out.

Out of the corner of his eye, Morgan saw a volley of arrows arc toward the target.

"Not bad," she told the archers. "But you can do better."

Realizing Davey was still lying in the dirt, Morgan dropped his targe and extended his hand to help him up.

"Good sparrin'," he mumbled, distracted by the activity in the adjoining field. "Carry on."

While his men continued to do battle, he leaned against the fence, removing his gauntlets, to watch Jenefer work.

She was a dedicated instructor. Patient. Observant. Generous with her praise, yet unforgiving of flaws. Under her direction, his men thrived, improving with each subsequent shot.

He wished he could do as Bethac suggested and keep her as his archery master.

But she was a warrior and might be a laird in her own right one day, with a husband and a clan and children of her own. She could have no interest in becoming his hireling.

Besides, he thought, as he watched her demonstrate a shot at close distance—swiftly drawing back the bowstring and firing in one direct, forceful movement—he wasn't sure he could endure living in such close quarters with the beautiful, tempting warrior lass.

His jaw clenched with frustration, and his heart ached with regret. If only things had worked out differently... If only Alicia hadn't returned from the grave...

He knew it was a wish that bordered on blasphemy. And yet he couldn't help but imagine how much better all their lives would be if she'd only stayed dead.

As if God had heard his wicked thought, a bolt of lightning streaked across the heavens, followed shortly by thunder. Rain began to pelt the earth.

His men quickly gathered their weapons and headed for the armory.

Jenefer sent the archers off with their bows and quivers, then went to collect their arrows from the target.

As the rain started to fall in earnest, everyone scattered for shelter until only he and Jenefer were left, standing in the downpour.

When she turned and saw him, her face was bleak. The fire in her eyes was dimmed by sorrow, and the rain seemed to make tears upon her cheek.

He too felt as if the raindrops made a mockery of his anguish, drenching him with wet misery to match his mood.

They continued to stare at each other, careless of the drowning deluge. A jagged bolt of light speared the black clouds, and neither of them flinched. Thunder crashed over their heads, and they stood their ground in brazen defiance.

It was as if they both knew they could be struck by lightning at any instant. Yet it was worth the risk to stand here, sharing this rare moment.

The rain increased until it pounded the sod, pinging off his plate armor and making a halo of mist around her. And still they stood, two souls lost in a maelstrom not of their own making.

They were kindred spirits, he realized, warriors, children of the storm. Born in battle. Tempered by fire. Hardened by misfortune.

They wouldn't let a mere storm defeat them. And he'd be damned if he'd let anything stand in the way of their love.

When they came together, it was in a collision as dramatic as the thunder clapping above them. Heedless of who might witness their perfidy, they dropped everything and rushed forward, meeting across the wattle fence.

He buried his face in her hair.

She seized his cotun in her fists.

When she turned her face up to his, her eyes burned with a fire that defied the drenching downpour. She lowered her gaze to his mouth and, without uttering a word, demanded he quench her thirst.

It was wrong.

He knew it was wrong.

He was married.

His loyalty belonged to another.

And yet, when Jenefer looked at him like that—as if there were no other man in the world—he could no more resist her than he could resist breathing.

With a groan of defeat, he slanted his mouth over hers, feasting on her sweet and welcoming lips.

She tasted like the storm. Wild and wet. Wave after wave of passion washed over him. And he never wanted the deluge to end.

Jenefer felt like she was drowning in Morgan's embrace. And yet she would willingly die in his arms, just to feel the desire flowing from his lips to hers.

She clutched at his clothing, willing him to come closer, to mold his body against hers, to delve deeper into her mouth with his delicious tongue.

They kissed as if they battled, straining against each other, grunting with effort, attacking, retreating, and attacking again.

Despite the storm raging within and around them, drenching their clothing and soaking their skin, a molten heat built at her very core. Warmth sparked in her heart. Smoldered through her veins. Enflamed her senses and brought her body roaring to life.

Blind and deaf, aware of only each other, they might have easily become lost in the maelstrom of their emotions.

But in the next instant, a flash lit up the sky, and a crack of thunder split them apart.

His eyes smoldered into hers as his chest heaved with fervor.

Breathless, she raised trembling fingers to her lips.

He glanced up at the sinister clouds and then reached out to clasp her by the waist, lifting her over the low wattle fence. He took her hand and loped toward the shelter of the stables, pulling her along with him.

The stables were abandoned except for two cart horses. The stable lads had likely gone into the keep, out of the storm.

In one of the empty, hay-sweet stalls, Morgan hauled her into his arms, swooping down on her mouth again. His fingers rasped down her cheek and along her throat. His knuckles collected the droplets of rain on her bosom. With a lusty growl, he slipped her kirtle off her shoulder.

"God, I want ye, Jenefer," he breathed between kisses.

"I want you as well," she said, gasping.

She threaded her fingers through his wet locks, cocking his head to twist her frantic lips across his. Her body burned with craving. Her soul ached for him.

But even as they engaged in blissful sensual combat, Jenefer warred with her conscience. Like a loyal guard, her damned honor stepped in to raise a shield against what she wanted most.

In her heart of hearts, she knew the truth. Nothing good could come of this. No matter how much she cared for Morgan, no matter how deeply he touched her, the yearning she felt was bittersweet.

She dreamed of an impossible conquest. Longed for something she could never have. Theirs was a cursed love, star-crossed and hopeless.

As long as Lady Alicia lived, Morgan belonged to her. Nothing on heaven or earth could change that.

Neither she nor Morgan were foolish enough to sacrifice their integrity, their fealty, or their honor for a moment's pleasure.

Still, resisting the Highlander was harder than defying the ocean's current. It was so much easier to float along on the thrilling wave of desire surrounding her.

But she had to stop this before it led them both to ruin.

"Nay," she rasped out, breaking free of their kiss.

Morgan's beautiful eyes were glazed with yearning. She had to look away, lest she be drawn back into his whirlpool of lust.

"Nay," she repeated, lowering her head and closing her eyes against temptation. "We mustn't."

"Why?" he murmured, stepping toward her again.

She placed a hand on his chest to stop him. "You know why."

After an interminable moment, his heaving chest sank. She glanced up then and saw his expression change from desire to disappointment. Her heart broke as she experienced the same emotions.

When his face fell and he withdrew, nodding at her with a clenched jaw and somber acceptance, she wanted to weep.

They watched in silent separation as the downpour diminished to a drizzle.

Meanwhile, Jenefer's eyes welled with their own warm rain as she thought about the future. She knew she couldn't remain at Creagor. It was sheer torture to be so close to Morgan and not to be able to touch him, to kiss him, to make love to him.

As for Miles, if she spent one more day with the babe—smelling his soft scent, snuggling his warm neck, peering down at his precious smiling face—she would die of heartbreak when she left.

First thing on the morrow, she decided, she'd steal away. She'd be violating her oath not to flee. But sometimes honor demanded difficult decisions. Better she should leave and break her knight's vows than stay and make Morgan break his marriage vows.

CHAPTER 59

Alicia shuddered from the cold and turned her face up to the roiling clouds, letting the rain pelt her bruised face. Fate must be smiling on her indeed, to create a foul storm just as she emerged from the trees that bordered Edward's castle.

When the people of Firthgate saw her stagger into the keep—as wet as a drowned rat and shivering, her face still marred by injuries—her pathetic appearance would doubtless move them to mercy.

The English would never suspect she'd been the one to slay their lord.

And when she told them her story—that she'd been snatched from the keep by savage Highlanders who'd crossed the border, that they'd murdered Edward and her midwife Godit, that they'd taken her prisoner—they would readily believe it.

She'd name her abductor.

She'd disclose his location.

And she'd tell the English that the keep where the Highlanders were staying was ill-prepared for war.

No English soldier worth his spurs could resist such a prize. She'd bring them a perfectly good excuse to attack a poorly defended Scottish holding.

In exchange, her rewards would be threefold.

She'd absolve herself of Edward's murder.

She'd punish Morgan for choosing that bloody wench over her.

And she'd earn admiration and respect from the English for her part in delivering to them a Border castle claimed by the Scots.

Once she was rid of Morgan, she'd find out who stood to inherit Edward's holding. It would be a simple matter to court a new lover, to seduce her way into the bedchamber of the new lord.

As it turned out, her plan worked even better than she expected.

The new lord was Edward's hotheaded brother, Roger. Not only was Roger enraged by Edward's death, but he was eager to avenge it. When Alicia presented him vengeance on a silver platter, he gathered his army at once to launch an assault on Creagor.

By the time they crossed the border into the Scottish woods, the rain had stopped. By the time they reached Creagor, it was dark. They made a hasty camp in the haven of the forest, planning to attack in the morning.

Alicia had insisted Roger take her along, ostensibly to be his guide and to gain him easy entrance to the castle. But as she peered through the trees at the stately keep that would soon fall to ruin, she thought about Morgan and his cold countenance when he'd refused her in favor of that conniving wench.

He wouldn't be so indifferent to her now. Not when she brought with her the new lord who'd come to seize his castle. Morgan deserved as much. And she couldn't wait to see his face. In fact, she wouldn't miss it for the world.

The castle was still slumbering when Jenefer stole from the nursery bed.

It was better to leave now.

Before Miles woke to tempt her with his irresistible grin.

Before she had to explain anything to Bethac. Or argue with Feiyan. Or face Morgan's despair.

It was bad enough she had to reckon with her own.

Even after all the tears she'd spent last night, her eyes welled as she thought about the mac Giric clan.

To think she'd imagined Highlanders to be wild savages, vicious and brutal, who ate live rodents and bartered away their own children.

Never had she met a man who cared so tenderly for his child. As for Bethac, her gruffness hid the softest heart. And the archers she'd helped to train were patient and hard-working, the best apprentices she could hope for.

She knew if she delayed to bid them farewell, she might never leave.

Tiptoeing to the window, she peered out the shutters. The stars were invisible, obscured by a blanket of cloud that hung all the way to the ground. But the night had turned from coal black to iron gray. Soon the bakers would arise to warm the ovens for bread.

She would be gone before they woke.

Just as she turned away to take her cloak from the hook on the wall, she saw a movement in the mist, between the trees. She froze, staring hard at the spot.

After a moment, when nothing changed, she decided it must have been an owl or another animal on a late night hunt.

She started to close the shutters when she saw the motion again. Withdrawing into the shadows, Jenefer watched with astonishment as a pale figure emerged from the fog.

It couldn't be.

Alicia had returned.

Jenefer's heart plummeted.

She'd been so certain the woman was gone forever.

Surely Alicia didn't believe Morgan would take her back. Surely Morgan wouldn't consider forgiving her.

Yet, as she watched Alicia creep across the frost-rimed grass toward the gates, Jenefer had her doubts.

Morgan might be big and brave and brawny. A formidable warrior with a heavy targe and a thick cotun.

But Jenefer knew his *true* fatal flaw. Inside that armor beat a heart full of honor and compassion. Morgan would sooner cut off his own hand than harm his wife and the mother of his child. No matter how much she deserved it. He wasn't so foolish as to throw caution to the winds. But his soft heart might leave him open to attack.

Someone had to watch his back.

The guards had been warned. They were not to let Alicia through the gates. But they'd surely alert Morgan of her return. And he'd go down to meet her.

Jenefer intended to be there when he did.

Miles began to stir fitfully in his sleep, as if he could sense his cruel mother was near. Before he could wake the others, Jenefer lifted him from his cradle and soothed him back to slumber against her breast.

Then, holding fast to the precious babe and peering through the crack of the nursery door, she watched for a messenger.

She didn't have to wait long before young Danald knocked on Morgan's door. But instead of following the lad downstairs, Morgan headed toward the nursery. Jenefer barely had time to retreat from the door before he came through it.

Startled to see her awake, he stopped short.

She hugged Miles close, wary of Morgan's intentions. "What are you going to do?"

"Give me my son," he replied.

"Nay."

His brows rose in surprise, then lowered. "Give him to me."

"Don't do this, Morgan."

Cicilia and Bethac, disturbed by the noise, began to stir.

"What is it ye think I'm doin'?" he asked.

"Don't give him to her," Jenefer said, clinging to the babe. "Don't give Miles to that madwoman."

From her pallet, Cicilia gasped. "Ye wouldn't give the bairn to Alicia?"

"What? Alicia?" Bethac shook the cobwebs from her head. "He's not that foolish. Ye're not that foolish, m'laird. Right?"

Morgan frowned, no doubt irritated that he had to explain himself. "Nay. I'm not *completely* witless. I'm not givin' him away. But Alicia is at the gates. And she's his mother. She deserves to say one last farewell."

The three women exchanged meaningful glances, probably thinking the same thing.

Bethac said it aloud. "I don't trust her, m'laird. Neither should ye."

"I don't," he said, "which is why I won't let her within the walls." He straightened with pride. "And I'll be the one holdin' Miles. No one will protect him like I will."

Jenefer was somewhat placated by his answer. And she couldn't help but notice he'd called his son Miles. He might think Alicia deserved to say goodbye, but he no longer considered the babe hers.

"Take your claymore," Jenefer blurted.

Morgan arched a mocking brow, doubtless considering it a ridiculous notion to arm himself against a wisp of a wench like Alicia. He reached out and spoke with gentle insistence. "Give me my son."

Plagued by misgiving, Jenefer could nonetheless think of no reasonable argument to prevent him. She reluctantly handed Miles to his father.

As soon as the door closed behind him, the worried chatter began.

Cicilia clasped a hand to her bosom. "Do ye think he'll keep Miles safe?"

Bethac patted her arm. "I know he'll try."

"But will he succeed?" Jenefer said, biting her nail.

"What are we to do?" Cicilia said, sniffling.

"There's naught we *can* do. Morgan is the bairn's father," Bethac said, struggling to her feet. "But I've got a bad feelin' about this. I don't trust Alicia."

"Alicia?" Jenefer scoffed. "I don't trust Morgan."

Cicilia began wringing her hands.

Bethac shook her head. "That devil woman has ways o' steerin' Morgan," she said, "makin' him feel he's done somethin' wrong."

Jenefer nodded. "And if she does that...if she makes him think Miles needs to be with his mother..."

"Do ye think he might give him o'er to her?" Bethac clapped a hand to her bosom.

A wail of woe escaped from behind Cicilia's hands.

Jenefer scowled at the lump in the bed that was Feiyan. How her cousin could manage to sleep through the commotion, she didn't know. But Jenefer had heard enough.

"I'm not going to let that happen," she promised.

She shouldered her quiver and plucked up her bow.

"What will ye do?" Bethac asked.

"Whatever I need to."

"Wait!" Bethac interjected, seizing Jenefer's arm. "Whate'er ye do, lass, don't harm her. Morgan will ne'er forgive ye."

Jenefer nodded. She realized that. But Miles' safety was more important than Morgan's forgiveness.

She climbed to the top of the castle wall walk where she could keep an eye—and an arrow—trained on the treacherous woman.

True to his word, Morgan didn't let Alicia into the keep. He motioned his approval to the guard at the palisade gates and met her just outside the wall.

At first, they appeared to be having a civil discussion. Morgan held Miles securely in his arms. Alicia's head was bowed in a semblance of remorse.

Then she dramatically burst into tears, burying her face in her hands.

Morgan took a step forward, extending one hand to her.

She suddenly clutched his hand in both of her own and sank to her knees, like an urchin begging for bread.

"Shite!" Jenefer spat, knowing Morgan was about to be sucked into the whirlpool of pity Alicia had created.

When Alicia stretched her hand toward Miles, Jenefer tightened her grip on the bow.

"Oh nay, you don't," she muttered.

Before Morgan could surrender the babe for whatever it was Alicia had pleaded for—a last embrace, a final kiss, a fond farewell—Jenefer sent a shaft spiraling into the ground between them.

To her satisfaction, they both visibly started.

"Back away, wench!" she called down. "Or my next arrow will find your deceiving heart!"

Alicia came to her feet then. But she didn't recoil in fear or enlist Morgan's sympathy or make a desperate grab for her babe. Instead, she gave Jenefer an icy glare and then turned toward the palisade gates.

Jenefer followed the woman's gaze through the swirling gray haze. And her eyes widened in horror.

Alicia hadn't come alone. Dozens of soldiers began pouring through the gates, like ants boiling out of a nest.

CHAPTER 60

Morgan didn't notice the soldiers at first. Clutching Miles protectively to his chest, he was too busy glaring up at the meddlesome lass atop the wall.

Damn the wench! That arrow had come far too close. What if it had gone astray? Her gesture had been reckless and unnecessary. Hadn't he told Jenefer he wouldn't let his wife have Miles?

"Run!" Jenefer suddenly screamed at him.

He scowled. What was she carrying on about now?

"Run, damn you!"

He scowled and stood his ground. Was she giving him orders?

Only when he turned back toward Alicia did he finally see the hostile army charging toward them through the fog. Jenefer must have been ordering them to attack.

His first thought was for his wife. He couldn't let harm come to her. Lunging forward, he seized her around the waist. Ignoring her protests, he hefted her up in his free arm. He lumbered through the inner doors, shouting at the guards to bolt them behind him.

The guards managed to seal the entrance with only moments to spare, before the horde could force its way in. Even so, there was a loud rumbling as they crashed against the wooden doors.

He set Alicia down and turned to her in concern.

"Are ye all right?"

She gave him a cautious nod.

It appeared the army of Rivenloch had come at last.

With no time to waste, he began calling out orders.

"Davey!"

The eldest Campbell was already emerging from the armory. He was only half-dressed, but his claymore was firmly in his grip.

"Gather the men," he commanded, "and arm heavily."

"Aye, m'laird."

"John! We'll need a cart to reinforce the doors," Morgan ordered. "William, post archers at the four towers."

"Aye, m'laird."

"And William..."

"Aye?"

"No arrows are to be released except on my orders."

William's face fell in disappointment, but he nodded, "Aye, m'laird."

If there was to be any hope of peace, Morgan needed to make sure there were as few casualties as possible, something Jenefer apparently hadn't considered when she'd given the order to Rivenloch to charge.

It was tempting at that moment to hand Miles off to his mother. The lad was beginning to fuss. Things were about to get chaotic. Morgan needed his full concentration to defend the keep. And a bairn had no place in the midst of a siege.

But at that moment, Jenefer came tearing across the grass toward him. Her bow was in her grip, and her quiver of arrows bounced against her back.

"Nay!" she yelled, as if she'd read his thoughts. "Give Miles to me!"

He looked daggers at her. Give his heir to Jenefer? Was she jesting?

The lass may have been loyal and devoted to Miles. She may have soothed the bairn's fears and stopped his tears.

But this was war. That was her clan out there. There was no telling what she might do to salvage the castle and save her people. He'd be a fool to hand over his heir.

Instead, he turned toward young Danald, who had just arrived in the courtyard and was still tying up his trews. "Danald, lad, take my son. Gather the women and children in the great hall. Keep them safe."

The lad straightened with pride. "Aye, m'laird."

"Nay!" Mid-stride, Jenefer drew her bow, aiming at Danald.

The lad's eyes widened as she rapidly closed the distance.

Morgan felt his heart drop to the pit of his stomach.

God's eyes! Was the lass going to shoot Danald? Was she so intent on taking custody of his son that she'd kill anyone who got in her way?

Desperate to save Miles, Morgan quickly stepped between the archer and her target. With trembling hands, he placed the bairn in Danald's arms. "Go!"

Then he wheeled back around to deal with Jenefer.

Jenefer watched in dismay as Morgan put his precious son into the hands of a lad who couldn't even tie his trews properly.

What was he thinking?

It was bad enough that Morgan had dragged his murderous wife into the courtyard. But now he was leaving his sole heir under the protection of a beardless boy?

Her arrow was still trained on the lad. But it was an idle threat. She dared not shoot him now, not while he had Miles in his arms.

Focused on the retreating lad, she was stunned when Morgan suddenly knocked her bow aside with a powerful sweep of his arm.

But it was nothing to the shock she felt when the Highlander seized her by the throat in his steely grip.

Stunned by the fierce rage in his eyes, she dropped her bow.

Then he lifted her up by the throat, leaving her feet to dangle. The quiver fell from her shoulder, scattering her arrows.

He wasn't quite choking her. But she couldn't exactly speak. One hard squeeze of his fingers, and he'd throttle the life out of her. And by the fury in his gaze, she wondered if he might do just that.

She scrabbled at his hand, trying to pry his fingers loose. They wouldn't budge.

"Ye're comin' with me," he bit out. "And unless ye want to see your clan slaughtered before your eyes, ye'll do as I say."

She blinked. What the devil was he talking about?

"Do ye understand?" he said.

Nay. She didn't understand. Not at all. But when his fingers tightened on her neck, she gave him as much of a nod as she could manage.

Out of the corner of her eye, she saw Alicia mince by, heading casually toward the great hall where the women and children were gathering. The evil witch gave Jenefer a knowing smirk as she passed.

Jenefer twisted in Morgan's grip, trying to choke out an alarm and stabbing a frantic finger toward the departing Alicia. But Morgan only gave her a silencing shake.

Rage quickly erased her fear of strangling. She began kicking at the Highlander. Maybe he'd drop her long enough for her to warn him he'd just set a fox loose among the hens.

But she could get no purchase to get in a good kick. Instead, he dodged her flailing limbs and circled her waist with his free arm, setting her on his hip. He finally released his grip on her throat, but before she could cry out, he clamped his hand over her mouth to keep her quiet. His clansmen cleared a path for him as they crossed the yard.

"Make no trouble," he said as he climbed the steps to the wall walk, "and there will be no bloodshed."

Trouble? What kind of trouble could she make? Her weapons were strewn on the courtyard grass. She was helpless to free herself. Hell, at the moment, she couldn't even scream obscenities at him.

"Ye said ye were a woman of honor," he said. "I expect ye to tell the truth."

What the devil was he going on about? With his hand locked over her mouth, she couldn't even spit out a few choice oaths, let alone concoct a good lie.

"I won't have ye tellin' your uncle I harmed ye in any way."

Jenefer froze.

Her uncle?

What did her uncle have to do with...

Her eyes widened as she realized his mistake.

Morgan thought the invaders were from Rivenloch. He thought they were her uncle's men.

She strained against his grasp, making urgent sounds behind his palm.

"Aye," he muttered, "I know what ye're goin' to say. We trysted. 'Tis true. But I hardly think ye can claim ye were harmed."

He stifled her scream of frustration.

"Fine. I did take your virginity. But ye know very well 'twas partly your idea. *Mostly* your idea."

She emitted an irritated squeal.

"Really?" he asked. "Ye're goin' to argue the point?" He shook his head and sighed as he climbed the last two steps. "Maybe 'tis best we say nothin' about it at all."

She attempted to speak in a rational tone, intending to tell him the army below was not Rivenloch. But, muffled by his hand, none of her words could be understood.

"Anyway, the important thing," he said, "is for him to see with his own eyes that his nieces are safe and unharmed."

She closed her eyes to smoldering, sarcastic slits.

"Oh come now, lass," he chided. "'Tisn't so much to ask."

He was just approaching the middle section of the wall when there was a call from below.

"Who is the lord of this castle? Show your face!"

He peered over the edge and boomed back, "I am Morgan Mor mac Giric o' Creagor, rightful laird o' this keep."

"Then before this day is through, Morgan Mor, I'll have your head on a pike!"

She felt Morgan start in surprise.

He recovered quickly.

"There's no need for that, m'laird," he said. "I think we can come to a fair agreement."

"A fair agreement?" the man sneered. "For murdering our lord?"

"What?"

"You slew Lord Edward, my brother, while he slept. Now you will pay."

Dumbfounded, Morgan loosened his grip on her. "What the hell?" he murmured.

"'Tis what I've been trying to tell you, you overbearing lummox," she said, extricating herself. "That's not Rivenloch."

CHAPTER 61

Three thoughts coursed through Morgan's head in the space of an instant.

The invaders were English.

They'd come for blood.

And his clan's forces were badly outnumbered.

It didn't take long to guess who had led the English to believe that it was he who'd slain their lord. And, curse his honor, he'd let the conniving woman into Creagor.

Now what could he do about it?

If he let war break out, he'd surely lose. With his small army, he couldn't hold the castle for long.

As hopeless as it was, he'd have to try diplomacy.

"Who is my accuser?" he called down.

"Roger of Firthgate," he barked. "And I'll be carving that name into your flesh."

His men roared in solidarity.

"Roger, ye've got the wrong man," Morgan shouted. "I've ne'er set foot in England."

Their reply was an earth-shaking charge against the doors.

"Hold!" Morgan shouted. "I have no quarrel with ye. Can we not settle this like reasonable men?"

Again they banged against the doors.

Morgan glanced down at the heavy-laden cart blocking the doors from the inside, rocked by the blow. Three of his strongest men were currently managing to hold it in place. But for how long?

"What proof do ye bring o' this crime?" Morgan tried.

"My brother's blood is on your hands, you filthy Highlander!" Roger shouted back.

Roger's soldiers, fueled by bloodthirst and beyond reason, sent up a bellow, rattling their weapons upon the doors.

Beside him, Jenefer was clearly done with diplomacy.

"Amor vincit omnia, my arse," she muttered. "I'm rounding up the archers."

He stopped her with a hand. "They're already posted atop the towers."

"The towers? We need them all at the front wall."

He shook his head. "We can't leave the flanks unprotected."

"But they're not at our flanks. Not yet," she argued. "We need a show of force. Make them think there are more of us."

He creased his brow. She had a point.

He nodded. "Fine. But I'll do it. I need ye in the hall with the others."

"Ballocks," she scoffed. "You need me up here."

He leveled a brow at her. "I won't argue with ye, lass. I'm—"

"Good. Then 'tis settled. You handle the men-at-arms. I'll command the archers."

"Jenefer," he growled as she headed for the stairs. "Jenefer! If ye don't go straightway to the great hall of your own accord, I'll have the Campbell brothers toss ye in on your arse."

"They can try," she called back.

He shook his head. With the enemy at the door, he didn't have time to discipline the lass. Nor could he spare the Campbell men to enforce his threat.

"M'laird!" John cried. "They're fellin' a tree for a batterin' ram!"

Morgan ran his hand across his jaw. The hotheaded English commander apparently wasn't going to waste time with a siege. He wanted blood. And he wanted it now.

Morgan had to save his clan. Even if, in the end, it required a sacrifice.

"Jenefer!" he shouted, loping after her.

He caught her by the shoulder and whipped her around toward him. Her expression was full of fire and determination.

"What?" she snarled.

Her anger disappeared when she saw the genuine concern in his eyes.

"Do as I say," he pleaded, "I'm beggin' ye."

"Damn it, Morgan, I can do this," she told him. "I can fight."

"Aye, ye can," he admitted, "better than most o' my men. But I need to know ye're safe, because..."

He looked into her spark-filled green eyes, burning with a passion for justice. And honor. And life.

And he told her the truth.

"Because I love ye."

Jenefer thought there was nothing he could say that alter her from her course.

She was wrong.

His declaration—fierce and sweet—caught her completely offguard.

She'd been prepared to defend her skills. It was something she did all the time. Men seldom believed a mere lass could hold her own in battle.

But Morgan wasn't questioning her abilities. He'd just admitted she was an accomplished warrior.

Instead, he'd attacked her with something she'd never had to defend against before.

Love.

Granted, it was a love that could never be. A love full of heartache. A love doomed by honor and circumstance.

But it was a love that was pure and true.

Her throat closed. Her vision blurred with tears. Her heart melted as she was overcome by her own deep, doomed feelings for him.

She wished she could freeze time and let his words wash over her, bathe in the waters of his affection, relish the tender moment they shared.

But she knew it was useless to water a tree that would never bear fruit.

Besides, there was no time for selfish emotions.

This was war.

Right now, she had to consider what was best for the clan. If there was any hope of surviving this attack, Morgan needed her skills, her experience in battle, and her knowledge of the Borders.

She hated to waste precious time arguing, especially when what she truly longed to do was return his words of affection. But she had to convince him she could be of more help atop the wall than locked in the great hall with dozens of helpless...

She knitted her brows.

Helpless? They weren't helpless. Every one of those Highland lasses had faced hardship with a backbone of iron.

Bethac. Cicilia. Feiyan.

How could she have forgotten Feiyan?

They could help defend Creagor.

Morgan would wring her neck when he discovered what she planned. But in the end, it just might win the war.

"Fine," she said, lowering her shoulders. "I'll go to the great hall." Then she pounded his chest with the back of her fist, piercing him with her gaze. "But you promise me…"

"Aye?"

"You survive, Highlander."

Without waiting for his reply, she wheeled and fled down the stairs and across the courtyard, gathering her weapons on the way.

In the great hall, Lady Alicia ambled through the gathering crowd. The women were flitting around the room like agitated hens.

At first, she'd been horrified to be trapped on the wrong side of the castle wall, with Morgan instead of Roger. But now she saw it might have its advantages. Like a lucky chunk of bread, she'd landed butter-side-up once again.

Without a doubt, Roger's army would win. They far outnumbered Morgan's forces at Creagor. And they had more provisions. Whether they chose to lay siege or attack—and knowing Roger's temper, she would wager on the latter—they would triumph.

Since Morgan had no idea that Alicia was allied with the English invaders, she'd be perfectly safe until Roger declared victory and came to rescue her.

To ensure Morgan's trust, she created a new tale for herself. And naturally, once she confided in a few maids, the myth spread like fire in a hayfield among the gossipmongers of the mac Giric clan.

Within half an hour, everyone had heard that poor Alicia, wrongly accused of murder, had been pursued by the English and followed here to Creagor. She'd been fortunate to elude them. And terribly grateful to Morgan for rescuing her from the avenging horde.

But there was still a problem. She hadn't confronted Morgan himself.

He might accept her story as the truth. He might be convinced of her innocence.

But what if Roger's knights disclosed the tale she'd told to *them*—that Morgan himself had committed the murder of Lord Edward?

She chewed on her nail.

She needed a safeguard.

Across the hall, beside the fire, young Danald sat, balancing Morgan's son on one knee. As he jostled the chuckling infant up and down, Danald was grinning like a fool.

With a calculating smirk, Alicia sauntered over to the hearth, keeping a watch out for that intrusive maidservant, Bethac. Warming her hands over the low flames, she glanced at Danald.

Forcing her lips into an indulgent smile, she sat beside him. "Isn't he the most beautiful child?"

Danald's grin froze at once.

Shite. He must have been warned about her. The lad gave her a polite nod and cradled the babe against his chest.

She made another attempt. "'Twas so kind of Morgan to take me back," she said softly, running her finger fondly down the babe's spine. "After all, a babe should be with his *real mother.* Don't you agree?"

Danald's face clouded.

Alicia silently cursed again. How could he agree? Danald was an orphan, raised by a milkmaid.

"Or at least," she added diplomatically, "someone who loves him like a real mother." She twisted a finger in the curls at the back of the babe's neck. "And that I do."

Danald still looked guarded.

She lowered her eyes and clasped her hands in her lap, asking gently, "You don't believe what they're accusing me of, do you? The English?"

Danald cleared his throat, obviously uncomfortable. "I only know the laird entrusted me to keep his bairn safe, m'lady."

"And you're doing a fine job of it," she said with a watery smile, "for which both of us are grateful. I only wish..." She broke off with a sob, then murmured under her breath, "I'm not a murderer. I swear to you, Danald. I wouldn't hurt a soul. I wish he'd believe me."

Danald, extremely ill-at-ease now, gulped and glanced around the hall. "I'm sure... I'm sure the laird will do what's right."

She smiled through her tears. "I'm sure you're right." She placed a tender hand on the lad's shoulder. "At least *you* believe me, don't you, Danald?"

What else could the lad say? "Sure, m'lady."

She reached out to stroke the full length of the babe's back with her knuckles. "I'll confess," she whispered. "I miss holding the wee babe."

He said nothing. When her hand slipped farther down to contact Danald's forearm, she let her touch linger.

"You wouldn't...you wouldn't let me hold him? Just for a moment? I promise I won't move from this spot."

Danald's brows came together with worry. "I don't know, m'lady. The laird—"

"I won't tell him. It can be our secret." She bit her lip, letting the tears well in her eyes. "It may be the last time I can hold my son."

Before he could answer, the doors to the great hall crashed inward, slamming against the walls and bringing the room to silence. In strode that infuriating, bow-wielding wench to waylay Alicia's plans.

Grinding her teeth in frustration, she withdrew from Danald and the infant. She'd have to adjust her strategy. She sank into the shadows to wait.

CHAPTER 62

"**h**ear me!" Jenefer called out, securing the door behind her and holding a hand up for quiet. "I bring grave tidings."

The room rapidly silenced. But when she looked into the fearful faces of the clanswomen, she wondered if she was doing the right thing. These weren't the Rivenloch maids, who were accustomed to staring death in the face. They were ordinary women—wives, mothers, milkmaids. Living in the remote Highlands, they'd probably never endured a siege or waged a war.

Still, they were strong, as tough as thistles. She could see that by their callused hands and determined faces.

"'Tis the English who storm our gates."

Gasps and epithets filled the hall.

She waited for them to silence.

"Ladies of mac Giric, I need your aid. The *laird* needs your aid," she said. "I won't lie to you. The English have a stockpile of resources. More soldiers. More weapons. And more experience. But what they don't have is the courage and heart of the clan mac Giric. And sometimes that's more important than experience."

She perused the faces before her. They were looking at her with trust. She didn't want to put them in danger. But she needed their cooperation.

"Those are our men out there, she said. Then she paused, realizing what she'd said. *Our* men. No matter that she'd known Morgan only a few days, that he belonged to another, that their love was hopeless. She still thought of him as hers.

Straightening with pride, she said, "They need our help. And we can give it. Now is your chance. Show me what Highland lasses are made of."

Her challenge got their attention.

"Do you have the courage to fight alongside your kinsmen?" she asked. "Or will you cower here behind closed doors?"

A few took offense at her remarks and stepped forward.

"I'll fight."

"I don't cower."

"I can throw a punch as well as any man."

Several lasses chimed in in agreement.

"What about the rest of you?" she asked. "Will you let the English spill the blood of good Scots soldiers? Or are you brave enough to spit in their faces?"

By the snarls of outrage, Jenefer quickly learned that Highlanders had even less tolerance than Lowlanders for the English.

But despite their growing enthusiasm for the fight, Jenefer wouldn't put the lasses' lives at risk. She wasn't a fool. They had no battle experience. And their laird would have her neck if she endangered his clanswomen.

So she quickly laid out her plans.

"Our best chance against the English is to convince them not to invade. We have to intimidate them, make them believe we're not worth the battle."

"Us?" someone said. "Intimidate them?"

"Aye," she said. "We may not have the strength of wolves. But we have the guile of wildcats. If we can make ourselves look larger than we are, we might make the

English reconsider a frontal attack and convince them to lay siege instead."

Once she explained what she wanted them to do, the lasses' faces lit up at the prospect of such wily subterfuge. They quickly dispersed to follow her instructions.

Jenefer's attention was drawn to the hearth, where the young lad still held Miles safely in his arms. Perhaps Morgan had been right to trust him. She gave him a nod of approval, communicating that she had faith in him to keep the bairn safe.

He gave her a solemn nod in return.

Then she bolted up the stairs. She'd seen no sign of Feiyan, and she needed her cousin's aid.

Bethac and Cicilia met her on the steps as they scurried from the nursery.

"Who is it?" Bethac hissed. "Who's stormin' the gates?"

"The English."

Cicilia gasped.

"Where's Feiyan?" Jenefer asked.

"She's not with ye?"

"Nay."

Bethac's brow wrinkled. "I saw her climb into bed last night."

Jenefer nodded. "And she was sleepin' this morn when…" A sudden, nasty twinge of foreboding seized the back of her neck. "Bloody hell," she muttered, pushing past the lasses on the stairs and hurtling along the passageway.

She knew what she'd find even before she exploded through the nursery door. She tore the coverlet off the bed. The lump she'd believed was her cousin was just that—a lump.

"Shite."

Feiyan had deceived them. It wasn't the first time she'd used such a ploy to make an escape. The slippery wench must have stolen from the nursery and fled. But when? And to where?

The last Jenefer had seen of her cousin was when she'd returned from the practice field last night. Even then, she couldn't be sure the lump in the bed beside her had been Feiyan and not just carefully arranged bedlinens.

Could Feiyan have gone after Alicia? Had she been intercepted by the English? Was she lurking in the woods?

Damn her devious cousin! She'd picked the worst possible time to disappear.

Jenefer blew out a steadying breath. Then she whirled and exited the nursery. There was no time to dwell on obstacles. She'd just have to lead the battle on her own.

Alicia, hidden in the shadow of the hearth, had heard enough.

She didn't think the Highland women were capable of pulling off the lass's rash scheme. But enough doubt nibbled at the corners of her confidence to convince her she definitely needed to ensure her own safe escape.

With everyone rummaging through bedchambers, collecting men's clothing, the great hall was essentially deserted except for her, the lad, and the infant. From her secluded spot, Alicia could easily reach the small iron shovel used for scooping out ashes. So while Danald babbled to the babe, pointing to the happily crackling fire, she coiled her fingers around the handle of the shovel.

"Danald," she called softly from behind him, drawing the shovel back like a club.

He jerked at the sound of her voice. "Oh! M'lady! I'd forgotten ye were ther—"

As he turned toward her, she swung forward. The flat of the shovel struck his temple with a dull thud. He dropped like a stone. The child spilled out of his arms, hitting the hard floor.

She let go of the shovel and scooped up the infant. He was still and silent. She thought he might be dead, killed by the impact. Not that it mattered. She only needed Morgan to *believe* his son was alive.

After a moment, however, the lad began to squirm. His face turned red, and he opened his mouth to wail in protest.

She smothered his cries against her chest before they could draw too much attention. Then, with her head bowed, clinging to the shadows of the hall, she skirted past the gathering women and slipped out the door.

The courtyard was in chaos.

Men raced back and forth with swords, bows, pikes, and shields, shouting orders.

The penned sheep milled in a panicked circle.

Chickens flapped in the rising dust.

Archers stood atop the front wall, their bows at the ready.

A heavy cart blocked the entrance, and three strong men pushed their backs against it. But a jarring blow from outside rocked the gates, forcing the men to scramble to slide the cart back into place.

It wouldn't be long now. Roger and his men would break down the gates. They'd charge in with gnashing teeth and slashing broadswords, leaving carnage in their wake.

But she'd be fine. Her safety was assured. She had control of the most valuable mac Giric asset. Morgan would surrender his castle, his clan, and even his life for his precious heir.

With strangely maternal calm, she stroked the back of the infant's downy head. His cries were loud, desperate, insistent. But they couldn't be heard above the din of the coming battle.

"Shite," Morgan muttered as he watched the men shove the cart back against the gates.

They couldn't hold out forever. The English axes had made a crude battering ram out of a fallen tree. Eventually, the repeated pounding would splinter the wooden doors.

He'd hoped to force the invaders to a siege rather than an attack. Once tempers cooled, he might be able to negotiate for peace.

But it was clear that wasn't the situation. Their blood was hot. Their thirst for revenge was urgent. Alicia had probably told them that the keep was ill-prepared for battle. That Morgan's resources were limited and his men were few. It was only a matter of time before they breached the courtyard and started spilling clan blood.

He couldn't let that happen. He eyed his claymore, propped against the wall. Eventually, he might have to surrender the keep. Or bargain with his own life to save the lives of his people. But he didn't intend to surrender without a valiant fight.

Abandoning diplomacy, he instigated battle tactics, using a castle's first, best line of defense.

"Archers, take your positions!" he yelled.

As one, they snapped to attention along the wall. Morgan was impressed with their new discipline, something they'd doubtless learned from the master archer who'd been working with them.

"Aim!" he called, peering down at the invaders. "Draw!" Hearing his command, the English raised their shields to form a protective armor of sorts, resembling a giant scaled dragon. "Loose!"

The handful of arrows rained down. Most of them bounced off or lodged in the overlapping shields. But one shaft managed to find a crevice between the shields, piercing a man in the shoulder.

At this rate, with so few archers manning the wall, even if they managed to hit their mark every time, they'd be lucky to claim a half dozen victims before they spent all their shafts.

Morgan scowled, scraping his hair back with one hand. This wasn't going to work.

As he racked his brain, trying to think of a better strategy, more clansmen arrived to populate the wall. He narrowed his eyes. They were carrying a strange assortment of objects—rocks, pots, crockery, clay vessels, iron pans, cooking spoons. A few even brought jordans.

It was only when he looked closer that recognition dawned. They were dressed in men's clothing. But they weren't men. They were the lasses of the clan, come to join the fight.

It didn't take him long to guess whose idea that was.

"Jenefer," he grumbled.

Furious that she'd convinced the mac Giric clanswomen to leave the protection of the great hall, he prepared to order them back.

But before he could intervene, one of the lasses hurled a stone at the English. Another pitched a ceramic bowl. Two more heaved an iron cauldron over the wall.

He heard a yelp and peered over the edge. One of the Englishmen had been knocked flat by the cauldron. The commander beat a retreat as more rocks and pottery hailed down upon them.

The lasses celebrated their moment of victory with silent glee, their eyes shining as they ducked back from the wall to let a second wave of women take their place.

Even if he didn't approve of the risk, Morgan had to admire their cleverness. Not only had they made the English believe they were confronting a larger army of men, but they'd managed to fend them off with their makeshift weapons.

The strategy wouldn't work forever, of course. The English quickly perceived that the falling objects might be annoying, but they were fairly harmless. Soon they began shooting back at the culprits who were dropping them.

Morgan had to act to keep his clanswomen safe.

Suddenly, from his left flank, he heard a familiar female voice. "Fall back!"

Damn the wench! Why was Jenefer standing at the embrasure, directly in the line of fire? It was far too risky. Anything could happen.

No sooner did he have that thought than he saw something fly past her shoulder.

An enemy arrow. Sharp. Deadly. And far too close.

CHAPTER 63

organ's heart seized. His breath caught. His knees turned to custard.

Jenefer, however, didn't even flinch.

"Archers, move in!" she ordered.

His jaw went slack. He didn't know whether to be mortified or outraged. How dared the lass interfere with his command? What gave her the authority to tell his men—and women—what to do?

"Take your best shots!" she shouted.

His brows collided. He whirled toward her with clenched fists.

But Jenefer, fully engaged in battle, was blind to everything but the war being waged on the ground below.

Before he could bellow at her to go back to the great hall, he heard the random twang of bowstrings, followed by distant groans of pain. He ventured a glance over the battlements. To his surprise, the mac Giric archers had wounded several of the attackers.

He looked at Jenefer in wonder.

"Second wave!" she called out.

Though he was tempted to haul the lass off the wall, Morgan couldn't argue with the effectiveness of her strategy. While the English, unprotected by their shields, attempted to recover from the archers' attack, the lasses rushed forward to hurl stones, cups, and pots down at them.

As the English flinched and dodged the projectiles, unable to form an effective wall of shields in the confusion, the mac Giric archers took over again, stepping in to shoot at them.

To further confound the enemy and make their arrows harder to defend against, the archers didn't release all at once in a volley. Instead, Jenefer had apparently directed them to choose a specific target and shoot when they had a single victim squarely in their sights.

Once their arrows were spent, with very few of them wasted, the archers withdrew from the battlements.

"And again!" Jenefer shouted.

The lasses moved forward in unison to pelt the foe with hammers and pans and platters. Those English who were foolish enough to fight their way through the falling objects were subsequently picked off when the archers took over.

It was ingenious.

Morgan looked at the lass with new respect. She *was* a warrior maid. Not only could she handle a bow. She could wage war. Indeed, he'd never seen a more capable commander.

He was about to tell her so when a sudden hard impact made the stones shudder beneath his feet.

Jenefer turned and caught his eye. "The doors!"

Morgan's heart plummeted as his glance landed on the cart blocking the entrance. It was tipped at a dangerous angle, and his men strained to keep it from flipping. The rough point of the battering ram was visible between the splintered rift in the doors.

He clenched his jaw. He needed to get down there.

"Go!" Jenefer barked. "I've got this!"

He hesitated.

He couldn't leave his soldiers in the hands of a lass.

Could he?

In the end, it was Jenefer's steady, self-assured gaze, burning like fire, that convinced him.

"I've got this," she repeated. "Go."

He knew she was right. With a nod and an exhale to settle his nerves, he snatched up his claymore and raced down the stairs.

Stepping into the courtyard was like marching into hell.

Time screeched to a halt, dragging at Morgan's boots as if he slogged through sludge, while he took in the turmoil around him.

In his shifted reality, panicked livestock kicked up clouds of dust at a snail's pace while their keepers labored to keep them penned.

As if they moved through thick sap, breathless lads raced back and forth, fetching weapons from the armory.

Scowling men-at-arms shrugged slowly into their cotuns, snarling drawn-out oaths at one another to whip up their courage for the hand-to-hand battle to come.

At a sluggish pace, sweating servants piled barrels, chests, casks—anything heavy they could find—onto the cart to give it weight against the oncoming tide of English soldiers.

Then, in the midst of it all, appearing through the rising silt like a calm angel, rose Alicia. Oblivious to the pandemonium, she seemed as tranquil as the eye of a storm.

In this strange, stretched time, it felt to Morgan like he stared at her in puzzlement for an eternity, unable to comprehend her peace.

And then he glimpsed the bairn in her arms.

A prolonged, painful, rasping gasp racked Morgan's chest. His precious son was in the clutches of the one who saw him, not as an innocent child, but as a hostage. Alicia was no heavenly being. She was the Angel of Death.

A calculating smirk slowly bloomed on her face. Her eyes closed down to scheming slits. Her hand drifted up to the back of Miles' head.

An impotent roar choked Morgan's throat as he saw his son frozen in time—red-faced, body arched, crying in terror, and helpless in the witch's grasp.

In that protracted instant, he tried to gauge whether he could cross the courtyard to recover his son before she did him harm.

But before he could act, a mighty crash and a loud, grinding noise jarred him back to real time.

His gaze flew to the entrance of the keep.

The battering ram had splintered the doors.

The wheels of the cart were skidding back under the pressure, despite the efforts of his men to anchor them.

One more blow would let the English into the breach.

"To arms!" he bellowed to his men, brandishing his claymore as he thundered forward.

Jenefer heard the horrendous crack and felt the wall shudder. The English had burst through the doors.

It was time to change tactics.

"Archers, disperse along the walls!" she cried. "Guard the doors!"

The archers abandoned the battlements, facing inward and finding the best vantage points to keep the entrance in their sights.

As for the women atop the wall, though they would have no parapets to hide behind when the English streamed in, Jenefer felt they were safer up here than sitting in the great hall, waiting like lambs to be slaughtered.

Apparently, they agreed. Not a single one fled down the stairs. Instead, the determined lasses hefted up what projectiles remained in their arsenal and prepared to launch an attack inside the walls.

For one moment, her breast swelled with pride.

Then, with a brutal punch of its wooden fist, the battering ram shattered the doors. Her chest caved as the breath hissed from her lungs.

The cart keeled over and smashed onto its side. A man who didn't dodge fast enough screamed as the weighted conveyance crushed his leg.

But what wrenched at her heart, making it knife sideways, was the sight of Morgan down there, in the thick of things. He and his men stood before the doors, baring their teeth and brandishing their claymores.

Too soon, like angry wasps knocked from their nest, the English began to swarm through the narrow opening and over the overturned cart.

She swallowed down her fear and stiffened her spine. *I've got this,* she'd boasted. Now there was no turning back.

At her direction, the women flocked to the section of wall directly above the attackers, lobbing rocks and dropping pitchers on them as they came through the entrance.

Her archers, aided by the disarray the women sowed, performed expertly. They wounded nearly half of the invaders as they slipped through the gap.

The English lucky enough to evade their arrows were met by Morgan's claymore-wielding giants.

As for Jenefer, she gave herself the singular mission of keeping Morgan safe. She shot at anyone who came within a yard of him, not even noting or caring that she might have killed a man for the first time.

By some miracle, the Highlanders repelled the first wave of invaders and righted the cart again. Once the injured man was carried away, five men-at-arms shoved the cart up against the splintered doors and held it there with their backs.

It wouldn't keep the enemy out forever. But now maybe Roger would think twice about the cost in casualties if he attacked again. A dozen bodies lay strewn about the courtyard, feeding the grass with English blood.

But one person in the keep wasn't pleased with the outcome.

"Nay!" Alicia screamed, frowning in fury at the carnage.

Only one thing could make her that angry, and that was having her plans foiled. She must have been counting on the English to seize Creagor and take Morgan. She expected them to rescue her. Which confirmed that it was she who'd misled them, telling them Morgan had committed the murders.

Afire with rage at Alicia's betrayal, Jenefer drew her bow, aiming at the treacherous woman's back.

Then she hesitated.

She remembered what Bethac had said. Morgan would never forgive her for shooting Miles' mother.

Her hands faltered on the bow as she saw Morgan turn toward Alicia, his blade still in hand, his chest heaving, his face grimy from battle.

Still Jenefer fought the urge to slay the woman where she stood.

But Alicia shifted her posture then, enough so Jenefer could see the bundle in her arms.

Alicia had Miles.

He writhed in her arms, bleating to be free.

Jenefer's heart plunged. Her hands quaked. A knot of horror clogged her throat.

Bloody hell. What if Jenefer had fired that shot and accidentally hit Miles?

Before her grip could slip, before she could do something she'd regret, Jenefer lowered the bow. But her fingers still trembled on the grip. And her gaze as she kept Alicia and Miles in her sights could have pierced steel.

"Let me out!" Alicia snarled, clinging tightly to the babe.

At that moment, Danald came stumbling out of the great hall. He gripped his head in one hand.

"M'laird," he grunted, "I lost him. I lost..." He stopped as he took in the situation and saw who had taken the babe from him. His brow clouded. "'Twas ye. Ye took Miles."

Now all the men-at-arms faced her. Their blood was hot from battle. Their grim blades were bare. What was one more victim?

Alicia must have sensed their hunger for violence as well. It fueled her desperation. She slid a dagger from her belt.

"If you don't let me go," she bit out, "I'll kill him. I'll kill your heir."

CHAPTER 64

Morgan felt all the air go out of his lungs.

Could Alicia do it? Kill an innocent child? Her own flesh and blood?

A few days ago, he would have thought it impossible. But now...

"Back away!" she ordered.

The eyes of everyone in the courtyard were fixed on Alicia as she clutched Miles. Frozen in shock, no one moved a muscle.

"Back away, I said!"

They shuffled back. Morgan stood his ground, but slowly and carefully set his sword on the grass. Maybe—if he could calm her down and avoid falling apart—he could talk some sense into his wife.

"Listen to me, Alicia."

"Stand back," she warned, pressing her dagger against Miles' pale wee neck. "I'll do it."

"Please," Morgan choked out. "Whatever's happened, whatever ye've done, I can help ye. There's no need to go back to the English. I can keep ye safe here."

The last thing he expected was Alicia's jangling laughter.

"You fool," she said. "'Tis the English who are going to keep me safe from *you*. You're the coldblooded killer who murdered their lord and stole my infant."

Of course. He'd forgotten. Alicia had neatly pinned the blame for her crime on him.

He could deal with her treachery later. For now, all he cared about was safely retrieving his son.

"Now out of my way," she growled.

Morgan couldn't let her leave with Miles. If she did, he knew he'd never see him again.

"Please, Alicia," he said. "Can't we talk this over? Leave the bairn here. I'll give ye safe passage beyond the wall."

She smirked at his offer. "Ye'd have a knife in my back ere I reached the door."

"Nay. I swear. Only don't take him."

"I need some assurance you won't come after me," she explained. "You wouldn't want anything to happen to poor wee...what are you calling him now?"

Yards away, Danald snapped, "Miles!" Though his tone toward Alicia was venomous, he probably blamed himself for the bairn's capture.

Morgan issued a steely promise to her. "If ye take him away, I'll hunt ye down, I swear. I'll follow ye to the ends o' the earth."

She raised her dagger, reversing it in her hand and letting it hover over Miles' belly. "Maybe I'll get rid of him to save you the trouble."

One downward thrust would end Miles' life.

"Nay!" Morgan's cry was hoarse and full of torment.

In the end, he had to admit defeat.

She wouldn't negotiate with him.

She didn't want to stay at Creagor.

And he couldn't convince her to surrender Miles.

He couldn't even risk taking the bairn by force. He saw now that Alicia had no feelings for her son. She had no feelings for *him*. He wondered if she had feelings for anyone save herself.

The slow march toward the doors was interminable. Alicia warily advanced, clenching her hand around the dagger that threatened Miles' vulnerable body.

Morgan and his men followed her at a safe distance, waiting for her to make a mistake.

Trip up somehow.

Falter.

Drop her guard.

Change her mind.

Anything that would give them the advantage.

But she never stumbled. Never veered from her course. Never hesitated or had second thoughts.

She took a dozen tortuous steps.

Then, on the thirteenth, the sudden earth-shuddering crack of the battering ram made everyone jerk in distraction. Everyone except the highly focused archer who sent an arrow spiraling through Alicia's upraised forearm.

The thud at the doors didn't garner as much attention as the tortured scream Alicia emitted when she felt the arrow's wicked bite.

The dagger fell from her hand. Her eyes rolled wildly as she stared at the shaft impaling her and the blood dripping down her arm. While she staggered in shock, Morgan rushed forward, easily snatching Miles out of her arms.

Then he scanned the battlements to see who had shot the arrow.

A lone archer lowered a bow.

Jenefer.

The mist swirled around her like smoke off a fire. Her face was grave, graver than he'd ever seen it. She must know the risk she'd taken. If her shaft had drifted by so much as an inch, she might have killed Miles or one of the men behind him.

He wanted to be vexed with her. But the truth was she'd saved Miles' life.

He gave her a nod of gratitude. And he prayed he'd live long enough to thank her properly.

The battering ram thudded against the doors again, opening the crevice. The men shoved the cart forward, sealing it again.

Soon he'd have to prepare for a second round of hand-to-hand fighting. He needed someone to take his son to safety.

He glanced at Jenefer again. As if she'd read his mind, her gaze dropped to Miles, and she started down the steps.

But he shook his head, stopping her.

He wouldn't waste her talents.

Anyone could look after a bairn.

There was only one Jenefer, master archer.

"I need ye on the wall," he called to her.

She nodded and immediately started issuing commands to a group of lads on the wall. "You lads! Gather all the arrows. Pry them out of the dead if you have to. Quick! Bring them up to the archers."

Meanwhile, Morgan spotted Danald, who stood apart, twisting his cap in his hands.

"Here, lad," Morgan said, "I need ye to take Miles."

"Are ye certain, m'laird?" Danald asked. "I failed ye once. Lady Alicia—"

Behind Morgan's shoulder, Alicia screamed in agony.

Two of the Campbell brothers had taken mercy on her. They'd broken off the arrow head and were pulling the shaft out of her arm.

"Won't be seizin' anythin' for a while." He placed his son in Danald's hands.

The lad gave him a solemn nod and fled with Miles to the safety of the great hall.

Alicia screeched again, this time in outrage. The Campbells were tearing her fine leine to use the linen for a bandage.

The next crash against the doors came with an ominous creak. One or two more hits, and the doors would not only open. They'd splinter off their iron hinges. Then there would be no trickle of English soldiers through the entrance. There would be a flood.

"Archers at the ready!" Jenefer shouted from above.

"To mac Giric!" Morgan bellowed, brandishing his claymore to embolden his men.

They roared in response.

The Campbells had no more time to tend to Alicia. They handed her the bandage, leaving her to bind her own wound.

Jenefer's throat thickened with pride as she watched the archers all along the wall nock their arrows in perfect unison. Her eyes welled with tears of admiration as she saw the mac Giric lasses reassemble above the entrance, armed with whatever they had left.

How could she ever have imagined they were dimwitted savages? These Highlanders were fierce and brave, loyal and resourceful, a clan anyone would be proud to claim.

She only prayed she wasn't condemning them to death.

She drew her own bow, watching the doors, determined to defend them with her last breath.

Then she felt a strange tingle at the back of her neck.

Something was coming.

She dared not look away from the doors. But the sensation persisted.

Swiftly, what began as a prickling became a sound, as if someone were calling to her.

Hardening her jaw against distraction, she kept her focus on the entrance as the battering ram once again tried to break through the thick oak.

Again the men-at-arms were able to hold back the beast, shoving the cart firmly against the doors. But the oak had splintered partially away from the heavy iron hinges. The doors wouldn't withstand one more pummeling.

In the few moments the English would need to regroup, Jenefer eased the tension of her bow and stepped to the battlements. Still feeling the queer shiver along her neck, she cast a glance toward the palisade gates.

The field was thick with fog. An archer could shoot an arrow and never see where it landed. But she thought she glimpsed something stirring in the mist.

Figures.

She blinked her eyes to make sure she wasn't imagining the shapes.

And then she saw clearly that they *were* figures. Dozens of warriors marching through the gates and toward the castle.

She held her breath, fearing they might be English reinforcements.

And then she glimpsed the familiar banner emerging from the fog.

"Rivenloch," she breathed, her heart leaping with hope.

When she recognized her cousin Feiyan leading the charge, she knew at once that rescue was at hand. And when she spied Hallie and all the parents at Feiyan's flank, armed and armored for serious battle, she knew the English were finished.

"Rivenloch!" she cried, grinning in triumph when she turned to call down to Morgan. "Rivenloch is coming!"

It didn't occur to her that Morgan would perceive Rivenloch as the enemy.

His face fell. His shoulders dropped. His mouth turned down, grim but resolute. Still, he lifted his claymore in defiance, as if to proclaim he wouldn't lose Creagor without a fight to the death.

"Nay!" she called to him. "They're here to give aid!"

He still looked skeptical. His men reflected his uncertainty.

"Feiyan brought them," she tried. "She and Hallie are here with dozens of warriors."

"'Tis true, m'laird," William called down from the wall. "I can see a whole army comin' through the gates."

Jenefer noticed the English had ceased their attack. She peered over the battlements to see what was happening.

The English were muttering among themselves, a few frantically pointing at the incoming soldiers. Someone finally recognized the banner, and startled barks of "Rivenloch" circled their ranks.

No doubt they knew the Border clan by virtue of their reputation. Since the English couldn't fight on two fronts at once, they were forced to abandon the battering ram and turn to engage Rivenloch.

"Archers, to the walls!" Jenefer commanded.

While the English awaited Rivenloch's arrival, the archers were able to wound a few unwary soldiers.

Meanwhile, Morgan and his men waited in the courtyard. When the moment was right, they would move the cart and attack the English from the rear.

"At my signal!" Jenefer called down to Morgan.

Never doubting her for a moment, he answered with a curt nod.

She held her arm aloft, calculating how long it would take Morgan's men to move the cart and get into place.

Rivenloch's charge was awesome to behold. Jenefer, accustomed to being in their ranks, had never seen the army from this vantage point. She was astounded by their power to intimidate. The mass of warriors stormed toward the castle, shoulder-to-shoulder, shield-to-shield, brandishing their blades with a mighty roar.

"Archers, halt!" she cried as Rivenloch drew near. In the coming melee, the risk of shooting an ally was too great.

At the clash of the first two blades, Jenefer signaled Morgan with the drop of her arm.

Morgan ordered the cart rolled aside. The doors sagged inward. His men wrenched them out of the way. Then they began to engage the enemy from the rear.

Jenefer watched from the battlements, her bow at the ready.

It wasn't difficult to distinguish the armies of Rivenloch and Creagor.

Rivenloch's warriors were fitted with polished armor and flawless chain mail, armed with painted shields and gleaming broadswords.

But Creagor's soldiers, despite their simple cotuns and trews, their crude targes and well-used claymores, fought ferociously.

Morgan was magnificent. With one powerful shove of his targe, he knocked three English foes onto their arses. With a sweep of his claymore, he sent another man sprawling.

At the fore of the battle, Jenefer saw Hallie fighting with cold, calculating menace, slashing one man's thigh and another man's arm with two expert blows.

Next to Hallie, Feiyan raised one of her heavy forks, catching and snapping off an enemy blade with the flick of her wrist.

Her Uncle Pagan used his shield to shove a knight toward her Aunt Deirdre, who dispatched him with ease.

Feiyan's mother, Miriel, leaped about like lightning, stinging victims with a needle-like dagger, while her father, Rand, finished them off with thrusts of his broadsword.

And Jenefer's own mother and father, Helena and Colin, sent up showers of sparks as they crossed swords with their foes, bellowing out curses and howling in triumph.

The tide was turning.

They just might win this battle.

CHAPTER 65

In his heart, Morgan was fighting for his life and the lives of his clansmen. But he had to admit that repelling the English from the gates of Creagor gave him great satisfaction.

He also had to admit he was glad Rivenloch wasn't his foe.

Well-equipped and seasoned, menacing and effective, the army was the most impressive he'd ever seen.

To his surprise, he glimpsed Feiyan leaping among the fray. And he recognized Hallie as she hacked at the legs of a soldier who got too close to Feiyan. There were other female warriors in their midst. One of them saluted him after dispatching an enemy who'd taken a swing at Morgan's head.

The battle didn't last long. Morgan's men had advanced mere yards past the broken doors when Roger realized he was outmatched.

"To Firthgate!" the English lord cried. "Retreat!"

Rivenloch's forces could have slaughtered every last one of them as they turned their backs and funneled through the palisade gates. But Lady Deirdre was merciful. She gave orders not to pursue the fleeing army, allowing them to bolt to safety before closing the gates behind them.

That was fine with Morgan. The English had been deceived by Alicia, just as he had. They couldn't be blamed for seeking out justice for their lord's murder. On the other hand, they'd think twice before crossing the border to attack Creagor again.

As he watched the English flee, Morgan heard a sharp scream of rage from the courtyard behind him.

"Nay!" Alicia shrieked. "Cowards!"

He strode back through the splintered doors to see what was amiss.

Eager to welcome her clan, Jenefer had come down the stairs to the yard as well.

Alicia stood between the two of them, spitting mad. She'd clearly expected the English to seize the castle and oust Morgan. Her plans had been foiled. Her rescuers had abandoned her.

If she weren't such a villain—making Morgan believe she was dead, killing her lover and her midwife, blaming Morgan for the murder, goading the English into attacking Creagor, threatening the life of his son—he might have felt sorry for her.

She had nowhere to go now. She'd managed to bind her gruesome wound. It had stopped bleeding. But her hand hung limp at her side. She might never recover from the damage to her arm. And her one hope of escape was retreating out the palisade gates.

"Come back here!" she screamed, her face purpling.

"Why would they?" Jenefer scoffed.

"Ye betrayed them, Alicia," Morgan said, "just as ye betrayed me."

He expected Alicia to try manipulating him again. To concoct a new, twisted version of events. To beseech him to forgive her.

He didn't expect her to lash out at him. But her eyes were wild with fury. Venomous with revenge.

"This is *your* fault!" she barked.

He tightened his jaw.

"You *knew* I couldn't abide the Highlands," she spat. "You *knew* I was miserable. And yet you did nothing."

His fist tensed on the hilt of his claymore.

She was right. He'd known for a long while how unhappy she was. He'd hoped that she'd grow to love his home. He'd hoped that having a bairn to care for would make her forget her loneliness.

"'Tis *your* fault I fled into the arms of another," she insisted. "What else was I to do?"

He scowled. He knew he couldn't be blamed for Alicia's disloyalty. But was there a kernel of truth in what she was saying? Could he have done more to keep her happy?

Her voice softened with bitterness. "At least I left you the babe."

That was true. She could have taken his heir with her. It was a sacrifice most mothers couldn't have borne.

Jenefer, however, didn't see it that way.

"You mean the babe you threatened to kill?" she snarled.

In an instant, Alicia's eyes transformed from rueful to furious. "And *you!* You meant to steal his son from him!"

"What?" she exploded.

"You wheedled your way into his household," Alicia bit out. "You knew if you commanded his heir, you could command his castle." She peeled her lips back from her teeth and erupted in a mirthless cackle. "Well, the jest is on you. That babe you're so desperate to protect?" She turned back to Morgan with a whisper that was cruel and full of malice. "'Tisn't even yours."

Alicia's words hit him like the blow of a lance, collapsing his chest and piercing his heart.

It couldn't be true. Miles had to be his. Morgan loved the wee bairn.

Stunned, he couldn't move. Couldn't speak. Couldn't breathe.

Jenefer apparently could. She reared back her fist and plowed it straight into Alicia's face.

Alicia dropped like a stone.

There was a collective gasp of horror from the clan.

Alicia, not quite struck silent, was reduced to mumbling curses harmlessly into the dust.

Morgan wanted to feel pity for her. Instead, he felt satisfaction as Jenefer shook the pain of impact from her knuckles.

"Don't listen to her," Jenefer said. "Of *course* Miles is yours. You know that. She only said that to provoke you." She stepped toward him, confiding, "I knew he was yours before you ever said a word. Remember? He has your eyes. Your smile. Your air of command."

That he did. Miles could summon Jenefer to do his bidding with a single wail.

Alicia had heard enough.

She'd been utterly humiliated at the hands of that usurping whore. Irreparably wounded by her arrow. Laid low by her punishing fist.

Now the wicked woman had the gall to malign her to the clan and to her own husband.

Damn the wench! Alicia was mistress here. *Lady* Alicia mac Giric. And she wasn't going to put up with any more.

She might be bleeding and battered. She might be reduced to crawling in the dust like a lizard. But she would rise like a dragon.

While the two lovesick doves cooed over her, Alicia blinked to clear the dazed fog from her eyes.

While they murmured sickeningly sweet reassurances at each other, she rooted through the grass with her undamaged hand.

While they bent their foolish, unwary heads together, her fingers finally found and closed around the dagger she'd dropped.

She grinned through bloody teeth.

She might never regain Morgan's affections, not after the lie she'd told him about his son. But if she couldn't have him back, neither could the scheming bitch who was clamoring for his affection.

Mustering her strength for one bold attack, she scraped the knife across the ground toward her and tested her wobbling legs.

As she moved, her weight shifted to her injured arm. She bit back a groan and blinked away the red haze of pain.

Then, with strength born of vengeance, she surged up all at once, stabbing toward the belly of the unsuspecting wench.

Time dragged to a slog as Alicia perceived the next moments in isolated flashes of detail.

The thrust of the knife in her left hand.

The insipid chatter of the woman.

The sudden sharp turn of Morgan's head.

The widening of his eyes.

It was strange, she thought. She'd never known the exact color of his eyes. But she could see now that they matched his beloved Highland scrub. Brown. Green. Gold.

Then her attention was distracted by the loss of her target.

Morgan was shoving the wench aside with his left arm, moving her out of range.

Alicia's brows drew together in frustration.

It wasn't fair.

She deserved this. She deserved revenge.

With one last burst of effort, she angled the dagger, hoping to at least maim her victim if she couldn't kill her.

But her lunge was cut short as Morgan's claymore came down, colliding with her blade.

The impact of steel on steel jarred her, sending a shudder up her arm.

But she held tight to the dagger. She'd be damned if she'd let herself be disarmed again.

Before she could recoil for another strike, Morgan knocked her aside with the flat of his blade.

Weakened and off-balance, she staggered sideways. She fell onto her injured arm, which collapsed beneath her.

For an instant, she lay stunned on her belly. Numb. Confused. Unable to sort out what had just happened.

It made no sense.

Even Morgan's words as he towered over her at first had no meaning to her.

"That's the last time ye'll attack the ones I love," he proclaimed.

Then the truth of what she'd done sank in.

Strangely, she felt no pain.

All she felt was disbelief and a curious, comical irony. Morgan didn't know how true his words were, she thought.

And even when the dagger lodged in her chest made it difficult to breathe and drew a filmy gray curtain over her eyes, she couldn't help but see the black humor of it all.

She rolled onto her back, barely hearing the chorus of horrified gasps around her.

As she laughed with the last of her breath, her eyes rolled. She released her fingers from the dagger in her heart and felt blood gurgle from the wound.

CHAPTER 66

I t was hard for Jenefer to feel sorry for Lady Alicia. After all, the woman had fallen on her own dagger in the act of trying to stab Jenefer.

But her gaze flew to Morgan in concern. He'd been the one to push Alicia aside. Would he think she'd died because of him?

His expression was grave as he stared down at his dead wife. For a long while he didn't speak. No one spoke.

Finally he muttered, "Take her away. I don't want Miles to see her like this."

Three servants rushed to do his bidding.

"Miles doesn't need to know," Jenefer assured him. "'Twas an accident. Bury her in hallowed ground, someplace he can visit her when he's grown."

He didn't reply.

"Morgan," she insisted.

Still he didn't answer.

"'Twasn't your fault," Jenefer murmured. "You know that, aye?"

He said nothing, only staring bleakly at the ground, stained by his wife's blood.

It would take more to jar him from his spiraling guilt.

"Morgan, listen to me," she said, seizing his arm. "I know you. You're a man of honor. I know you gave her everything you had. A home. A title. A child. I know you tried to make her happy."

He swallowed.

"And how did she repay you?" Jenefer asked. "With petulance. Disloyalty. Dishonor. Betrayal." She shook her head. "For the love of God, the woman feigned her own death. She broke your heart. She abandoned her own son. She murdered her lover and then blamed you for it. She threatened to kill Miles. And if you hadn't prevented her, she would have..." Her voice caught as the truth of how close she'd come to death sank in, then added under her breath, "She would have killed me."

Morgan blinked, awakening from his daze. He looked at her as if seeing her for the first time.

"Jenefer," he sighed. He knitted his brows in concern. "Are ye hurt?"

She shook her head.

"I'm alive," Jenefer told him in no uncertain terms, "because you did what you had to, to save me."

Then there was no more time to discuss what he'd done and why he'd done it. Rivenloch was coming through the doors.

For Jenefer, it seemed like weeks had passed since she'd been among her clansfolk, months since she'd seen her parents. In the last few days, a lifetime of events had forged her into a different woman.

So, in light of the tragic situation, it was with measured cheer that she greeted her kin.

"Morgan Mor mac Giric, this is my clan," she said. "The laird, Deirdre, and Pagan Cameliard, Miriel and Rand la Nuit, and my parents, Helena and Colin du Lac.

He nodded respectfully. "My thanks for your help."

"Of course," Deirdre replied.

Her mother, Helena, stepped forward, sizing him up from head to toe. She crossed her arms and arched her brow. "Unlike you Highland folk, constantly quibbling among yourselves," she told him with a sniff, "we Lowlanders *always* fight together against the English."

"Hel!" Deirdre gave Helena a chiding cuff on the shoulder. "Put your sword away. The battle's over."

Her uncle Pagan scowled at Morgan from beneath stormy brows. One hand rested casually on the hilt of his sheathed sword. "So you're the one who took our daughters hostage?"

Jenefer's father, Colin, ever the peacemaker, came between them with a disarming smile. "Now, Pagan, if I know my daughter, she likely fueled the fire." He gave her a wink.

Before Jenefer could issue a halfhearted protest—he *was* right, after all—her aunt Miriel spoke. "We would have been here sooner, but Feiyan advised we approach with stealth."

Her uncle Rand perused the courtyard. "'Twas a wise decision, daughter," he said to Feiyan. "Aside from the doors, the castle is largely intact."

"Feiyan!" Jenefer cried as Feiyan wove her way through the ranks of Rivenloch knights. She'd never been so glad to see her pesky cousin. "How did you escape? When did you...?"

"I saw soldiers in the woods last night," Feiyan said. "I thought it was Rivenloch, come to rescue us. I went out to warn them not to attack."

Morgan stopped her. "Went out? What do ye mean, ye went out?"

Feiyan shrugged. "'Twasn't hard to get the palisade guards to fight. While they were quarreling, I slipped out the gates."

Her answer didn't please Morgan. He frowned.

"Once I found out the soldiers were English," she continued, "I fled to fetch Rivenloch."

"And you found Hallie?" Jenefer asked. She'd seen her cousin in the battle.

Behind Feiyan's triumphant smile, her face darkened. "Aye. She was at Rivenloch all the time, as we thought."

"And Colban?" Morgan asked.

"Here," his man said. The Rivenloch knights cleared a path for him.

"Colban!" Morgan cried in relief.

But judging by Colban's face, Jenefer thought it looked like he'd *lost* the battle.

And when she spied Hallie in the entryway—her face smudged with blood, her eyes resolute—standing in cool silence, she couldn't help but wonder what had happened between them.

She'd have to wring the story from Hallie later.

For now, other things were more pressing. Burying the dead. Tending to the wounded. Repairing the damage.

The two clans worked together for several hours, restoring the keep enough to make it secure. Meanwhile, Bethac had the cooks prepare supper for the hungry warriors.

It was early afternoon when they crowded into the great hall. Sitting elbow to elbow at the trestle tables, they feasted on thick mutton pottage and barley bread. And they swapped glorious stories of past battles.

Jenefer, ravenous after the skirmish, paid more heed to the stew than the boasts. But after she'd finally eaten her fill, she asked the one thing she was most anxious to know.

"What news from the king?"

Morgan's hand tightened around his eating dagger.

He narrowed his eyes at Deirdre. If the Laird of Rivenloch had brought news from the king herself, it must not bode well for him. Glancing at Colban's bleak expression, Morgan expected the worst.

Ballocks. After everything he'd been through over the past several days, he didn't think he could endure more bad tidings.

Lady Deirdre's face was unreadable as she wiped her mouth, set her napkin aside, and rose from the table.

She turned to her husband. "Pagan?"

He pulled a sealed document from his gambeson and handed it to her.

"First of all," Deirdre said, holding it aloft for all to see, "I hope all of you understand this is the will of the king and not the decree of any one clan." Her ice blue gaze landed on Morgan then, and her voice was forthright, sincere, and reassuring. "As far as mac Giric and Rivenloch, this document affects neither our loyalty nor our friendship."

Morgan nodded in agreement. The two clans had fought side-by-side, after all. Nothing could break the bonds of war.

Then she turned away.

"By order of the king, Castle Creagor and its surrounding lands are hereby awarded to Lady Jenefer du Lac of Rivenloch."

His clan's whispers of shock and disappointment circled the great hall as she handed the decree to Creagor's new laird.

Morgan's heart sank.

Then bitter bile rose in his throat.

How could the king do such a thing? How could he take away the prize Morgan had been awarded?

He and his clan had traveled over a hundred miles from the Highlands to get here. They'd already settled in. He was finally beginning to feel like Creagor was his home.

God's eyes. His clan had even shed blood in defense of the keep.

The king's betrayal filled him with rancor. How could a beardless boy, sitting miles away in his royal robes, steal Morgan's future with a single stroke of his pen?

His clan gave voice to his ire. There was a swell of muttering and cursing from the mac Giric soldiers that was becoming a risk, even if they were no longer armed and hot from battle.

It was up to him to rein them in. And keep them safe.

He came to his feet.

"Heed my words, mac Giric! The king has spoken and made his will known." He held up his hand for silence. "By all rights, Rivenloch could have marched on Creagor and forced us out at the point of a sword. But they did not."

Even as he said the words, he knew Rivenloch would never have attacked, not while Jenefer was in his ranks.

"Instead," he continued, "they've been merciful, fightin' by our side." To his horror, his voice cracked on the last words as he recalled how proud he'd been of Jenefer's expert command of his archers. Not daring to look at her, he cleared his throat. "We owe it to them to return to the Highlands without delay."

"The sooner, the better!" Colban barked.

Morgan narrowed his eyes at his loyal companion. He'd never seen Colban so grim. What had happened to him at Rivenloch?

Soon his clan was joining in with comments of their own, like monks trying to make good wine from sour grapes.

"I'll be glad to be far away from the bloody English!"

"'Twill be good to see real mountains again."

"We can be back and settled ere winter comes."

"The siege stores will be good for the journey home."

"...home..."

"Home."

Morgan tightened his jaw.

His heart was breaking.

He told himself it was because he'd grown to love Creagor. He would miss its rolling hills and green grass.

He blamed the pain on all of his recent losses. The loss of his right hand man. The loss of his wife. And now the loss of his holding.

He tried to believe his sorrow was because his son would never know his mother, never grow up in his grandfather's castle that was his birthright.

But deep in his heart, he knew the truth. He knew the source of his anguish. It had hair like honey silk and eyes of fiery emeralds. It went by the name of Jenefer.

At least she would be happy. She was getting what she wanted. What she'd wanted all along.

He sat back down, refusing to look at her. He couldn't bear to see her smug smile. Not now. Not when he knew it would be the last he saw of her.

"Wait!" Jenefer said.

What she did next shocked them all.

She pushed the document back across the table toward Deirdre.

"I don't want it. I don't want Creagor."

Jenefer had spoken on impulse. But it was true. She didn't want to win the castle this way. Not at the expense of the clan she'd come to care for. Not if she'd be stealing it from the man she loved.

She was sure she was making the right decision.

Until her mother glared at her, her eyes flickering with dangerous fire. "What do you mean you don't want it?"

"I mean, Mother, you can tear this up."

The fire in her mother's gaze flared even brighter as she leaned toward Jenefer. But Deirdre pushed her back with an arm across her chest.

"What's happened, Jenefer?" Deirdre demanded.

Jenefer lowered her eyes, lifted her chin, and shrugged.

"Nothing," she said. "I've just changed my mind."

She wasn't about to divulge the truth. That she'd fallen in love with the Highlander. That she adored his precious son. That his clan—Bethac, Cicilia, William, Danald, the Campbell brothers, all of them—felt like family to her.

She didn't have the heart to take the keep from Morgan. Not after everything he'd lost.

Her mother's temper erupted then. "Changed your mind? Changed your *mind?*" She pounded a fist on the table, rattling the ale cups. "Listen, lassie. Your father and I didn't just traipse the length of Scotland to curry the favor of a king scarce out of his swaddling just to have you change your mind. Your cousin didn't barter away—"

"Hel," Deirdre warned. "That's enough." She turned to Jenefer and spoke with an air of firm but fair command. "What the king has decreed and set his name to is final. 'Twas negotiated and hard won. You cannot refuse such a gift. Not without incurring the king's wrath."

Jenefer knew she was testing her aunt's patience. Her mother looked ready to carve her up with her eating dagger. Even her normally calm cousin Hallie stared at her with glacial rage.

Feiyan and her mother Miriel, however, murmured together. In unison, they crossed their arms and arched their brows. Then they gave Jenefer secret, knowing smiles.

"Of course, the English could attack again," Miriel mused. "You'll need a fighting force to keep Creagor safe."

Feiyan added, "Servants to set up your household."

Miriel nodded. "Someone to purchase provisions and livestock."

"And probably a dozen cooks," Feiyan said with a smirk, "to keep up with *your* appetite."

Ordinarily, Jenefer would have cuffed her cousin for that remark. But she was beginning to understand their veiled message.

Maybe she didn't need to send the Highlanders away just yet. She could definitely use their help.

When she turned to Morgan, her heart pounded, belying the casual tone of her words. "What say you? Will you stay on?"

His face was grim. Of course it was. He'd just been told that the castle he'd risked life and limb to defend had been taken away from him.

But her throat ached. What if he said nay? How could she bear the thought of never seeing him again?

"'Twill take a few days to prepare for the journey home." His voice was ragged with bitter defeat. "But we'll delay no more than that. We must leave ere winter comes."

It wasn't much. But it was something.

Jenefer would just have to use every weapon of seduction in her arsenal in the coming days to convince him to stay.

CHAPTER 67

Beneath the tangle they'd made of the coverlet, Morgan felt Jenefer arch in ecstasy.

Her fingers clawed at the bedlinens.

Her astonished mouth fell open.

Between his legs, he felt the blood surge to his hungry beast, caught within the cage of her womb.

She moaned in need.

He growled in impatience.

They gasped together in growing wonder.

Then, just as he feared another instant of delay would make him explode, she shook with tremors of rapture, releasing him to shudder in his own welcome relief.

Their passion spent, they fell back on the bed in happy, breathless exhaustion. Again.

It wasn't the first time he'd made love to Jenefer in the week since their battle with the English.

It was, however, the most comfortable location. With a fire crackling on the hearth and morning storm clouds outside the window, his bed—*her* bed now, he reminded himself—was definitely his favorite place for bedding.

Last eve, they'd trysted in the straw. Jenefer had lured him to the stable, telling him she wanted his opinion on enlarging it to accommodate knights for the tournaments she planned to hold.

Yesterday morn, they'd discussed reorganizing the armory and wound up swiving on a pile of targes.

The day before that, she'd led him down to the pond, explaining how it could be dug deeper for bathing. Naturally, she'd had to show him how shallow it was, peeling off every stitch of her clothing and wading into the freezing water. He'd had to warm her up afterward in a nearby thicket.

What she lacked in experience, the lass made up for in ambition. And her creativity was keeping him distracted from his responsibilities.

Yet the longer he delayed getting his clan ready to leave Creagor, the less he felt like leaving.

He could definitely get used to this.

If he lingered much longer, he'd *have* to get used to it. The lass's appetite for love, like her appetite for food, seemed insatiable.

But he was running out of excuses to remain. And he knew it was pure selfishness that made him wish to stay.

He sighed as he glared up at the ceiling.

Yesterday, a small contingent of servants from Rivenloch had arrived to complement Jenefer's household. In addition, her mother had gifted her with a flock of sheep, a few cows, assorted fowl, a pair of oxen, and even a handsome destrier. Six knights and six archers had moved into the armory with their weaponry.

Soon she wouldn't need his protection.

Meanwhile, Morgan only tortured himself with procrastination.

Disgruntled, he rose up on his elbows. "I should go."

"Go? What do you mean, go?" Did he imagine the subtle note of panic in her voice before she tempered it with a coy smile? "Don't be daft. We haven't even had breakfast yet."

He had to smile at that. "After breakfast then, I suppose."

BR&DE OF F&RE

But he knew he couldn't delay the journey home forever.

"You're not thinking of leaving *today,* are you?" Her voice seemed artificially bright. "I mean, look at the clouds. There's sure to be a downpour. If you go now, your clan and your livestock will be forced to slog through the mire and sleep in the mud."

He glanced out the shutters. To be honest, the clouds looked no more threatening than on most days in the Highlands.

But the temptation in the bed beside him—Jenefer's wide emerald eyes, her rosy lips, her lush tresses, the gentle curve of her bare shoulder—proved too great to resist. He supposed one more day couldn't do any harm.

"Perhaps on the morrow then," he said, content to blame his delay on the weather.

"Aye, tomorrow," she said. "Or the next day. Though it does seem like winter has set in."

"Does it?"

"Oh aye." She shook her head. "When I think of you stranded in the mountains in the ice and snow with Miles…"

"Perhaps we *should* stay a while longer." He pensively scratched his jaw. "For Miles' sake."

"Aye!" she cried. Then she tempered her enthusiasm with a shrug. "I mean, you'd certainly be welcome to stay here."

"Just until the weather clears."

"Of course. Once the weather clears, you'll want to be on your way. I'm sure you're eager to return."

But that was just it. He *wasn't* eager to return. He'd come to Creagor with all intentions of staying. That hadn't changed. If anything, he had more of a desire to stay than ever.

He was even fairly certain she *wanted* him to stay. Why else would she be swiving him in every corner of the keep?

And why would she be making the flimsiest of excuses to keep him at Creagor?

If she wanted him, why had she not asked him to marry her? After all, Morgan was free to wed, now that Alicia was gone.

The question was, did Jenefer want him for a husband? Did she envision him as her loyal, lifelong companion? Or was he only a pleasant diversion?

She must realize he couldn't go on being her lover. He was too proud for that. He wouldn't disgrace her by keeping her as his mistress. They'd taken enough liberties in that quarter as it was.

For the sake of honor, they had to become husband and wife.

And it had to be her idea.

Otherwise, no one would ever believe he was marrying her for love. They'd assume he was marrying her to reclaim Creagor.

Nay, as inconvenient as it was, it had to be Jenefer who proposed marriage.

Jenefer sighed in equal parts bliss and frustration.

How much more seduction would it take before the stubborn Highlander proposed marriage?

She let her gaze roam over the man in the bed beside her, the bed clearly meant for two.

Loki's rod, Morgan was devilishly handsome. Incredibly gifted. Breathtaking and mouthwatering. But more than that, he was noble and good and strong and fair. Any woman would be lucky to have such a man in her bed.

To have him as her husband...

Damn it, she was getting desperate.

She was running out of excuses to keep him at Creagor.

Every night, she found herself praying for bad weather.

And as wicked as it was, she even considered breaking the wheel of one of his carts or setting fire to his supplies to delay him.

She watched him as he stared at the ceiling, deep in thought.

Not for the first time, she wondered why she couldn't confront Morgan the same way she confronted everything else. Without hesitation. Without artifice. Directly. The same way she released arrows. Straight and to the point.

Why was that so difficult when it came to addressing Morgan?

She should look him in the eye. Stand firm. Speak frankly.

But the truth was she was afraid of his reply. She was afraid he might not feel the same way she did.

What if his heart didn't race every time she walked into a room?

What if his breath didn't catch every time she smiled at him?

What if his soul didn't ache at the thought of never seeing her again?

Delaying that conversation kept hope alive for her, she realized. Hope of a lifetime with him. Hope of being a mother to Miles. Hope of adopting this clan as her own.

She'd been utterly charmed by Morgan's son. She'd grown terribly fond of Bethac and Cicilia. She'd bonded with the mac Giric archers as if they were her own men. And Morgan... There were no words to describe the love she felt for him.

How could she watch them walk away forever?

If Morgan refused her, they *would* walk away. And all her hopes would be dashed.

But why *wouldn't* Morgan wish to go home? He'd lost his wife, and he already had an heir. What use did he have for another? In the Highlands, he probably had a whole bevy of willing lasses he could swive to his heart's content, without commitment or even affection.

Jenefer hoped he wanted more than that. She wanted to believe he loved her.

He'd told her so once.

But words spoken in the heat of battle couldn't be trusted.

She swallowed down fear. She couldn't put off the confrontation forever. The longer she waited, the harder it would be.

"Morgan!" she blurted before cowardice could curb her tongue.

He turned to her in startled concern. "Aye?"

His captivating eyes, still smoldering from passion, made her stumble over her words. "I... I..."

She glared at the ceiling. She couldn't do it. She suddenly realized it was too soon. It would be too easy for him to tell her nay.

If she could only keep him at Creagor a little while longer. Maybe until spring. Long enough to fall in love with her...

CHAPTER 68

Morgan held his breath, waiting for Jenefer to finish.

Was it possible she'd finally stopped beating around the bush and intended to ask him to be her husband?

She'd averted her gaze. Her fingers were clasped together tightly enough to snap a birch arrow in half.

At last she seemed to screw up her courage.

"I have a proposal—"

"Aye!"

"What?" She blinked at him.

"Ye said ye have a proposal?"

She blushed and looked at her hands. "Aye. I'd like to propose...that you stay on for a few months to train my men in using the claymore."

His eyes flattened. "Train your men?"

"Aye. If 'tisn't too much to ask."

Her clan had admired the great swords the mac Girics carried and were forging claymores of their own. They'd need someone with expertise to teach them how to use them.

"Fine," he said. "As long as I'm here, I'll train your men." He narrowed his eyes at her. "Anythin' else ye'd like to propose?"

She licked her lips. "I... I'll need to buy calves in the spring. I could use your help with negotiating a good price."

"Right. Coos. And claymores." He arched a brow. "And?"

She bit the corner of her lip. Then she lifted her gaze to rove slowly over his body. The calculated desire smoldering in her eyes almost reignited the fires of passion in him. Almost.

When she ran a finger coyly down his chest, her message was clear. She didn't want to speak any more of proposals. She wanted to swive him again.

His flesh was willing enough. But he had to stay strong. He wasn't going to continue warming her bed if she was only going to tease him with a future of meaningless dalliances.

He plucked her finger from his chest and returned it to her.

"Coos and claymores ye can have, lassie. Couplin', however, is goin' to take a different kind o' proposal."

Jenefer wasn't sure if his words were a rejection or an invitation.

"What are you saying?"

"I'm not content to be your...paramour."

Her heart caught. She knew it. Why would he be content with one woman when he could have whomever he wished? Bitterness twisted her pain into ire as she said, "You seemed content enough a moment ago."

"Aye," he said. "But I want more."

"More," she echoed. "I see." She nodded as hurt and anger sharpened her tongue. "This isn't enough for you."

"Nay, 'tisn't."

"Fine."

"Fine?"

"Go then."

"Go?" He seemed genuinely puzzled. "Go where?"

"Home!" She snapped the coverlet back and swiveled her legs over the edge of the bed. "Back to your Highland lasses!"

"My what?" He sat up in alarm.

She began collecting her discarded garments. "Heaven forbid I should keep you here when you've got a bevy of wenches waiting for you—"

"A bevy o' what?"

She swept her kirtle from the floor and pulled it down over her head.

"But I'll tell you this," she said, stabbing her arms into the sleeves and wrenching it down over her hips. "None of them will ever care for Miles the way I do." She snatched her surcoat from the foot of the bed and snagged her hose from atop his discarded leine. "None of them will train your archers with such dedication." One boot she found beside the hearth. She had no idea where the other one had gone. She could hardly see for the tears of anger blurring her eyes. "And none of them will love you as much as..." To her horror, her voice broke.

"Aye?"

"It doesn't matter," she muttered, scouring the chamber for her missing boot. "You obviously don't care for me."

"What?" He burst from the bed in an explosion of linen. "Why do ye think I've been swivin' ye for the past sennight?"

"Sheep swive all the time. I don't think *they* care all that much for each other."

"Sheep. *Sheep?*" He looked at her in disbelief. "Bloody hell, lass! I told ye I loved ye that day we fought the English."

She shook her head in dismissal. "'Twas in the heat of battle. You wanted me to go to the great hall. You would have said anything to get me to do your bidding."

"If I'd only wanted ye to do my biddin', I'd have dragged ye to the hall myself."

"Fine. Maybe you *did* love me," she said. "But now you've apparently changed your mind."

He blinked, incredulous that she should say such a thing. "What?"

"You said you didn't want to be my... What did you call it? My paramour."

"That's true. I don't."

She gave him a smoldering glare. He'd stabbed her in the heart already. He didn't have to twist the damned knife.

"Then we understand one another," she bit out.

"Nay," he growled. "I don't think we do."

He tore the linens from the bed, knotting them around his waist.

Then he slowly advanced on her, all scowling brow and clenched fists.

"What about ye?" he demanded. "Is that all ye want?"

He took a threatening step forward.

She dropped her clothing and took a judicious step backward.

"A Highland warrior at your beck and call?" he snarled.

He ambled toward her, menacing her with his words as much as his size.

She retreated, staying carefully out of range.

"A man to warm your bed on cold winter nights?" he sneered.

His last step trapped her against the wall.

"Someone ye can command to come hither," he breathed in a husky whisper, "when ye've got an itch that needs scratchin'?"

She gasped at his crude words, which both angered and aroused her. Then she shoved at his chest.

The massive brute barely budged.

He caught her wrists in a steely grip, pinning her against the wall.

"Do ye know," he bit out, holding her as much with his demanding gaze as with his powerful body, "ye've not once said ye loved *me?*"

She blinked. Was that true? Had she never told him how she felt?

"That's not possible," she decided.

"'Tis."

"Surely I—"

"Nay."

"When we were—"

"Not once. Not even in the heat o' battle."

She lowered her eyes under his scrutiny, mildly abashed that she'd overlooked such a crucial thing.

"Fine," she said. "Well, I do."

"Ye do what?"

"I...care for you."

"Bethac *cares* for me," he scoffed. "Is that the best ye can do?"

"Fine." She blew out an irritated breath and mumbled, "I love you."

"What was that?" He cocked his ear toward her.

"You heard me."

"Did ye say ye loathe me?" The glimmer of mischief in his eyes made her heart melt a little. "Because that's what I heard."

"You know what I said," she murmured.

"Sorry, nay. I couldn't quite—"

"Oh, for the love of Thor... I love you!" she shouted. "All right?"

He grinned, releasing her wrists.

She gave him a chiding punch in the chest for looking so smug. Then she demanded, "So what are you going to do about it?"

"Me? Well, if ye'd only stop dawdlin', proposin' this and proposin' that..."

Her jaw dropped. How dared he accuse her of delay. She'd been seducing him for days now.

He continued. "If ye'd just aim, draw, and loose instead o' dallyin' with your bow..."

"Dallying with my...?" She felt her veins fill with fire. Was that what he thought she was doing? Dallying? "Fine. You want a bull's-eye? I'll give you a bull's-eye," she said. "Marry me!"

"I will!"

"Wait. What?"

"I said I will."

Her mouth clapped shut. Was that all it took?

She might have gone on staring at him in shock, but she was startled by the sudden sound of cheering from the nursery next door.

Morgan scowled. "What the devil?"

They didn't bother getting fully dressed. They stole out of the bedchamber door as they were and crept to the nursery.

Bethac greeted them at the crack of the nursery door. She was grinning from ear to ear.

"Congratulations," she said with a wink. "Though it took ye long enough."

Jenefer sighed. How much had the maidservant heard? They'd have to be certain to close the shutters from now on when they were grappling...either with words or under the bedsheets.

Then Bethac swung the door wide to reveal the guests crowded into the nursery.

Jenefer was mortified.

Her aunt Deirdre was holding Miles, smiling gently down at the wee lad.

Hallie sat on the bed beside her, looking on in cool, quiet reflection.

Cicilia was closing the shutters. When she turned, her face was alight with pleasure.

Feiyan and her mother Miriel were warming their hands at the hearth, looking both satisfied and conspiratorial.

Her mother Helena stood with her arms crossed. Her expression was grave, but a smile tugged at the corners of her mouth.

"What are you doing here?" Jenefer blurted.

"We did give you a sennight," Deirdre said, tickling the babe in her arms. "Didn't we, Miles?"

Her Aunt Miriel shrugged. "We figured if it didn't happen today..."

"We might have to intervene," Feiyan finished.

"If what didn't happen?" Morgan asked.

Miriel didn't answer him, speaking to her sisters instead. "I told you they wouldn't read the document."

Deirdre nodded. "You were right. And it turns out 'twas for the best."

"The document?" Jenefer asked, growing annoyed with her aunts.

Feiyan answered. "The document from the king."

Helena stepped forward, eyeing Morgan up. "We decided to wait for a sennight. If by then the two of you weren't wed or dead, we'd return to prod things along."

Morgan's brow had clouded. He probably didn't like the way her mother had said "prod," as if she meant to jab him with her sword.

Jenefer wasn't happy about her kin's interference either. "What about the document?"

Hallie rose from the bed. There was a sad wistfulness in her voice as she said, "The important thing is you've chosen to wed."

Cicilia couldn't contain her glee. "Now wee Miles will have a mother!"

Bethac joined in. "And we can all stay here at Creagor, aye?"

Her mother's eyes gleamed. "Think of the fighting force you'll have, combining your two armies."

Bethac clasped her hands in delight. "And the brood o' wee bairns ye'll make to carry on the clan name."

Even Miles voiced his opinion, cooing from Deirdre's lap.

The nursery filled with happy chatter as everyone began to discuss the future. Details for the wedding feast. Plans for meeting Morgan's parents. Schedules for upcoming tournaments. Alterations to the castle. Arrangements to take turns caring for Miles, whom they'd all come to adore.

Jenefer couldn't stay disgruntled for long. Especially when she let her gaze slip over to Morgan.

He was everything she'd ever wanted in a husband. A man of honor and discipline. Kindness and strength. Fierce. Gentle. Handsome. Powerful. Fair.

Like a straight arrow married to a flexible bow, their union would fly true and go far, bringing harmony between their clans.

Peace along the border.

A lifetime of love and loyalty and adventure.

"Amor vincit omnia," she murmured.

Love conquers all.

Perhaps the Rivenloch motto wasn't so wrong after all.

By the sparkle in his eyes and his heart-melting grin, it seemed Morgan agreed.

epilogue

"It isn't right!" Jenefer snapped, dropping the document onto her bedsheet-covered lap.

She was suddenly furious. With the king. And with her kin.

Her rage was palpable enough to wake Morgan, dozing beside her.

"What is it?" he murmured with a yarn, still drowsy from the honey mead they'd imbibed at their wedding feast. That and a night full of lovemaking. "What's wrong?"

"Did you know about this?" she demanded, shoving the document under his nose and crossing her arms over her naked bosom.

Rising up on his elbows, he squinted at the parchment. But with the candle on her side of the bed, he couldn't make out the words.

"I can't... What does it say?" he asked.

She hesitated. Gazing at his adorable mussed hair, his half-lidded eyes, and the concern etched between his brows, she couldn't help but feel her anger soften. After all, she had no reason to be vexed with *him.*

He couldn't possibly know what the document said. The king's decree had been sealed for a month, forgotten in the flurry of wedding plans. Since they were wed now, she'd finally opened it, figuring she should know exactly what it said.

But her pardon of Morgan's complicity didn't mitigate her anger with everyone else who knew what it contained.

She took the document back.

"According to this," she said, poring over the words, "The king 'hereby grants the lairdship of Castle Creagor and all its lands thereto'..." She skipped the boring description of the holding. "'to Jenefer du Lac *upon the condition of her marriage to Morgan Mor mac Giric.*'"

"What?" That woke him up.

He seemed just as outraged as she was. He reached across her to grab the candle and took the document to examine the words himself.

She sulked. "My inheritance was apparently secured with the promise of a wedding between us. My kin knew all along. And they didn't say a word."

"'Twas to be a political alliance then," he said in disappointment, lowering the document to rake his hair back from his furrowed brow. "Not a love match."

"Why?" she asked bitterly. "Why would they do that? Why would they bargain away my..."

She couldn't finish the thought, because she knew that wasn't quite accurate. She'd given Morgan her maidenhood freely, of her own accord.

Besides, most marriages between powerful nobles were political alliances. That anyone fell in love after a forced marriage was a rare occurrence.

"Why didn't they tell us?" she wondered aloud.

There was a long silence before he answered, "I think I know."

She lifted her brows in askance.

"We would have refused the match," he said.

"What?"

"Think about it. If your kin had shown up and said that in order to win Creagor, ye'd have to wed me..."

"I would have turned them down." She'd already decided she didn't want to win Morgan by force. She only wanted him if it was of his own free will.

"As would I," he said. "I couldn't have ye always wonderin' if I only married ye for your castle."

She nodded, beginning to understand. "Feiyan. It had to be her idea."

"Your cousin?"

"She knew I had...feelings...for you. She must have told everyone that the match could be accomplished without force."

"Without force."

"Aye. 'tis the same thing she says about her fighting. That there's greater power in diverting a foe's own force and using it against them."

"So ye're sayin' they had faith in the power of our love."

She nodded.

Morgan studied the document more closely. "There's more."

"More?"

"Your cousin's betrothal was bargained for as well."

"What?" she exploded. "Feiyan?"

"Hallidis."

She gasped.

Hallie's hand in marriage seemed too great a price to pay for one border castle. The man who married Hallidis Cameliard of Rivenloch would inherit a valuable prize indeed. After all, she was in line for the lairdship after her mother.

"Hallie's to be married?"

"So it says."

She snatched the parchment away. "To whom?" she asked, quickly scanning the document.

Finally she found the name.

"Nay."

Her heart sank. No wonder Hallie had seemed so glum and resigned when she returned to Creagor. She must have known what was in the king's decree.

"What's wrong?" Morgan asked. "Who is it?"

"Archibald Scott."

"And who is Archibald Scott?"

"He's at least a decade older than Hallie. And he's..." How could she describe Archie? "He's a vain popinjay. A weakhearted coward who faints at the sight of blood." So she remembered from one of the Scotts' visits to Rivenloch years ago.

Morgan grimaced. "I'm sorry for her. If it's any consolation, she probably expected as much. Powerful clans are always pawns in the king's game. 'Twas the same way with Alicia and me."

"Aye, and Hallie will do her duty," Jenefer agreed. But she didn't approve. And if there was a way to prevent this travesty of a match, she wouldn't hesitate.

"Wait," Morgan said. "Ye don't suppose..."

"Aye?"

"My man Colban has been miserable, mopin' about like an orphaned pup. He said he might leave Creagor after the weddin'. I thought he was only upset to lose me to a wife." He lifted a brow. "Ye don't think somethin' might have happened between them in the woods, on the way to Rivenloch?"

"Between him and *Hallie?*" Jenefer asked in disbelief.

In matters of the heart, Hallidis was practical and dispassionate. She didn't have a romantic bone in her body. Jenefer shook her head.

"Maybe a skirmish or two," she said. "But when it comes to love, my cousin is about as warm as ice."

"Ye're probably right," Morgan decided. "And Colban's only restless, goin' off on an adventure. By the time her returns, he'll likely have swived every maid between here and Stirlin'." He took the candle and parchment from her, reaching across her to place them back on the table. "And speakin' o' swivin'…"

Any lingering doubts Jenefer had about Hallie and Colban vanished as soon as her new husband claimed her with a soul-searing kiss.

Unlike their earlier trysts, which were wild and frenzied, this time their coupling was sweet, slow, full of languid touches and soft sighs. Morgan sank into her with tender care. And she rose gently up to meet him.

But soon their bodies began to strain and tremble. Their desire grew as taut as a bowstring. And when they could no longer hold back the arrow of their passion, they released their love skyward, sending it across the heavens in a beautiful arc of pleasure.

Before they could float completely back to earth, the music of their mingled gasps was interrupted by a muffled cry from the nursery.

"Miles," they said in unison.

Then they grinned.

"At least he waited until we were finished," Jenefer breathed.

Morgan withdrew with a groan and rolled off of her. She missed him at once.

But they had a whole lifetime of coupling ahead of them. Miles, however, wouldn't be a babe for long.

As she slipped from the bed and into her kirtle, she gave Morgan a wink. "I'll be right back."

"I'll be waitin'."

He laced his fingers behind his head, displaying the magnificent muscles of his arms and exposing his broad and powerful chest. Lord, he took her breath away. It was hard to believe she'd once considered him a ruthless savage. Even harder to believe he was her husband.

"Before ye go, wife, there's just one thing I need to know," he said, narrowing his eyes in smoky challenge. "Ye didn't marry me for my handsome son, did ye?"

She smiled and gave him a shrug. "Not entirely."

He chuckled.

When she reached the door, she turned to him. "But ye must promise me one thing, Highlander."

"Aye? What's that?"

"Promise me you won't trade your handsome son for a coo."

The End

Coming soon...

BRIDE OF ICE

The Warrior Daughters of Rivenloch, Book 2

Thank you for reading my book!

Did you enjoy it? If so, I hope you'll post a review to let others know! There's no greater gift you can give an author than spreading your love of her books.

It's truly a pleasure and a privilege to be able to share my stories with you. Knowing that my words have made you laugh, sigh, or touched a secret place in your heart is what keeps the wind beneath my wings. I hope you enjoyed our brief journey together, and may ALL of your adventures have happy endings!

If you'd like to keep in touch, feel free to sign up for my monthly e-newsletter at www.glynnis.net, and you'll be the first to find out about my new releases, special discounts, prizes, promotions, and more!

If you want to keep up with my daily escapades:
Friend me at facebook.com/GlynnisCampbell
Like my Page at bit.ly/GlynnisCampbellFBPage
Follow me on Twitter @GlynnisCampbell
Follow me on Instagram @glynniscampbell
Follow me on Goodreads @glynnis_campbell
Follow me on Bookbub @glynnis-campbell
And if you're a super fan, join
facebook.com/GCReadersClan

About the Author

I'm a *USA Today* bestselling author of swashbuckling action-adventure historical romances, mostly set in Scotland, with more than 20 award-winning books published in six languages.

But before my role as a medieval matchmaker, I sang in *The Pinups,* an all-girl band on CBS Records, and provided voices for the MTV animated series *The Maxx,* Blizzard's *Diablo* and *Starcraft* video games, and *Star Wars* audiobooks.

I'm the wife of a rock star (if you want to know which one, contact me) and the mother of two young adults. I do my best writing on cruise ships, in Scottish castles, on my husband's tour bus, and at home in my sunny southern California garden.

I love transporting readers to a place where the bold heroes have endearing flaws, the women are stronger than they look, the land is lush and untamed, and chivalry is alive and well!

I'm always delighted to hear from my readers, so please feel free to email me at glynnis@glynnis.net. And if you're a super-fan who would like to join my inner circle, sign up at http://www.facebook.com/GCReadersClan, where you'll get glimpses behind the scenes, sneak peeks of works-in-progress, and extra special surprises.

Made in the
USA
Columbia, SC